BETRAYED

a novel

BETRAYED

a novel

rosey dow &
andrew snaden

PROMISE
PRESS
An Imprint of Barbour Publishing

© 2001 by Rosey Dow and Andrew Snaden

ISBN 0-7394-2091-7

Published by Promise Press, an imprint of Barbour Publishing, Inc., P.O. Box 719, Uhrichsville, Ohio 44683, http://www.promisepress.com

 Member of the
Evangelical Christian
Publishers Association

Printed in the United States of America.

DEDICATION

We wish to thank the Lord, first of all,
for leading us into this joint effort.
Thanks to our families for their cheerful encouragement
and for their willingness to read several rewrites.
Special thanks to Carrie Wood and Joyce Hart
for their parts in making the dream happen.
We couldn't have done it without you.

PROLOGUE

A cool breeze skipped across shimmering oranges and reds; a brilliant sunset reflected on gentle waves. The wind caught Laura McIvor's copper hair and wrapped it around her face. Darryl Hansen brushed it away from her cheek. Her emerald eyes locked with his, and her heart fluttered. Would he do it now?

But no, his boyish face broke into a broad grin. He clasped her slim hand and tried to lead her down the beach. Laughing, she jerked away. A gull called to its mate as her feet pounded the sand. She glanced over her shoulder to see if he chased her.

Grinning, he shouted, "Hey! Come back here!" Five strides later, he grabbed her elbow, and she spun around into his arms, their laughter fading as, chin to chin, their eyes met again. He paused for a taut moment as foamy surf whooshed across their toes.

Slowly he drew away. Lacing his fingers with hers, he aimed for an iron bench facing the Pacific. When she sat, he kept hold of her hand and dropped to one knee before her.

"Laura," he murmured, "I was wondering. . ."

"Yes?" She felt as though she were melting into his indigo eyes. She'd been waiting months for this question.

His breathing was slow, expectant. "Will you marry me, Laura McIvor?"

She paused while a wave crashed onto the sand and flowed back, a white froth. "Yes, Darryl Hansen," she breathed. "I will marry you."

Suddenly, he grabbed her shoulders. His fingers dug into her flesh.

"Stop! You're hurting me!" she cried.

He began to shake her. The sound of surf and smell of salt retreated. Light burned against her eyes.

"Miss McIvor, wake up!" A harsh male voice broke through her consciousness. "I'm Special Agent Sam Perkins of the FBI. We're going to search your room."

Wincing, Laura forced her eyes open. The stench of stale tobacco choked her as she peered at the granite face of a big man with gray at his temples. Laura twisted hard and broke free of his hands pressing her shoulders. "Who are you?" she screeched, pulling further away.

"FBI, Ma'am." He whipped out his identification and held it in front of her face. "This is my partner, Paul Newberg." As tall as Perkins, Newberg looked like he pumped iron four hours a day.

"What. . .What's going on?" Laura asked, clutching the blanket to her pounding heart.

"We're executing a search warrant in relation to the alleged criminal activities of your father." While Perkins spoke, doors slammed against their frames in the far recesses of the mansion. Men's voices drifted in from the hall.

Laura sat up. Pulling her knees against her chest, she had the odd feeling that the men in her bedroom were a nightmare. Any second now, she'd be back on the beach with Darryl. When they started dumping her clothes onto the carpet, she knew the nightmare was reality.

Daddy's criminal activities? He was a computer scientist, probably the most brilliant in the country. As far as Laura knew, he was guilty of nothing more than having no personality.

A porcelain cat shattered against the foot of her sleigh bed, followed by a bottle of perfume. With the breath-snatching odor came a fury that chased away her initial fear. She shouted, "Would you mind being more careful with my things!"

Perkins's expression darkened. "After what your father's done, don't expect much, Lady."

"You're insane! He hasn't done anything."

Wiping his palms against the legs of his black fatigues, Perkins ignored her and slid back the closet door. Laura's mouth formed a hard line as her business suits landed on top of the growing pile that represented her normal, secure life. She clamped her teeth together when Newberg's size elevens trudged across silk and rayon to pull open a door on the left. An instant later, every stuffed animal from her collection bounced into the wreckage.

Tigger fell on his head. She got him when she was eight. Pooh landed on Tigger's belly and rolled to a resting place on a white silk blouse with a boot print on it. Bear ricocheted off a wall and ended up at the base of her hope chest.

A gift on her first birthday, Bear had been a special friend all her life. Though Laura had turned thirty-two last May, some nights he still slept in her arms.

"Perkins."

The agent followed Newberg's pointed glance to the stuffed animals on the floor.

"What do you think?" His words held malicious meaning.

Perkins rubbed a wide hand over his chin. "The warrant says search everything that could hold a computer disk. Go for it."

A grin slid across Newburg's face. He pulled a jagged knife from its sheath and stabbed Tigger. Horrified, Laura watched her childhood friends being hacked to shreds. When Newberg reached for Bear, she let out an anguished cry.

Newberg crumpled to his knees as Laura's body crashed against the backs of his legs. The knife flew behind the bed. Gripping Bear, Laura bolted for the door. Perkins twisted to grab her, but his hand slipped off her satin pajamas.

"Come back here!" he bellowed.

Laura pounded down the arched hallway and lunged into her parents' room. Her face slammed into yellow FBI letters on a black jacket. The agent spun, then held himself in check before he drove the rifle butt into her face.

"Leave her alone!" Alice McIvor shouted, her slim form coming upright from a Monterey chair. Laura rushed into her mother's arms.

Red-faced, Newberg strode toward Laura, his hand outstretched. Laura clutched Bear to her chest. She slipped behind her mother's stiff back.

"Give me the toy!" Newberg demanded.

Laura glanced around for a way to escape.

"What's going on?" the guard asked.

"We think there might be something inside the bear," Perkins told him. "She let us rip open every one of them except that one. There's got to be a reason she's protecting it."

"I've had him all my life," Laura ground out through clenched teeth. "There's no way you're going to hurt him."

Newberg and the guard grabbed Alice McIvor and yanked her away from her daughter. When Perkins reached for the stuffed animal, Laura whipped around to press her body against the plastered wall, pinning Bear to it. The FBI agent spun Laura around. Mrs. McIvor screamed. Delivering a well-placed kick to his groin, Laura sprinted toward the door.

Newberg's heavy hand bit into her upper arm. Laura stumbled, and he pinned her to the Navajo rug. Alice McIvor broke free like a lioness protecting a cub and sank her teeth into the back of his neck. The other two agents dove in to help, and the bedroom became a frenzy of screams, curses, and flailing limbs.

Jonathan Corrigan's deceptively boyish face had a grim cast as he followed the macadam driveway through two acres of manicured lawn. For over a year, he'd worked this investigation. He almost had the case cracked, but a piece of the puzzle was still missing. Last night, he pleaded with the director to give him more time. He should have saved his breath, because this morning the CIA had informed the FBI about the activities of Harrison McIvor.

A friend at the Justice Department had tipped Corrigan off when the search warrant was issued. He'd burned rubber getting here. Rounding a curve, he saw four black sedans crowding the space before the Spanish-style villa. Cursing silently, he thumped the steering wheel with a fist. All he could do now was damage control.

Corrigan knew every detail of the white stucco house with arched doors and windows. Below the clay-tile roof, he could see shadows of men moving about the bedrooms on the second floor. He knew which belonged to Laura, which belonged to her parents. The estate was more than a computer scientist could afford. It had drawn attention that Harrison McIvor would have been smarter to avoid.

Corrigan's powerful legs crossed the tiled patio in three bounds. He flashed his ID, and the FBI guard stood away from the door.

The instant Corrigan stepped into the front entry, he heard hoarse screams from upstairs. A gaping hole in the living room plaster told him this was a revenge search. McIvor had made fools of the powers that be.

They were repaying him by destroying his home.

Corrigan bounded up the curved staircase, using the iron rail to boost his momentum. There was no point in holding secrets any longer. Everything had been blown wide open.

In the master bedroom, Schwarzenegger-Newberg and Greer, a short, stout African-American, had Alice McIvor pinned against the bedroom wall. The refined lady was writhing and crying, desperate to get to her daughter.

Laura's face was pressed into the carpet, Perkins with his knee on her back, digging under her. Her face was blue, soaked with sweat and tears.

"Get off of her!" Corrigan bellowed.

His face equally covered in sweat, Perkins looked up. "Not 'til she gives me the bear."

Corrigan's sharp kick brought a howl of pain. Clutching his side, Perkins rolled off Laura as Corrigan turned his attention to the agents holding Mrs. McIvor. "Let her go."

Newberg released the woman into Greer's care and moved toward the CIA agent. "Now, just wait one minute. You've. . ."

Newberg's head snapped back as Corrigan grabbed his windpipe. "I'm not negotiating with you morons. The girl has nothing to do with it. Now get out!"

Newberg gulped and rubbed his throat. When Corrigan shot a sharp look at Greer's brown face, he released Alice McIvor. She rushed to her daughter, and the women retreated to the safety of Mrs. McIvor's bed, crying in each other's arms.

Sending killing glances at Corrigan, the FBI agents shuffled out of the room.

Corrigan righted an antique chair and placed it near Laura. Sitting, he reached for her hands. She turned loose from her mother and faced him, dropping the bear to the quilt as she moved.

She watched him, grateful for a rescue, but full of questions he had hoped he'd never have to answer. The original plan was for him to disappear with his secret intact and not even testify. The FBI had sure fixed all that.

"You okay?"

Laura nodded. Without thinking, he gently brushed a tear from her cheek. What was he doing? The game was over. No need to pretend he loved her. But as he looked into those shimmering emerald eyes, he felt

BETRAYED

a deep, fierce dread.

"What's this about, Darryl?" Her words, a mere whisper, cut him to the core.

How could he tell her that the candlelight dinners, soft looks, and tender words had been the CIA's means of getting close to her parents? He let his eyes drift over her flushed face, down to her quivering lips; and he felt like pond scum.

"What's the reason for this?" Mrs. McIvor broke the spell.

Corrigan shot a sharp glance at the older woman before returning his gaze to Laura's fragile face. Her desperate expression clung to hope like a drowning man to a bit of passing driftwood. She silently begged him to make it all right.

"Who are you?" Laura whispered.

Corrigan released Laura's hands. He took a deep breath and forced himself to speak the awful truth. "My name is not Darryl Hansen. I'm a member of a law enforcement agency that's investigating your. . ." he glanced briefly at Mrs. McIvor. . . "your father."

Laura's eyebrows knit together. "You're not a high school PE teacher?"

"No."

"You're leaving me?" She spoke slowly like someone half awake.

Her soft words sliced through him. Why did he feel so guilty for doing his sworn duty?

Suddenly, he noticed that Laura's cheeks had turned translucent white. Was she going into shock? He wanted to reach out and hold her close. Instead, Alice McIvor tightened her arms around Laura.

Laura reached for Bear and stared at him for a moment that seemed like forever to Corrigan. Raising her chin and blinking, she said, "The talks and the walks," she swallowed convulsively, "the hugs were all part of your job?"

Color rushed into Laura's face, and Corrigan shied further back into the chair. "I wouldn't put it like that. You're a wonderful person. I. . ."

"The shared secrets, the dreams. . .were just playing along?"

Corrigan bit his bottom lip. "If I could only tell you what was at stake, you'd understand."

"The flowers? Did you use your money, or the government's?"

His silence gave her the answer.

A sharp crack echoed through the house. Corrigan touched his cheek

BETRAYED

where the imprint of a hand blossomed a brilliant red. He clamped his jaw until the muscles protested. He was a CIA agent. He couldn't afford to have feelings.

He stood up and strode out of the bedroom before she could see the pain in his eyes. Laura's bedroom door stood ajar. He paused and caught a whiff of Elige perfume. He had to get out of there.

When he reached the bottom of the stairs, six FBI agents watched him.

"Your face looks a little red there," taunted Perkins.

Corrigan ignored him.

"Got any more hearts lined up to break, or you taking a holiday after this one?" asked another.

Corrigan shouldered between them, refusing to be baited.

"Hey, how was it being undercover with her?" Perkins called after him, laughing.

Corrigan spun on his heels. Perkins's head snapped back, and blood gushed from his nose.

Corrigan's flinty eyes darted from man to man. Each stupid grin vaporized. Finally, he turned again to Perkins. "Where is Harrison McIvor?"

Pressing a handkerchief against his nose, he muttered, "He wasn't here."

Corrigan's top lip curled into a sneer. "Oh, that's obvious. You've torn the whole house apart, and the only suspect you came up with was a stuffed bear. Well, Hotshot, if you'd bothered to touch bases with me, I could have told you Harrison wouldn't be home tonight. After this fiasco, he'll be out of the country within hours. That man has the power to bring this nation to its knees. Don't you think he has an escape plan?" He clenched a meaty fist, begging one of them to make a move. "You've destroyed a year's work."

A moment later, he picked his way through the debris and paused at the door. "Let me make this perfectly clear: If any one of you so much as lays a finger on that girl, I'll be back."

Half an hour later, Laura pulled loose from her mother's arms, clutched Bear to her chest, and wandered back to her own room, her feet shuffling as if they wore chains. The bedroom door clicked shut behind her. Skirting the mound of clothing on the floor, she brushed past her overturned hope chest. Her no-hope chest.

BETRAYED

Leaving the lights on, Laura crawled into bed and pulled her knees up to her chin. She folded the blankets over her head, Bear next to her face. Once again, he soaked up her tears.

CHAPTER ONE

Corrigan glanced at Special Agent Sam Perkins beside him at the window. The big man lay aside his infrared binoculars and reached for yet another piece of pizza from a flat box on the floor beside him. Of all the slobs he had to be hooked up with, Jonathan Corrigan had to get Perkins. It also irked Corrigan that the CIA was legally bound to work under the FBI on this investigation. The thought of taking orders from Perkins turned Corrigan's stomach. He returned his attention to the street below and especially to the apartment across from them.

The pizza box shuffled across the dusty floor, propelled by Perkins's foot. "Wanna piece?"

"Leave it for the rats," Corrigan grunted. The apartment was a dump. During the night, they could hear the disgusting rodents traveling inside the walls. Corrigan took secret delight that the rats bothered Perkins. The FBI agent came from a comfortable suburban home. Jonathan grew up on a farm. Rats were nothing to him. As a boy, he'd potted his fair share with his .22 rifle.

But Perkins hated them. Corrigan had almost split a gut when a rat had run across Perkins's feet. The FBI agent practically jumped out of his skin and even pulled his weapon. City folk.

Perkins spoke again. "Sure you don't want some pizza?"

"No, thanks."

"Oh, yeah, I forgot. You're one of them health nuts."

Corrigan's mouth showed irritation. "I'm not a health nut. I just shy away from food that makes my belly look like a balloon." He glanced at

BETRAYED

Perkins's gut hanging over his belt.

The other man caught the move. "What are you saying? I'm out of shape?" When he shifted in the chair, his coat opened to reveal more evidence against him. "I can take care of myself when it counts."

Corrigan choked back a comment that Perkins hadn't done so well with Laura McIvor two years ago. The next instant, her face flashed across his mind. The building in front of him blurred, replaced by a beach scene. Their favorite spot. Warm wind, soothing waves, and her emerald eyes close to his. He remembered the softness of her skin as he brushed her hair aside, the tenderness of her lips as he. . .

Corrigan forced his attention back to the lighted windows of the building across the street. He had to stop torturing himself. It was over. It had just been a job, nothing more.

"I still don't see why you have to be here," Perkins said for the fifth time that day. "It's not like the FBI can't handle a few terrorists."

"None of you speak Arabic. I've spent the last eighteen months in Lebanon watching these guys. No one knows them like I do."

Perkins grunted. "So says you."

"That's right. So says me."

Finishing his pizza, Perkins picked up a copy of *Sports Illustrated*. Corrigan continued watching, wishing again he could have bugged the apartment across the street. They'd tried it once, but the suspects had simply swept the place with an electronic scanner. A few minutes later, the FBI's listening device was swimming toward the city sewer. Corrigan had to settle for visual surveillance.

"Seems you're not the only one who wants pizza tonight," Corrigan told his FBI partner a few minutes later.

At the entrance to the apartment building, a delivery boy got out of a dark Hyundai with a lighted sign on top of it. Slim and young, a baseball cap shielded his face from the blue-green lenses of the binoculars.

Corrigan said, "Some guy is going into the building with one of those big pizza-warming envelopes."

Perkins grabbed his own sights. "So what?" he said. "Someone's getting pizza."

Corrigan shifted his attention to a video display linked to a hidden camera in the dingy third-floor hall across the way. Soon the delivery driver's long-legged, loose-limbed stride brought him into view.

Perkins craned his head around Corrigan's back to watch the monitor as the kid stepped into the apartment. In less than two minutes, he left with the orange warming envelope hanging at his side.

"Looks like our boys got hungry," Perkins said, returning to his magazine.

"They must love MacDuff's pizza. How many times has this been? Half a dozen?"

Without answering, Perkins returned to an article about the Los Angeles Kings moving if they didn't sell more season tickets.

Half an hour later, Corrigan stiffened. "They're going out," he said. "Why would anyone go out at midnight just after eating delivery pizza?" He squinted into the eyepiece. "One of them has a briefcase."

"They probably want fresh air. I'll have someone follow them."

"I don't think we should take that chance. Our guys might lose them."

"I'd hate to blow our cover for a false alarm, Corrigan. They might just as easily be going to get some antacid. MacDuff's pizza is pretty brutal. I don't know how that place stays in business."

Corrigan rubbed his unshaven face. He glanced at his wristwatch's glowing LED numbers. Midnight wasn't really that late. But something was nagging at him. Something staring him in the face! Corrigan swore. "Do you know what today's date is?"

Perkins glanced at his own watch. "January 17. Why?" He flipped a page.

"Ten years ago today we started bombing Baghdad in Desert Storm."

"No, we started bombing on the sixteenth. I remember, because my nephew's birthday is January 16," said Perkins.

Perkins straightened up in his seat, his belly jiggling. "You think they'd be that obvious?"

"You want to take a chance?"

Perkins lifted his wrist and spoke into his cuff. "They're on the street. Pick them up." He looked at Corrigan. "If nothing comes of it, you go down with me."

Corrigan bit back his lower lip. People might die, and all Perkins cared about was who'd get the blame.

Corrigan watched below as a dozen agents propelled themselves from doorways and parked cars. The terrorists started running like fleeing calves in a rodeo. Less than eight seconds later, their noses scraped the pavement. Corrigan grinned. Those agents could have taken a ribbon in a real event.

BETRAYED

A dozen people gathered around, gaping at the men prone on the sidewalk.

"Tell those guys not to touch the briefcase," Corrigan said.

Perkins hesitated.

"Tell them not to touch the briefcase!"

"Hey, I'm in charge here, not you. I'll decide what's to be done."

Corrigan stood and faced Perkins, intimidating him with his six-foot one-inch, two-hundred-and-ten-pound frame—no fat. "How's your nose?" It was all he had to say. Perkins would never forget the day on the McIvor estate when Corrigan's right hand had flattened his face.

Perkins lifted his wrist. "Clear the area and call the bomb squad. The briefcase may contain explosives. Leave it alone."

Before Perkins finished talking, Corrigan bolted out of the apartment and charged down the stairs. When he burst out the door, the onlookers were rushing in opposite directions, the word "bomb" popping out like corn thrown in a hot fireplace.

Corrigan sprinted a hundred yards and drew up, sucking air, hands on hips, relieved that the leather case was still intact. It could contain enough explosive to incinerate at least one building. Still flat on the ground, the prisoners eyed him warily. They flinched in unison when he ran his hand over the clasps on the case. Did they flinch because they were scared or to mislead him?

Glancing up and down the street, he saw just what he needed: a twenty-four-hour check-cashing place. He grabbed the briefcase and dashed toward it.

CIA identification in one hand, briefcase in the other, he stormed into Instant Cash. Two female clerks and a bald desk jockey looked up when the door slammed back.

"Everyone out!" Corrigan shouted.

Standing, the manager stepped around the desk. "Officer, two of us have to remain. There's a lot of cash here."

Corrigan nodded toward the briefcase. "I've no time to argue. This may be a bomb." He set off toward the thick metal door at the back of the room and almost bumped his nose on a door made of steel bars. He turned back, looking for the manager, but the place was empty.

Pulling his Glock 21 from under his left arm, he fired half a dozen shots into the lock mechanism. When the door swung free, he set the briefcase on the cement floor and pulled the heavy vault door closed.

Only the manager could lock it, but Corrigan was counting on its weight to absorb a significant amount of the blast. If he were wrong, he'd never have to answer for his decision.

Drawing a six-inch knife from a sheath at his ankle, Corrigan took a deep breath. He had a fifty-fifty chance that the side he'd chosen would be clean. He made a long incision and started breathing again. A hole the size of a videotape revealed three sticks of dynamite connected to a timer. Any kid with Internet access could do better than that. It was his worst nightmare.

After carefully disconnecting the alarm clock, he pushed hard against the steel door and bounded out of Instant Cash to where the perps sat in the back of a police cruiser.

Perkins stood nearby—chest out and chin up to let everyone know that the arrest had been his idea. Running hard, Corrigan reached for the FBI agent and dragged him out of earshot.

"We've got a problem."

Perkins pulled away. "What are you talking about?"

"The explosives in that case could only wreck a few cars and take out some glass. It's a decoy."

Twelve hundred miles away, Shannon Masterson pulled a strand of blond hair to the corner of her lips and curled up on the worn love seat in her Bellingham apartment. She picked up the remote and flipped on the TV. At least this was free entertainment. She couldn't even afford a movie.

A year ago, she had had such high hopes for her computer consulting business. To date they were just hopes. Local businesses seemed bent on using Puget Information Systems, Inc., which had a dozen programmers on its payroll.

Shannon's sketchy background was the problem. She couldn't show her master's degree from MIT or glowing references from Silicon Valley giants. Those kudos belonged to Laura McIvor, and Laura McIvor was dead. She had to be. After the widespread media hype about her father's treachery, there was no way she could get a job in the U.S. Shannon could only show prospective clients how good she was—if she ever got a chance.

She flipped through thirty channels. The Sunday evening choice boiled down to *Touched by an Angel* reruns or a basketball game. Shannon chose the basketball game. She still didn't trust herself with emotional programs. Tears came too easily. She glanced at the stack of unpaid bills piled beside her on the scarred table and wished some angel would touch her pretty soon.

It was a good game. The Sonics were up on the Lakers by ten points. At a commercial break, Shannon uncurled long legs and padded to her microscopic kitchen for a Diet Pepsi. Her fridge looked more like a dishwasher.

At halftime, Shannon jumped when the phone jingled. Her heart sped up. She had no friends in Bellingham. The call could mean only one thing—business. Snatching the receiver, she forced her soprano voice to speak slowly and professionally.

"Masterson Consulting."

"Hi, is Gary there?" the voice asked.

Her heart dropped into her stomach. "Sorry, wrong number."

"You sure?"

Looking around her tiny bachelor apartment with a wry grin, Shannon answered. "I'm sure."

"Must've misdialed then."

"Must've." Shannon hung up.

Seconds later, the phone rang again. She snatched up the receiver. "Hello."

"Gary there?"

"No, nothing's changed since last time."

"Is this 555-1433?"

"Yes."

"Well, this is the number he gave me."

"Well, I can assure you there is no Gary here. He must have given you the wrong number."

"Yeah, I guess so."

As soon as she had snuggled back into the love seat, the phone rang yet again. She snatched the receiver, "Gary's not here!"

The voice was soft. She wasn't sure if it came from a man or a woman. "Uh, hi. I'm looking for Shannon Masterson."

Shannon went cold. A customer. Her very first potential customer, and she'd just yelled at him or her. "Sorry. I just got a couple of wrong-number calls. I thought that's who you were."

"Uh, no. I'm computer systems manager for Archon Energy, Ltd. My name's Ted Booregaard. Look, I realize it's Sunday and all, but I was wondering if you were available. We've got a problem with our payroll program, and the checks have to be ready by tomorrow noon. I called our usual firm, but all I got was voice mail."

Shannon forced herself to breathe slowly. Could she come? Was he kidding? Then again, she couldn't let him know how hungry she was. "Well, you're right; it is Sunday. Tomorrow won't do?"

"Most of our crew is union. It's my head if they decide to walk when their checks aren't ready."

Shannon paused for effect. "I'll be there in half an hour."

"Great. Our building is on the corner of Kentucky and Cornwall, across from the high school. Someone will meet you at the front door."

She set down the receiver and rubbed sweaty palms across her faded jeans. Pulling her only good outfit from the closet, she laid it on the bed—a white silk blouse and a gray A-line skirt that ended just above her knees. She slid her arms into the sleeves of a matching jacket and scrutinized herself in the mirror. Copper roots showed at her blond hairline. Time for another rinse.

Slipping on black low-heeled pumps, she picked up her shoulder bag and unlocked the dead bolt to let herself out. Securing the door behind her, Shannon tapped down two flights of stairs and made her way to her trusty Ford Tempo on the street. She paused in front of it. A streaked hood and cloudy windows made it look eighteen instead of eight years old. Before she met a new client, it would have to be washed.

She pulled in a corner of her thin lower lip, debating. The automatic car wash cost five dollars. At this point in her life, it might as well be a hundred dollars. Slipping her key into the door lock, she remembered a do-it-yourself place nearby on Ellis Street. She'd never been there before, but how hard could it be?

Three minutes later, she pulled into a brightly lit washing bay. She stepped out of the car, her shoes squishing against the wet concrete floor. She saw the control box and instruction sign on the other side of her car. She walked over to the control box and was pleased to learn that one dollar bought a wash. She had four quarters in her purse and no time to stop at a bank machine.

Shannon plugged the coins into the slot, then jumped back as the steel wand on the floor leapt to life, shooting water all over the place. She managed to corral it by stamping on it, but not before it had soaked her nylons and skirt. She stamped her foot and let out a small scream. It was all his fault. If Darryl Hansen hadn't ruined her life, she could take her car to an automatic wash. His face popped into her mind, and all Shannon could see was red. Given a chance, she'd claw those playful blue eyes right out of his head.

Forcing her anger aside, Shannon turned the high-pressure stream of hot soapy water toward her car. The dirt melted away in front of the wand. This was great. Hey, she might never use an automatic car wash again.

She worked from the front to the back, then toward the front again. The water slowed to a dribble while she sprayed the right front wheel. She walked back over to the panel and switched the lever to rinse.

Nothing.

She turned the switch back and forth half a dozen times. Still nothing.

The Ford Tempo looked like a giant marshmallow. Shannon dropped the wand and hurried to the phone-booth type office where a teenage girl sat on a stool. Working hard on a piece of gum like a cow on its cud, the girl flipped back a long strand of greasy hair and said, "Yeah? What is it?"

"The car wash quit working."

"What did you do to it?"

Shannon's eyebrows raised along with her chin. "I put in my quarters and washed my car. When I turned it to rinse, it quit."

The attendant stuck out her bottom lip and blew her limp bangs away from her eyes. "You gotta put more quarters in."

"But it says one dollar for a wash."

The girl looked up at the ceiling and shook her head. "If you read the small print on the bottom of the sign, it says a wash is two minutes. You've got to put more money in."

"I don't have any more money, and the job's only half done."

Ignoring her, the teen turned a page of the magazine and dove in.

Green eyes flashing, Shannon stormed out of the office and jumped into her car. *A wash is two minutes. How was I supposed to know that?* Slamming the car into gear, she pulled onto the road—ignoring the honks of the car she cut off—and headed toward Archon Energy, suds flying behind her like a foamy wake from a speedboat. Maybe Mr. Booregaard wouldn't meet her himself. Maybe a security guard would let her into the building.

She pulled into a parking lot of about two dozen spaces in front of a three-story steel-and-glass office building. Putting on the parking brake, Shannon glanced into the mirror behind the sun visor. Her makeup was coming apart, but it would have to do. She was already late. Locking the car door behind her, Shannon dropped the keys into her bag as her heels clicked across the parking lot containing only one other car, a late-model Accord.

A stodgy man in a rumpled suit waited at the front door. He had an anxious expression and thin, gray hair cut short. His eyes immediately went to her water-stained skirt. When his forehead wrinkled, Shannon wondered if she was going to get past the front door.

"So, if this bomb is a decoy, what have they been doing in there all this time?" Perkins asked.

Corrigan glanced at the terrorists' apartment building. The answer had to be inside there. He broke into a jog.

"Hey!" Perkins cried after him. "Where ya going?"

Pausing briefly, he turned back. "To their apartment. Maybe we can figure out what they've been up to."

Tapping two other men from the Bureau—a Mutt and Jeff set—Perkins bounded after Corrigan, his belly bouncing with every stride. Slick with sweat, the stout agent paused, wincing, when Corrigan used the butt of his Glock to smash glass and reach through to unlock the door. "Why didn't you just buzz someone to let us in instead of busting up private property?"

Corrigan turned to Mutt. "You guys have already evacuated the building, right? Isn't that standard FBI operating procedure when a bomb has been found?"

Mutt nodded. Corrigan stared at Perkins. "Then who's going to answer the buzzer?"

Not waiting for a reply, Corrigan bounded up the narrow stairs. Three sets of heavy boots followed him. The men drew up at the door, and Perkins reached for the knob.

Corrigan's arm flew out, blocking him. "They may have booby-trapped the door."

The big man took a step backward. "We ought to wait for the bomb squad."

For an instant, Corrigan glared at the chipped door as though it could whisper its secret. He glanced at the lanky agent standing off to the left. "You're absolutely sure everyone's out?"

"Yes, Sir." His Adam's apple bobbed. "As soon as you grabbed that bomb, we started clearing the building."

"Good work." Corrigan glanced at three tense faces, considering, then said, "You all get out of here. I'm going in."

BETRAYED

Perkins shook his fleshy head. "No way. We wait for the bomb squad."

Corrigan moved within inches of Perkins's nose. "I'm going in now. Alone. There's not a second to waste. Hundreds, possibly thousands, of lives depend on it." His cheeks tightened with disgust. "I shouldn't have to tell you that."

The men from the Bureau glanced at each other. Their leader pursed his lips. He nodded at Mutt and Jeff, and they hoofed it to the stairs. Perkins stared at Corrigan. "What is it with you? You got a death wish or something?"

Corrigan gave no reply, but the words hovered in the stale air. Since the incident with Laura McIvor, Corrigan had played peekaboo with death for twenty-four months, requesting one dangerous assignment after another. What had happened to him?

Giving the men two minutes to clear the building, Corrigan screwed up his face—expecting an explosion—and kicked in the hollow panel before him.

The only bang he heard was the doorknob cracking a hole in the wall plaster. Brushing a fleck of wood from his face, he stepped inside.

Before him lay a living room containing a low-backed couch, a chair covered with nubby green fabric, and a coffee table that held the cigarette burns and coffee stains from twenty years before. Fast-food litter and empty whiskey bottles sprawled over faded carpet roses and every piece of furniture. Whiskey bottles? They had to be from previous tenants because these guys didn't drink. They took their Islam seriously.

In the kitchen doorway, he stopped, chilled to the core.

Segments of different-colored wires littered the table and floor. Shavings of a puttylike material dusted the entire tabletop. Corrigan lifted a gray sliver and touched it to his tongue. In a corner lay a pile of small boxes with pictures of a travel alarm clock on their covers. Instantly, he knew what had happened.

"All clear?" Perkins called from the hall.

"Yeah," Corrigan replied. Squatting, he counted the small boxes.

"What is it?"

"They've made timer-activated C-4 bombs."

"How did they get them out? We've seen everyone coming and going. Not one of them had so much as a paper bag in his hand."

Standing, Corrigan nodded toward the empty pizza boxes on the floor. "Everyone but the pizza guy."

Wearily rubbing his jaw, Perkins drew in a breath. "You think he was with them?"

"You're the one who said MacDuff's pizza is rotten. Why else would they buy so much of it? Very likely the pizza guy brought in the raw materials and took out the finished product."

"Someone has eleven timer-activated C-4 bombs out there?" Perkins asked. "Why, Corrigan?"

"Actually ten. One clock was used for the decoy. I think they want to make us feel what it was like to be in Baghdad during Desert Storm—the terror of explosions hitting at random." He glanced at Perkins. "It's a frightening experience knowing death is raining down on you, and there's not a thing you can do about it."

"Aren't these guys Lebanese? Why do they care?"

"They just lived in Lebanon. Two are Iraqi and the third is an Egyptian mercenary."

Perkins sank into a plastic kitchen chair and reached for a handkerchief to wipe his face. "Okay, Corrigan. I admit it. I'm over my head. What happens now?"

"I'm not sure." Corrigan opened scratched wooden doors and peered at the mold under the sink. "What we've got to do is work together for a change." He pulled out more empty whiskey bottles and empty bottles of cleanser, tossing them to the floor.

He stood and turned to Perkins. "We don't have a clear picture of the delivery guy, and we can be sure the car has been dumped. We have to beat these guys with our brains."

Perkins grunted as he got to his feet. "Now you've really got me scared. We've. . .actually, I've messed up pretty much every way an agent could on this one."

For the first time since he'd met him, Corrigan saw a hint of humility in Perkins's eyes. "Hey, don't beat yourself up too much. I should've clued you in on the pizza guy a lot earlier. We're in this together." Corrigan held out his hand.

Perkins shook it. "Okay, Partner, let's get on with it."

The two agents mercilessly trashed the apartment, tearing open the scant furnishings, kicking holes in walls, even to the point of ripping the toilet out. Dirty and covered with sweat, they finished their search empty-handed. Corrigan strode to the living room window and peered down at the police car holding the prisoners. What would their weakness be?

BETRAYED

According to their religion, even torture and death only added stars to their crowns in the hereafter. American tactics fell way short on that score. Psychological maneuvering was the only option—and a slim hope at that.

"I've got an idea," he told Perkins.

"What?"

"No time to explain." Corrigan slipped a notebook and pen from his pocket and scrawled some words.

He handed a slip of paper to Perkins, who raised shaggy eyebrows. "What you got cooking now?"

Corrigan grinned. "Trust me. It'll be good."

"I'll have to break a few laws to get this stuff."

"That a problem?"

Perkins shook his head and grinned. "Not at all." Stuffing the list into his inside coat pocket, he headed toward the stairs with Corrigan behind him.

At the street, Perkins jerked open the door of a dark Crown Victoria and left a strip of rubber as he tore out.

Corrigan turned to the half-dozen FBI agents standing nearby. "Take those three back to their apartment for questioning."

Without a word, the shortest one pulled open the door and motioned for the suspects to get out. Handcuffed, they shambled down the sidewalk, eyes down, seemingly submissive.

Corrigan sized them up as they passed him.

The oldest and by far the most dedicated was Ahmed al-Shahin. Medium height and refined, he was a prime suspect in several bombings. He had served ten years in an Israeli prison before his release as part of a peace treaty. Robust before his prison term, he was thin and gaunt. The Mossad had put al-Shahin through their worst, but he couldn't be broken. He lived only for revenge.

Next in line, Mustafa Farid was an Egyptian who'd never agreed with the Israeli/Egyptian peace accord. He ran a terrorist-for-hire business, and Iraq was his most recent customer. He was stocky with a thick, black beard, his dark eyes penetrating and angry. Farid was in it for the money. He might talk to save his own hide, but Corrigan doubted it. Better to rot in an American prison than spend the rest of his life running from the Iraqis.

The last terrorist was a slight fellow just over twenty years old. Saad Salih was a university student, a handsome kid with easygoing brown eyes who turned bad when a stray Gulf War bomb took out most of his family. Saad was the weak link. Corrigan knew he loved his only remaining family members, two sisters, with an obsessive, protective passion.

As he shuffled past, Corrigan planted a powerful hand on young Saad's chest and bent over to whisper in his ear. "You're playing with the big boys now," he said in Arabic. "By the time today is done, you'll have a whole new understanding of the word *pain*."

Sweat broke out on Saad's upper lip.

Corrigan just smiled.

CHAPTER TWO

In his mid-fifties, Ted Booregard's copper nose and blotchy skin told the world he was a hard drinker. His heavy jowls sagged almost to the knot in his tie when he leaned forward to run a pudgy paw through thinning gray hair. At the moment, he wore a deep frown.

When Shannon drew near enough to see his face, her spirit sank. She'd already failed inspection. She may as well go back to her car and leave.

Three strides later, she paused in front of him, chin high, ready for the worst. If she had to go, she'd go down fighting.

Staring at the water stains on her jacket sleeve and skirt, he muttered, "Computer geek."

"Excuse me?" Shannon's embarrassment suddenly changed to something more heated.

"You're a computer geek, all right," he said more clearly. A smile flitted across his soft features. The next instant, he noticed her sober expression and killed his own joke.

Shannon quietly exhaled, trying to squelch her flaring temper. Before her parents' arrest, she had dressed with the best. Clamping her teeth, she took a firm grip on her pride and squeezed it down. If she was going to eat, she had to work. Avoiding eye contact with her portly host, she edged past him into the vast lobby.

Glancing around at more glass and chrome, Shannon almost collided with a potted palm. Totally flustered now, she waited for the manager to take the lead.

Whatever Archon Energy did, they did it all over the world. Pictures of oil rigs—at sea, in deserts, in jungles, and on farm fields—covered the massive walls. Staring straight ahead, Mr. Booregaard plodded across thick rust-and-green carpet to a back wall lined with silver elevators, the center one standing open. He paused for Shannon to enter first.

When the doors wheezed shut, he fidgeted with his rumpled gray tie. "Have you ever worked with BASIC? I should have asked on the phone."

"Sure," Shannon replied, as though it were nothing. "BASIC is archaic, but some people still find it useful for some applications. I take it your firm still uses it."

Booregaard squeezed his fat lips together into a woeful expression. "Oh yeah, we're still using it. . .for our sins." A bell dinged, and silver doors slid open. Leading the way, he stopped before a solid metal door with an electronic lock. "I signed on here three years ago," he said as he shoved a plastic card into a slot and placed his thumb on a touch plate. "As soon as I saw what they had, I suggested they change to a network of microcomputers, but this outfit only spends money on things that make oil." He pulled open the door. "I call this monster T-Rex. Welcome to his lair."

Shannon's jaw dropped. Before her was a VAX mainframe at least fifteen, possibly twenty years old. Most programmers would have just said no and let Archon pay for its sins. Most programmers weren't a month away from being on the street.

The mainframe itself was in a glass-enclosed room that was temperature controlled with halon fire-extinguisher nozzles installed in the ceiling above it, the only suppression system that worked on these babies. Unfortunately, they would kill any human trapped in the enclosure as well.

He looked at her, unsure. "Are you positive you can work with this? I've got a degree in computer science but how to understand the source code for this thing is something I've long forgotten."

Shannon hid her dismay. This job could have her up all night. She smiled at Booregaard. "No problem." Her father had insisted she learn every programming language ever used, and BASIC was her first primer.

Shannon took a deep breath, then slipped her purse strap from her shoulder. "Show me which terminal you want me to use."

He led her to the far right corner of the room and flicked a hand at a scuffed work pod in traditional almond color—one of a four-man unit. Heavy and bulky equipment covered most of the tiny desk, with odd-sized notes completely covering the dividers. "Welcome to the magic portal," Booregaard said. "The place where miracles happen every day. If they didn't, we'd close down."

Shannon seated herself at the stiff desk chair and gazed at the green monochrome monitor showing a single phrase—END. She shook her head. She hadn't seen a monochrome for five years. Archon was past archaic. She glanced up. "When the system crashes, what does it do exactly?"

"It says our employee records are invalid. Go figure. Two weeks ago they're valid, this week they're not. It makes no sense."

Her fingers played lightly across the thick keyboard with a metallic, rattling sound. "Does Archon know that it costs more to maintain this relic than to replace it?"

Booregaard folded his arms. "I told them. I almost had them convinced until they called in Puget Information to do a study. Puget's report said that the total cost of reentering records, training personnel, and buying new hardware made a change unwise. They said Archon should wait five more years."

Shannon crinkled her forehead. "That's crazy."

Booregaard's face twisted into a cynical expression. He leaned closer. "Between you and me, I know exactly why they did it. We ended up forking over twenty-five thousand dollars to make this system Y2K compliant. What's really interesting is that they gave us a two-year warranty which expired a week ago.

"When I came in this week to run the payroll, she crashed. I phoned Puget, and they said I'm looking at about ten grand to have someone fix it on a rush basis. That kind of expense has to be approved by the board, and all the bigwigs are in Caracas at that big oil summit." He drew in a bushel of air. "So. . ."

Shannon smiled. "So you've spent the last three days trying to fix it yourself." Suddenly, she understood why he'd looked so dour when she arrived. Poor guy.

Booregaard nodded, his mouth quirked in on one side. "I know, pretty dumb. I guess you've probably figured out that my neck is on the line here. I've got a lot riding on you."

Shannon's smile widened. "We'll try and keep your neck just where it is. If you'll give me the access codes, I'll go to work."

Booregaard scrawled some letters on a green sticky note, then shuffled to a glass-enclosed office at the other end of the room, shoulders sagging, his body heavily swaying with each step.

Shannon felt relieved when the door bumped closed behind him. She hated for people to peer over her shoulder.

A couple of minutes later, she was inside the source code. Printing it out would take hours. Viewing it at a terminal was quicker. Fortunately, she already had a theory. As page after page scrolled down, her eyes moved with the text, looking for one particular word: GOSUB. As always, time stood still when Shannon sat at the controls. She loved this job.

Just over an hour later, on GOSUB command number sixty-four, she nailed it. Leaning back in her squeaky chair, she chewed the last bit of lipstick from her bottom lip. The system would be up and running in less than two hours. At the normal rate of seventy-five dollars an hour, she'd make a lousy one hundred and fifty dollars.

Booregaard would never know if she overcharged him, but she could not do it. After what happened to her parents, Shannon had made herself an ironclad promise. Her affairs would be as clean as Ivory soap even if she had to shut down her fledgling business. The alternative cost far too much.

Fingers flying, she repaired eighty-two lines of code, then signaled to Booregaard.

He practically leaped from his desk and rushed to her. "Something wrong?"

"It's fixed."

His eyebrows reached for his hairline. "Already? I mean, those Puget guys have never fixed anything in under two days. Are you sure?"

Shannon got up from the seat. "Try it yourself."

Booregaard sat at the console and keyed in his payroll program. When it loaded, he looked up at her. "What was the problem?"

"The way some programmers got around the Y2K program was to put in what's called a subroutine which tells it how to interpret the dates. Some GOSUB commands in your system pointed to an invalid line number, and the program didn't know how to process the employees' birth dates. I simply found the line number of the subroutine and redirected the commands."

"Any idea why it happened?"

Shannon brushed blond hair away from her eyes. "The subroutine is encrypted. I can't read it, but the problem has to be in there somewhere."

"Why is it encrypted?"

BETRAYED

"Probably because Puget people wrote the program. Since they own it, they don't want their unprotected code on client computers; otherwise, any programmer could copy it and spread it all over the world. Puget would never get paid for their property."

His face showed irritation. "If there's something wrong in their file, then they should have to fix it."

Shannon hesitated. "Without breaking their code, I can't prove it."

"Just great," he said, massaging the side of his face. "You're telling me this could happen again."

"I suggest you call them. Maybe they're aware of the problem and forgot to notify you."

Booregaard's mouth twisted. "Convenient for them, don't you think?" He stood. "How much do we owe you?"

"A hundred and fifty dollars. I can mail you a bill." Shannon had to force herself to mention a bill—she was almost out of groceries—but it was the professional thing to do.

He stared at her. "That's all?"

She slipped her purse strap over her shoulder and turned as though ready to go. "Of course. My rate is seventy-five an hour."

He stepped away from the desk, his eyes friendly for the first time since she'd arrived. "Have you got any business cards with you? I can't remember the last time I met an honest programmer."

Shannon pulled a stack of cards from her jacket pocket and held them out to him. "I'm sure you're exaggerating. It can't be that bad."

"Oh, yes, it is."

Fifteen minutes later, Shannon left Archon Energy with two hundred dollars in her pocket. Booregaard had paid her from petty cash and insisted she take more for working at night. Even better, Ted Booregaard had promised he'd call her again, and he'd tell his friends about her. Maybe she really had been touched by an angel.

Back in his trashed apartment with half a dozen agents swarming over the place, young Saad Salih sat with his feet shackled to chair legs. Heavy cuffs cut into his wrists, and the wooden chair back gouged his backbone.

Beside him, the Egyptian Mustafa Farid hunched on the ratty sofa. Mustafa's dark eyes were glowing embers. Grim resolve showed through his thick, black beard.

Twenty minutes ago, the Americans had dragged Ahmed to the back bedroom. From the shouts and groans filtering through the closed door, the leader of the terrorist troop wasn't cooperating.

Saad shifted to his left hip and tried to imitate Mustafa's stiff expression. The young American with the deadly eyes had promised him pain. Would Saad be able to stand strong when it happened?

Saad had always known they'd be captured. Ahmed had planned to have the Americans follow them while the fourth member of their team planted the bombs. In Lebanon, Ahmed had said, "Don't worry. When we're taken, they'll only deport us or put us in one of their prison hotels. Those Americans have soft bellies."

Ahmed was wrong. The dangerous American and his fat friend had told them from the start: no reading of rights, no negotiating. Whatever it took, Ahmed and his men would tell who had the bombs and where the targets were. Saad knew they'd never get anything out of Ahmed or Mustafa, and with the help of Allah, they'd never get anything out of him, either.

The door to the interrogation room thumped back, and the fat agent trundled across the faded tile in the hall, hitching his belt closer around his sagging gut.

"Any progress, Perkins?" a tall, skinny man asked.

He shook his head, sadly. "Nope, tight as a drum. We won't get anything out of him."

"Whatcha going to do?" asked a short guy on the other side of the room.

"Me?" Perkins asked. "Nothing. It's up to big-shot Corrigan of the CIA."

CIA? The word whipped through Saad's brain. Ahmed had told him that the CIA didn't work inside the U.S. What was a CIA agent doing here?

Crack! A pistol shot made Saad jump. Metal peeled a layer of skin from his wrists and ankles. In unison, five agents slowly looked down the hall. Perkins yawned and scratched his side.

Saad searched Mustafa's eyes and saw a flicker of fear that vanished the next instant.

Perkins sighed. "So much for that guy." He pointed his chin toward Mustafa. "He's next."

Two agents came at the man who looked like a young Fidel Castro.

BETRAYED

Mustafa arched his back and lunged toward the smaller of the two. Shorty stepped aside, and the tall, skinny one slapped the terrorist across the face with a crack almost as loud as the pistol. Mustafa reeled. One on each side, avoiding his thrashing legs, the FBI agents dragged him down the hall.

More groans and shouts. The men guarding Saad flipped through old newspapers as though they were deaf. The one who slapped Mustafa sent Saad an odd smirk that could be understood in any language—guess who's next.

The voices grew hoarse, then faded. Perkins returned. Saad gulped, his mouth like cotton.

"No luck?" Shorty asked.

Perkins chuckled. "These guys don't know how serious Jon is. They think he's kidding."

Another pistol shot. Sweat streamed from Saad's forehead and dripped down his cheek. His palms felt clammy. He couldn't breathe. Perkins moved so close to him that Saad could feel the big man's belly against his shoulder. "You've got an appointment, Kid. Let's not keep the doctor waiting."

Staying well behind the prisoner, Skinny uncuffed Saad's ankles from the chair and clipped his feet together with shackles. Rising painfully, he shuffled down the hall with an agent gripping each arm in a come-along hold. When Perkins pushed open the door, Saad gasped, and his knees buckled.

Turning his head away from bloody Ahmed and Mustafa stretched out on the carpet, Saad Salih forced his legs to straighten and swallowed back the hot bile rising in his throat. He mustn't show weakness before these infidels.

The big American's flinty eyes didn't blink as he stared at Saad, his words all the more menacing because of their gentle tone. "I hope you're smarter than them, Saad."

Perkins shoved him into a steel chair and tied him down. Breathing heavily from the exertion of bending over, he trudged to a kitchen chair in a far corner out of Saad's line of sight. "He's all yours, Corrigan. Let me know when you want me to leave."

Corrigan leaned down until he bumped noses with him. His voice boomed. "Where are the targets?" Saad tried to turn his head away, but powerful hands forced his face forward.

The young Iraqi kept silent, his breathing shallow and quick.

Suddenly, the American straightened and stepped back. He spoke in Arabic, soft and melodious. "Look, Saad, I'm not FBI. I'm CIA. I'm speaking Arabic because that FBI agent in the corner would arrest me if he knew what I'm saying." He moved closer. "I want to know where the targets are. I'll do anything to find out." His face moved down to eye level with Saad.

"I know you believe you'll go to heaven if I kill you. Maybe so. But consider this—what if you kill some Muslims today? Millions of Muslims live in the United States, and many work for government agencies."

Saad couldn't suppress a small smile. The idiots thought government buildings were the targets. He made an effort to straighten his face. Ahmed had warned him that the soft bellies would try that argument about killing Muslim brothers, but the American's words were foolishness. Allah would give any Muslims who died a martyr's reward.

Corrigan stepped back and paced, reasoning with him now. "You know, Saad, I understand why you're angry. It was terrible to lose your parents during the Gulf War. I understand your need for revenge. That's why I'm not going to torture you like I did those others." He flicked a hand toward the bodies behind him as though they were a trifle.

Saad swallowed. His tongue had glued itself to the roof of his mouth.

His tormentor stopped pacing and leaned down, still talking in Arabic. "You have to understand something. I need revenge, too. You're going to kill innocent people today, and someone has to pay. I'm glad you feel confident of heaven, because in a minute I'm going to ask the FBI agent to leave again. When I shoot you, my revenge still won't be satisfied, Saad. I know your sisters live in Lebanon. They have five beautiful children."

Corrigan pushed in, his breath mingling with Saad's. "After you're dead, I'm going to have the Israeli air force bomb their village. Are you willing to gamble your sisters' lives? Ahmed and Mustafa doubted my word. Don't make the same mistake."

Saad had prepared himself for prison, even death. But not this. In their presence he'd always pretended to be aloof from his sisters, Fatima and Hala. It was the Iraqi way with females. But his love for them was a living thing that squeezed his inmost being until he felt physical pain.

He glanced at the bodies of his dead comrades. If he gave the information, he'd destroy a glorious mission. His shoulders twitched, then his arms and his hands. The next moment he shook like a man in the throes of malaria.

BETRAYED

Corrigan nodded to Perkins. Coming out of his chair, the fat man shook his head sadly as he walked past Saad. Three paces later, the door squeaked open, then closed.

Smooth steel pressed against Saad's temple. He gasped and looked up to see Corrigan's heavy hand next to his left eye, fingers wrapped around the grip of a Glock 21.

"Last chance, Kid," he said. "If I pull this trigger, your sisters die."

Saad wanted to scream. He could see the broken bodies of Fatima and Hala lying in the street, their blank eyes open to the rain. Allah forgive him; he couldn't bear it.

Working his tongue loose, he mumbled, "Craigmore School."

"Louder! I can't hear you."

"Craigmore School!" he shouted. Pure hatred—raging, consuming—swelled in his belly.

Corrigan's face turned the color of an old brick. "You filthy beasts targeted a school?"

"Five schools." Saad's features twisted. "It's time for Americans to know how it feels to have children die."

The CIA agent took a spiral-bound notepad from his pocket. "Tell me their names. If one kid dies, so help me, I'll take out more than one Lebanese village."

Three seconds later, Saad spieled off the names, and Corrigan charged out, leaving his prisoner tied.

Alone in the death room, Saad's anger turned against himself. He felt dirty. Surely they'd threatened Ahmed's family, and he hadn't broken.

He hung his head to hide furious tears when Perkins came back to unfasten Saad's wrists and ankles from the chair.

Ahmed moaned.

Saad's head snapped around.

The second moan came louder.

"Ahmed!" Saad shouted. He yanked at the last cuff still about his ankle, trying to get to his friend. His senses whirled. He felt faint.

Perkins chuckled. "They're not dead. We smeared them with paint and put them to sleep."

Groaning like an animal in pain, Saad lunged for the Beretta holstered under Perkins's arm.

"Hey!" Perkins shouted. Running footsteps sounded behind him.

The fat man managed to get his hand on Saad's wrist, but the young

BETRAYED

Iraqi had the gun. He twisted around and squeezed the trigger twice as Corrigan charged into view. The gun bucked in his hand, and his tormentor fell. Saad's face hit the carpet, and he felt his tied ankle crack. The pain was nothing. He almost enjoyed it. The American had paid.

CHAPTER THREE

Shannon squinted at a shaft of sunlight streaming through a crack in her bedroom drapes. Irritated, she snuggled deeper into the covers. It was no use. Once she woke up, that was it. No snoozing for this girl.

Rolling over, she glimpsed the ten twenty-dollar bills stacked on her nightstand. She sighed and stretched. It was going to be a great day. First on her to-do list was dropping her suit at the cleaners, then she'd rewash the Ford Tempo. On the way home, she'd treat herself to a tall cup of Muffin Mania's cinnamon hazelnut coffee and a fat muffin.

After a quick shower, she pulled on her most comfortable faded blue jeans and a Seahawks sweatshirt. Bellingham stayed much colder than California where she used to enjoy T-shirt weather year-round. Sitting in front of her vanity mirror, she applied light makeup and smiled, remembering last night. If Ted Booregaard turned out to be as good as his word, she may just be in business.

Swiping up her suit hanger and purse, she started out of the apartment. Before she could open the door, the phone rang. Shannon stared at it. Two calls in less than twenty-four hours?

She dropped her purse and lifted the receiver. "Masterson Consulting."

"Shannon Masterson?" a woman's throaty voice asked.

"Yes."

"I'm Olivia Donner. I got your name from Ted Booregaard. He says you're pretty good at programming."

"That's nice of him to say so," Shannon said.

"How about microcomputers? Do you know hardware, Windows Millennium, that kind of thing?"

"I'm very familiar with microcomputers and related software."

"What a relief! My technician was in a car accident last night and. . ."

"I'm sorry to hear that," Shannon said. "I hope he'll be all right."

"Oh, yes. God was with him. He'll be off work for six weeks, though. He broke his right hand. If you haven't had breakfast yet, could we meet somewhere and talk?"

Shannon paused for effect. Microcomputers and their software were way below her skill level, but who cared? "That will be fine," she said.

"How about the Muffin Mania at Cordata Place?"

"Perfect. When would you like to meet?"

"How about quarter to ten?"

Shannon glanced at her watch. "Fine. How will I know you?"

"I'm wearing a light blue blazer with matching slacks and a white blouse. I have curly brunette hair, and I'm what people kindly call pleasantly plump."

Shannon suppressed a chuckle at the woman's honesty. "I'm about five feet, four inches, blond hair, and I'll be wearing. . ." She glanced at the suit hanging from her hand. "Blue jeans and a Seahawks sweatshirt. I'm sorry I won't be more presentable, but I was on my way out to wash my car."

"That's all right, Dear," Olivia said, good humor in her voice. "It's your brains I'm interested in. Besides, Bellingham isn't exactly New York City."

Shannon said good-bye and left the apartment wearing a brilliant smile. Things were finally looking up.

She dropped the suit at the cleaners and pulled into the car wash. Handling the high-pressure wand like a pro, she was on her way to Muffin Mania five minutes later.

The moment she pulled open the door, the warm aroma of coffee and fresh pastries closed around her. The place was bustling, every table full and a line at the high counter. At a corner booth, Olivia Donner sent her a big wave and smile that put Shannon at ease immediately. Pushing fifty, Ms. Donner had a pie face and round cheeks.

Shannon navigated through the crowded restaurant, avoiding elbows and skirting chairs. When she finally reached the corner booth, Olivia Donner took her hand. "Hi, Shannon. You're right on time." She eased herself out of the booth bench. "What will you have?"

"Black cinnamon hazelnut coffee and a blueberry muffin would be great," Shannon answered, sliding onto the cloth seat.

"Super. I'll be right back." Olivia trundled toward the counter. Pleasantly plump had been a gross understatement.

While she waited, Shannon idly listened to the TV mounted near the ceiling. The volume was just loud enough so that she could hear the newscaster over the noisy room.

Sally Epson spoke from the Channel 7 news desk. "FBI agents thwarted a terrorist attack on five elementary schools in the Los Angeles area early this morning. Unconfirmed sources say the agent responsible for uncovering the plot was critically wounded while apprehending the terrorists." A video clip showed a hospital emergency entrance, then focused on the injured man's face.

Shannon sucked in a quick breath. On the screen, Darryl Hansen lay on a stretcher, his eyes closed, his mouth twisted in agony.

Shannon shivered inside her sweatshirt. Her stomach wound itself into an iron knot. A dozen emotions washed through her as Darryl's stretcher disappeared through glass doors.

"Are you okay, Honey?" Olivia asked. She placed two tall mugs of coffee on the table; both with a muffin balanced on top. "You're as white as a ghost."

With a shaking hand, Shannon reached for her cup, hoping the hot liquid would stop her trembling. She glanced at the TV. "I think I just saw one," she murmured.

"Get him to surgery." Corrigan heard a man's voice. "He's started bleeding again. We're going to have to open him back up."

Corrigan gritted his teeth and prayed he'd pass out. His stomach was an inferno. An oxygen mask covered his mouth and nose. An IV ran into his arm. On both sides of the gurney, men and women in white shouted orders nonstop as they whisked him down a wide hall.

One of the hands holding the rail of the stretcher had a freckled forearm. Corrigan's pain-dazed eyes moved upward. Her face was turned away, but he saw that her cheek was lightly freckled as well. Her copper hair lay coiled into a thick bun.

Laura!

Mustering all his strength, he lifted his fingers and draped them over her hand. Since she was here, she must have forgiven him.

Glancing at his hand over hers, she turned and smiled down at him. When they slowed to enter a doorway, the nurse said, "Try to relax. We're going to fix you right up."

Corrigan moaned and clenched the bloodstained sheet. *Laura, where are you?*

Three wide lights glared into his eyes. Someone yanked off the plastic oxygen mask and replaced it with a black rubber thing. A masked man held up two hands while a nurse slipped latex gloves on them. The lights swirled and grew dim.

In his last moment of consciousness, Corrigan murmured, "How could I have been such a fool?"

Olivia sat beside Shannon and turned to look up at the TV screen. "Terrible thing, that. I caught the full newscast earlier. Those terrorists planned to set off a small bomb at one end of the school, then put a larger bomb at the other end where the children would run for safety. Imagine killing innocent children for some political cause! Boy, if they knew their Bible they'd never try a stunt like that."

"I guess not," Shannon said, still distracted by the TV broadcast. Laura McIvor had loved Darryl Hansen. Shannon Masterson did not. Sure, Darryl had tried to make up for what he'd done by arranging a new identity for her, but that could never, ever repay her for everything she'd lost.

"So, Honey," Ms. Donner said, while they sipped coffee and broke into their muffins, "tell me about your computer background."

Shannon shifted in her seat, trying to force her mind back to the interview. "I have a diploma in computer science from a correspondence college in Texas. I know it's not much, but I did learn well." A diploma provided by Darryl. One of the many things he'd done to make her false identity appear genuine.

"You must have aced the course, then some. According to Ted, you did in two hours what those crooks over at Puget do in two days."

"I wouldn't go as far as to call them crooks."

Olivia put her hand over Shannon's. "Honey, you don't know half of it. Two years before Y2K hit, Puget snatched up every decent programmer in the area. They hired one away from me. There was no way I could match the salary they offered. Once they had the market sewn up, they gouged every business around here."

She wrapped a pudgy hand around her cup and held it to her lips. When she set it down, she said, "Anyhow, let's talk about you and the job. Our focus is helping people pick out the right computer system. Then we put it together and load their software. We also do in-house and on-site training. Can you handle that?"

"Sure. I can build a system from the case up, load the software, and configure it for whatever the user wants. If they're into games, I can tweak it for that; if they're into business applications, I can do that, too."

"Sounds like you're the woman I'm looking for. Now, about your consulting business?"

"Will I have to put that aside while I work for you?"

Olivia broke into a broad grin. "Not in the least, Dear. I'm thrilled to have you. What I was thinking is this: As long as you can give me a day's notice, if you get a consulting job, go for it. I can only pay twelve dollars an hour, so it's hardly fair to hold you back. Can you live with that?"

"I certainly can."

"Great. When would you like to start?"

Shannon took a sip of coffee and slowly set the cup down. "How about tomorrow? I have a few things to do today."

His stomach was on fire. The flames spread down his legs and into his chest. Jonathan Corrigan clamped down on his lower lip and pried his crusted eyes open. He was in a dim hospital room, little flashing lights and beeps everywhere. He tried to lift his hand, but the movement created a fresh spasm, and he let it lay where it was. Four years ago, he'd taken a bullet in the arm, but that had never hurt like this.

What had happened? Their interrogation had gone so well. The kid confessed. There was time to stop the bomber. Then a muzzle flash. . . That's right. The kid had gotten Perkins's gun and shot him. The first shot had doubled him over. On the second one, he'd crumpled to the ground. Saad had hit him twice—in the stomach and the left leg.

Corrigan tried to lick his lips, but his tongue was too thick to move. His mouth felt full of last year's sawdust. Slowly, easily, he rolled his head to the right. . .and blinked.

Beside the bed his mother sat, chin on chest, eyes shut. As a young woman, his mother could ride, rope, and stare down a wild-eyed horse with the best of them. Age had finally tapped her on the shoulder. Her raven hair was mostly gray, and her face had more lines than when he last saw her five years ago. He was on his way to an assignment, and they had exchanged harsh words about his lifestyle and his job. She had always expected a lot from him, the eldest son.

He looked up at the tiled ceiling, hot tears welling up. He was Jonathan Corrigan, a tough, street-smart CIA agent. Thirty-three years old and on his way to making section chief. But tied to an IV stand and a catheter bag, his middle covered with bandages, he felt like a six year old, weak and scared and so glad she'd come.

"Mom," he croaked.

Her rough hand brushed at that sweet moon-shaped face, then returned to the armrest. She had always slept deeply.

Jonathan closed his mouth and worked his tongue around, trying to develop some saliva. He didn't get much, but it was enough. "Mom!"

She blinked, looked at him, and came out of her chair the next instant. "Jonathan. Honey, you're awake!"

"Water," he rasped, his eyes pleading.

She shook her head, her face filled with concern. "Sorry, Son. All you can have is this." She held up a pink sponge on a stick—a weird lollipop—and reached for a Styrofoam cup. Filling it from a carafe on the bedside stand, she swished the sponge in water and placed it against his lips. When he opened she swabbed his mouth.

"How did you get here?" Jonathan asked, struggling to concentrate. "How did you know?"

"You were on national television, Jon. The same afternoon a nice man from the FBI flew up to Bellingham to get me." She lifted his free hand and cradled it in both her own.

"Who was he?"

"A fellow by the name of Perkins. He was very kind."

Jonathan tensed. "He got me shot."

"He shot you?" Her mouth dropped open.

"He let a suspect get his weapon, and I ended up shot."

Mrs. Corrigan shook her head. "He never told me that. No wonder he was so kind. I hope you're not bitter toward him. I'm sure he didn't mean. . ."

Jonathan pulled his hand from her grasp, trying not to show the pain it cost him. "Let's not go there. I don't need a religious lecture right now."

Her eyes lost some of their life. "Of course not. Sorry."

He let his eyes close and drifted into a morphine haze. Religion. He'd

BETRAYED

had enough of religion to last him a lifetime. Sunday school, church, youth group—he'd done it all. He'd even believed it for awhile. Until Dad.

Warren Corrigan and his son had been inseparable. Jonathan's first memories were of riding with Dad on the tractor. Later, he rolled out before dawn to help Dad hook up the milking machines. It wasn't a chore. Working with Dad was better than meat and potatoes to a growing boy.

When Jonathan reached thirteen, he stood shoulder to shoulder with his father, tossing hay bales, competing to see who could stack the most. Dad always won. . .until the summer Jon turned seventeen.

The day started out as usual, tossing bales from the field to the hay wagon. "Getting tired, old man?" Jonathan asked, laughing. It was an old joke, but one they both enjoyed.

"I can still beat a young pup like you," Warren called, his face glistening with healthy sweat. Suddenly, he bent over with a coughing fit that left him on the ground gasping for air. Jonathan rushed to him, supporting him, more scared than he'd ever been in his life.

When he could talk, his father said, "Hay fever." He held out his hand for a pull up. "That's all it is. Hay fever." Pulling a blue bandanna from his back pocket, he wiped his face.

The rest of the summer, Warren had to stop often to rest. At night, Jonathan lay in bed unable to sleep, listening to his father cough.

In September, Warren Corrigan stepped from a doctor's office with the verdict in his hand. Lung cancer.

Like everyone else, Jonathan begged God to heal his father. Watching that powerful man waste away into a shell, Jonathan's prayers changed to accusations. How could God give lung cancer to a man who never smoked in his life? A man who worked in the fresh air all his days? How could God let him suffer?

The heavens stayed silent. His father died. Jonathan's mother and his younger brother, Danny, had grieved, but then they seemed to accept his father's death.

Jonathan came apart. He refused to bathe or change his clothes. He wept for days and spent long hours in the woods, tramping nowhere. When his mother mentioned counseling, he took a shower and tried to act normal; but the rage still gnawed him to this day, popping out at odd times. It was then that Jonathan decided the only religion he needed was the religion of self.

In spite of it all, Mom still prayed. She still believed her husband's death would work out to the glory of God. Her faith and his anger were drawn swords, always clashing.

When Jonathan awoke, the room was brighter. Light came through the window. This time his mother stood nearby, watching him. She touched his forehead. "You've been sleeping a long time. How do you feel?"

"Rotten." He tried to swallow, and she reached for the lollipop sponge.

"How bad am I?" he asked as she swished it in water.

She swabbed his mouth and didn't answer.

"How bad, Mom?" His voice grew louder, more insistent.

She laid down the sponge. "Let me get the doctor."

"No!" he gasped. "You tell me."

She shook her head, a frightened expression on her face. "I don't know how to explain it. I'll get the doctor." She strode from the room, still quick for her fifty-five years. In short order, she returned with a balding man in a white lab coat.

The doctor stopped near his arm, his manner professional. "I'm Dr. Alfred Henley." He began lifting Jonathan's eyelids, shining lights in his eyes, touching here and there.

"How bad, Doctor?"

"Patience, young man. I'll let you know in a moment."

Dr. Henley paced to the end of the bed and lifted the blanket. "Hold that for me, will you, Mrs. Corrigan?"

Jonathan couldn't see what was happening. Panic hovered near the surface.

"What do you feel?" the doctor asked.

"You're pressing your finger against my left foot," Jonathan replied, impatient. What was Henley up to?

"Thank you, Mrs. Corrigan. You may lay the blanket down now." He returned to the head of the bed. "You can't have solids for a few more days. The first bullet caught you in the stomach, fragmented, and tore through your bowels. You lost a few inches of small intestine, but you shouldn't have any significant long-term effects."

He pursed his lips, choosing his words carefully. "As for your leg. You have some nerve damage."

Jonathan felt a cold chill. "But I'm okay. I mean, I could feel your finger."

BETRAYED

Dr. Henley slipped a sharp instrument from his coat pocket. "I pricked you with this, not my finger."

Corrigan looked at the pick like it was a cobra. "What does that mean?"

"Your leg is numb. You'll be in a wheelchair for awhile, and you'll need therapy."

"But eventually I'll be okay." It was a statement, not a question.

Dr. Henley returned the sharp piece of steel to his pocket. "With nerve damage, it's hard to say. If you work hard, you'll be able to walk with some impairment. More than that, I can't promise."

Jonathan leaned back into his pillow, his chin stretched up, his teeth tight. How could he be a field agent if he couldn't run? He squeezed his eyes tight, holding back the emotion that wanted to break him down. Obviously, the Divine Creator wasn't finished with him yet. A little more torture for Jonathan Corrigan.

His mother's mellow voice shattered his make-believe calm. "Son, we'll pray for healing."

He raised his head to glare at her. Rage colored his words. "Do you still pray for me every day like you promised?"

"Of course." Her brows drew together, pain in her hazel eyes.

"Were you praying for me the day I got shot?" His voice grew louder, full of blame. "Thanks a bunch, Mom. Pass my compliments on to God."

Sandra recoiled as though he had struck her. Tears filled her eyes.

The doctor stepped between her and the bed. "Mr. Corrigan, you have a lot to be thankful for. One of the fragments missed your spinal cord by a millimeter. Another barely missed your femoral artery. You could have been paralyzed from the waist down or else bled to death in three minutes. You're getting things out of perspective."

Feeling a rush of shame, Corrigan glanced at his mother, tears coursing down her weathered cheeks. The last time he'd felt this bad was after he told Laura McIvor he didn't love her. His eyes filled as he lifted his hand toward his mother. She stepped up to clasp it. "I'm sorry, Mom," he whispered.

She leaned down to press her cheek against his, and the dam broke loose.

CHAPTER FOUR

Alistair Crane liked the fine things in life. An Inuit carving from Nunavut particularly fascinated him. The smooth figure fit neatly into his palm. His feminine fingers felt across the face of the mother and rested on her sleeping child. In his younger days, owning a piece of artwork worth ten thousand dollars had been a pipe dream. Not anymore. Through skillful maneuvering, Crane had turned Puget Information Systems into a gold mine.

Leather upholstery, brass ornaments, and the best view in Bellingham, his company leased the entire top floor of the Baker building. His thin lips pulled into a tight grin. Everyone had laughed. "Why Bellingham?" they asked.

Why not? It was big enough to have enough sheep for him to fleece but small enough not to have any talent smart enough to figure out what he was doing.

A knock at the door made him drop the bit of jade into his pocket as he called, "Come in."

His stocky security chief, Bart Dagg, paced in and closed the door behind him. A former FBI agent who'd left the Bureau under shady circumstances, Dagg made the perfect coconspirator.

Crane yawned widely.

"Too much racquetball this morning, Chief?" Dagg asked, taking a seat in front of the desk.

"The usual," Crane said, stretching his stiff legs. He'd give the morning game a couple more weeks to get rid of his baby paunch. If racquetball didn't do the job, he'd hire a trainer. He glanced more closely at Dagg. "You look like a man with something on his mind."

The security chief rubbed his prominent forehead before answering. "Maybe."

Crane sat up. "Speak English."

Dagg looked uncomfortable. "We got a call from Archon Energy last week. When we quoted the standard ten grand quick-service fee, they declined."

"You're kidding." Crane reached into his jacket pocket for a pack of mints.

"Cross my heart, Boss." He ran stiff fingers across his bald head. "We decided to let them stew a few days. They left a message on the weekend voice mail, and the tech supervisor called them back. They said the problem was solved."

Crane's heart rate elevated slightly. "That's impossible." He turned to his laptop and opened the Archon Energy file. On the bottom right corner of the screen, he entered a password and read a string of text. "There's absolutely no way. That virus could never be broken by the likes of Booregaard. He's too dense."

Dagg clasped powerful hands and asked, "If not Booregaard, who?"

"That's what I'm about to find out." Crane lifted his phone and punched in Archon's number. "Ted Booregaard, please." Hitting a button to activate the speakerphone, he tapped on his rosewood desk while he waited.

"Ted Booregaard here," a voice crackled.

"Hi, Ted, it's Alistair Crane. I heard you had a problem last week. Everything all right now?"

"Yeah, the program's working like a charm."

"I'm glad you were able to fix it."

"Not me. It was some young gal with a new consulting business. I managed to catch her at home last night. She's a real whiz. She did in two hours what you wanted ten thousand dollars to do. Seems like an excessive fee, don't you think?"

Alistair felt slight panic but deliberately slowed his breathing before answering. "Most definitely. You have to understand that our tech people were giving an estimate. That was the top end. If it only took our people a couple of hours, you definitely wouldn't have been charged ten thousand." What he wouldn't tell Booregaard is that the technician would have made sure it took at least two days.

"Well, that would be a first," Booregaard said. "Hey, she mentioned you might already be aware of a flaw in the program and have some kind of patch file. Do you?"

"I doubt it's a flaw in the program. If she only needed two hours to fix it, it was probably an input problem. If we'd worked on it, we would have been able to show you what went wrong. If it happens again, we'll sort if out for you."

Booregaard's breath buzzed into the phone. "If it happens again, I'm calling her."

Crane almost choked but managed to keep his voice calm. "I'm sorry to hear that, Ted. We've always considered Archon one of our best clients. It seems harsh that one little incident like this would cause you to lose faith in us."

"Yeah, whatever. All I know is she was there when I needed her, and it didn't cost ten grand either."

Crane's fingers tapped double-time. "Well, Ted, you certainly have the right to deal with anyone you want. I feel so terrible about this that I'm putting a note in your file that for the next year, all technical support for your company is free."

There was a pause. "You're serious?"

"Absolutely. Customer satisfaction is number one."

"Well. . .I'll give it some thought."

"You do that. By the way, what was this young gal's name?"

Booregaard chuckled. "Why? So you can hire her and leave me with no options?"

"I am always on the lookout for sharp minds. You know that."

"You'll probably find out sooner or later. Her name's Shannon Masterson. She goes under the name of Masterson Consulting."

"Thank you, Ted. I hope we'll be in touch again. I can't over-emphasize how much we value your business." He gently set down the receiver.

Dagg's thinning eyebrows rose. "A year of free technical support? Since when do you give anything away free?"

"Since now. Under no circumstances do we want someone else poking around our program. If this Shannon Masterson ever figures out what we've done, we'll be doing time, my friend. That would be much worse for you than for me."

Dagg shifted uncomfortably. "What do you want me to do?"

"For now, just find out who she is, and have someone keep an eye on her. Maybe she won't cause trouble. Then again, maybe she will, and we'll have to do more."

"How much more?"

Turning his dark eyes on Dagg, Crane said, "Whatever it takes to make sure she doesn't know enough to squeal. It's really up to her, isn't it?"

Dagg let loose a cruel chuckle and sauntered out of Crane's office.

Shannon tingled with excitement. She was actually sitting in Madge's Cut and Curl, the last chair on the left. Yesterday, she couldn't afford a car wash. She never dreamed that today she'd have sixty dollars for a new hairstyle. She'd pinched pennies for so long, this time she was going for the max.

Slender and well-worn, Madge paused, the gray bottle of coloring poised over Shannon's head. "Why on earth did y'all dye your hair?" she asked in a Midwestern drawl. "I can see from the roots that your natural color suits you perfectly. Sure you don't want me to change you back to what you were before?"

"No," Shannon answered too quickly. She smiled to soften her hasty response. "You know what they say; blonds have more fun."

Madge's tired face cracked into a smile as she ran a hand through her own bleached mop. "So they say, but I'm still waiting. Well, here goes." She squeezed purple fluid into Shannon's hair. "Did y'all hear that the fella who saved those kids in California is from around here?"

Shannon woke up. She stared at Madge in the mirror. "How did you find that out?"

"It was in the afternoon paper. Seems someone from around here recognized him. There's even a picture."

"Really?" Shannon gazed at her own reflection, but all she saw was a man's agonized face on a TV screen. Her emotions were all over the map. She dug her nails into her palms. She would never let him hurt her again, even if it was just thinking about him.

Madge stretched a plastic cap over Shannon's drenched hair. She stepped back to wash her hands and said over the spraying water, "If he's anything like his picture, he's a hunk."

Shannon looked away. "He's not that great," she mumbled.

"Oh, you saw the picture already?" Madge asked, reaching for a towel.

"Yes, um. . .no. . .um. . .oh, never mind."

Madge's eyebrows arched. "You all right, Honey? You're as red as my lipstick."

Desperate now, Shannon said, "Please, just do my hair. I don't feel like talking." She locked eyes with Madge in the mirror.

"Sure," the hairdresser said, a wise expression on her face. "My lips are sealed." She glanced at the timer on the counter and pulled off the plastic cap. "Come on over to the drier, Honey."

When Madge left her to see to the next customer, Shannon suddenly noticed the afternoon paper lying on the table beside her. She started to reach for it, then pulled her hand back. What did she care?

The next instant, she snatched it up. There he was, younger, in a uniform, with that disarming grin. "Local Boy Thwarts Terrorist Plot." Whose heart did he break to do it? She scanned further down and caught her breath.

There was his name. Jonathan Corrigan. Her fingers touched the lettering. He grew up in Bellingham. But where was he now?

When Shannon left the beauty salon, her silken blond hair and new cut gave her a carefree appearance, but her mind still churned with emotion. She paused outside the plate-glass window lettered Madge's Cut and Curl and dropped two quarters into a machine holding the *Bellingham Herald*. Tucking the paper under her arm, she headed for the Ford Tempo. She had to get home. She felt a good cry coming on.

Standing upright from the brick wall of Chan's grocery where he'd been leaning for the past half hour, Rory Critch followed Shannon Masterson down Meridian Street's busy sidewalk. He blended in well—medium height, medium build, dark hair, blue eyes. No one noticed him, but he sure noticed the gorgeous blond ahead of him. Shadowing Shannon Masterson would be a pleasure.

Jonathan was sick to death of sucking ice cubes, but at least they were better than those awful sponge lollipops. Doc Henley said it would be a couple of days before he could take liquids, then a couple of weeks before he could eat soft food. One good thing about being a hero, the government had gone all out providing him a first-rate room, complete with cable TV.

Unfortunately, nothing on the tube interested him. He was a man of action, and staying in bed was driving him crazy. Exhausted from his unpredictable mood swings, his mother had gone out for some fresh air. Corrigan knew why she'd left, and he couldn't blame her.

A soft knock at the door drew his attention from the sitcom he wasn't watching. The next moment, Corrigan looked into the face of Jack Fitzgerald, Assistant Director of Operations of the CIA. The powerfully built African-American smiled as he entered the room. "Jonathan, you're looking good."

Corrigan returned a wry grin. "Thanks. You'll excuse me if I don't stand." He picked up the remote and flipped off the television.

Fitzgerald chuckled. "How long 'til you're up and about?"

"Two weeks if I behave."

"Will you?"

Corrigan glanced down at his bandaged thigh. "I'm at the mercy of a ruthless nursing staff. Every time I step out of line, they come at me with a needle or a bedpan. Believe me, I'll behave."

Fitzgerald eased into the vinyl lounge chair near the side of the bed. "Have you been following the news?"

"Yeah." Disgusted, Corrigan stared at the dark TV screen. That machine had made a bad situation worse. Practically every American in the United States could recognize him on sight. Worse than that, sooner or later, he'd have to speak to the media. So far, the FBI had kept them at bay, but once he left the hospital he was on his own. He was a celebrity.

Corrigan muttered, "This is the worst of all possible outcomes."

"I wouldn't say that," Fitzgerald said, lifting his left ankle and resting it on his right knee. He grinned. "In the worst case, you'd be dead." He grew serious. "I guess you've already figured out what we're going to have to do."

"Kill me?" Corrigan asked hopefully.

Fitzgerald's grin returned. "I wish."

"Why not? I can see the headline now." He spoke in a monotone, one hand tracing imaginary type in the air. "Hero Jonathan Corrigan died in the hospital today from internal bleeding, a complication from his stomach wound. The nation mourns the loss of this great man." He dropped his hand and looked at Fitzgerald, brow lifted. "How about it?"

"No can do. If we kill you, that means plastic surgery, new identity, falsification of documents, not to mention breaking your sweet mother's heart. Besides, it's not necessary."

"Sure it is. I want to get back to work. I can't do it while I'm a celebrity."

"Yes, you can."

Corrigan's eyebrows lowered. He looked menacing, even in his blue dotted hospital gown. "What have you been drinking for lunch, Fitzgerald? There's no such thing as a world-famous spy. You've got to kill me and make me someone else."

"Your spying days are over, Corrigan." Fitzgerald spoke softly, but Corrigan heard his words with the deep impact of a death knell.

He asked harshly, "Then what will I do?"

"Public relations."

Corrigan sat up. A wide sweep of his hand knocked a water jug to the floor. He never glanced at it. "Not on your life! I'm a field agent!"

Fitzgerald shook his dark head. "The director has reclassified you to public relations. You make us look good."

Jonathan's breath sounded ragged. "Don't put me behind a desk. I'll be section eight in two days!"

Fitzgerald put both feet on the floor and leaned forward, his words coming quick, his tone aggressive. "Look, you've got a gimpy leg. How can you be a field agent if you can't run? Are you going to shout to someone who's chasing you—'Hey, I'm a cripple'? 'If you don't let me go, I'll file a lawsuit for discrimination'?" His voice softened. "Face it, Corrigan, your spying days are over. Take this assignment. It pays better, and you can have a life."

"I don't want a life," he ground out, wishing he had something to throw. They couldn't do this to him.

"I'm sorry I had to get rough with you, Jon, but you have to face facts."

"If I refuse the transfer?"

Fitzgerald raised both hands, palm up. "You get a pension at half salary."

Corrigan's expression turned stubborn. "That's what it'll be then."

Fitzgerald stood. "You're not thinking straight. We'll talk again in a couple of weeks." He put out his hand, and Corrigan shook it—reluctantly. "We'll talk again," he emphasized. He left the room, a sad look on his refined features.

As he left, a delivery girl carried in a narrow vase of daisies and placed them near Corrigan's shoulder on a table. "Have a great day!" she chirped and hurried away.

BETRAYED

Ignoring the flowers, Corrigan flipped on the TV. He needed some noise to crowd out his angry thoughts. Six days ago, he was a top-level agent; today he was a public relations man. All because of that idiot, Perkins.

The door opened a crack. "Anybody home?"

"Get out!" Corrigan shouted, without waiting to see who was there.

Fat as ever, Perkins stepped inside. His navy suit looked like it had been slept in. "I won't stay long, Corrigan. I just came by to say that I'm sorry for what happened." He spieled off the words as though he'd memorized them. "If there's anything I can do for you—anything—you just name it."

Corrigan's blood pressure went off the chart. "How dare you show your face in here, Perkins?" he bellowed, breathing like he'd just finished a two-mile run. "You want to do something to make me feel better?"

"Yeah, you name it." Perkins took one step into the room.

Corrigan wrapped his hand around the vase of daisies.

"Die!" The vase crashed just above Perkins's head, showering him with water and broken glass. "You've ruined my life, you scum! Get out!"

Shocked, Perkins backed away and scooted from the room.

Five minutes later, a red-haired nurse walked into the room dragging a blood pressure machine behind her. She found Corrigan holding his pillow over his face, moaning in a grating, guttural tone that told of agony far greater than physical pain.

CHAPTER FIVE

Two weeks later, Jonathan's face creased into a reluctant smile when his brother Danny burst into the hospital room without knocking. "Today's Homecoming Day!" Danny announced, beaming.

Danny Corrigan stood four inches over six feet and weighed in at a hefty two-hundred-thirty pounds. Today, he wore a gray T-shirt that stretched across his muscular chest, his biceps pulling the sleeves taut. He kept his dark hair in a military cut that made his Dumbo ears stand out.

Four years separated the boys, and they had never been close. Danny had leaned more toward his mother. Jonathan had idolized his father. After college, Jonathan joined the Navy SEALs, and Danny did a hitch in the marines. That's as far as the similarity went. Danny had married a lovely blond named Rita, and they now had two daughters. After his discharge, he joined the Seattle police force—a job that kept him close to his family and his mother.

Jonathan had disappeared into the secret world of the CIA, and the Corrigan men hadn't seen one another for ten years. Danny's wife and kids were only photographs to Jonathan. He'd never met them. Danny had surprised his wounded sibling by showing up when their mother had left Los Angeles to prepare the farmhouse for Jonathan's arrival.

Danny took a seat beside the bed. "You aren't talking, Bro. Aren't you glad to get out of here?"

Corrigan stared at him. "Are you kidding? I'm jumping up and down on the inside. My leg just won't cooperate." He craned his neck to look out the window at the grounds below. "It's the treat waiting for me on the lawn that's got me down."

Danny laughed. "Oh, the press. You've got to meet them sooner or later. Better sooner while you're still in a wheelchair. They'll have more sympathy."

"Right." He wasn't buying it. He'd watched the evening news and winced as a mike-wielding reporter interviewed grieving parents, the camera coming in for a close-up of their tear-blotched faces. If those guys had sympathy, they kept it under wraps.

"Mom's tearing the house apart, looking for a red carpet to roll out when you get there," Danny said, chuckling. "If she can't find one, she'll weave one." He leaned back and clasped his hands behind his head. "I haven't seen her this excited since my wedding."

Jonathan stayed sober. "I hope she doesn't go to too much trouble. I have to go to the farm because the doctor won't release me unless I have someone to look after me and a therapist besides. At least Uncle Sam's picking up the tab for the therapist." He reached for his tan polo shirt lying over the end of the bed. "Personally, I'd rather go back to my apartment in Langley."

Sitting up, Danny's tone became defensive. "What have you got against Mom? Is it so bad that she wants to baby you a little? After the way you've treated her, you should be glad she'll even talk to you."

Corrigan frowned. "It's not Mom."

"Then what?"

Corrigan hesitated, his lips puckered. "Let's forget it," he said finally, slipping the shirt over his head.

Skirting the empty wheelchair parked beside him, Danny moved onto the edge of the bed, one leg on the floor, the other hanging down. "Let's not. Look, Jonathan, I'm not a kid anymore. I'm a man, and I'm your brother. Spit it out."

Corrigan concentrated on his four buttons. "It's the place."

"The farm?"

"Everywhere I look, I see Dad."

Danny nodded, his face sad. "You should be glad the farm reminds you of him. You had great times together." He looked away. "I wish I had some of your memories."

Jonathan gazed at his brother's gentle face. "That's not what I remember, Danny. When I'm on the farm, all I see is a ghost of the man I knew, wandering listlessly about the grounds, wasting away." He swallowed and drew in a labored breath. "I don't remember the good times."

His brother touched his shoulder. "I'm just a dumb patrol cop, but I've got enough smarts to know that you've got to deal with this before it gets you."

Jonathan tried to smile. "I know. I'll try."

A dark-haired nurse with a small, perky face popped her head through the doorway. "It's time, gentlemen," she called, her voice lilting.

"Be right there," Danny said, sliding off the bed as she darted out. He glanced at Jonathan. "Wow, what a knockout."

Jonathan chuckled. "Hey, you're married. You shouldn't notice."

"Hey, you're not married; you should notice. Did you get her number?"

Jonathan shook his head. "All I know about her is that her name's Vicki." He stood on his good leg to tuck his shirttail into dark twill pants. "Unfortunately, I associate all the women here with a dozen embarrassing situations, most of them painful."

Danny chuckled. "Ooookay. Well, let me help you into the chair."

Jonathan held out both arms as his brother stood across from him. Grabbing Danny's shoulders, Jonathan gently shifted into the waiting wheelchair.

"I'm glad you can use your leg a little," Danny said. "I doubt Mom could move you."

"Actually, I can walk a few steps. The hospital wants me to leave here in a wheelchair for some sort of insurance reasons."

"You can walk?" Danny demanded. "How come no one told me that before?"

"I practice when no one's looking. I swear these nurses would keep me bedridden forever if they had their choice." He lifted a manila envelope from the table—his release papers and instructions.

"Hey, Bro, you're not a bad-looking guy," Danny said, taking hold of the handles behind Jonathan's shoulders. "Maybe the nurses want you to stay awhile." He set the chair in motion.

Jonathan felt his spirits lift a little as they wheeled out of the room he'd called home for the last three weeks. When they rounded the corner, hospital staff and patients lined the hallway to clap and call out their good wishes. He raised his hand in a loose salute, nodding his thanks while he tried to control his emotions. After all he'd been through, this kind of display got him choked up.

The elevator had been held for them, and they wheeled right in. Vicki stepped inside behind them and touched the white button marked Lobby.

"You married?" Danny asked her, his voice teasing.

Jonathan scowled and tried to catch his brother's eye. Danny ignored him.

"Uh, no," she answered, reddening a little.

"Dating anyone?"

"Why are you so interested?" she bantered back. "Isn't that a wedding band on your finger?"

"Sure is, Ma'am," Danny said proudly. "I've got two gorgeous little girls, too. It's him." He pointed to Jonathan. "He's got no one."

"Shut up, Danny," Jonathan growled. He glanced at the nurse. "Sorry, Vicki."

Her giggle grew to a laugh. "Don't be sorry. There was actually a running bet at the nurses' station on which of us you'd ask out." She smiled into his eyes. "We were all disappointed when no one won."

Jonathan laughed—his first hearty laugh in a long time. "I'd like to make you the winner, but. . ."

"There's someone else," she finished.

"Yeah." He spoke the word softly, almost to himself.

"Who?" Danny jumped in, greedy for more information.

Corrigan stared at the shiny door ahead of him and kept his lip buttoned.

"C'mon, Jon, give!"

"Nope." He shot his brother a look that put a cork in his questions.

Conversation died until the trio reached the front doors of the hospital. Across from the covered portico, someone had set up a small stage. Corrigan nodded at the rows of chairs filled with men and women wearing press badges. "That my firing squad?"

"Afraid so," his brother answered, turning loose of the chair to take a closer look. "There must be fifty of them."

"I'll leave you now, Mr. Corrigan," Vicki said. "Take care of yourself." With a parting smile she headed back to the elevator.

Danny gave the chair a shove, and the sliding doors parted. Jonathan shielded his eyes from brilliant sunshine. A deep breath of the cool February air smelled wonderful after the recycled air inside the hospital. The moment he came into view, a cheer mingled with gentle applause.

People parted as Danny wheeled him up the ramp toward a podium holding a wide bundle of microphones.

Fitzgerald met him at the top. While shaking hands, he leaned forward and asked in a stage whisper, "Have your plans changed?"

"Not that I know of," Corrigan answered blandly.

"We'll talk again," Fitzgerald said, standing back.

Corrigan scanned the sea of faces, then leaned toward the microphone. "You'll have to excuse me for not standing, but the hospital says I have to stay in this wheelchair until I'm off the property. I will be happy to answer some of your questions, though." It wasn't really a lie. He could stand, for about a minute.

Questions came at him machine-gun style. Nothing in his training had prepared Corrigan for the intensity of the press. If this were friendly fire, he would hate to be the enemy.

"Mr Corrigan, from your comment I take it you can stand. Are you close to a full recovery?" asked a young woman in a red dress.

"Give me a few weeks, and I'll be at the Olympic tryouts," he said, grinning.

A grizzled man in a rumpled suit shot his hand into the air. Jonathan gave him the nod. "Bart Olafson, *L.A. Times*. Is it true the FBI botched this operation?"

"That's not true." It wasn't false either, but Corrigan didn't need any enemies.

The same man dove in for a follow-up. "Sources say the weapon that shot you belonged to an FBI agent. Is that true?"

"I was on the floor bleeding. I didn't pay much attention." Perkins owed him more than one favor now.

"How did you get hardened terrorists to reveal their targets?" asked a thin, gray-haired man wearing wire-rimmed glasses and a badge with CNN in blue letters.

Corrigan grinned. "I said, 'Pretty please,' and then they told me everything."

Laughter wafted from the crowd like a gentle breeze.

Tiring after fifteen minutes, he gave the last question to a middle-aged, sharply dressed woman sitting in the center of the pack. "Mr. Corrigan, June Smyth from *Women's Universe Magazine*. Tell me, what kind of woman does America's hero like?"

Jonathan's brain unhitched for an instant. Everything he said would be on the afternoon news. Here was a chance to talk to Laura. What could he say?

Wetting his lips, stalling for a few more seconds, he finally answered, "A woman who would understand my failures and accept my apology."

"Mr. Corrigan, you sound like you're talking about someone specific," Ms. Smyth said, her smile inviting him to say more.

Jonathan smiled, friendly but definitely closed.

"That's enough, ladies and gentlemen," Danny said. "Jonathan's got a flight ahead of him, and we need to get going."

"Please, one last question," the lady from *Universe* magazine persisted.

Jonathan nodded, wondering what kind of hardball she had waiting for him this time.

"If the people of the United States could give you one thing as a reward for what you've done, what would it be?"

Jonathan considered. Not a bad question. "The people of the United States," he said, "could not give me anything. But you, the press, could."

"What would that be?" a young Asian-American man called out.

"My privacy," Corrigan said, his words clear and strong. "Several law enforcement officers have been pulled off active duty to guard my apartment, my mother's home, and this hospital from the press. If you could give me anything, it would be that you respect my privacy and leave me alone."

A portly man pushed forward. "Bryce here, NBC. You will not hear from our network again. If you wish to talk, Sir, call us."

Bryce's comment set off a storm of pledges. No one would harass the man who had saved the children.

On his way to a waiting limousine, Jonathan felt relieved at the reaction of the press to his request, but the question uppermost in his mind was, would Laura hear him and would she understand?

A hundred miles off the coast of Taiwan, Captain Zheng Zhengqiu barked an order to his second in command, and the People's five-hundred-fifty-foot guided missile cruiser yawed sideways. Zheng's lips pressed into a hard line, anticipating the glory in store for China. No more missed targets or fouled detonations. Thanks to Chinese Intelligence, their weapons now equaled those of Russia and NATO. Best of all, today China would give the Taiwanese a little surprise.

Zheng had orders to put half a dozen cruise missiles directly over Taiwan and destroy an old freighter on the other side—a demonstration to take the starch out of the Taiwanese navy. One day, Taiwan must return to Mother China. Zheng's chest puffed out. That day lay just ahead.

With his ship parallel to shore, Zheng entered the tiny control room where four officers sat at computers, the brains of the ship. Closing the door behind him, Zheng barked, "Lock onto the target!" The weapons officer's fingers danced along a gleaming keyboard. He turned toward his captain and gave a single stiff nod.

Two seconds later, the ship's communications officer spoke into his headset directly to Beijing, "All ready." Touching the headset, the young man looked at his captain and nodded.

Zheng's lower teeth showed as he called out the Chinese equivalent of "Fire!"

Two cruise missiles vaulted from the ten-thousand-ton ship, the backlash making it rock. Zheng's chest expanded still further, his gleaming gold buttons taut on blue serge. It was a great day for China.

Four minutes after the launch, a low, grating sound erupted from every loudspeaker on the ship. Red lights flashed at the weapons station. Seated next to the captain, Min An, the weapons officer, had his face two inches from the glowing green monitor, his fingers a blur of motion over the keys.

Zheng leaned toward him. "What has happened?" he demanded.

The glass screen clouded with Min An's breath. He reached up to wipe it clean.

"What has happened, you fool?" Zheng shouted. Four pairs of eyes turned toward Min, aghast that he hadn't answered his captain immediately.

"Sir," his voice trembled, "the missiles veered off course."

Zheng's throat closed. His jaw was a vise. It was an outrage.

Min An hit a few more buttons. A moment later, his voice rose an octave. "They've turned toward us!"

Zheng shoved the weapons officer out of his seat and took charge of the console. Feverishly, he entered code after code, but nothing changed. The radarscope traced the path of the runaway missiles now ten miles away. Now five miles. Seconds ticked by. Desperate, Zheng pushed the yellow self-destruct button.

With a roar like heavy thunder both missiles exploded, and China's oversized firecrackers fizzled into the sea.

Face tight, back straight, Zheng stalked out of the control room,

BETRAYED

making eye contact with no one.

"Should we fire the next two?" Min An called after him. Ignoring the question, Zheng stormed onto the deck. He glared at the sky, certain that an American spy satellite had seen it all. Instead of recording China's triumph, it had witnessed China's shame.

Leaving First National's late drive-through window as the teller drew down the shade, Shannon aimed her Ford Tempo toward Hansen's Super-Save. She found a parking place near the door and grabbed an abandoned cart in the slot next to hers. Life had changed dramatically these past three weeks.

Olivia Donner's sales had almost doubled since Shannon arrived, and last night Olivia had invited her to stay on the payroll as long as she wanted.

Not much had happened at Masterson Consulting, but Shannon wasn't concerned—she was working at what she loved best and making lots of friends doing it. Two weeks ago, Olivia invited Shannon to Bellingham Bible Church, and—surprising herself—Shannon had accepted.

On her first visit, she sat in the third row with Olivia, glancing around at padded burgundy pews and carved wood on the platform. Suddenly, she drew up short and stared at Ted Booregaard on the first row, smiling and shaking hands with everyone who passed him.

When she mentioned him to Olivia, the woman's round face shone. "Ted found the Lord three years ago. He used to be a heavy drinker, but look at him now." She nodded, taking personal satisfaction in the man's achievement. "He's been off the stuff ever since. He's got a great job; his family's happy." She glanced at Shannon, her eyes glowing. "That's what it's all about."

Shannon smiled and nodded. She wasn't sure what "found the Lord" meant, but she felt a comforting warmth at the ancient clapboard church with its old-fashioned steeple. The next week, she'd felt drawn to come again.

After the second Sunday morning service, Charlene and Miriam Cassidy asked Shannon out to lunch. Olive-skinned sisters who looked enough alike to be twins, Charlene and Miriam were legal secretaries who worked for different firms. A gifted mimic, Miriam kept the girls laughing.

"So anyway," Charlene said over dessert, "this young lawyer, Bobby

Meese, joined the firm last fall. He was fresh out of law school, so he had to work twelve hours a day. Guess who got assigned to him—me." She looked at Miriam, who stifled a giggle.

Charlene continued, "Because the poor guy's bushed all the time, I kept having to remind him of his trial dates." Her thin dark brows stretched upwards. "Do you think he was thankful?"

"No," the two sisters said in unison.

"How rude," Shannon said, cutting into her pumpkin pie.

Charlene added sugar to her latte and stirred. A warm hazelnut aroma spread outward with the steam. She said, "I guess he figured that his law degree made him some sort of god. Whenever I'd remind him of an appointment, he'd snap, 'I know.' "

Miriam added, "If it hadn't been for Charlene, that guy would have been late for court every time."

"Anyhow," Charlene continued, "one day I was sick, so there was no one to hold little Bobby's hand. He missed a date with Judge Elvira Thompson—the dragon lady. Fortunately for him, I'd called the court clerk that morning and told him Meese wouldn't be there."

"What if he'd shown up?" Shannon asked.

The two girls laughed. "Not likely," Charlene said. "The next morning, I returned to work, and Judge Thompson called." She glanced at her sister. "You finish it, Miriam."

The other girl had an impish grin. "It wasn't really Judge Thompson. It was me. I can do the judge's voice pretty good."

Shannon's eyes grew round. "You didn't!"

Miriam giggled. "I asked him why he hadn't been in court the day before. I asked him if it was too much trouble for the rising star of Bellingham law to show up for his pretrial motions. I asked him if there were any good reason why I shouldn't consider contempt charges."

"What did he say?" Shannon asked, laughing and aghast at their audacity.

"It was hilarious. He bumbled on about being tired all the time, working so hard as an associate, and how his secretary had been sick so there was no one to remind him. He was like a little baby slobbering all over the phone.

"When he got through, I said that if his secretary kept him on time, he'd better treat her real nice, because if he ever missed a court date again, he'd be counting bars from inside a county cell."

BETRAYED

Charlene picked up the story. "Half an hour later, Bobby Meese showed up at my desk with a vase full of daisies and asked me how I felt."

"We cured that boy good, didn't we, Charlene?"

"And how!"

Shannon still laughed whenever she thought of what they'd done. She and the Cassidy sisters had been friends ever since.

Skimming down the lighted sidewalk in front of Hansen's, Shannon stopped and looked at the sign. Hansen's. Is that where Darryl got his false name? A grocery store? She shook her head and pushed on. The shopping cart contacted the black rubber mat, and twin doors slid back, welcoming Shannon to a brilliant world with a million tantalizing choices. She was one lady with plenty of money and a raging appetite.

In the produce department, her eyes locked onto California strawberries—out of season and expensive. Picking up a carton, she caught a whiff of them and was lost. She bought half a pound and made sure she picked up a can of aerosol whipped cream to go with them. Lettuce wasn't cheap either, but a large head still ended up in the basket.

Half an hour later, Shannon stood in the checkout line. Ahead of her, a frazzled young blond in a rumpled T-shirt and jeans had a squirming baby boy on her hip and a two-year-old girl hanging on her leg. The woman struggled to transfer her groceries onto the belt.

"I can hold the baby if you'd like," Shannon said, beaming at the little boy. He wore a blue jacket with the front unzipped.

The mother looked relieved. "Would you?" She held out the boy, about six months old. "His name's Scotty."

Shannon took the baby and made googly sounds with him. Each time Scotty smiled, she smiled, and a pang shot through her. She was almost thirty-five. Would she ever have children? In her twenties, a career had seemed vital. Now she wasn't so sure. If things had turned out different with Darryl. . . No, Jonathan was his name. Or was it? Until she knew differently, he would be Darryl to her.

She gazed into the baby's face pretending some features were hers, others were Darryl's. This child in her arms could have been theirs. Placing her face next to his hair, she caught that distinctive baby scent and felt a tug deep inside her.

She jiggled Scotty and made a funny face, miffed at herself for getting sentimental and determined not to show it. This was not the time to get blubbery. She had a life to rebuild.

When her grocery cart was empty, Scotty's mother held out her arms, and Shannon reluctantly surrendered the child. Placing bagels, strawberries, and milk on the conveyer, Shannon smiled at the checkout girl, an African-American teen with her hair crocheted into tiny braids. The scanner beeped as each item passed it. Halfway through Shannon's groceries, the beeps stopped—everywhere. Almost in unison, the cashiers groaned.

"What's the matter?" Shannon asked the frowning clerk who held a box of macaroni over the sensor.

She shook her head, making her crocheted braids swing. "Computers are down—again."

"This happen a lot?"

"This is the third time since last Thursday. Mr. Hansen is going to blow a gasket."

That moment, a tall man—a bald dome above his eyebrows—came rushing out of the front office. He made his way to each register in turn, punching buttons and getting nowhere. When he reached Shannon's checkout, his narrow face looked pale, and sweat gleamed on his forehead.

"Maybe I can help," Shannon said.

His gray eyes locked with hers. "How?"

"It looks like a software problem. I happen to be a computer programmer."

He turned to the keypad in front of him, tapping loudly. Nothing. He said to Shannon, "I appreciate the offer, but I've already called our regular company."

"When will they get here?"

He exhaled sharply. "Three or four hours."

"Do you mind my asking what company you use?"

"Puget Information."

Shannon felt like an anxious racehorse bumping the starting gate. She moved one step closer, her eyes alight. "Tell you what, if I fix it before they get here, you pay me a flat fee of five hundred dollars. If I don't fix it, you pay me nothing."

"Sounds to me like you're telling fairy tales." He pinned her under a stare. "How do I know you won't foul it up more and double Puget's bill?"

"Have you heard of PTL Computers downtown?"

"Sure, that's Olivia Donner's place. She used to do our stuff before we went with Puget."

"Well, I work with her. She's at the store late tonight. Give her a call, and see what she says."

Hansen cocked his head, his mental gears working. "Wait right here." He trotted into his office cubicle. A couple of minutes later, he appeared at the doorway and motioned for her to come in.

Shannon held a hand out toward the checkout girl and asked, "Would you mind watching my groceries?"

"I'll put them back," she answered. "Last time this happened, we were down a full day."

"Not today," Shannon said, flipping hair off her face. She marched to Hansen's tiny office and took a seat at his desk. The system was more up-to-date, but his problem was similar to the one she'd discovered at Archon Energy.

Thirty minutes later, initializing sounds came from six registers, and Ronald Hansen almost kissed her. He reached for his checkbook. "Young lady," he said, beaming, "here's your five hundred dollars, and whatever's in your cart is free."

"Thank you," Shannon said, delighted. She dropped the check into her purse and found a business card. "If this happens again, feel free to call me day or night."

Rory didn't know much about Puget Information Systems, but he knew Mr. Dagg would want to know that Shannon Masterson had magically fixed Hansen's computers. Leaving his post outside the grocery, he started his battered, smoke-spewing VW Beetle and drove to Dagg's favorite bar.

Back at her apartment building, Shannon made three trips to haul six bags of groceries to the second floor. She flipped on the TV to listen to the news while she unpacked everything. The lettuce remained on the counter with carrots, celery, and tomatoes. She placed a T-bone steak next to the stove. Though not much of a meat eater, Shannon was determined to celebrate in style. A check for five hundred dollars burned in her purse.

She unpacked the strawberries, washed them, and sliced them into a bowl. The six o'clock news came on, and Shannon stood transfixed. There he was again. Wasn't there anyone else in the United States they could put on evening television?

"Sally Epson reporting." Good old Sally Epson. Petite, perfect hair, upturned nose, plastic smile, and always talking about superhero Jonathan Corrigan.

"Get a life," Shannon murmured toward the screen. She opened her tiny fridge and pulled out the aerosol can of whipped cream.

"In our top story, local hero Jonathan Corrigan finally speaks, and boy, what he has to say. . .when we return from these messages from our sponsors."

Scowling, Shannon sliced the end off a pound cake and placed it on a saucer. What could Darryl say that a person could believe? People were so stupid.

She spooned strawberries over the cake, tense, waiting for the advertisements to end. She should stop torturing herself and shut the TV off, but she felt a morbid fascination. What lies would Hero Hansen tell this time?

The news began again with a close-up of Corrigan on a platform, answering questions with his usual smug demeanor. Whipped cream can in hand, Shannon moved over to the TV and turned up the volume. A well-dressed woman had the floor. "Mr. Corrigan, June Smyth from *Women's Universe Magazine.* Tell me, what kind of woman does America's hero like?"

I know what he likes, Shannon thought, shaking the can with vengeance. *A woman as dumb as a fence post and as gullible as a two year old.*

Corrigan hesitated, then smiled softly. "A woman who would understand my failures and accept my apology."

Shannon yelled at him, "How dare you even think it! What do you take me for? A celery brain?" Tempted to throw the can at the screen, she remembered the possible consequences just in time. Instead, she aimed the nozzle at the glass and painted Darryl a white beard. Still not satisfied, she added a white toupee.

"You big creep!" she shouted. "I'd brain you with this thing," she waved the can near her left ear, "if I could get close enough."

A loud thump came from the ceiling above, but Shannon ignored it. Let the whole world know for all she cared. "I'll never forgive you!" she cried. With a shaking hand, she turned off the TV and paced back to the kitchen. Squeezing whipped topping over the strawberries, she reached for a fork. Half the shortcake concoction had disappeared before Shannon realized that she'd just eaten dessert and forgotten to cook dinner.

Alistair Crane didn't care for the Lumberman's Bar and Grill. It was a bar frequented by grimy men who worked with their hands. But, if he had to meet Dagg's little spy, Crane definitely didn't want him at his country club.

He pushed open the door, and the cloying odors of cheap beer and cigarette smoke made him wince. Music pounded him from hidden speakers.

Basically, Lumberman's was one big room with about fifty oak tables, served by women who didn't know they were past their prime. In a dark corner, Dagg stood up and waved to get Crane's attention. What a choice spot for a meeting. How could anyone hear in this place?

Navigating his way past lumberjacks, mill workers, and farmers, Alistair reached Dagg's table. Pulling out a chair, he didn't acknowledge the greeting from Dagg's spy. The less he had to do with that pimply-faced greaseball, the better. Hadn't anyone told the kid black leather jackets and slicked-back hair had gone out decades ago?

In front of Dagg sat a small wide glass half filled with amber liquid. Critch had a brown bottle with a green label. The moment Crane sat, a tall waitress with fiery hair paused by their table. "What-ya having?" she asked, watching Crane.

"A root beer," he said shortly. When she left he glanced at his watch.

Dagg nodded at Critch. "Spill it."

The young man had a nasal whine. "Well, I was following the broad like you guys asked and. . ."

"Wait just a moment," Crane interrupted. "I never told you to follow anyone."

"Well, he did," Critch said, pointing at Dagg. The ex-FBI agent slapped Critch's hand down.

"Don't point."

"If he told you to follow her, then say him," Crane advised.

"All right, all right. Dagg told me to follow the broad. I trailed her to Hansen's where she parked in the third row. . ."

"Cut to the chase," Dagg growled. "Tell him about inside the store."

His greasy face twisted. "Man, you guys don't admire good work." He gestured with the bottle in his hand. "Okay. I'm over by the magazines watching her at the checkout when all the cash registers died." He grinned, showing a broken front tooth. "Old man Hansen started running around like a girl who's lost her engagement ring.

"My target talks to him for a bit, and he goes into his office. He comes to the door, waves to her. She goes in, and half an hour later they're back in business." He took a swig. "I figured it was important, so I came to

Mr. Dagg here right away."

Dagg flipped a twenty in Rory's direction. "Lose yourself until I call you."

Snatching the money up, Rory sauntered two tables away to join a couple of hard-faced women.

As soon as he left, Dagg asked, "You figure she fixed Hansen's system?"

"Definitely. I checked with tech support. Hansen called for help, then a little over half an hour later, he cancelled the call. He was scheduled for a surprise today. It had to be her."

"How much do you think she knows about us?"

"Since she only needed half an hour, she knows exactly what we've done. It's only a matter of time before she's tempted to decipher the encryption. Once she does that, we go to the cooler."

Dagg shredded his napkin. "That's not going to happen."

"Can we take her out?" Crane asked.

"That I'm not sure of yet. My man in Texas found her hometown today. Shannon Masterson currently resides in a graveyard in Galveston. She died from leukemia at the age of eight."

Crane's expression changed. "You don't say." He sipped his root beer.

"Before we take action, I've got to know why she's here. There are four possible reasons for a new identity. First, she's hiding from the law. I doubt that. This is a professional job. I checked out the Social Security number and it's solid. Only someone deep in government could do that.

"Maybe she's in witness protection. That means she testified in some big case. But was she a criminal or an innocent bystander? If she's dirty, the Feds won't notice what happens to her; but if she's clean, we'd best be real careful."

"You said four reasons," Crane reminded him.

"The fourth is the one that's got me worried. She might have a friend with connections. A year or so ago, some Russian Mafia guys grabbed a teenage girl to sell her in the white slave trade. The kid came from a single-parent home, no important relatives or friends, or so they thought. It turned out her uncle was undercover with the CIA, and by the time the agency was finished, five of the Russkies were dead. If she's a case like that, and we ice her, prison will be the least of our worries."

"Find out who she is, and why she's hiding," Crane said, "and do it yesterday."

"What do you suggest?" asked Dagg. "We just walk up and ask her?"

A sinister grin came over Crane's face. "No, we dig a little deeper, that's all." He pulled his cell phone from his pocket, flipped it open, and punched in a number. Leaning close to the wooden paneling, he clapped his left hand over his ear, straining to hear. "Do you know who this is? . . . Good. . . What's your schedule like this Sunday? . . . Excellent. Let's meet then." He nodded. "Yeah, same as usual."

Closing the phone, he smiled at Dagg and said, "Call Critch."

CHAPTER SIX

The Lear jet touched down softly at Bellingham International Airport and taxied to the small terminal. Corrigan groaned when he looked out the portal and saw a crowd around the outdoor gate. "I thought they said they were going to stay away."

Across the aisle, Danny leaned far over Jonathan to peer through the window. "That's not the press."

Corrigan stared up at the underside of Danny's jaw, "Who is it then, the IRS?"

Danny chuckled. "You're the local hero, Jon. That's your welcoming committee."

Jonathan's eyes narrowed. He scowled at a hundred people pressed against the chain-link fence, waiting for the jet to open its door. "There's a reporter out there. I can smell him."

"I doubt it." Danny returned to his own seat. "The local paper might be out there, but that's all."

As the engines whined down, a dark-suited man wearing wire-rimmed shades stood and stepped back to Jonathan's seat. "Sir, we'd like to exit the aircraft first and give the crowd a look over."

"Sure, Larry," Corrigan answered. "We'll sit tight."

Four Feds lumbered out of the aircraft. From his window, Corrigan watched them barking instructions to the local police. A corridor of troopers and FBI agents pushed through the center of the crowd and opened it up. Ten minutes later, Larry strode across the tarmac, shoulders stiff and square. He climbed the steps and paused three paces from the cockpit

BETRAYED

door to say to Corrigan, "All clear, Sir."

A stout nurse wheeled a chair next to Corrigan's soft leather seat. Jonathan recoiled when he saw the wheelchair. "I'm not going out in that."

"Why not?" Danny asked, standing. He seemed to fill half the cabin. "Everyone knows you're injured. They love you more for it."

He spoke every word distinctly. "I'm not riding in that chair."

Jonathan clamped his jaw in a characteristic show of stubbornness. Waving Danny and the nurse away, he pushed himself to a standing position with his good leg. Grunting heavily, he said, "I've got my cane. If you'll let me lean on you, I can make it."

"You'll be sorry, Jon. Believe me."

Jonathan stared at him.

"But, Sir," the nurse said.

Turning to her, Danny shook his head. "It's no use, Miss Haskins. He's always been like this."

Gripping his brother's shoulder from behind, Corrigan hobbled down the aisle. When he stepped into the cool sunshine, intense pain shot through his leg. His stomach ached awfully. He managed a weak smile and a half wave at the cheering crowd.

The narrow stairs were agonizing. Danny went ahead. Gasping, Jonathan leaned against his broad back.

"This is a dumb idea," Danny whispered fiercely when they were halfway down.

"Just keep going," Jonathan urged. Sweat broke out on his forehead. The crowd was still cheering, hands waving, faces smiling. Then they started to blur and spin.

Jonathan shook his head, trying to get his eyes to quit playing tricks. An icy chill washed over his head and back. The pavement came up to meet him. Suddenly, Danny's meaty arms wrapped around him. Through a gray mist, he heard shouts and voices filled with concern.

One voice, a feminine soprano, stood out above the others. "Let me through! I've got to see him!"

Jonathan shook his head a second time. He was dreaming again. That voice couldn't be hers. He'd left her in Phoenix.

When he regained consciousness an hour later, a familiar, lined face hovered over him: Dr. Parker, his former family doctor. Looking down, Jonathan saw a blue stethoscope pressed against his bare chest. Six gray circles stuck to his torso, little wires trailing from each. On his arm, a black cuff inflated automatically, then released.

Corrigan tried out a shaky grin. "Doc Parker," he whispered, "long time no see."

The snowy-haired physician adjusted his glasses and frowned. "You haven't changed much, Jonny boy. You never did know when to quit."

"Man, you sure scared us." Pale and drawn, Danny spoke from a chair off to the side.

Jonathan looked around. A pale green curtain surrounded him, the scuffling and rattling of a hospital emergency room wafting through it. His gaze stopped at Danny. "What happened, Bro?"

Dr. Parker answered the question with a question of his own. "What harebrained impulse caused you to refuse your wheelchair?"

Keeping his eyes away from the doctor's stern expression, Jonathan quirked in the corner of his mouth. "What can I say, Doc? It was stubborn pride."

"Well, pride doesn't cut it with me. When you're in my care, you will obey my orders to the letter or have a room in this hospital for the next month."

"Aw, come on, Doc," Corrigan said, moving his hand. "I'm not that sick."

Parker opened a metal folder. "This is your chart from L.A." He glanced inside and let it close with a clack. "You're sicker than you think." Moving closer to the gurney, he said, "The choice is yours. Will you stay here or go home?"

Corrigan tapped his fingers against the sheet. Sniffing the antiseptic atmosphere around him, he thought of the farmhouse—its sculpted log walls and crackling fireplace, the soft sofa and one of Mom's thick afghans across his legs. A moment later, he nodded curtly, giving in with poor grace. "Your terms, Doc. You've got me by the throat."

Parker smiled for the first time. "Fine. I've already got a nurse for you. She'll stay at your home for at least a week to make sure you behave yourself. She'll also do the therapy prescribed on your chart." He peered at Corrigan over his glasses. "Do I need to put this in writing?"

"Aw, Doc. I'm not that bad."

"How about the time you broke your arm and busted the cast off after two weeks because it felt better?"

BETRAYED

Corrigan grimaced. "I was only thirteen."

"As far as I can see, you've gotten taller but not one whit smarter since then."

A tall, svelte blond with reddish highlights in her hair poked her face through the privacy curtain.

Parker glanced at her. "Hello; you're right on time." He looked down at Jonathan. "This is your nurse, Andrea Kramer." Turning back, he said, "Andrea, this is one tough cookie. You think you can handle him?"

Her pearly teeth showed as she smiled and stepped through the green drapes. "Sure, Doctor, I've had experience with this one. I'll keep a lid on him." She beamed at Jonathan.

The patient lifted his sagging jaw. "Hi, Andrea," he said, giving her his lopsided grin.

She stepped closer to the bed and leaned over to look into his eyes. Her voice had a soft, husky quality that made him want to hear it again. "Hi, Jon. It's been a long time."

Corrigan forgot the clanking of metal doors, the squeaking of rolling carts, the soft voices of people passing by. She still had that brilliant smile and that daring look he'd always found irresistible. Everyone from his class at Bellingham High School would remember what he had almost forgotten—that Jonathan and Andrea had been an item for more than two years.

Reaching for her left hand, he saw that it was bare. "It's been longer than I thought."

Dr. Parker cleared his throat. "In any case, you'll stay here the night for observation."

Andrea smiled. "I'll come back when you're released tomorrow."

Olivia Donner frowned as she watched Shannon pick at her chef salad. The young woman looked lovely in a silky dress the mottled color of autumn leaves. Looking deeper than Shannon's snappy new hairstyle and shimmering lip gloss, Olivia sensed that something troubled her new friend.

"You don't like Denny's salads?" Olivia asked, finally. "We can get something else if you want."

Shannon looked up. She had fatigue lines around the eyes. "Huh? Oh, no, this is fine. I'm not really hungry." She tried a loose-lipped smile, then gave it up.

Olivia laid down her fork. "Look, maybe I'm putting my nose in where it doesn't belong, but I'm worried about you, Shannon. Maybe if you'd share your problem, you'd feel better."

Shannon pushed a tomato slice out of the way and stabbed a crest of lettuce coated with ranch dressing. "Things couldn't be better, Olivia. I've got regular work, and I'm expecting more consulting business since I fixed Hansen's system glitch. What more could I want?"

Olivia smiled gently, her cheeks bulging out. "How about a man?"

Instantly, Shannon's eyes flashed. "Why would you ask that?"

"I'm sorry, Dear," she said. "I crossed a line. Forgive me."

Shannon reached out to squeeze her hand. "I'm sorry I snapped. I'm not upset at you."

"I'm no great expert on romance," Olivia said, reaching for a napkin in the metal holder, "but the way you mope around, it's like you've got a broken heart."

Shannon's eyelids flickered. "That's not it exactly. My problem is family related, and I'd prefer to keep it to myself." She made an effort to eat her salad and the conversation dwindled.

Finishing her spaghetti, Olivia prayed for Shannon. More than one morning the younger woman had come to work with eyes puffy from weeping.

Suddenly, Shannon asked, "What does it mean, 'Come unto Me everyone who's heavy laden, and I will give you rest'?"

Olivia looked up startled. Where had that come from? "Are you talking about the pastor's message this morning?"

She nodded. "I didn't understand it completely. If God takes people's burdens away, then why do so many Christians seem unhappy? It sounds to me like that verse doesn't really work."

Olivia thought for a moment before answering. Here was the opportunity she'd prayed for. She rubbed her wide chin, then let her hand fall to the veneered tabletop. "When you came to work for me, which of your burdens disappeared?"

Shannon cocked her head, thinking. "Well, the lack of money for one."

"Nothing else?"

"Umm, well. . .I had something to fill my days."

"That's it?"

"I guess so."

"I'm sorry to hear that," Olivia said softly.

"What more could there be?" Shannon asked, stirring her coffee.

BETRAYED

"Lots more. Did you have any friends in Bellingham before I hired you?"

Shannon shook her head. Their waitress—a woman with biceps like a bodybuilder—stopped by their table with a pitcher of tea to refill Olivia's glass.

"Thank you, Dear," Olivia said, smiling. When the waitress left, she continued, "You have dozens of friends now. You've got me as a friend, there are the church people, and besides them, our regular customers have taken you in like family."

Looking like a kid getting a scolding, Shannon nodded. "Yeah, I guess you're right."

Olivia pushed a little harder, her tone gentle. "Have you ever felt that you have nothing to offer?"

Shannon glanced at her friend, lips twisted. "Only about every day or so."

Olivia smiled. "Ted Booregaard told me that when his system crashed, he'd never been so tempted to start drinking again. He may have done it if you hadn't been there. You made the difference."

"Really?" Shannon smiled for the first time that morning.

"Absolutely."

Olivia ran pudgy fingers through her curls. "Can you see what I'm getting at, Honey? Your life is so much better now, but you still act sad and worried sometimes.

"Christians do the same thing. God takes many of their burdens, but sometimes they hold on to one or two." Her face creased into a broad smile. "God promises He'll never leave us." She leaned forward. "You can trust Him."

Shannon eyes lit up at that phrase.

"He wants to be your Friend. Do you want me to show you how He can be?"

A wall came up, and Shannon looked away. "I'd like to think about it."

Olivia dug around in her suitcase-sized purse and pulled out a well-worn New Testament. She slid it across the table. "Here, take this and read the Gospel of John. If you have any questions, give me a call." She caught the eye of the husky waitress and beckoned to her, then grinned at Shannon. "How about joining me? I'm having a giant slice of cherry cheesecake for dessert."

Grinning as usual, Danny Corrigan pushed a blue wheelchair into

BETRAYED

Jonathan's second-floor room at St. Joseph Hospital. This place was much more plush than his sickroom in L.A., complete with brocade curtains and a wide, soft recliner.

Dressed in a blue shirt and khaki pants, Jonathan lay on the bed with the top half elevated to forty-five degrees. When he glared at the chair rolling toward him, Danny chuckled, his tone wheedling, "We're not going to have trouble with the patient today, are we?"

The patient sat up suddenly. "When I get better, I'm going to wrap that wheelchair around your head."

"Watch out, Bro," Danny said, pausing to flex his powerful arm. "Things have changed since we were kids."

Jonathan shook his head. "You watch out." He swung his sock-clad feet to the floor and slipped them into brown loafers. "I know some moves that'll put you on your can in three seconds."

"Oh, yeah?" Danny's eyes widened. "In a couple a' months I'll make you eat those words." He parked the chair near Jonathan's knee. "In the meantime, we gotta go and eat baked chicken. Mom's got a huge Sunday dinner planned."

"Who's coming?"

"It's a surprise." Danny's grin reappeared.

Jonathan groaned. "I don't think I can handle a crowd. I feel as weak as a newborn calf."

"Oh, there won't be that many guests. No more than half a dozen people."

"Does that include our baby-sitters from the Bureau?"

"No, but I wouldn't be surprised if Mom sends them a plate."

"Neither would I." Jonathan glanced at the open door and asked, "Where's Andrea? I thought she was coming out with us."

"She's gone ahead in her own car. She'll be there for lunch."

Pivoting on his good leg, Jonathan swung into the wheelchair, and Danny pushed him to the elevator. Except for the tall, dark agent following five paces behind them, the hallway stood empty. Jonathan swiveled his head and asked, "Where is everyone?"

Danny chuckled. "Getting used to the limelight, huh?" He pushed the elevator button as the FBI agent stepped in with them. As soon as the doors closed, Danny said, "Bellingham is a great town. You know that. A lot of people feel bad about what happened at the airport. The word is out that you want privacy. You're looking at it."

Outside the hospital entrance, a black stretch limousine waited, the usual group of men standing around, wearing dark glasses, talking into their wrists and trying to look like ordinary Joes.

Corrigan eyed them. "I wonder how long those goons are going to follow me around."

"When they're convinced the Iraqis aren't going to bump you off," Danny said, opening the car door.

Jonathan grunted. "There's little chance of that."

"Why not?"

Corrigan glanced at him. "Ever hear of the need-to-know principle?"

Danny waited while he got settled then closed the door, folded the chair, and stowed it in the trunk. The car purred and moved ahead with a floating sensation, an FBI agent at the wheel. They tooled through town and headed north until streetlights and sidewalks faded into grassy fields and barbed-wire fences. When they reached the lane winding through half a mile of pastureland, Danny glanced at Jonathan beside him. "There's. . . uh. . .something I've got to tell you."

Jonathan stared at him, sensing something was wrong. "What is it?" he demanded. "C'mon, spit it out."

"It's one of the guests. Well, she's not really a guest. I mean she is, but not for just today."

Corrigan's forehead furrowed. "What are you talking about?"

"Since my beat is in downtown Seattle, I work a lot with street kids. About six months ago, I busted a sixteen-year-old girl named Roxanne— nice girl, pretty, smart as a whip. She got involved with the wrong bunch, and I had to book them all for B & E." He cleared his throat. "That's breaking and. . ."

"For Pete's sake, Danny! I got out of kindergarten almost thirty years ago!"

Danny flushed. "Sorry, Jon. I didn't mean to insult your intelligence." The car entered a thick stand of pine trees. Bare branches and evergreen limbs formed a dappled shadow pattern on the hood and windows of the limo. The house stood in the center of forty wooded acres. When their father cleared this land, he had decided to leave a wide patch of the trees around the house. It had been a good decision. Jonathan loved those trees.

"As I was saying," Danny continued, "Roxanne had no permanent address, and her parents were deadbeats. It was a slam dunk she'd go to juvenile detention to live with a bunch of lowlifes. I told Mom about her and asked her to pray. Mom said that she would and asked me a few questions. I thought that was it."

Jonathan leaned forward, his hand on the front seat. His face had an I-can't-believe-this expression. "I already know what you're going to say."

"You got it." His brother nodded. "While I was in court waiting for Roxanne and her friends to be sentenced, the defense lawyer stood up and announced that Roxanne had a new guardian. Then Mom marched down the aisle. . ."

Jonathan stared at the ceiling of the car and shook his head.

". . .And the judge took one look at her—tough as an old board, a right arm bigger than his—and gave custody to Mom as long as Roxanne's on probation."

"Has she been giving Mom fits?" Corrigan demanded, staring at him.

Danny shook his head as though he were relieved to have something good to say. "Actually Roxanne seems to be getting along fine." He gazed out the window as though the trees suddenly fascinated him. "Mom didn't want to tell you while you were so sick, but that's why she had to get back home. She didn't feel right leaving Roxanne with Billy and Ida for too long." Farm workers, Billy and Ida McRae lived in a cottage on a corner of the property.

Jonathan let out an irritated gasp. "What was Mom thinking? She's too old to deal with a teenager, especially a delinquent."

"She considers it a ministry."

"Oh, yeah," he said sarcastically. "I forgot about that."

The car floated around a sweeping curve. Soon the house would come into view. "It's what she believes, Jonathan," Danny said. "You have to respect that."

"Right." Corrigan passed a hand across his face. "Why did she decide to do her charity work just when I'm coming home? Honestly, Danny, I don't feel like hearing any whining and sassing right now. If the girl pulls that I may just put her over my knee. Especially if she's rude to Mom."

When Danny didn't answer, Jonathan let his back relax against the seat, his eyes on the wide tree trunks flipping past his window. That kid better not give him any lip, or she'd get a hard lesson from Old Father Corrigan.

From his vantage point in the loft of an abandoned barn situated across the road, a watcher who called himself Ben observed the limousine followed by a dark Caprice as they pulled into the Corrigan driveway. His powerful binoculars couldn't penetrate the tinted glass to see who was inside the limo. It didn't matter. Corrigan had to be in there. Getting close to the CIA agent would be tough while the FBI stayed around, but he had to chance it. Too much was at stake.

CHAPTER SEVEN

Guiding her Ford Tempo out of the Denny's parking lot, Shannon remembered her talk with Olivia at lunch. With both her parents in prison for treason, Shannon had her fair share of burdens. Why hadn't they considered what would happen to their only daughter if they were caught?

And Darryl Hansen had so completely taken her in. One moment she was about to be engaged, the next moment she had her identity erased. Soon afterward, she had landed in a strange city with a good chunk of cash and a blank page to fill in all on her own.

She sighed, easing into traffic and immediately changing lanes to make a left at the light. Was it possible that Darryl really had cared for her? Why had he said that on TV?

Deep in her thoughts, she drove home on automatic pilot, somehow managing to stop for every red light and make the correct turns. Parking in her numbered space in front of the apartment building, she felt the world closing in on her. Could God really take such a heavy burden away?

Digging out her apartment key as she walked, she pushed open the door to the redbrick building. She no longer needed a key to open the outer door. The Wilson teens on the third floor had kicked it in when they forgot their key. That was a month ago, and the landlord still hadn't bothered to repair it. She clumped up the dark stairs, wishing she could afford better digs.

When she inserted the key into the dead bolt, her door creaked open under the light pressure. She froze, every sense screaming. Her heart thumped like a jackhammer. She swallowed and tried to breathe.

She started to push into her apartment. . .then stopped. How many times had she yelled at a TV character, "Don't go in there, you fool! He's waiting around the corner. Call the cops!"

Spinning on her heel, she trotted downstairs to Mr. Iverson's apartment and pounded on the wooden door, the varnish worn off where her hand hit.

Somewhere inside, bottles clinked. Then came language that made her ears tingle. Wouldn't that manager ever come? She pounded louder, bruising her palms on the wood.

Shuffling footsteps ended at the door. One chain lock slid off, another chain lock, a dead bolt, and the door opened. A gnarled face covered with thick, white stubble appeared in the opening. The smell of stale whiskey and cigarette smoke hit her in the face when he spoke, forming the words carefully, each one drawing out longer than normal. "Whadda ya want? It's Sunday. Can't it wait?"

Shannon cried, almost hysterical. "Someone. . .no. . .my apartment. . ."

His watery eyes tried to focus. "Can't you see I'm busy?" He rubbed an arthritic hand across the front of his T-shirt, once white, now gray.

Eyes wild, Shannon gulped, then breathed deeply, forcing herself to be coherent. "Someone broke into my apartment."

The old man's hunched frame straightened up. His jaw tightened. "I warned those kids to stay away from you. You're the nicest tenant I have ever had." He paused a second, considering, then said, "I'll be right back."

Leaving the door ajar, he trundled into his apartment. Liquor bottles covered the dining room table and littered the filthy carpet. A moment later, he returned with a weathered baseball bat in his hand.

"Shouldn't we call the police?" Shannon asked, wincing at the sight of the bat.

Weaving, the old man stared at her, amazed. His words ran together. "Why? So they can give those Wilson boys some milk and cookies?" He got louder as he spoke. "Not a chance. If I survived Korea, I can survive those punks. Let's go."

Shannon followed Iverson up the narrow staircase, staying a few steps behind him. She should have called the police first.

When he reached her apartment, he held up his hand. "Wait here. I'll make sure everything is all right."

Using the bat, he shoved her door open the rest of the way, then walked in with his club high, anxious to score a grand slam. Waiting in the dusty hall, Shannon heard him muttering obscenities. A few minutes later, his blotchy face appeared at the door. "Come on in, Missy. No one's here."

Harsh in the glaring light of an afternoon sun, her couch cushions lay in tatters, her few dishes broken and scattered across the floor. The little fridge lay on its side, its contents running over the scuffed tile. The mattress hung half off the bed, its stuffing spread throughout the room like a grotesque snowstorm. Crumpled clothes lay everywhere.

A brown lump next to the couch caught Shannon's attention. Moving closer, she bent over for a better look. On his back, spread-eagled, Bear's torso lay wide open, his life's blood spilled out around him.

Moaning, Shannon's knees buckled. She felt Iverson's stiff hands on her shoulders, guiding her to a wooden kitchen chair that had escaped destruction.

Her eyes stayed on the bear. The Feds had never found what they wanted from her father. Had they found her and come back to finish the job? Was it coincidence that this happened the day after Jonathan Corrigan came to town?

Covering her face, she wept, her gasping sobs muffled yet strong. Mr. Iverson awkwardly patted her back. His voice had tightened up. "It'll be all right, Missy."

Raising her head, she spotted a pile of clean tissues on the floor by the window, the torn box nearby. She left her chair to pick up a handful and wipe her face.

Iverson asked, "Is anything missing?"

Shannon looked about and groaned. "My TV and electric piano are gone."

"Those little. . ." He looked at her. ". . .Monsters."

Shannon stifled a hysterical laugh. After the language he'd used that day, why turn into a gentleman now?

The bat hanging from his hand, he headed for the door, saying over his shoulder, "I'll be right back." A moment later, he pounded up the stairs to the next floor. From the apartment above her came muffled yelling, erratic thumping, and slamming of doors.

Red-faced and panting, Iverson reappeared. "The little brats deny it. I looked through their place, and I didn't see your stuff."

Shannon's eyes fell on Bear. "Thanks anyway, Mr. Iverson, but it probably wasn't them."

He looked around, spotted the phone on the floor, and paced toward it. "We've got to call the cops."

Shannon knelt beside Bear and began gathering up his stuffing. Maybe major surgery could save his life. She wiped fresh tears with the back of her hand. What did they think she had? Any answers would be in her father's head, not hers.

When his parents' log home came into view, a surge of excitement passed through Jonathan, surprising him. His father had built the house, using timber from the logs felled on their property. A stickler for detail, he had scribed each one, so they fit tight.

With two stories visible, the house had a solid concrete foundation and a full basement that gave it three floors with a wide front verandah and large deck that ran off to the left. A red steel roof added drama to the yellow-orange logs.

Almost twenty-five years before, that roof had caused a stir among their closest neighbors, particularly Pat Murray and Seth Poulson.

"Shouldn't you use cedar shakes?" Murray had asked, watching from the ground, one thumb under the strap of his faded overalls. Dad had nodded to be polite and kept slapping on sheets of coated steel.

Half an hour later, Poulson had said, "You really ought to use shakes. They look best with a log house."

"No doubt you're right," Dad had called back, staying at the job.

Just a ten-year-old boy, Jonathan had waited until his father came down for lunch. Munching a bologna sandwich, he'd asked, "Why aren't you using shakes, Dad?"

His father had leaned toward him, his eyes crinkling as he smiled. "Someday you'll understand, Son."

Dad was right. Two winters later, Murray lost his house when embers from the wood furnace ignited the shakes. Four years after that, Poulson had to replace his roof because he hadn't kept his shakes treated, and they rotted. Dad had grinned and shook his head when he saw Poulson's pickup truck pass the Corrigan place—the back piled high with coated steel panels.

Coming in from the barn, Dad would look at that steel roof and say, "She ain't pretty, but she'll last longer than I will." Those words turned out to be tragically true.

The steep roof wouldn't have made the cover of *Architectural Digest,* but it looked beautiful to Jonathan today.

Sweeping out of the woods in the limo, headed for that house, Jonathan sucked in a slow breath and felt his whole body relax. He was really home. If any good had come from his wounds, this was it. They forced him to come home.

As the car drew close to the wide front porch, a massive dog with a bearlike head came at the car, barking wildly.

"Gus!" Jonathan cried. "Is he still around? He must be twelve years old."

Danny grinned. "He's just as lively as ever. He follows Roxanne around like he was still a puppy."

The front door burst open, and Sandra Corrigan trotted to the top of a new ramp where the steps used to be. She dabbed at her eyes with something white. A curly redhead appeared at Sandra's right hip. A curly blond head leaned against the other side.

Jonathan leaned toward the window. "Say, Danny, are those. . . ?"

He grinned broadly. "Yep. My girls."

"They look like you did when you were a kid," he said, smiling. "How old are they now?"

"Janine is eight, and Mary is six."

Jonathan glanced at his brother. "Is Rita here?"

"Uh-huh." He nodded. "She can't wait to meet you."

Corrigan seemed to grow. His shoulders squared off and his head lifted as though drawn by a string at his crown. He burst out, "This is great!"

Danny cocked his head. "You serious? At the hospital you said you didn't want to come here."

Jonathan paused, shocked at the change in himself. He gazed at his brother, a new light in his eyes. "I've never been more serious in my life."

Danny's big hand pressed against Jonathan's forehead.

Jonathan jerked away. "What are you doing?"

"Checking your temperature. You must be delirious." He chuckled deep in his chest and pulled the door latch as the car stopped.

When Danny stepped out of the limo, his daughters rushed, squealing, into his arms. With a whoop, he scooped them up and spun them around, their laughter like musical chimes. Finally, he dropped to his knees, holding them close while they covered his cheeks with loud kisses.

Waiting inside the open car door, Jonathan held up his hands in a feeble attempt to ward off a Gus attack. Wagging his stub tail twice a second, the giant hound tried to act like a lapdog, licking Jonathan's face and leaning into his chest.

"Howdy, old fella!" Corrigan said, rubbing the dog's head. "Missed me, did ya?" His heart was glad that Gus remembered him, but his stomach didn't like the dog's attentions.

Finally, Sandra came to Jonathan's rescue and got hold of Gus's collar. "Back, Gus!" she called, pulling firmly. "Out of the car!" Turning back to lick her free hand, Gus retreated and Jonathan breathed.

Holding two tugging hands, Danny stood up and looked at his mother. "Where's Rita?" he asked.

"Down at the horse barn with Roxanne," she answered, stepping toward the limo. "We'd best get Jonathan inside. He's probably worn out."

Danny turned to his brother. "Girls, this is your uncle Jon." Mary stuck her index finger in her mouth and shied behind her dad, but Janine stepped forward, her slim arm outstretched. Jonathan gently shook her hand.

"I'm Janine," she said, watching him, her busy eyes curious.

"I'm Jonathan." He smiled softly. "How do you do?"

"I'm great." Her eyes flickered toward his leg. "How are you?"

The smile stretched wider. "I'll be fine."

Danny pried himself loose from his offspring as the driver opened the trunk and set the chair to the ground. Flipping open the seat and locking it down, Danny pushed it to the open door, saying, "Okay, Janine, step back. I'm going to help Uncle Jon get into his chair." He got it into position. "Nice and easy now, Jon. Let's not have an accident and spoil your homecoming."

Waiting until he got into the chair, Mom let Gus go and bent over him for a hug. "Welcome home, Son."

He swallowed the lump in his throat so he could whisper, "It's good to be home."

"Janine, go down to the barn and tell Mommy and Roxanne we're here," Danny said when Mom turned Jonathan loose. He grabbed the handles on the chair and turned it around.

Skinny as a blade of grass, Janine sprinted the forty yards to the horse barn, her sister three strides behind her. Barking, Gus followed them, his round belly bouncing with each stride.

Jonathan watched them, his gaze lingering on the wide barn door. Many fond memories hid in that barn and the corrals behind it.

The mouthwatering smell of baking chicken wafted over them as Danny rolled Jonathan through the front door. Once inside, other odors caught his attention—fresh paint and dust, like a construction site.

"Have you been painting?" he asked his mother.

"Come and take a look," she said proudly.

"Turn loose, Danny," he said. "I'm driving from here." Taking charge of the wheels, Jonathan propelled the chair down the hall. Past the living room, the kitchen—where Danny left them—and on to his father's study at the end of the hall.

Rolling inside, he looked around. It was no longer a study. His maple bedroom furniture stood there with a new queen-sized bed at center stage. A wide door stood open to the right. He wheeled toward it. "What's in there?"

Mom came near the back of his chair. "It's a wheelchair-accessible bathroom."

He looked up at her, chagrined. "You shouldn't have spent the money on this, Mom. I won't need it for long."

Wearing that decided expression he knew so well, she stepped around to look him in the eye. "You don't like to be fussed over, Jonathan Corrigan. If I hadn't done this, you'd try to use the powder room down the hall and hurt yourself." She glanced at her watch. "Besides, several handicapped people attend our church. Now I have a friendlier place for them." She stepped toward the door. "Don't worry; it won't go to waste."

Jonathan reached the dining room in time to see Danny hugging his slender wife, her honey-colored hair swishing against her shoulders. When her husband let go of her, she turned and smiled at Jonathan.

"Hi, Rita," he said, liking her right away. "I'm glad to finally meet you."

She darted a glance at Danny then back to him. "I wanted to come to the hospital, but someone had to stay with the girls." She reached down and gave Jonathan a warm hug. "Welcome home."

There came that pesky lump in his throat again.

Rita moved away. "I've got to see that Janine and Mary wash their hands."

As she passed, Danny pinched her.

"Oh!" Her cheeks turned brilliant red. "Danny Corrigan! In front of your brother?" She pushed his chest, and he took a step backward, arms flying wide. Laughing and dodging another attack, she skipped out of the room.

BETRAYED

"Don't worry about Jon," Danny called after her. "He's been wearing long pants for at least a year or two. He knows the score." He chuckled.

Jonathan moved the wheelchair near the table to keep his face turned away. His loss hit him with fresh force. *Laura, where are you? Will I ever see you again?*

A sharp knock, then Andrea strode in wearing a black jumpsuit with a glittering blazer in maroon, green, and gold, her wide heels loud on the oak floor. "Hello, Jonathan," she said, beaming at him as she swept a mop of thick, blond hair from her face. "I hope I'm not late."

"We're just getting the gang together for lunch," Danny said, moving toward her. "Would you like to see your room?"

She slid the strap of a massive leather handbag from her shoulder. "My suitcases are in the trunk of my car." Letting her eyes linger on the muscles under his green T-shirt, she said, "I'm sure you can handle them." She held out her keys.

"No sweat." Danny said. He hurried out, the door thumping behind him.

Andrea sank into a chair next to Jonathan. "How's my patient? Exhausted yet?"

He tried to smile. Now that she mentioned it, he was a little tired. "I'll live," he said. "Just don't fuss over me, okay? Mom will do plenty of that. I can't take it if you do it, too."

Her smile faded, "Sure, Jon. I was just being friendly."

"I didn't mean to snap at you," he said, feeling bad. "I guess I'm more tired than I thought."

"No problem." She put her hand on his bare arm. "This is Andrea, remember?" He caught a sudden whiff of Charlie perfume.

That moment, Mom appeared, carrying a wide bowl of succotash. She drew up when she spotted Andrea. A moment later, she nodded at the newcomer. "Hello, Andrea." Her lips smiled but her eyes didn't. "Have you seen your room yet?"

"Danny's getting my things from the car," she said, standing as the door opened. "That's him there."

"Just leave your suitcases in the hall for now," Sandra Corrigan said. "We're about to sit down." She placed the bowl in the center of the table.

"Do you want us to sit anyplace special, Mom?" Jonathan asked.

"We removed a chair from that spot for your wheelchair, Jonathan," she said. She nodded at a chair two places down from her son. "You can sit there, Andrea."

Mom hurried back to the kitchen. The rest of the gang arrived before she returned. Janine pulled out the chair next to her uncle Jon. Mom sat at his other side, between him and Andrea.

Arriving late, Sandra's ward, Roxanne, came through the back door with Gus close behind her. About five feet eight, she had soft features and black hair that fell to her hips. She was out of breath. "Mom, we'll have to keep Gus inside," she told Sandra. "He wants to bite the FBI men outside. I had to drag him in." She patted the dog who was sitting beside her. He grinned upward as though proud of himself.

Sandra frowned at Gus. "Will you look after him, Roxanne? I've got enough on my mind without having to run after that giant fur ball." She tsk-tsked at the dog, her eyes smiling in spite of her frown. "You're more trouble than you're worth, you know that, Gus?" she said.

Wagging his stumpy tail, he gave a short bark.

After washing her hands, Roxanne sat across from Jonathan. When he tried out a friendly smile on her, those cobalt eyes were sentries, guarding the door to her soul. Gus lay down by the door, his wide nose lying between two wide paws.

"Danny, would you say the blessing for us?" Sandra asked when everyone had taken a seat, and the meal began.

As usual, dinner was outstanding—baked chicken that fell off the bone and a sweet-potato casserole that used to make Jonathan want a third helping. Unfortunately, doctor's orders forced him to limit himself to only mashed potatoes and applesauce with a tiny serving of diced meat.

Danny's oldest daughter held a chicken bone out toward Gus. The dog stood up.

"Janine! Not while you're at the table!" Rita called. "And certainly not a chicken bone."

"Why, Mommy?"

"Because it can splinter and choke the dog."

The girl lay the bone on her plate, and Gus went back to his corner, his black eyes alert.

"Uncle Jon, is it true you're a spy?" Janine asked, watching him closely.

He picked up his water glass, buying some time. "Who told you that, Sweetheart?" he asked.

"It was on TV." Her face had a wise look like she was eight going on twenty-five. "They said you're a spy, and you saved a whole bunch of kids."

He shifted in his chair, wishing that Danny would help him out with an answer. "Many people helped those children," he told her finally. "Not just me."

Her brow pulled down, and her mouth pulled up. "Have you ever shot anybody?"

He darted a look at her father who was munching a dinner roll and talking to Andrea. How should he answer the child?

"You know, like James Bond," Janine persisted.

"I told you she was too young for that movie," Rita told Danny. Finally tuning in, her husband's expression darkened, his eyes on his daughter.

Jonathan leaned toward the little girl, speaking softly. "No, Janine, I've never shot anybody." He'd broken limbs, noses, the odd jaw, true. He hadn't needed a gun to get the job done.

"How do you catch crooks if you don't use a gun?"

Whew! This kid was more persistent than a snapping turtle clamping on a stick. "By being smarter, Janine," he told her. "It's what's up here that really counts." He tapped his temple.

"Daddy shot someone," little Mary piped in, bursting with information. "A bad man was going to hurt this lady and—um, Daddy was there, and he shot him to save the lady."

"That's enough talking about shooting, girls," Rita announced, passing the pickles to her husband. "This is supposed to be a welcome-home dinner for Uncle Jonathan." She turned to Roxanne. "How do you like Maranatha School?" she asked.

"I like it," the girl mumbled. It was the first time she'd spoken.

"Have you made any friends?" Andrea asked, smiling.

"Some." Eyes down, she pushed at her food with a fork.

"How are your grades?" Danny asked.

His mother said abruptly, "Roxanne is doing fine."

"Meet any boys?" Janine chirped, her voice hopeful.

Roxanne blushed and squirmed. "Uh, a couple."

"That's enough, Janine!" Rita said, staring down her eldest.

Roxanne gave Rita a thankful glance.

"So, Danny," Jonathan said, speaking loudly, "how's life on the Seattle force? You haven't told me about your job yet."

From there the topic turned to a dozen cows Mom wanted to sell and the farm's daily milk production.

Twenty minutes later, Sandra Corrigan stood up. "I've got an apple pie in the kitchen."

Danny groaned and rubbed his stomach. "Why didn't you tell me that before?"

Everyone laughed.

Suddenly, an FBI agent in a dark suit burst through the front door and into the dining room. "Everyone stay where you are!"

Gus lunged toward the man, growling like the bear he resembled. "Down, Gus!" Danny yelled. Scraping back his chair, he grabbed the dog's collar and pulled him toward the kitchen. "C'mon, boy. In here." He urged the animal inside and closed the door. Barks and scratching came from the other side.

Another agent dressed in black combat fatigues, an assault rifle held high across his chest, followed his partner in and positioned himself by the nearest window, peering around the edge.

"What's going on?" Corrigan demanded.

"Perimeter alarm," the first one said. "We have an intruder."

CHAPTER EIGHT

While waiting for the police to arrive, Shannon sat Indian style on the floor and cradled Bear. Gently, she pushed white cotton into his empty abdomen. With great care, she squeezed the fabric together, then sewed it closed with needle and thread from a travel kit in her purse. A quarter way into the job, the fabric tore away from the stitching. He was as old as Shannon was, and the fabric had become brittle. Biting hard on her bottom lip, she whispered a curse on whoever had done this to him.

Laying him on the carpet, she searched the kitchen floor and found a roll of brown packing tape. Using a short strip, she patched the bear's wound the best she could, leaving a lumpy ugly scar.

A light tap on the doorframe brought Shannon around, her heart racing.

"I'm Wesley Anderson, Bellingham police," the young man said, stepping inside. His head barely cleared the top of the door. A freckle-faced redhead, he looked like an overgrown boy. He glanced around the apartment. "What happened?"

Shannon stepped closer, craning her neck back to look up at him. "I got home from lunch and found the dead bolt broken."

He grabbed the door and flipped the lever on the lock. Nothing happened. "I see."

"Should you be touching that? What about fingerprints?"

Jotting something in his notebook, Officer Anderson shook his head. "This isn't going to make you happy, but B & E is a minor crime.

We don't do fingerprints anymore. We just take a statement and hope to find your stuff."

"You're kidding."

"I wish I was."

First Shannon felt like screaming, then she realized that this was a stroke of good luck. What if the CIA or FBI was involved, and the Bellingham police caught on? Wouldn't that blow her identity wide open?

"I'm really sorry, Miss Masterson," he said. Shannon looked into his eyes and saw genuine warmth there.

He cleared his throat. "Can we sit down? I need to ask you a few questions."

Shannon looked around and spotted a kitchen chair on its back in the hall. Anderson saw it at the same time and reached it in four strides. Lifting it with one hand, he placed it near its mate in the living room, knee to knee.

He asked the usual—name, phone number, what had been taken, any known enemies. That one was a laugh. How about the CIA and the FBI for starters? "None," was the only safe answer.

Ten minutes later, he got up to poke about—moving articles and looking under furniture while Shannon stayed in her chair. Her trembling had stopped, and she watched him in a detached way, like the apartment belonged to a stranger.

"Strange kind of B & E," he said, on his knees by the sofa.

She crossed her arms tightly across her waist. "What do you mean?" she asked.

"I know they stole some things, but this destruction looks more like a search."

She chewed her bottom lip, her eyes frightened. "I know."

Wesley looked surprised. "You do?"

Shannon swallowed. What an idiotic thing to say. She laced her next words with heavy sarcasm. "Anyone who lives in a penthouse like this must have a bundle of cash stashed away."

Officer Anderson chuckled. He stood and placed huge hands on slim hips. "There's only one thing left to do here."

"What's that?"

"Start cleaning up." He strode to the kitchen. The next moment, water splashed into the sink.

She darted after him. "What are you doing?"

He smiled down at her. With that mischievous, boyish expression, he reminded her of someone from her past.

"I'm going to help you get this place straightened up," he said. "Unless you don't want me to."

"No, it's not that." She let out a quick breath. "I can use the help. That's obvious enough. But don't you have to get back to work?"

"Nope." He checked his watch. "In ten minutes I'll call in my report, and they'll punch my card." He squirted white soap into the sink.

Shannon bent down, picking up plastic plates and glasses, her taupe-colored pumps crunching over broken glass. For the first time she realized that she still wore her new dress from church that morning.

She set the dishes on the counter. "If you'll excuse me a minute, I'll change into work clothes."

He smiled and turned off the water. "Take your time. I'll tackle that fridge while you're gone."

Picking through the jumbled pile in front of her dresser, Shannon had a sharp impression that she was reliving that painful day two years before, a victim of the FBI's heavy hand. Was this a repeat operation or the work of some new invisible enemy?

She shivered. Why was this happening to her? She was the kind of person who returned extra change to a careless cashier. She put money in the parking meter even when the attendant was off duty. Life was definitely unfair.

Glimpsing her Seahawks sweatshirt half under the bed, she snatched it, along with her favorite jeans and sneakers, and locked herself in the bathroom to change. The sink contained a sludgy mass of broken cosmetic bottles and smashed lip gloss containers; cough medicine and chalky white antacid smeared the linoleum.

Trying to avoid looking at the litter around her, she carefully draped her dress over the shower rod to keep it from getting stained. Sliding into her clothes, she ran stiff fingers through her short hair to repair the damage the sweatshirt had caused, then pulled on her shoes.

When she reached the kitchen, Officer Anderson had his indigo coat and tie off, his shirtsleeves rolled up to the elbow. The fridge sat in its former position, and he held two plastic bowls over the trash can, shaking them.

"Welcome to the palace," he said. "How about some music? Do you have a radio?"

"I'm not sure. I'll look," Shannon said, her mood lifting. Having someone to share the work made the task so much easier, especially when he was fun to be around. She found her clock radio with its cassette cover torn off and carried it to the kitchen. Miracle of miracles, the radio came on. She tuned in an easy-listening station, and Glenn Miller's music filled the room.

She smiled "That's much better, Officer Anderson. Thanks for suggesting it."

"Please call me Wesley," he said, dipping his hands into the steaming water. Dishes thumped and suds sprayed under his energetic movements.

"Call me Shannon." She looked around. "Let me find a broom. I can't stand things crunching under my feet."

When the dishes lay neatly in the cabinet, Wesley said, "I'll scrub this floor next."

"You'll spoil your uniform."

"No problem," he said, grinning. "A few water spots won't be anything new for these pants." He glanced in corners and peered at the jumble outside the kitchen door. "Do you have a mop and a scrubbing brush?"

"Sorry, no mop, but there's a scrubbing brush around here somewhere." She paused and looked up at him, realizing again how tall he was. "I still can't understand why you're doing this."

His expression grew serious. He spoke gently. "I live alone, too. I know how I'd feel if I came home and my place looked like this." His lips formed a soft curve. "Besides, what do I have to do tonight besides baby-sit my television?" His blue eyes smiled and seemed somehow close. "I want to help you. Is that okay?"

"Thank you, Wesley." She felt a slow warmth fill her as she lifted a bottle of cleanser and handed it to him. Maybe there really were some good people left in the world.

On the Corrigan homestead, Ben's face smashed into the forest floor. He took in a mouthful of dirt. When he rolled over, dried pine needles slid down the back of his pants. He sat up, trying to figure out what hit him. Sunlight glinted against a thin wire. A perimeter alarm.

He'd counted six FBI agents on the Corrigan property. In minutes they would zoom in on him. Could he cross the open field and return to the abandoned barn? Not likely.

He stood up, desperately scanning the area for a place to hide. The forest lawn had no bushes to crawl under. He had only one direction left.

Ben raced a hundred yards northeast of the wire to a large pine with thick branches. Unfortunately, the first limb was ten feet up. Wrapping arms and legs around the tree trunk, he shimmied upward. His leather jacket and jeans gave him some protection, but the rough bark scraped his hands and face. The acrid smell of pinesap filled his head. Stabilizing himself with his legs, he grabbed the lowest limb and hauled himself up.

Running steps came closer. Moving like a ghost, he slipped up the tree, placing a dozen wide branches between himself and prying eyes below. Fifty feet up, he stopped, schooling himself to breathe silently when his chest cried out for gallons of air.

Twenty feet to his left, two agents paused—one wide and one high.

"This is the spot," the stocky one said. He had a deep voice.

Neither spoke for the space of five breaths.

"I don't see anyone," the tall one answered.

Sounding disgusted, Chubby said, "It was probably a deer or a coyote."

"We should look around some, anyway. We'd have to pay the piper if something happened to that big-shot hero during our watch."

Chubby swore. "If you ask me, Gary, this detail is total overkill."

"You've got that right. You'd think this guy was the president."

"As far as you bozos are concerned, he is the president." It was a third man—tall, big, and mad.

"Perkins!" Gary said, acting pleased. "How you doing?"

"I'm doing fine," Perkins barked. "But you won't be if I hear any more bellyaching about this detail. The president made it clear that if anything happens to Corrigan, whoever goofed up will be doing wiretaps until he retires."

Heavy footfalls retreated. Chubby muttered a few choice words. "Boy, are his shorts in a knot!"

"Didn't you hear?" Gary asked.

"What?"

"It was Perkins's gun that nailed Corrigan. He let a terrorist grab it."

"Is that why he won't go near the house?" Chubby asked, starting away.

Following him, Gary said, "You've got it. If Corrigan saw Perkins, he'd probably shoot on sight."

They moved out of earshot, but Ben didn't move. His tripping the perimeter alarm was a lucky break. Corrigan's guards weren't taking their job seriously. If he was careful, he may get close enough for a shot. He preferred to shoot during the day, but night wasn't out of the question. He had the equipment; he just didn't have much time.

Corrigan stared at the agent who'd stormed their dinner table and bellowed, "Perimeter alarm! Are you guys insane? These woods are full of deer. They'll set off the alarm twice an hour." He paused to take a breath and looked at his nieces. Their eyes were round and scared. The rest of the group stayed stock-still at the table, as though waiting for the main event.

"Whose brilliant idea was this, anyway?" Corrigan went on.

The agent hesitated.

"Whose?" Corrigan pushed.

"Hey, Jonathan, relax," Danny said. "They're trying to do a job."

Corrigan turned his outraged stare toward his brother. "Danny, you grew up here. Surely you know those alarms aren't worth dirt."

"They'd rather be safe than sorry."

Jonathan's face turned red. He jerked his head toward his bedroom. "Come with me, Bro." He swung his chair away from the table.

The agent blocked Jonathan's path. "Sir, please stay in the room. We have to ascertain if there is a threat."

"Move."

The agent backed off, and Jonathan led Danny down the hall. As soon as the two brothers reached the bedroom, Jonathan motioned for Danny to shut the door. "The Iraqis are not a threat, Danny."

"What are you talking about? You're the reason their buddies are on ice. They're bound to come after you."

"Look, I'm going to tell you something. If you ever repeat it, even to your wife, you'll have a cell next to those terrorists."

Danny drew back. "Are you serious?"

"Absolutely. Even the FBI doesn't know this."

"Okay, Jonathan, you're the boss. Whatever you say won't leave this room."

Corrigan opened his mouth, then paused. Watching his brother, he made a spider motion with his hand, then put his finger to his lips. "On second thought, I don't think I should tell you."

Danny's face assumed a deadpan expression. "You probably shouldn't," he said. "Whatever it is, if it makes you feel the house is safe, it's safe."

"Good. It's nice to have my judgment trusted. Hey, it's stuffy in here. Let's go outside and get some air."

"Great idea."

Jonathan wheeled toward the front door. The FBI agent stepped in front of him. "Sorry, Sir, we still haven't secured the grounds."

Jonathan spoke slowly. "Get out of my way."

"Sir, you have to let us do our job."

Corrigan snickered. "Your job. You guys are probably in a sweat over some poor coyote who smelled my Mom's baked chicken." He lifted a tight fist. "Move!"

"Do as he says," Danny said. "I'll be with him."

Jonathan looked over his shoulder at his brother. "No danger of a coyote attack with that big moose on my side."

Reluctantly, the agent stepped away. Jonathan wheeled his chair across the porch and down the ramp. He sucked in pine-scented air. Though February, the breeze felt deliciously warm. He tried to move farther into the yard, but the chair bogged down in the gravel driveway. "This is just great. How am I supposed to get around?"

Danny grinned. "We were going to wait until later to show you this, but now is as good a time as any." He trotted to the garage about fifty feet from the house. A minute later, the roar of an engine came through the open door, and Danny burned out of the garage on a four-wheel Polaris all-terrain vehicle. He skidded to a stop near the wheelchair.

Jonathan groaned. "Where is Mom getting all this money?"

Danny let out a loud laugh. "This little gem didn't come from Mom. It came from Bellingham Power and Sports. It's a loaner until you get on your feet."

Jonathan's eyes lit up. "Really?"

"Yeah."

"Cool!"

"Hop on," Danny said. "I'll drive."

Jonathan shook his head, his face full of life. "Not in a million years. People have been pushing and pulling me for weeks. That baby is going to make me mobile. Off you get."

With a feigned pout, Danny got off the machine. "Need a hand?"

"I'll get on that thing if it kills me."

Using his cane, Jonathan righted himself. He turned his back to the four-wheeler and eased onto its long, padded seat then swung his right leg over. The next moment, he was in charge of the machine.

"Get on," he called to Danny.

Ignoring the warning on the bumper not to carry more than one passenger, his brother hopped on behind him.

"It's an automatic," Jonathan yelled over the gunning motor.

"That's right," Danny called into his ear, "no clutch."

"Thank Bellingham Power and Sports for me." With that, Jonathan turned the throttle, and the ATV tore down the driveway, leaving a shower of stones and dust. An exasperated guard yelled after them, but the men didn't hear him.

The years rolled away. Jonathan and Danny were kids again, the wind sailing around them as they tore down the driveway ending in the narrow cattle trail to the pasture. Five minutes later, eyes full of absolute delight, Jonathan came to a stop in the middle of a one-hundred-acre field. "This should be far enough," he said, laughing.

"You really think your room has a bug?"

"No, but I'm not taking any chances. I wasn't kidding. What I've got to tell you only half a dozen people in the U.S. government know. You can never repeat it."

Danny got off the ATV and leaned against the front fender, facing Jonathan. "I hope you know what you're doing, big brother. I'm not so sure I want the responsibility of knowing whatever it is. But if you think it's necessary, you've got my word. I'll never tell a living soul."

"That's good enough." He switched off the motor and leaned both arms against the steering wheel. "It's like this."

Scrubbing the bathroom floor, Shannon looked up when Wesley appeared at the door, the vacuum cleaner rolling in front of him. "It's almost eight," he said. "I'm starving. How would you like to go to the Blue Coat Inn for some supper?"

She rocked back on her heels, brushing hair from her eyes with her wrist. "I'm dressed for the McDonald's drive-thru, Wesley. I can't go to a sit-down restaurant now."

He rolled the vacuum farther down the hall. The closet door creaked. A moment later, he returned and leaned a forearm on the doorjamb. "I live ten minutes from here. I could go home and shower while you get ready. I'll come back and pick you up." He smiled hopefully. "How about it? I don't feel like opening a TV dinner tonight."

She sighed and got to her feet, bone weary but also famished. "I'll meet you there in about an hour. Okay?"

BETRAYED

His face showed his delight. "Great! See you then." He stepped away, and the front door bumped shut. The new lock—purchased and installed by Wesley two hours ago—closed with a loud click. Shannon hurried to slip the chain into its slot.

Why was she hesitant to ride in Wesley's car? She reached for the bottom edge of her sweatshirt. A shower would feel heavenly.

On the other side of the country, CIA director Elijah Stone surveyed the landing area below him. His Jet Ranger hovered over a cabin nestled in the wilderness on the backside of the Poconos. Three choppers already sat on the ground. Since all four of the people attending this conference were helicopter pilots, they could meet far from prying eyes.

Stone hadn't given out this location until they were all in the air. This was too big to chance a leak. For the first time in history, America had a chance to destroy the military standing of China, Russia, and a dozen other nations in one fell swoop. Nothing must stop it from happening. Not even the so-called ethics of the secretary of defense.

Reducing power, Stone lowered the chopper to a vacant spot and shut down the engine. As he scuttled from the helicopter, a gust of cold wind knifed through him. Jogging to the log cabin, he held a briefcase in one hand and a hard-shell black suitcase in the other, both banging his knees as he ran.

He'd borrowed the cabin from an air force colonel who thought Stone wanted some R&R. A solid growth of timber separated this place from the nearest human being by ten miles. There was only one way to get here, and Stone had just used it.

He pushed open the plank door on the cabin, and the smell of wood smoke caught the edge of his consciousness. Good. Someone had enough sense to light a fire. The cabin was rugged but neat, no curtains or rugs. In a dark corner, two cabinet doors and a chipped sink made up the kitchen.

Stone nodded to the other occupants, two men and a woman. Following orders, no one spoke. First he had to sweep the place for bugs. He was taking no chances that someone had this hideaway under surveillance for some other reason. An unseen listener would ruin everything.

Stone opened the black suitcase and pulled out some electronic equipment. He flipped a couple of switches and moved about the room.

Finally satisfied that it was clean, he put it away.

This humble cabin held four of the most powerful people in the United States. Sitting on the leather sofa was Gary Jefferson, the tall, balding African-American who directed the National Security Agency. Beside him sat Major General Tony Feretti, a bull of a man with a stiff shock of black hair, who chaired the Joint Chiefs of Staff. Secretary of Defense Nancy Cartwright had a chair at the thick plank table. Elegant and refined, Nancy looked like an aristocrat, but she was one of the first women in U.S. history to go under fire as a naval aviator. Her military record was impeccable.

"Nice of you to join us," Cartwright said. Her deep voice held a tinge of irony.

"Sorry for the delay," Stone replied. "I hung back for awhile to make sure no one followed us in."

"Good thinking," Feretti said. "We can't afford to let this get out." His tone made one think of coarse-grained sandpaper.

"So, Director," Cartwright said, making a point of checking the time, "what is so imperative that it merits these extreme measures? I had to cancel four important appointments."

Stone joined her at the table, his words coming fast. "Three days ago, the Chinese fired two cruise missiles at Taiwan."

Cartwright's eyes widened. "That's old news, Elijah. The report came over my desk that same day."

"Hear him out, Nancy," General Feretti rasped. "There's more." He leaned forward, his elbows resting on his thighs, his expression intent.

Stone continued, "The interesting item is that the missiles held true for approximately four minutes before altering their course back toward the sending ship."

Cartwright crossed her legs. "The Chinese have never been famous for their accuracy."

Stone said, "Shortly after that incident, we fired a couple of our cruise missiles with the same exact results."

The men waited for her reaction. They were disappointed. She simply stared at Stone.

Jefferson spoke for the first time, "Harrison McIvor's missile guidance system has shut down. Our smart bombs, ICBMs, Tomahawks, and pretty much everything using computer guidance has just turned to garbage."

"He's right," Feretti said. "We set off ballistic missiles from both land

and submarine with the same results. They travel for four minutes then turn back upon the launching site."

Cartwright's face turned pale. "How many people know about this?"

"That's the good news, Ma'am," Feretti said, wryly. "As soon as we realized what was happening, I called off all further testing. I told my staff that the reason was budget restraints."

Jefferson said, "As you know, two years ago Harrison McIvor and his wife went to prison for selling that technology to the Russians, the Chinese, the Iraqis, the Israelis, NATO, and who knows who else."

"It's a worldwide crisis," Stone said tersely.

Feretti said, "Sooner or later someone is going to fix the glitch and gain nuclear supremacy."

"How did he do it?" Cartwright asked. She'd suddenly aged by ten years.

Stone nodded toward Jefferson.

The dark man spoke clearly. "During Desert Storm, several of our high-tech missiles malfunctioned. Since we had to do the Y2K thing anyway, after the war we contracted Dr. McIvor to rework our high-tech systems. He's the most brilliant weapons specialist in the world."

Cartwright said, "Tell me you did a security check."

"Yes, Ma'am." Jefferson nodded, his head gleaming. "Nothing showed up to give us the first clue that McIvor was dirty." He paused to draw in a deep breath and continued, "His task included reprogramming software and overhauling hardware. When he finished, we could blow an eyelash off a gnat." He turned toward Stone. "C'mon, Elijah, give us the rest."

Stone picked up the ball. "Last night, our people found an encrypted program within the guidance system that seems to be the source of the trouble."

"We've got the best programmers in the world," Cartwright said. "Crack the code."

"We've been working around the clock," Jefferson told her.

Stone added, "Harrison McIvor is fluent in eight languages, including Navajo and an African tribal language.

"The key could be a little-known language, a seemingly random set of numbers, a book, anything. Our computers are firing away with every combination of symbols, languages, and numbers they can find, but with no success. Breaking that code could take years."

Cartwright drummed short, manicured nails on rough oak. "Buy

McIvor off. Threaten him."

Stone said, "He wants ten billion dollars and full pardon for him and his wife."

"Unacceptable," Cartwright said firmly. "You'll have to find some other way. Try negotiating with him. Ten billion and a pardon are out of the question. But something lesser may work." She glanced at the faces across the room. "Here's a thought. Why don't we just reinstall our old programs?"

Feretti exhaled slowly. "For starters, they aren't Y2K compliant. In about six months, we could probably get them ready, but they still wouldn't interface with our launch systems. You see, McIvor changed both the software and the hardware. Our programs won't work with his hardware. Some of that hardware is in orbit. We'd need several shuttle missions to change it."

"You're sure the Chinese and Russians also have this problem?"

"Yes, Ma'am," Stone said.

"The encryption could be broken at any time," Jefferson added.

Cartwright looked at Stone. "I thought you just told me it would take a couple of years."

"I said it *could* take a couple of years. We also could get lucky and hit the right combination—like a slot machine."

"So could the Chinese," Cartwright murmured.

"Exactly," Jefferson said.

Watching her closely, Stone said, "If McIvor came to CIA headquarters, and our boys worked him over. . ."

Cartwright pursed her lips. "For your information, Mr. Stone, pounding a U.S. citizen to make him talk happens to be illegal."

"But, Ma'am," Feretti said, indignant, "he's breached national security."

"General Feretti," she turned cold eyes toward the sofa. "You will have to find some other way."

She stood and adjusted her long, navy coat. "That's all the time I can spare, gentlemen. I've got a cabinet meeting in," she checked her watch, "two hours. I'll brief the president." She looked at Stone. "Elijah, keep me posted. Mention the Pocono Project, and I'll know what you mean." She nodded at the others and left the room.

Feretti rose and moved to the window. Within minutes, the helicopter's engine revved, and it moved skyward. "She's in the air," he said, turning toward the room.

Jefferson spoke to Stone. "What about McIvor's daughter? That's a bit of leverage you didn't mention."

The CIA director gave his friend a cynical grin. "You have a devious mind, Mr. Jefferson." He reached for the handle of his briefcase. "We're working that angle even as we speak."

CHAPTER NINE

Alex Popov yawned as rain pelted the windshield of his 1999 Ford Cougar. He put his hands behind his head and leaned back. The lineup at the Sumas, Washington, border crossing stretched long. He was in a hurry, but his years of KGB training had taught him to relax. Appearing rushed would only attract the attention of the U.S. Customs officer.

Yesterday's phone call had surprised him. Now a Canadian citizen, Popov was a professional hockey scout. For the last ten years, he had traveled throughout the U.S., Canada, and Europe, searching for hot young talent. With the Cold War over, he'd assumed Mother Russia would have no more use for him. Apparently, he was wrong.

Last evening, a courier had brought him a long envelope containing photographs of Jonathan Corrigan and Laura McIvor. His orders were simple. Keep an eye on Corrigan. Where he goes, you go. If he connects with the woman, follow her, then contact the boss. Whatever Popov did, she wasn't to be harmed. Someone in Russia would take care of that. They didn't say why they wanted her, but Popov knew who she was. He remembered the McIvor trial.

The line of traffic moved slowly, cold rain making the wait miserable. Bored, he flipped the radio on, and a religious station out of Seattle blasted him with gospel music. He frowned and hit the seek button. Foolishness, pure foolishness. Did they really believe that rot? That's what he liked about hockey. You didn't run into too many fanatics.

Eventually, his turn came. He drove up to the booth, and a young brunette beamed at him. "Mr. Popov. How are you today?"

"Fine, Linda. And you?"

She patted her mouth and faked a yawn. "Usual."

"Well, someone has to protect the United States. Might as well be you."

"Might as well. Your business in the U.S?"

"I'm off to Seattle to watch the Thunderbirds take on the Cougars from Prince George."

"How long will you be staying?"

"Not sure. A couple of weeks, maybe longer. I'll probably check out the teams in Portland, Spokane, and the Tri-Cities."

"I'll put you down for two weeks then. If you're held up, just notify us."

"Will do."

"Happy hunting!"

Popov's tobacco-stained teeth showed as he smiled. "Thank you." With a wave, the Russian operative headed south through the small town of Sumas. The speed limit said twenty-five, and past experience told him they meant it. It wouldn't do to get a traffic ticket.

Exiting the town, he worked his way over to Highway 9. The term "highway only" loosely applied. The narrow road had farms on each side. When the speed limit increased to forty-five, he started to make good time. That is, until a farm truck stacked with trash pulled out in front of him and settled in at thirty-five miles an hour.

Popov slammed the brakes, fishtailing on the wet pavement. He laid on the horn and cursed the yokel ahead of him. Why couldn't he have waited? That driver had to know he was holding up traffic.

Popov took a couple of deep breaths to calm himself. Anger was pointless. He'd just have to wait for a chance to pass. Unfortunately, oncoming traffic was heavy with many Canadians returning home after the weekend. Close to the rear of the truck, Popov peeked out every now and then, waiting for just the right chance to pull out.

The truck hit a bump, bounced hard, and part of its load fell over the tailgate. Popov swerved, but his left front tire still cut through the trash. An explosion followed by a *thud-thud* sound told him that he'd just lost a tire.

Easing partway onto the narrow shoulder, Popov drove an extra fifty feet to a wide farm driveway. There was no way he could change the flat beside that country road. Traffic was too heavy.

Slamming the door, he stormed to the trunk, all thoughts of staying calm forgotten. The Russian stared at the trash truck grinding south,

BETRAYED

shook his fist, and swore a red streak.

Popping open the trunk, he hauled out the spare and wheeled it to the front of the car, returning for the jack and tire iron. Ten minutes later, Popov tossed the tire, jack, and tire iron back into the trunk. He'd drop the flat tire off at the first garage he came to and pick it up on his way home. Still muttering about stupid Americans, he reentered traffic and headed for Bellingham.

"The reason the Iraqis are no threat to me," continued Jonathan, still seated on the ATV in the middle of the pasture, "is because they were the ones who helped us hunt down the terrorists."

Standing by the front of the small vehicle, Danny's eyes widened. "Come again?"

"The Iraqis knew of four independent terrorist cells who planned major hits on the U.S. in honor of Desert Storm's tenth anniversary. They gave us the names and locations of three of them, but they only had sketchy information on the fourth. That's the one I tracked down."

"Why'd they do that?"

"You ought to know that one, Bro. We have a different president now. The new guy in the Oval Office has made it pretty clear—touch us and we'll hammer you. If any of the terrorist hits had succeeded, cruise missiles and smart bombs would be on the menu. The Iraqi economy can't afford to have more power plants and oil refineries blown away."

Danny scratched behind his wide ear. "Who'd a thunk it!"

"At the same time, the Iraqis don't want to alienate the extreme fundamentalists. Those terrorists would strike at Iraq if they thought they'd been double-crossed. If anything happens to me, the Arab world will find out how we got the lead on the terrorists. Iraq is in a no-win situation. We want to keep it that way. So keep your mouth shut."

With motions to match his words, Danny said, "Zippered shut, key thrown away." He shifted positions, leaning an arm on the handle bars of the four-wheeler. "Hey, what happened to the other three terrorist groups?"

"They didn't make it out of Lebanon alive."

"No kidding. How come you didn't whack the guys that ended up in L.A., too?"

"We only knew one of them. I followed him to the U.S. where he met the other two. Unfortunately, when you get to U.S. soil, you can't just whack people. We'd thought of deporting them but weren't sure if we had them all. As it turned out, we didn't. There are no certainties in my game, Danny. Fortunately, this time it turned out right."

"Thank God," Danny said.

Jonathan looked at stormy clouds rolling overhead. "Yeah, we probably should thank God." He pressed his hand over his stomach. "I hate to break up the party, but I feel sick."

"You look kind of pale."

Jonathan's eyelids drooped for a second. "I think I've overdone it." Raindrops spattered his face.

"We better go in," Danny said, moving to the back of the ATV. His voice sounded like an echo coming from a distance.

Jonathan tried to turn the throttle, but the effort was too much for him. He leaned against his brother. The wind had chilled with the rain. Jonathan shivered. Danny's body felt warm against his back as the big man reached around him to handle the controls.

"You're a great little brother," Jonathan slurred as the four-wheeler moved ahead.

"You're an idiot," his brother replied. "Mom is going to put me on bread and water for this."

In a sea of pain, Jonathan clamped back a moan as the machine bumped across the field. When they reached the house, Danny parked the vehicle and hopped off. He slid beefy arms under Jonathan's legs and behind his back.

The door flew open, and Sandra Corrigan descended upon the two of them with the same expression she wore thirty years earlier when they'd cornered a skunk under the corncrib and tried to dig him out by hand.

"What do you think you are doing?" she demanded, hands on hips.

"Nothing, Mom," Danny said, edging past her with Jonathan in his arms. "He just got tired, that's all."

The next moment, Andrea appeared and took control. "Get him to his room." She followed closely behind them as Danny shambled down the hall. "What on earth possessed you two?" she asked, blue eyes flashing.

"They're worse than kids," Rita called from the kitchen door. She tried to speak lightly, but worry put an edge to her words.

Danny eased Jonathan onto the nine-patch quilt, and Gus came up to sniff his hand. Raising limp fingers, Corrigan patted the dog's snout.

Andrea shooed everyone but his mother from the room. Her deft hands working quickly, she wrapped a black cuff around his arm and inflated it. Next, she pressed a stethoscope against his chest and listened, frowning in concentration. While she waited for a temperature reading, she very gently probed his stomach, watching his face for a reaction.

"How is he?" his mother asked. "Should we call an ambulance?"

"No ambulance," groaned Jonathan around the thermometer.

Andrea smiled at Sandra Corrigan. "He's just exhausted. After complete rest for twenty-four hours, he'll be okay."

"I think we should call the doctor," Sandra said, moving closer to touch his hand. "He may have pulled something loose."

Jonathan took the thermometer from his mouth. "I'm okay, Mom," he said, his voice breathy.

Andrea picked up a prescription bottle and dumped a blue pill into her palm. Reaching for the water glass on the bed stand, she said, "Mrs. Corrigan, please go back to your guests. I'll keep watch over him. It's my job."

Corrigan could tell that his mother didn't like to leave him alone with Andrea, but to his way of thinking, this situation had some definite benefits. Raising up, he swallowed the pill, then relaxed back on the pillow. "Go on, Mom," he said, his voice stronger. "Everyone is waiting for dessert. Just make sure Danny doesn't eat it all."

Sandra gave a wan smile. "I'll check on you later." She went out, leaving the door ajar.

The moment she left, Andrea's eyes flashed. "What did you think you were doing, Hotshot? You think it's funny scaring everyone?"

He made a face. "Aw, come on, Andrea, lighten up."

She stared at him, unsmiling.

"You're still sore, aren't you?" He felt better by the minute.

Andrea's eyebrows rose high. "About what?"

"About me breaking up with you before the senior prom."

"Are you crazy?" She was even more beautiful when she was mad. "That was fifteen years ago. I don't hold a torch that long." She leaned closer, light glinting on her pale hair. "Not even for a hotshot like you."

"I'm sorry, Andrea," he said, truly contrite. "I've regretted that incident a dozen times since then."

Suddenly, she smiled softly. "So have I."

"Forgive me?"

"Sure." Her fingertips brushed his cheek as she stood. "Now get some rest." She pulled a quilt over him and moved away to draw the heavy drapes.

His eyes drifted closed, and a deep sigh escaped his lips. He expected to

BETRAYED

dream of a tall, svelte blond, but strangely the girl he met there had hair the color of burnished copper.

A few minutes to nine, Shannon's Ford Tempo reached the parking lot of the long, low restaurant with a giant sign out front reading, Blue Coat Inn. She drove around the building, searching for a parking space and hoping Wesley was already there. If not, he may not find a place to park. She slid into the last available space—next to the dumpster—and got out, tucking the back of her cream blouse into dark teal pants.

The moment she stepped inside, Wesley came to his feet at a two-person table near the door. He wore a black turtleneck with a gray blazer. His hair looked auburn under the low lights.

Relieved to see him, Shannon smiled as she slid into the seat and dropped her purse to the floor. Two long menus lay on the table.

"I ordered coffee," he said, beaming at her. "I happen to know that the T-bone here is out of this world." He looked up. "Here comes the waiter now."

Gentle music soothed Shannon's jangled nerves. Though clients filled every table, the place had the hush of quiet distinction—mellow laughter and the soft clinking of glass and silver.

When they'd ordered, Wesley opened the creamer and dumped it into his coffee. "How long have you lived in Bellingham?" he asked.

"About a year," Shannon said, stirring sugar into her own cup.

"Are you from California?"

"Phoenix."

"And before there?"

"Texas." She arched an eyebrow. "Hey, am I a suspect here?"

He grinned. "Can you blame me for wanting to know more about you? We've worked our heads off for about six hours straight, and I've had the time of my life."

Shannon blushed. "Sorry. I guess I'm still edgy." She sipped coffee, forming her next words. "I'm originally from Texas."

"C'mon. With your accent?"

"Why, thank you," Shannon replied in a thick drawl. "It's so nice of y'all to say so."

He stared. "That's how you normally talk?"

"Not anymore," she said in her usual voice. "It took me months to learn to talk like this, but I stuck it out." In truth, she'd worked hard at developing the Texas drawl for times such as this. Darryl had insisted on it.

"Why?" Wesley asked, surprised. "I think it sounds great."

"What's the first thing that comes into your mind when you hear a Texas accent?"

His shoulders came up. "I don't know—horses?"

"Exactly. When I open my mouth, I don't want customers to think horses. I want them to think of a professional computer consultant."

"You saying Texans don't know computers?" he asked. "Tell that to Ross Perot."

"That's not what I meant," she said, impatient. "Look, I'm a single woman trying to build a business. I can't afford any hindrances. In this part of the country, the accent was a strike against me."

"I never thought of it like that." He finished his coffee and pushed the cup away. "So, are your folks into computers as well?"

"Are your parents cops?" she asked sharply. This conversation was heading south fast.

Wesley held his hands up. "Hey, I was just trying to get acquainted."

Their food arrived, breaking the tension. Steak and fat baked potatoes smothered with sour cream captured their attention for a full ten minutes.

"Hey, Anderson!" A short, balding man stopped at their table. "I must have left ten messages on your machine. We've got to talk."

Wesley's head jerked around. "Hi, Boswell," he said, his voice smooth. "I've been out all day. I'll call you in the morning."

Dark, deep-set eyes stared at the young policeman. "See you do." Without a glance at Shannon, he headed for the door.

Wesley smiled. "He's the coach for the force's basketball team. They want me to play, but I don't have time. Boswell has been on my case for weeks." He stabbed a last morsel of steak. "Didn't I tell you this T-bone was great?"

While they waited for strawberry pie to arrive, he said, "The piano is sitting empty tonight. I wonder where Solly is."

"I play a little," Shannon murmured, eyeing the baby grand in a corner nearby.

"You don't say!" Wesley smiled, eyes bright. He stood. "Let's hear what you can do."

She blushed. "Not here, Wesley. I couldn't."

BETRAYED

He reached for her hand. "Sure, you can. I know the boss here, and he'd love it." He tugged. "C'mon."

She let him draw her from her seat, and she slid onto the gleaming bench as Wesley snapped on the light overhead. Automatically, her fingers tinkled out "Moonlight Sonata," then drifted into a short piece her father had written for her years before, a gift for her twelfth birthday.

"Say, that's good," Wesley said, smiling down at her.

Dreamy from the music, she smiled softly; happy times—almost forgotten—came over her. As the last note faded, she slid from the seat. "Concert's over." Light applause wafted through the restaurant.

He clasped her elbow. "This has been an over-the-top night for me."

In a warm glow, Shannon nodded. It was a special night for her, too.

Later, dipping a fork into her dessert, she said, "You've heard my life story. What's yours?"

He leaned back in his chair, one arm resting on the table. "I used to work a beat in Las Vegas, but when my parents were killed in a car accident five years ago, I had to get away. Someone told me the Bellingham force was hiring, so I came up here." He smiled. "Now I'm glad I did."

"I'm so sorry about your parents." Shannon was deeply moved. "I know what it's like to be alone in the world." She swallowed and looked down. "It's horrible."

"You don't have to be alone anymore, Shannon." His hand reached out to cover hers.

She jerked her hand away.

"I'm sorry." There was that little-boy expression again. "I'm always such a jerk around pretty women. I knew I'd do something to spoil everything."

It was Shannon's turn to feel bad. "I didn't mean it that way. I'm just not ready for a serious relationship right now. I've got too many things to get settled first."

He leaned toward her and looked deeply into her eyes. "I want to help you, Shannon. Will you let me?"

Something inside Shannon wanted to respond, but another man's face rose up just behind her eyes. She looked away. "It's late," she said, reaching down for her purse. "I'm awfully tired."

"I'm sorry. I shouldn't be keeping you out after such a hard day." He picked up the check and hurried to the register. A few minutes later, he held the door open, and Shannon paced through it.

"I'm parked around back, next to the dumpster," she told him, reaching into her purse for her keys. They turned the corner of the building, and Shannon stopped, her heart racing. The parking space was empty. Her car had vanished.

CHAPTER TEN

At Shannon's dismayed cry, Wesley stared at the empty parking space and asked, "You're sure you parked there?"

Shannon looked up at him. Already at the breaking point, her temper flared. "I know where I parked my car!"

"Sorry." His face filled with concern. "I just wanted to make sure. You'd be surprised how many times we get a car reported stolen only to find the owner forgot where he parked it."

Shannon glared. "Do I look that dumb?"

Wesley held up his hands. "Hey, not in the least. Just part of my cop training."

"Then do your cop thing, and find my car!"

"Don't get mad at me. I didn't steal your car."

Immediately, Shannon's expression eased. "I'm sorry. First my apartment and now this." Tears filled her eyes. "Why is this happening to me?"

Jaw tense, he said, "I intend to find out." His voice softened. "First, let's get you back inside. You're shaking. You need to sit down."

Dazed, she felt his hand on her arm and followed him inside the restaurant. Wesley seated her at their table near the front of the restaurant. "I've got a cell phone in my car," he said, leaning down to look into her face. "I'll make the call from there."

"Thanks." Shannon wiped at her eyes with the back of her hand. The people moving around her were blurry shadows, the noises faint echoes. Maybe it was true. The sins of the fathers were visited on the children. Suddenly she remembered something. Wesley!

She popped out of her seat and ran to the door. Pushing it open, she saw him near the edge of the parking lot. "Wesley!" she called.

He spun to face her. "Yeah?"

"Don't you need to know what kind of car and the license number?"

He slapped himself on the side of the head then jogged toward her. "Boy, some cop, huh? I guess I'm kinda upset, too."

When he reached her, he pulled out his notebook. "So, give me the description." He wrote down the details as Shannon gave them to him. "Great. Now go back inside, and I'll come for you as soon as I get this in."

As he started to turn away, Shannon put a hand on his sleeve. "Thanks."

He smiled into her green eyes. "My pleasure." With that, he stretched his long legs toward his vehicle.

Back in the restaurant, Shannon returned to the table. A dark-haired waitress near Shannon's own age stopped with a coffeepot in one hand and wad of tissues in the other. "Here." She handed Shannon the tissues. "Would you like some coffee?"

"I won't be staying long," she said, "but thanks for these." She blew her nose.

"He can be a pretty decent guy when he wants to be," the waitress said.

Shannon stared at her. "What?"

"Didn't you just have a fight with Wesley?"

"No. Someone stole my car."

The woman's face blossomed scarlet. "I'm so sorry. The way you ran out, I thought. . .you and him. . ."

Shannon shook her head, trying to concentrate. "We're just friends."

The waitress looked across the restaurant then turned back to smile at Shannon. "Stay here as long as you like, Honey. I'm sorry about your car." She hurried away.

The double doors of the restaurant swung open, and Wesley strode in, his expression intense. He sat down across from her and clasped her hands. "They've found your car."

"Great!" She let out a relieved sigh. Looking closer at him, she asked, "Why the sad face?"

"It's in a ditch."

"Wrecked?"

"Probably. They found it on a country road."

Rage came out in a rush. "Why would someone wreck my car?"

"Probably some teenagers took it for a joyride. It happens."

Shannon pulled her hands away and clenched her fists. "The miserable. . ."

Wesley's huge hands swallowed her fists. "Try to calm down. You're going to give yourself a stroke."

"I want to see my car." She got to her feet, and Wesley followed her outside. In the night air, Shannon pulled her coat tightly about her. It must be near freezing. When they reached Wesley's haggard Toyota Camry, he held the door for her and closed it with a thump. She stared straight ahead as he got in beside her.

Pausing before he started the car, he asked, "Are you mad at me?"

Shannon jammed her lips together. "I'm mad, but not at you."

They drove in silence. Wesley guided the car out of downtown Bellingham onto Guide Meridian. Turning left on Waldron, they drove a short distance past the New Beginnings Church to the accident spot. The orange strobe of a wrecker played across their faces and mingled with the flashing blue and red of a Bellingham police car.

Wesley said, "I'm glad the car is still in our jurisdiction. Any further out and the sheriff's department would handle it."

"Why does it matter?"

Wesley parked the car twenty feet behind the wrecker and turned to face Shannon, his expression serious. "It means I can give this my personal attention." He reached over and squeezed her hand.

"Thanks for caring," she said quietly, still staring ahead. She felt for the door latch beside her and got out, her pumps crunching over loose gravel on the shoulder. The closer she walked to the Ford Tempo, the more furious she became. Shoulders tense, eyes blazing, she walked over to the wrecker operator while Wesley left her side to talk to the officer on the scene.

"How bad is it?" she asked.

Grease-covered and wearing blue coveralls, the man with the truck had a flattened nose and a mop of salt-and-pepper hair. "I just pulled it out of the ditch," he told her. "Let's have a look-see." He held out a blackened hand. "My name's Jerry." He followed Shannon's eyes to his hand, and his face broke into a sheepish grin. "Sorry." He wiped his hand on his dirty overalls but didn't offer it again.

Shining a powerful flashlight, Jerry circled the Ford Tempo. The right side had several deep scratches and a long dent. The right front fender lay crushed against the wheel.

Leaning over the fender for a closer look, he said, "That'll probably interfere with the wheel turning. It won't take long for a body shop to straighten it, though."

"I can't afford a body shop," Shannon said, her voice brittle.

Jerry glanced up at her. "I can see from the car that you're not exactly rolling in dough. You have insurance?"

Shannon shook her head. "Not theft coverage."

"Tough break." He aimed his light at the interior, and Shannon gasped. The seats had been ripped apart, the dash torn open.

Shannon's fury brought up hot tears. "Why won't they just leave me alone?" She covered her cheeks with trembling hands.

"Hey, Honey, it might not be that bad." Jerry slid his large frame behind the driver's seat and turned the key. The Ford Tempo's motor jumped to life. "That's what I thought. It's just banged up."

Wesley came up behind her and put his arm around her quivering shoulders. "How bad is it?" he asked.

Shannon took a tissue from her purse and pressed her nose. "Someone destroyed it on purpose."

Wesley left her to peer at the front end. "You won't be able to drive it like that."

"I've got an idea," Jerry called from the inside of the car. Turning the wheel enough so that it barely scraped the fender, he managed to turn the car so it sat sideways on the road. He lumbered to his wrecker and pulled a massive hook toward the Ford Tempo. Attaching it to the bent fender, he motioned for everyone to step away, then he returned to his truck and pulled a lever. The winch turned, the chain pulled taut. Seconds later, the fender creaked and groaned. The metal backed away from the wheel.

Jerry walked over to inspect the job. He smiled at Shannon. "See there," he said, smacking his hands together.

"That's great, Pal," Wesley said, "but she can't sit in that seat."

Jerry rubbed his jaw. Shannon watched him, feeling like an extra at her own show.

The mechanic said, "You're right, Mister. I'll be right back." He disappeared into the cab of his truck and soon returned with two rolls of silver tape.

"What's that?" Shannon asked.

"Duct tape, a poor man's upholstery repair kit." Working smoothly and quickly, he wrapped it across the back of the bucket seat and across the bottom. When he finished, he stood up and said, "At least it will do until you can get a new seat." He grinned. "Or a new car."

She touched her purse. "How much do I owe you?"

"Nothing."

"I'm not that broke," she protested. "I can't afford a body shop, but I can afford a towing job."

Jerry smiled. "Ma'am, do you see the name on the side of my wrecker?" He shined his flashlight on it.

Shannon read, "Jerry's Towing and Wrecking." She looked at him, puzzled.

"Five years ago, God made it possible for me to start my own business when a wealthy Christian said the Lord told him to lend me enough money for a truck and a garage. I tell you, the first day I sat in that truck, I told the Lord that anytime I came across someone in need, the tow would be on Him." He grinned, his eyes kind. "It's God's tow truck. He said not to charge you, and I ain't charging you."

Shannon's eyes filled again. Her anger simmered down to low. "Thank you, Jerry. I'll never forget you."

He saluted with two fingers, pulled himself up into the truck, and drove away. The police car followed him, leaving Shannon and Wesley alone on the solitary road.

The temperature had fallen since they arrived. When Wesley spoke, his words came out in white gusts. Shannon squinted up at him in the glaring white pool made by his car's headlights.

"I hate to say it," he said, "but this is the second time today that someone has torn up your belongings looking for something. Is there anything you ought to tell me?"

She looked into his eyes—so close, so concerned for her—and murmured, "I can't."

Ben would have preferred to wait, give it a couple of days, let things cool down. But time was something he just didn't have. He would have to get near Corrigan under cover of darkness. With night equipment slung over his shoulder, Ben crawled down the ladder of the barn's hayloft and slipped out the crack between the wide double doors. After the close call with the FBI earlier, he'd moved his car down the road instead of keeping it in the barn.

From the barn to the tree line of the Corrigan property was a long way. Crawling was not his favorite occupation, but for his home it was worth it.

BETRAYED

He must not be caught. Too much depended on him.

Soaked from the earlier rain, moisture from the grass permeated his jeans and dark jacket in seconds. The field hadn't been cut in years, and the rotting grass underneath smelled musty. This pleased him. Tall grass concealed him all the more.

Pulling with his elbows and pushing with his knees, straining to see through the faint moonlight, he reached the ditch separating the road from the field, the most dangerous point. If the FBI agents were waiting in the woods, they might spot him.

Crawling down, then up the ditch, Ben started his slow slither across the gravel road. Rocks dug into his body, gouging his skin through his clothes. He winced but didn't complain. The payoff would be worth it. This job wasn't personal with him. Corrigan happened to be in the way of what Ben desperately needed. Money.

When he was within three feet of the edge, headlights streaked down the road toward him. Left with no options, Ben scrambled into the other ditch, cursing under his breath. If the special lens had been damaged, getting a clear shot would be impossible.

He lay in the ditch, freezing in six inches of water but afraid to move. As the vehicle drew closer, the headlights went out. The car passed him at a crawl. Was it FBI? Police? Had they seen him? Ben flattened deeper in the muddy water, grinding his teeth against the cold, tensed against the moment when a roving spotlight destroyed his hopes.

Gravel crunched under slow-moving tires, torturing him. *Just get it over with,* he repeated in his mind, chanting it again and again.

Finally, the car rolled past Corrigan's driveway and sped away. Ben slowly released his breath. It was forty-five degrees outside, and he was drenched.

Pulling himself out of the ditch and flopping down on his belly, he continued toward the tree line, trying not to shiver, clenching his teeth to keep them from chattering and giving him away.

Ten long minutes later, he reached the safety of the forest. Now to pass through the dense, dark woods without tripping another perimeter alarm. Slipping on his night-vision goggles, he inched ahead. As long as he moved slow and kept scanning for wires, he should be all right.

He stopped often to listen. So far, the night air carried only the hoot of an owl and the howling of coyotes in the distance.

Fifteen minutes later, he saw lighted windows twinkling through the trees. Only another fifty feet to reach the edge of the clearing. He'd wait there. Shooting through a window wasn't the best, but hopefully it would be good enough. He eased forward, placing each foot with care.

An upstairs light went on, and an attractive blond appeared in the window. She moved about, touching her hair and smoothing her narrow skirt as if she knew someone was watching her. Was she doing that for the benefit of the FBI agents guarding the house? Ben hoped so. If she had their attention, they wouldn't notice him.

Crouched behind a tree, his leg got a cramp. He desperately wanted to move, but movement attracted attention. Didn't Corrigan ever look out a window?

The front door opened, spilling a yellow shaft of light across the dark verandah. Ben retreated further behind the tree, one eye peeking out. His heart started to race, elated, as light glinted off a metal wheelchair. Corrigan was on the verandah. Perfect.

Shifting slowly to the side of the tree, Ben lifted the sight to his eye. Beautiful. He slowly squeezed. . . *Crack!*

Bark sprayed Ben's face. Something sharp stung in his shoulder. He dropped to the ground as three more bullets whistled over him.

"Stop! Don't shoot! I'm unarmed!" he screamed.

"Come out with your hands up!" a voice boomed from the dark side of the house.

Moving slowly, Ben raised his arms. His left arm refused to go all the way up. His left shoulder felt wet. It was on fire.

"What's going on?" shouted Corrigan.

Ben moved into the driveway illuminated by the yard light. Boots crunched gravel behind him. The next instant, Ben's face smashed into the stones covering the driveway. His arms were yanked behind him and handcuffs clamped on.

"Intruder," a deep voice called.

Ben felt hands grab under each of his armpits. He grunted as pain shot through his shoulder. "Hey, take it easy! I've been shot."

Popov almost laughed when he saw the old barn across from Corrigan's driveway. It made him forget his anger at the tire store earlier that afternoon.

"It'll only take fifteen minutes to fix a flat," said a short, fat kid with *Mark* embroidered on his overalls. "Why don't you wait?"

What would another fifteen minutes matter? So, Popov waited.

Mark disappeared into the repair bay, then waddled back, frowning. "Did you drive on this tire after it blew?"

"Yeah. There was no place to pull off the road."

"Thought so. I can't fix it. The sidewall is trashed."

"Put on a new tire then."

The kid scratched his ear with pudgy fingers. "I'm sorry, Sir, but I can't do that."

"Why not?" This guy was getting on Popov's nerves.

"You're driving on Goodyear tires. We don't sell Goodyear. It's best if all your tires have the same tread."

Popov's temper blossomed. "I don't care. Put anything on."

Mark pursed his lips and shook his head. "Nope. If I put the wrong tread on and you have an accident, you'll probably sue us. You'll have to go to a Goodyear dealer."

Seething, Popov watched the kid set the bare rim in the trunk of his car. To make matters worse, Mark then gave Popov such lousy directions that he spent an hour finding the road to Corrigan's place. And Americans told jokes about Russians being inefficient. Bah!

Popov reached the road just after dark. A couple of hundred yards from Corrigan's driveway, he found a gate to the field. Lights off, he drove to the abandoned barn and parked inside.

Climbing into the loft, he pulled out his night goggles and waited, glad he had brought along a sleeping bag. The night air already chilled him to the bone, and he couldn't risk running the car for heat. In the morning, he'd call the consulate in Seattle and ask for help. This was definitely a two- or three-man job.

CHAPTER ELEVEN

During the commotion in the driveway, a tall, bulky man stepped from the darkness at the side of the Corrigan house. In the dim light, his eyes were black shadows in a stone face. He stopped inches from the shivering Ben and stared at the camera hanging around his neck. "A photographer!" he ground out. He curled up a giant fist, and Ben shrank back.

The big man said, "I ought to knock you into next week. You know how much trouble you've caused?"

All Ben knew was that he was cold and wet and hurting something fierce. Could it get any worse than this?

"Perkins? Is that you?" In his wheelchair at the bottom of the ramp, Corrigan looked ready to explode.

Perkins dropped his fist to his side. His expression turned sheepish. "Yeah, it's me," he muttered, turning toward the wheelchair.

Corrigan's face twisted with rage. "What are you doing here, you big lug? No wonder this operation has been going haywire! Trip wires in the woods, people busting into our dining room."

Like a kid facing a switch-wielding father, Perkins trudged toward Corrigan. Before he reached him, the porch light flared on, and the front door swung open. A man built like a refrigerator lunged out. On his heels came an older woman in a housecoat, and the blond Ben had seen in the window. Her golden hair around her shoulders, she wore a dark silk wrapper that covered her chin to toe yet left little to the imagination.

"What's happened, Jonathan?" the older woman cried, rushing toward him. "Are you hurt?"

During her hug, he said, "I'm fine, Mom. Those goons were the ones shooting."

"Who was out there?" the bodybuilder asked.

"I don't know, Danny. Some guy. They've got him in the driveway."

Leaning to one side, Danny squinted through the darkness toward Ben, who squirmed in pain and humiliation.

"Come inside, Jonathan, and I'll take your blood pressure," the blond said, edging close as soon as his mother let go of him.

"Andrea, I'm fine." Corrigan turned his attention to Perkins. "What's a meathead like you doing here, Perkins? Don't I have enough trouble?"

"I requested this assignment," Perkins answered, trying to summon up some dignity.

Corrigan choked. "What incompetent bureaucrat agreed to that?"

"The director."

Corrigan froze for a full five seconds. "You're yanking my chain, Perkins. He knows how I feel about you."

More heated, Perkins said, "He also knows how bad I feel about my goof up. He knows that I have a good reason to make absolutely certain nothing else happens to you."

Corrigan's eyes became slits as he glared at the tall man in front of him. "You think protecting me means chasing every deer that touches your perimeter warning?" He let out a harsh laugh. "You can't even run up a flight of stairs without needing oxygen."

"Jonathan," his mother scolded, "there's no need for that. Agent Perkins is a fine man. We have coffee in the kitchen every morning." She smiled at the self-conscious agent standing near the ramp.

"It's true, Mom," Corrigan insisted. "Look at him."

Perkins threw back his shoulders. "For your information, since that terrorist operation in L.A., I'm down twenty pounds, and I can run two miles. I haven't had pizza for almost a month."

"Give me a break," Corrigan said. His tone revealed that he knew he was being unfair, but he didn't want to admit it. He gestured toward Ben. "Well, anyway, show me what you caught."

Perkins nodded to the two men holding Ben, who was shaking like a leaf in the wind. They brought him forward. When he reached the lighted porch, Andrea gasped, "He's been shot!" Moving quickly, she disappeared into the house, her slippers slapping the floor.

Noticing Ben's camera, Corrigan said, "This another one of your grandstand plays, Perkins? Shooting a photographer?"

"I saw light reflect off a lens. It could have been a rifle scope."

Lips twisted, Corrigan shook his head.

"He did the right thing," Danny said. "You're acting like a spoiled kid, Bro. Ease up, will you?"

"Stay out of this, Danny."

"I'd like to. . .except for one thing. You're wrong, and he's right."

Corrigan focused on Ben. "What do you have to say for yourself, Cameraman?"

Andrea reappeared with a black bag in her hand. "He's not saying anything until I get a look at his wound. He's bleeding." She looked at Corrigan's mother. "Sandra, can we take him inside?"

"Most certainly, Andrea." She stepped to the door and held it open, looking at Ben expectantly. "Bring him in, gentlemen." She looked at Danny. "He's freezing. Get him a blanket from the linen closet."

Hustling him inside, the agents led Ben to a yellow kitchen chair and let him sit. Gus was growling again. Roxanne hustled him upstairs to her room.

Watching the prisoner, the agents stood—hands behind hips—against the wall. The rest of the group crowded into the room. The kitchen was large but not large enough for ten adults.

Andrea forced her way between broad shoulders and drew a chair close to the prisoner. "Remove his cuffs," she said.

Perkins hesitated.

"Remove them," Corrigan said, bumping the backs of knees until he found an open space to wheel into the kitchen. "What can he do, throw the camera at us?"

Perkins produced the key and removed the cuffs. Ben could feel the big man's breath as he leaned over him. When his hands were free, Andrea stripped off Ben's jacket and shirt. Danny arrived with a thick quilt, and Ben snuggled into it, his shoulder exposed.

Andrea pressed a pad over the wound until the bleeding stopped. She poured antiseptic on it, and he groaned. "Almost done," she said, smiling sympathetically. "You'll have a story to tell your wife tonight."

Pulling a penlight from the bag, she peered at the wound while Ben held his breath, afraid she'd decide to touch it. He blew sandy brown hair off his clammy forehead and wished he were in a hot tub drinking hot chocolate.

"You've got a fragment in there, but it's too deep for me to get." She smiled at him. "You're lucky. It's just a flesh wound. I'll bandage it, and the FBI can take you to the hospital."

Corrigan asked, "Who are you anyway?"

"That's Ben Cahill," Sandra Corrigan said.

Corrigan looked at his mother across the oak table. "You know him?"

"Sure. I didn't recognize him at first, but I do now. He's with the *Bellingham Herald.* He came out and took some pictures when the paper was doing a feature on the local dairy industry." She smiled kindly at the pale young man. "How's your baby, Ben?"

He sent her a sideways glance. His voice was strained. "How do you know about Jason?"

Sandra spoke gently. "My whole church knows. Our pastor was at the hospital the day he was born. We've been praying for the little guy ever since. How's he doing?"

Ben's eyes glistened. He tried to steady his voice. "We have to fly him to L.A. for heart surgery."

Corrigan's forehead creased. "What's this all about, Mom?"

His mother replied, "Ben's little boy almost died two days after he was born. He has a hole in his heart. It's been touch and go ever since." She looked at Ben. "How old is he now?"

His lips quivered. "Two months."

Corrigan looked the man in the eyes and said, "That's tough, Pal, but why are you sneaking around our home with a camera? I thought the press agreed to leave me alone."

Ben felt like a slimeball. "The press did. The tabloids didn't."

Fire ignited in Corrigan's eyes. "You're trying to get a picture of me for a tabloid? Of all the dirty. . ."

Gulping, Ben cut him off. "We don't have enough insurance to cover Jason's medical bills. A single shot of you could bring enough to pay for the surgery, my wife's motel bills in L.A. while he's there, everything."

Sandra said, "I'm not a rich woman, but I have some resources. Why don't you let me help? I'll tell my church, and I'm sure they'll take up an offering."

Ben stared at her, shocked. "Why would you do that? You don't even know me."

"Because she's a super lady." A dark-haired teenage girl stepped up to the table. She put an arm across Sandra Corrigan's shoulders. "I'm going up

BETRAYED

to bed now." She leaned down to hug Sandra and kiss her on the cheek.

"Good night, Roxanne," Sandra said, smiling softly. "I'll check on you later."

When Roxanne left, Danny said, "I can pitch in a few bucks for the surgery."

"Me, too," Andrea chimed in.

Jonathan held up a wide palm and said, "That won't be necessary."

Everyone looked at him, surprised.

"Why not?" his mother asked.

"Because I'm going to let him take the picture."

"That could trigger a media frenzy," Danny said.

"Not if we do it right." Corrigan's expression showed he was thinking hard. "He'll take the picture as if I'm unaware. When it's published, we'll shout the house down. No one will know Ben had my permission."

Ben looked from one to the other as they discussed the fate of his only child. The situation seemed unreal, like a bad dream. Andrea brought his shirt and jacket—partly dry now—and he slipped them on.

"I don't advise this," Perkins said, shaking his head. "You'll invite a hundred more glory seekers out here."

Corrigan chuckled. "As if what you think matters to me. Let's go, Mr. Cahill."

Stunned, Ben followed Corrigan down the hall and out to the verandah. The younger man gripped his upper arm with his right hand, trying to hold it still and hurry at the same time. He wanted to get home in the worst way.

Corrigan spoke to Danny in the doorway. "Turn off the light. He might as well snap the picture the same way he planned it originally." The light went out.

Still not believing what was happening, Ben stepped across the gravel. Corrigan brought his chair to the edge of the porch. Looking off to the left, he sat like a statue.

As Ben focused the camera, the rest of the group moved onto the porch. Leaning over his chair in her silk wrapper, Andrea paused to speak to Corrigan, and Ben quickly snapped the shutter. His pain faded as excitement took over. A woman like that in his picture would surely double its value.

Monday morning, Shannon shuffled around her apartment with red, bleary eyes. Morning traffic moved on the street outside, calling her to join it, but the only thing she wanted to join was the borrowed foam mattress on the floor. Sunday had been the second worst day of her life.

She frowned at her reflection in the bathroom mirror as she applied makeup to hide circles under her eyes. The CIA had to be responsible for the mass destruction of her life. She remembered Darryl joking about how the FBI would rather let a criminal go free than jaywalk to catch him, but his CIA unit—specially selected by Director Stone—had no such compunctions, Darryl had told her. They'd do what they had to, and Shannon felt certain that included a slash-and-burn illegal search.

Picking up her black shoulder bag, she yawned deeply. If there was ever a day to call in sick, this was it. Afraid to sleep, she'd lain awake most of the night, hearing intruders who weren't there.

In spite of everything, she had to go to work. Saturday had been a record day at PTL, and she had five computer systems to build today. At least she could spend the day in the back room out of sight. For that reason, she wore a comfortable pair of jeans with her Seahawks sweatshirt and sneakers, a quilted green jacket over all.

She skipped down two flights of stairs and stopped short beside old Mr. Iverson working on the front door of the building. "Hi," she said with cheerfulness she didn't feel.

He turned and smiled up at her. Still unshaved and wearing a dingy T-shirt, his eyes were alert. "Hi yourself, Miss Masterson. I'm replacing the old lock. We can't have just anyone coming into the building, can we?"

"How will I get in later?"

"Don't worry," he said. "I'll leave it unlocked until I can get keys cut for everyone."

Stepping aside, he held the door for her. Shannon moved down the short flight of steps and over to her car. The morning was chilly. Heavy fog hung over the city. Traffic moved slowly, but Shannon still had time to swing up to Muffin Mania for an extra-large coffee and a muffin to go. Navigating her wounded Ford Tempo downtown, Shannon found a parking space on a side street a couple of blocks from the store. She turned off the ignition and paused to eat her blueberry muffin.

Sipping coffee, she slung her leather purse over her shoulder, got out, and locked the door. She stared at the key in her hand and laughed at herself. *Who'd steal it now?*

White fog lay low over the city, making her skin feel damp, her hair limp. Striding down the sidewalk, Shannon sipped the French vanilla brew—hot and strong—and felt that first rush of caffeine put some life into her tired blood. The way she felt today, six cups would get her through to closing time.

Meridian Street was quiet. Most of the stores didn't open for another hour.

Outside a hardware shop, she stopped and turned around. Was someone following her? She looked at the Muffin Mania cup. "You're good for keeping me awake, but you're murder on my nerves."

Continuing on, Shannon took a dozen steps when a heavy hand landed on her shoulder. She let out a small scream, her heart going like a jackhammer.

Eyes bulging, she whirled around and looked down into the milky eyes of a gnarled old woman wearing three winter coats and enormous rubber boots, a shopping bag in her left hand.

The woman jerked away. "Sorry, Miss," she rasped. "I didn't mean to scare you."

"Where did you come from?" Shannon asked, trying to catch her breath.

The old woman passed a thick hand over her filthy face. "Could you spare something so I can get some breakfast? I didn't eat at all yesterday."

Shannon started to say no. After all, the bag lady would probably just drink up anything Shannon gave her. The next moment, Shannon remembered Jerry, the tow truck driver who had been so kind to her the night before. Reaching into her purse, she pulled out five dollars.

The old woman looked at the bill and hesitated. "That's too much," she said. "I only need two dollars for McDonald's."

Shannon pressed the money into her hand. "Then have lunch there, too."

The lady's mouth hung open. "Uh. . .thank you."

Shannon smiled and shook her head. "Don't thank me. Thank God." Now where had that come from? Was Olivia starting to wear off on her? Or was it Jerry?

The street dweller smiled, showing blackened teeth. "I will."

Suddenly, Shannon felt better. A few more feet and she'd be in her warm shop doing what she loved best.

A sharp pain jabbed her shoulder. Shannon spun around, hands wide, trying to catch her balance. She sprawled to the ground, and her coffee cup flew into the gutter. A skinny man with a stringy red ponytail stood over her, yanking her handbag and her shoulder with it. "Give me the purse, Lady!" he growled.

Common sense told her to give it to him, but the rage, always under the surface, boiled up and over. "No!" She jerked the bag and made him stumble. Stepping back, he kept his balance. She pounded his legs with her heels. He grunted but held on.

Shannon froze as a brown carved handle appeared in his hand. She heard a sharp click and saw a gleaming blade. With quick movements, he sliced the straps and sprinted away, the bag under his arm like a running back heading for a touchdown.

Vibrating with fury, Shannon jumped to her feet and set off after her attacker. In a surge of adrenaline-laced speed, she closed the gap between them.

When she was half a block from him, she heard a dull thud, and the man landed facedown on the sidewalk. Still racing, Shannon grabbed her handbag out of the empty street.

Hands covering his face, the mugger rolled over and moaned. Blood streamed from his nose.

Her breath coming in ragged gasps, Shannon stepped nearer to him. She had a strong urge to jump on him and beat him senseless. At the last moment, foot lifted for a kick to the ribs, she stepped back. She would not stoop to the tactics of those low-life slimeballs who were tormenting her.

Holding her purse cradled in both arms, Shannon marched away from the wounded thief, her sneakers eating up the distance down the sidewalk. A hand grabbed her elbow, and Shannon spun, fist ready. She froze when the bag lady beamed at her.

"No one notices us," she said and laughed. She stuck her boot far out, demonstrating what she'd done.

"Thank you," Shannon said, feeling an urge to hug her.

The old woman chuckled. "Don't thank me. Thank God." She shifted the greasy shopping bag to the other hand and shuffled off into the fog.

Her senses whirling, Shannon walked back to PTL Computers. She had a gut feeling that the thief had been hired. The man behind the crime lived on a farm outside of Bellingham.

She made a sudden decision. The time had come to confront big-time hero Darryl Hansen. She'd do it today.

CHAPTER TWELVE

Someone called him, but Jonathan refused to hear. He burrowed deeper under the covers, so warm and relaxed.

"Come on, Sleepyhead. You're not fooling anyone."

Blinking, he rolled over to face Andrea. "What time is it?"

"Nine o'clock."

He tugged the quilt higher. "Too early."

Andrea shook her head. "Sorry, Pal. If you're going to get better, we have to keep a schedule."

He stretched, savoring a few more seconds of comfort.

Dressed in a black T-shirt and sweatpants, Andrea pushed his wheelchair near the bed. She lifted a blue flannel bathrobe off a hook on the door and threw it to him. Grabbing his cane, Jonathan stood on his good leg and slipped his arms into wide sleeves.

A few minutes later, he wheeled his chair into the empty kitchen. "Where's Mom?" he asked Andrea, behind him.

"She drove Roxanne to school. She said something about spending this morning with the cows. The vet's coming or something. She took Gus with her." Andrea set a carton of milk on the table near the sugar bowl and spooned thick oatmeal into two dishes.

Corrigan grinned at her. "You mean we're alone?"

"Yep." Handing him his cereal, she sat across from him. "You're brother and his family shipped out about six this morning."

"That's too bad. I wanted to say good-bye to the kids."

Andrea smiled. "I'm sure they'll come again soon. Those girls thought you were the greatest thing since McDonald's Happy Meals. A family version of James Bond." Her eyes laughed at him.

Grinning back at her, he dipped into the sugar bowl.

When they finished the meal, Andrea took his empty bowl and gave him a wicked smile. "Ready for your torture session?"

"Now wait a minute." He pushed back from the table. "I don't like the way you're looking at me. What gives?"

She set the dishes in the sink and headed for the door. "Come and see."

Jonathan rolled after her into the living room. On the hardwood floor lay a couple of blue exercise mats.

"Take off your robe," she told him, moving to the other side of the room. "Then lie down on the mat."

He flipped the footrests up, put on the brake, and stood up, balancing carefully as he untied the robe. As an afterthought, he peeled off the pajama top, leaving only his T-shirt and pajama bottoms.

With the injured left leg dragging, he moved to the edge of the mat and eased into a squat—the left leg stretched out in front of him—and let himself fall backward onto the mat.

"That's excellent," Andrea said. "I didn't realize you had that much mobility." She studied him. "There's only one problem."

"What?"

"Your right leg is so strong that you're using it too much. The injured leg will only improve if you use it." She smiled. "Today is the day that happens."

Corrigan moaned. "Now I know why you had that gleam in your eye. Have a heart, Andrea."

She chuckled. "Believe me, this will hurt me more than it does you. . . not." She sobered. "I'll make it as easy on you as I can, but you're going to have to work. Hard."

"I gottcha." He stretched back. "Bring on your thumbscrews."

Andrea knelt beside him to stretch and push the injured leg until he was saturated with sweat.

"You're doing good," she said, leaning back

"Thanks," Jonathan replied, his voice muffled by the towel pressed over his face. He reached back to wipe his neck. "What drives me crazy is the constant numbness. It's like walking on a stick of wood. I just want to drag it."

Andrea brushed a strand of hair from her smooth cheek. "If you do that, you'll become permanently disabled. The leg feels numb, but the

BETRAYED

muscles are okay, and they can work. You've got to retrain them." She stood, watching him. "Now, how are you planning to get up?"

Jonathan thought about it for a moment. It wasn't his leg but his stomach that caused the problem. He couldn't do a sit-up.

Rolling to his side, he used his hands to push himself to a sitting position. With his strong leg bent, he came to his feet in one sweeping motion and stood swaying, arms out for balance.

"Excellent!" she said, reaching for the white terry-cloth towel draped around her neck. "Now, for the rest of the day I want you to walk every hour for five minutes. It's important you walk for only five minutes. If it goes well today, then we'll do ten minutes tomorrow and so on."

Jonathan looked at the sweat stains on his T-shirt. "I think I'll use my first walk to get into the shower." Touching the wheelchair as he passed, he hobbled down the hall. Boy, did it feel good to be mobile again.

Standing in the Corrigans' driveway at the edge of a grove of fog-covered pines, Shannon glared at two men in black fatigues with FBI in yellow on their backs. A tall, slim agent had his weapon across his chest, blocking the lane, while the stout one stood near her car and stared at her driver's license.

"What's her name, Carl?" asked the one holding the long black gun.

"Shannon Masterson." He handed her license back. "Sorry, Miss Masterson. You'll have to turn back."

Shannon's nerves were tense as a piano wire. "This is still a free country, and you can't keep me out. I'm not a spy or a crook, and I want to talk to Jonathan Corrigan."

"We've got our orders, Lady," the armed man told her, moving a few steps forward. "Don't make us get rough with you."

Tugging at the bottom of her coat, her hands itched for something to throw at them. "What are you going to do, shoot me?" she demanded.

Carl's nostrils flared. He stepped closer, towering over her. "I won't say it again. Get going."

Shannon's chin came forward. She didn't give an inch. "Just call him and tell him Laura is out here, and I want to talk to him."

His mouth quirked in on one side. "Oh, so your name is Laura now? Tell me, are you planning to feed us names until you find one on the list?" His scornful expression showed he doubted her intelligence. "In case you forgot, I've already seen your ID."

From the driveway, the other man said, "How much time have you got to argue, Lady? We've got all day."

Seething, Shannon pulled open the door of the Ford Tempo and flung herself inside. She slammed the door and reached for the ignition. *Of all the ridiculous!* Putting the car in reverse, she backed out of the long driveway. Across the road, the old barn lay shrouded in white mist that disappeared as she drove closer.

In those few minutes, Shannon's blind rage changed to cool calculation. From the look of the farm, it was massive. How many guards could they have over all that acreage?

She backed onto the road and aimed the Ford Tempo toward Guide Meridian, but at the first curve she pulled as far over onto the narrow shoulder as she could and cut the engine. She sat still for a moment, staring at nothing, considering her next course of action. Finally, she picked up her mutilated purse and got out, closing the door gently so it wouldn't make a noise.

Instead of heading straight across the pasture, she continued walking toward the highway, scanning the field and the grove of trees in the center of it. If she couldn't get to the house from the front, maybe she could come in the back way. With the fog to cover her, she had a chance. The man said he had all day, well, so did she.

Watching from the barn, Popov was chilled to the bone, but he didn't dare leave. Because of the fog, he couldn't see the driver in the Ford Tempo, but that was definitely a woman standing in the lane arguing with the guards. In another hour, the sun would start to burn through the heavy mist. He slid down the ladder and stood at the gap between the wide front doors. If she left, he could get a clearer look from here.

In a few minutes, she backed out the lane, but the windows of the car were too cloudy for him to get a good look. All he could see was a head covered by short blond hair. He focused his high-powered binoculars on the retreating Ford Tempo, memorizing the plate number.

When she parked a short ways down the road, he grinned. After a long, dull night, this job was finally getting interesting. In a few minutes, the woman got out of the car and walked away.

Popov studied her until she disappeared into the mist. She'd left her car, so she'd be back. When she came, he'd be waiting.

Swinging wide to the side of the property, Shannon jumped the shallow ditch beside the road and jogged across the field. The dew clinging to the tall grass soon soaked her pant legs and sneakers. Wrapping her quilted coat closer around her, she ignored her aching feet and plunged on. The woods lay a hundred yards ahead.

She slowed her pace when she reached the trees; afraid she'd trip over a fallen branch or a root. Fifty paces in, she came upon a thin silver wire and carefully stepped over it.

She reached the clearing and stopped, pulling in both lips, thinking hard. Ahead lay the side of a log house, its porch rail like grinning, taunting teeth. If she got that far, it would be nothing short of a miracle. She glared at the house as though it were to blame for her problems. Since Darryl Hansen had waltzed into her life, nothing had been the same.

Keeping in the trees, she wound around to the backyard and hunkered down, watching for guards. What was it with this guy that he had to have such heavy artillery around him? Was he public enemy number one or something? How important could one terrorist attack be?

The LED reading on her watch said ten-thirty. She'd been in these woods almost half an hour already. Peering around and seeing no one, she left the woods at a full run aimed for the back steps. She vaulted up the short stairs and slammed into the broad chest of Special Agent Sam Perkins, FBI.

"Whoa! Where do you think you're going?" He took a step back under the impact, grabbing her shoulders in the same motion.

"Let me in!" Shannon cried, fighting tears and struggling to get away. "I've got to see him." She twisted and yanked, desperate to get away. "Jonathan!" she shouted. "Jonathan, I have to see you!"

Perkins turned her arm behind her back and hooked his elbow high against her shoulder. "You want to fight, do you?" he ground out. "Keep at it, and I'll add some pressure."

Coming around with her free hand, she punched his Adam's apple. Whooping for air, Perkins coughed and gagged, but he didn't turn her loose.

"What's going on here?" a deep voice asked from the door. "Perkins, what are you doing to that girl?"

The big agent gasped and swallowed, unable to talk. Shannon slipped away from him and turned. Jonathan Corrigan stood framed in the door wearing a navy sweater and tan slacks. His jaw dropped, and his face paled. "Laura."

"Yes," said Laura. "Don't look so surprised." She glared at Perkins. "Still got this oaf doing your dirty work, I see."

Corrigan stared at her. "What are you doing here? I thought you were in Phoenix."

"Just can't tell the truth, can you?" she fumed. "You know perfectly well where I've been." She stormed toward him. "Haven't you done enough, you. . .home wrecker!"

He held up both hands as though warding her off. "Calm down. Let's go inside and talk."

"Yes, let's." She brushed past him and entered the expansive kitchen. Leaning against the oak table, she watched him limp into the room.

"You didn't do enough the first time, did you?" Her voice vibrated with anger.

"Would you take a breath and tell me what you're talking about?" His expression changed from shock to exasperation.

"Don't give me that! I've had enough of your phony playacting." Her mouth drew up as though her words tasted bad. "All I have to say to you is this: Leave me alone!"

He let out a short harsh laugh. "What do you mean? I haven't. . ."

"Done anything? Is that what you were going to say?"

"Yeah."

Laura sneered. "Can't you ever tell the truth? Is it so hard?"

"Not when it is the truth."

"Oh, please!" She looked around for something to throw. "You've done nothing but lie to me since the first day we met, Hero Hansen. I saw you on CNN—so pious that people think you're some kind of a saint." She glared at him. "I know different."

"If you'd just. . ."

"What? Fall into your arms or swoon or something?" Her eyes were emerald points. "Not in this lifetime, Darryl Hansen!" She sprang toward the door, fighting furious tears. She would not break down in front of him.

He reached out and grabbed her arm, stopping her. "In the first place," he said between tight lips, "my name is Jonathan Corrigan. It always has been and always will be."

She tried to jerk away, but he tightened his grip. "Let go of me, you liar!"

"In the second place," he went on, "I've never wanted to hurt you or your family. . .ever."

BETRAYED

For an instant, she met his eyes and caught her breath, stunned by their intensity. "Laura," he said, his voice harsh, "I hope I can prove that to you someday."

Pulling away, her voice sounded low, threatening, "Let me go and stay out of my life."

He turned her loose. She stumbled, caught her balance, and headed for the door. As she reached the porch, Jonathan yelled. "Perkins! Come here!"

When the big man appeared, still looking a little green, Corrigan said, "See that she gets off the property without having a Glock pressed against her spine, will you?"

Perkins turned to go out.

"Say, Perkins," Corrigan called after him, "I believe the score is now McIvor two and Big Man Sam zero."

Perkins shot him a heavy look and lumbered away.

Alone in the kitchen, Corrigan sank into a chair at the table and rested his face in his hands. For two long years he'd dreamed of meeting Laura again. Even his worst nightmares about her had never been this bad. Behind his closed eyelids he could see her furious face, her flashing eyes. She was the most desirable woman he'd ever seen. And the most unapproachable. He'd tried to forget her, but he couldn't. What was he going to do?

Two hours after she disappeared, the girl returned by way of the driveway. She walked directly toward Popov, who watched her from the shadowy barn door. A broad grin covered the Russian's face. It was the target, all right. The hair was different, but it was she. He let himself sigh and stretch a little. Finally, something in this operation had gone right. He watched her until she got into her car and closed the door.

Leaving the sleeping bag behind, Popov eased his stiff muscles onto the upholstered seat of his Cougar and hit the starter. Soft leather never felt so good. He was getting too old for this game.

Easing the car out the barn's rear door, he crossed the bumpy field to the gravel road. The Ford Tempo had already moved out of sight. If he didn't catch up before she came to the T at the end of the road, he may lose her. His powerful V8 motor shot the Cougar forward until he saw the Ford Tempo at the stop sign.

Popov eased back on the accelerator. Suddenly, he slapped himself on the forehead. His license plates. He should have switched them to Washington State plates. He couldn't afford to draw any unnecessary attention. Too late now. The hunt was on.

Popov followed her to Guide Meridian Road and on into town. As traffic grew heavier, he allowed a car or two to get between him and his target.

In the downtown business district, she slid into a parking space on the street. Popov drove past her to park a dozen spaces down. He jumped out of his car in time to see her blond head bobbing down the street away from him. Mingling with sidewalk traffic, the Russian observed her entering a store that had tall red letters painted on the front windows. He came closer, noting the name. PTL Computers.

Crossing the street, he found a damp, iron bench three doors down and sat, wishing for hot coffee and a fat piece of bread with some cheese. Instead, he pulled out a cigar and lit up his breakfast.

CHAPTER THIRTEEN

After awhile, the cigar went out and grew stale. In spite of brilliant sunlight, the air was still crisp, and Popov was still cold. Ready to take a chance, he decided to watch PTL Computers from a cafe down the block. Throwing his dead stogie into a metal trash can, he shuffled down the sidewalk, his hands pushed down into deep coat pockets. A hot shower would feel so good right now.

The restaurant smelled of old grease. A tired-looking Hispanic woman poured him coffee that could patch potholes.

Popov didn't care. The place was warm, and the vinyl-covered chair felt good. Best of all, the greasy spoon had a pay phone.

He could have used his cell phone to call the Russian Consulate in Seattle, but he didn't want to risk it. A landline was safest. He dialed an unlisted number, waited to be told the cost of the call, and plugged in four quarters.

"Hello," a guttural voice answered.

"You put an ad in the paper for lost dog?" Popov had never quite managed to get rid of his Russian accent.

"Yeah, you seen it?"

"I saw it in Bellingham."

"Whereabouts?"

"Running loose in the neighborhood. I'll keep an eye on it, let you know. Maybe you should send someone over there to take it back."

"Where should they meet you?"

Popov glanced at the back of a menu. "Bigfoot Burgers on Meridian Street."

"They should be there in two or three hours."

"Excellent," Popov said, and hung up the phone. He returned to his table and sipped his scalding coffee. The girl must work at PTL Computers. She'd been in there for an hour, and she was, after all, a computer specialist. His men shouldn't have any problem getting there before her workday finished.

Two hours, two burgers, and a bowl of soup later, Laura McIvor emerged from the store. Too soon! His backup hadn't arrived yet. Popov threw five dollars on the table and grabbed a take-out menu to get the restaurant's phone number.

Moving as fast as he could without attracting attention, Popov rushed to his Cougar. Fortunately, Laura McIvor took her time. Her head was bent down as though she was tired.

Popov's engine sprang to life. He shoved it into gear, watching his mirror to see when McIvor's car passed him. The battered Ford Tempo rolled up and stopped. The girl inside waved for him to pull out.

Popov swore. Why'd he get a Good Samaritan for a target? Still anxious about attracting attention, he smiled, waved, and pulled out in front of her. Driving was tricky, keeping one eye on the rearview mirror and the other on the road.

At the intersection, the Russian kept a sharp eye on the Ford Tempo's signal lights. They stayed dark. Good. He pulled through the intersection and checked his rearview mirror. She was gone.

Furious, he turned around in his seat and caught a glimpse of the Ford Tempo's rear fender disappearing to the right. Flooring the accelerator, Popov sped to the next intersection and cut right. He was doing twenty miles over the limit, but he had to chance it.

At the next intersection, he cut right and shot down the street. The light was red with three cars waiting to make a left turn. He got in line and drummed his fingers on the steering wheel.

When the light turned green, the first car edged out to the center of the intersection and waited. Twenty cars stretched out ahead of them. Four cars later, a gap formed, enough for the lead car to slip through, but the driver didn't go. Popov resisted the impulse to hammer his horn. At this rate, only one car would get through.

The instant the yellow light came on, Popov cut into the right lane, surged into the intersection, and cut ahead of the lead vehicle. An orchestra of horns followed him, but he didn't care. He had to catch that girl.

Weaving through traffic, he found her four blocks later. Grinning, he felt inside his coat for a fresh cigar. He had her now. The short burst of a siren made him jump. A flash of red and blue reflected in his mirror. He cursed in Russian. The cop must've seen that stunt back at the intersection.

Right signal on, the Cougar moved onto the shoulder. The cop whizzed by and edged in behind the McIvor girl. What was she getting a ticket for? Going too slow?

When she pulled over, a tall policeman got out of his car. He placed both hands on the Ford Tempo and leaned over to talk in the window. In a moment, he laughed and touched her shoulder.

Popov glared at them. If the girl's boyfriend were a cop, he'd have to be extra careful when he made his move. The Russian thought of the new life he'd crafted for himself. To fail would mean disaster.

After about five minutes, the cop banged on the Ford Tempo's roof a couple of times, waved, then returned to his cruiser. Popov eased back into traffic as soon as she started out.

They left the downtown core and ended up at a three-story apartment building with a parking lot off to one side. Popov waited across the street while she parked.

After she slipped into the building, Popov kept his eyes on the front windows. He was rewarded with a light shining at an open window on the second floor. Watching her come in her door and close it behind her, he reached for his cell phone to call for reinforcements. The next instant, his phone clattered to the floor of the car. There was no time to call. Pressing the accelerator, he shot into the small parking lot and around the building.

Laura felt like she wore lead shoes as she climbed the steps to the front door of her apartment building. Her confrontation with Jonathan had made her feel worse instead of better. Her mind told her that he was a dead issue, but her idiotic heart still wasn't ready to throw in the towel. Hearing his voice and feeling his presence had sharpened half-forgotten images to a razor edge—his blue eyes looking into hers, his hand on her arm, the fire inside him that drew her like a moth to a lighted candle. She stifled a groan. Going out to the farm had been the mistake of the century. Why couldn't she relax and let a relationship develop with Wesley? At least he was real.

Pushing open the door, Laura opened her mailbox and pulled out a couple of envelopes. A utility bill and an offer to Occupant for a credit card with a gazillion-dollar credit limit. Occupant must have a great credit rating. She didn't have one at all.

She couldn't wait to get into her apartment and flop down on the foam mattress. She'd have to get a real bed soon, but she was so tired the one on loan from Wesley would feel like a pink cloud. Between lack of sleep and the emotional strain, she felt at the end of her tether. She blessed Olivia for giving her the rest of the day off.

She inserted the key into the dead bolt, and the lock snapped back. As she pushed the door open and flipped on the light, her heart rate picked up—a silly reaction from yesterday's break-in. Opening the door, she looked around. No surprises this time. Closing the door, she turned to slide the chain. . .

Her face bumped the wood, and something sharp pricked her throat. Hot breath spoke into her ear. "Don't move, or I'll cut you."

Laura gave a tiny scream. Her knees buckled, and she collapsed to the floor.

A strong hand grabbed her under the arms and dragged her to the living room carpet.

Laura looked up and groaned. It was the pony-tailed freak who tried to steal her purse. Slipping the crudely tied straps of her handbag off her shoulder, she held it up to him. "Here, take it. Just go away."

His face contorted. "I don't want your stinking handbag." Grabbing the black leather bag, he slung it behind him. It slid toward the sofa. He dropped to one knee, holding the knife to her cheek. "I want some respect."

Fear in her eyes, she tried to shrink away, but his other hand grabbed her hair.

The knife pressed closer. "You tell me who you are, or I'll rearrange your pretty face."

"Why are you doing this to me?" she wailed.

His smile was cruel. "Tell me who you are!"

"Shannon Masterson," she whimpered.

"Wrong!" He moved his hand over her mouth, pushing her head hard against the floor. "I want your real name."

Starting to recover from her initial shock, Laura's brain clicked into gear. This is what she had drilled for—all those self-defense classes in

BETRAYED

Phoenix. She mumbled something.

He pulled his hand away, his knife hand relaxed as he waited for her answer.

Twisting her body with the force of desperation, Laura struck the arm holding the knife, knocking it to the side and throwing him off balance. A sharp kick to his stomach put him flat on his back. Jumping up in one lithe motion, she darted to the kitchen. She could hear him cursing, coming for her. Reaching around the fridge for her secret weapon, she turned toward the door, ready. When Ponytail dashed in, she scored a homer with the bat her landlord had left her.

He staggered, spun. . .and collapsed backward into the living room.

The apartment door clicked open. Bat at the ready, Laura peered around the corner. A man of medium height looked down at Ponytail. He had a thick neck and dark glasses.

"Who are you?" she asked, posing for another swing.

The man smiled, gold fillings covering his front teeth. He spoke with a deep, guttural accent. "I see him moving past window. I come to help you."

He ambled over to her window, sliding it open. "Bad lock. Easy to get in from the fire escape, no?"

"Who are you?" Laura repeated.

"Ah, a good question, Miss McIvor."

She gulped, feeling cold. "You know who I am?"

"Da. Your father's very famous where I come from. His daughter, if you not mind me saying, is very beautiful."

"My father." Laura spat out the words. "I don't have a father."

"Perhaps. But I'm sure he still loves you. That is why you must come."

Laura raised the bat higher. "I'm not going anywhere. I'm calling my boyfriend. He's a cop." Boyfriend? Had she really used that word?

The man's heavy face darkened. "Oh, but you will come." His hand slid into his overcoat and a pistol appeared. He nodded toward the long barrel. "That is called a silencer. I can shoot you, and no one will hear. You come with me."

Laura shook her head. "Not a chance. If you need me, you won't shoot me."

He stepped toward her.

"Another step," she said, "and I'll smash you with this."

He stood, arms at his sides, still smiling. "Smash away."

Laura whipped the bat at his head. He caught it in a huge hand and yanked it from her.

She backed toward the bathroom. "I'll scream."

He took a step forward. "You are right, Miss McIvor. I will not shoot you, but I will shoot anyone who comes to help you. Do you want that?"

She imagined Mr. Iverson crashing through the door only to be shot in the chest. "No!"

"Come," he said, as though reasoning with a stubborn child. "No harm will come to you. Your father is a smart man."

"My father is an idiot," she said, and she walked out ahead of him.

He kept close behind her on the stairs. She started to push open the front door when a voice called from behind them. "Wait, Missy, I've got your key."

She turned to see Mr. Iverson standing in his doorway. "I'll get it later," she said.

The manager gave her companion the once-over. "Everything all right? I heard some thumping upstairs."

Laura smiled weakly. "Everything's great."

"Who's this guy?"

Her captor spoke. "You not worry, old man. Old family friend. Right, Laura?"

"Yeah, that's right." Her voice sounded flat.

Iverson's eyes narrowed. "Okay. Well, see you later then."

"Yeah, bye."

They stepped out of the building, and the kidnapper grabbed her elbow. "This way. To the alley."

Laura bristled at his touch, but followed his direction. They went around the building to a long, dark car. He led her to the trunk and opened it. "Get in," he ordered.

"In the trunk?"

"I not taking any chances on you jumping out of moving car."

She leaned back, away from the car. "I'm not getting in there."

"Then I go back and shoot the old man." His face had a smile, but his eyes were deep pits showing a black soul.

Shaking and feeling sick at her stomach, she climbed into the trunk and the lid closed darkness around her. *God, are You there? Help me!*

Jonathan flipped through every channel on the satellite dish and found nothing to interest him. The dish had been another surprise. His mom had never let her boys watch much TV when they were younger, but because he was injured, she had a dish installed to give him something to do. This was much more than he deserved. Since his father's death, he'd been nothing but trouble for her.

Andrea was in her room reading. Since Laura's visit, she'd withdrawn from him. Shortly after Laura left, Andrea had come into the kitchen.

"What's happened?" she asked. "I heard shouting."

At the table, he pulled his hands away from his face, avoiding her eyes. "Nothing that concerns you, Andrea. Don't worry about it."

She watched him closely. "I heard a woman, Jonathan. Someone you know?"

He lifted his sad eyes to her. "Don't go there, Andrea. It doesn't concern you."

Her chin raised a fraction. "I see." She turned away, flipping a hank of hair from her face. "Excuse me for living."

That was the last he saw of her until time for their workout. Afterward, she disappeared into her room. No offer of a back rub or a board game today. What was it Jonathan's old SEAL commander had said? "We can't live with them, and we can't live without them!"

After today, Jonathan felt certain he could live without them.

The front door opened. "Hi, Jonathan, we're back." It was Mom, home after picking up Roxanne from school. Gus trotted into Jonathan's room to say hello. On his bed, Jonathan stroked his thick neck, feeling the coarseness of his fur.

Roxanne had a relationship with his mother that he never had. As a boy, he'd been his dad's shadow. Mom had been necessary but not all that interesting. Roxanne, like Danny, seemed to bask in the glow of Mom's affection.

His mother bustled into the room. "How are you feeling, Son?" She glared at Gus. "Go on, now. You shouldn't be in here."

The dog blissfully ignored her. Jonathan kept stroking.

"Better," he said. "I'm still walking my five minutes every hour."

"I don't mean that; I mean about earlier on." She watched him with that knowing look in her eye.

"I'd rather not talk about it." This was the third time she'd hinted about the woman intruder. Laura was a topic he couldn't deal with right now.

Roxanne breezed into the room wearing a white blouse and blue tartan skirt, her school uniform. Immediately, Gus trotted to her side. She knelt down to talk to him and run her hands over his face. The girl didn't look like a street punk, yet Jonathan doubted the kid could change that fast. He'd keep an eye on her.

"Mom, I was wondering. . .now that Mr. Corrigan is back, if I could . . .you know."

"Start riding lessons again?" she asked.

Roxanne's face lit up. "Yeah."

"Maybe tomorrow. Tonight I've got to work on the farm books, then get supper ready."

"I'll do supper," she volunteered. "We can have hamburgers. Please?"

Smiling, Sandra Corrigan shook her head. "You're improving, Dear, but I don't think it's fair to expose Jonathan to your cooking just yet."

"Can't I go riding by myself? I know what to do. I'll be all right."

"You are not an experienced horsewoman, Roxanne. Duke is a gentle horse, but he could still hurt you without meaning to."

"Duke?" Jonathan chimed in. "You've still got Duke?"

His mother nodded. "Of course. What did you think I was going to do with him?"

"I thought you sold him. I made it pretty clear I wasn't coming back."

She chuckled. "And I made it pretty clear I would keep praying until you did." She smiled sweetly. "I won. You lost."

"That's where you're wrong, Mom," he said softly. "In this case, I won, too. Coming home is always a winning move." He glanced out the window at the horse stable across the yard. "Boy, I'd sure like to see Duke again. Can I go with Roxanne to the barn?"

The girl let out a little squeal. Gus barked once.

Jonathan gazed at her, amazed. In a single second, this teenager transformed herself into a little girl, jumping and excited. How did kids do that?

Sandra laughed. "I think the problem's solved." She sobered. "As long as you don't wear yourself out, Jonathan. Promise me you'll make her come in when you get tired."

He held up his right hand, thumb in. "Scout's honor."

"I'll change." Roxanne dashed down the hall and up the stairs, Gus at her heels.

"Meet me at the barn," Jonathan called after her.

His mother stepped closer. "Are you positively sure you're up to this?"

"Sure, Mom. I'll take the ATV down there and sit on a hay bale. I

BETRAYED

can watch her ride from there."

She started to leave, then turned, "Jonathan, Roxanne still has a lot of hurt inside of her. Be gentle. She's a fragile little girl who needs lots of TLC."

CHAPTER FOURTEEN

Though her kidnapper's car looked long and sleek from the outside, Laura felt like a canned ham molded inside its trunk. Huddled in complete blackness, her senses came alive to every bump, every screech or groan from the vehicle, the smell of new carpet under her, and exhaust fumes from farther away.

Her prayer became a droning repetition of "Help me! Help me!" until after awhile she sank into a strange stupor, tense and waiting, yet her mind wandering. Scenes from her past flipped through her mind as though guided by a remote in the hand of a bored teenager.

Laura didn't invite Sally Michaels to her tenth birthday party because the girl had black teeth, and no one liked her. High school football star Scott Kilgor convinced Laura to help him cheat on a chemistry exam in exchange for a date to the prom. Then there were the white lies that she'd told her mother to explain why she was late coming home from school. Starfire Arcade had drawn her like a magnet back then. Now she wondered what she'd seen in it.

Laura groaned and moved her hand under her head to shield it from the jarring. She may as well give up. Even if she got out of this fix, everyone would know who she was sooner or later. Would Olivia still want Harrison McIvor's daughter serving her customers? Not likely.

With Laura's knee pressing into something metal and a hard thing jabbing into her back, she relived last week's conversation with Olivia after a rude businessman brought in his crashed computer for repairs. Laura had fixed the machine, but the man refused to pay. He claimed the

BETRAYED

computer was defective when he bought it. Olivia had smiled and said, "No charge."

"Why did you do that?" Laura asked her, once he left the small store.

Behind the glass counter, Olivia shook her head as though the incident didn't matter. "He thought the computer was defective."

Laura grew heated. "He's been surfing the web without protection. I yanked out six viruses. Didn't you tell him that?"

"He claimed he didn't get them from the net."

"And you believe him?" Laura knew better.

"Of course not." Olivia chuckled and reached for a candy bar from the rack beside the register. "I was born on a Tuesday, but it wasn't last Tuesday."

Laura moved a step closer. "Don't his lies make you boil inside?"

Olivia nodded. "If they didn't, I'd have a pair of wings and a halo." She gazed at Laura, warm depth behind her eyes. "But it's much easier to forgive him and move on."

Laura's expression grew intense. Her eyes flashed sparks. "I'd never forget his face. And if I ever got the chance, I'd get even."

Olivia lay her hand on the sleeve of Laura's blazer. "Let's think about this a minute, Honey. If I stayed mad at the guy, would that make him spend the rest of his life in agony because he lied to PTL Computers?"

"No," Laura had answered, a wry look on her face.

Olivia sank into her wide chair near the register and tore the end off the candy bar wrapper. She glanced at the troubled young woman leaning on the counter beside her. "Shannon, that man walked out of here thinking he got away with something." She shook her head, and her curls swayed. "God knows what he did, and God will take care of him." She threw the wrapper in the trash can. "Why should I torture myself with angry thoughts and push my blood pressure any higher?" Her gaze looked right through Laura. "The only one I'd be hurting would be. . .me."

Lying in the dark trunk, Laura's thoughts moved to Jonathan Corrigan. What had her anger gotten her? Sleepless nights, buckets of tears, endless agony. And he didn't even know about it.

At his house this morning, he'd seemed fine. She thought about that some more. Or did he? She'd seen something in his eyes when he grabbed her arm. His words came to her in a rush, "I hope I can prove that to you someday." *Prove what?*

BETRAYED

The car hit a bump. Laura's head thumped the top of the trunk. The thing in her back pressed harder. Half turning to reach behind her, she ran her hands over the object, trying to push it away. A tire rim. What else was in here? Feeling around, she identified a jack, a tire iron, and some kind of metal stick.

The car slowed, then stopped. The door opened. The kidnapper's muffled voice came through the trunk lid. "Be very quiet, Miss McIvor. If you yell, someone gets hurt."

A couple of moments later, she heard his voice farther away. The car door slammed, and they started moving again. Before he had put her in the trunk, he mentioned her father as though he had something to do with this. Was Daddy still tearing her life apart from his prison cell? Would it ever end? She lay her head back and moaned like a hurt animal.

The car swerved, and her hand fell on the jack again. Her instructor's voice spoke clearly in her mind. "The worst hindrance to self-defense is blind panic." Squeezing her eyes shut, she silently screamed, *"Think, Laura!"*

In a flash it came to her. Surely anything that had the power to lift a car could spring that lock. Groping about, she found the tire iron. At least her father had taught her how to change a tire. Feeling around the jack, she found the spot to insert the end of the tire iron and moved it up and down. Nothing happened. Was it broken?

She felt the end of the jack. It was the kind that turned! Starting to sweat from her exertion in close quarters, she wound the handle. The jack slowly expanded. Shifting her body out of the way, she slid the jack under the lock and rotated the handle.

Up it went, each turn a step closer to freedom. The top of the jack touched the lid. Metal strained, then the handle quit moving. The jack was as high as it could go. Frustrated—longing to beat the lid with her fists—Laura kicked out. Her toe struck the tire rim. *Ow!*

Biting her lips, grunting from fear and pain, she wound the jack down and twisted her body into impossible contortions to slide the tire rim under the lock. Exhausted and panting, she pushed with both legs and arms until it reached the right position. Aching to rest but afraid the car would stop again, she placed the jack on the tire rim and started over. Why had she wasted so much time dreaming?

Ages later, the metal above her squawked. A glimmer of light broke through a crack.

Suddenly, she stopped. What was she thinking? She couldn't jump onto the highway at seventy miles an hour. She'd have to wait until he stopped. *God, please keep him busy for just three minutes when we get there.*

Her calves ached from being cramped. She longed to stretch her throbbing back. How much longer?

The car slowed, and Laura tensed to an excruciating degree. Would she know when to move? If she waited too long, she'd lose her chance. The car swayed into a sharp curve. An exit ramp?

She tried to peek through the crack, but there wasn't enough room to see anything but light. The vehicle stopped. Laura rotated the jack handle a quarter turn, then paused. Traffic noises sounded fast, like a major highway. She decided to wait. On the third stop, she heard a bus starting up, and a woman shouting something. Fumbling in her frenzy, weeping and gasping, she yanked the handle around.

The lid popped up. A rush of cold city air washed over her as Laura lunged onto the pavement. She turned to run as a gray Caprice pulled up behind the Cougar, and two men sprang out.

Jonathan sat on a bale of hay while Roxanne fetched Duke from the wide, clean corral. She had her dark hair tied into a yard-long ponytail. Wearing jeans, cowboy boots, a western shirt, and a down-filled vest, she looked the part of a cowgirl except for the helmet his mother insisted she bring.

"Please, don't make we wear that," Roxanne had said, looking at the black helmet as though it were a black snake.

Sandra Corrigan's mouth was firm. "If you want to ride, you'll wear the helmet."

"But I've got this awesome cowboy hat." She held it up, a brown Stetson with a silver band. "Why can't I wear it?"

"That fancy thing won't do your head any good when you hit the ground."

Roxanne's entire body pleaded when she said, "Duke's so gentle. He'd never knock me off."

"Listen, little lady," Sandra spoke softly with authority in every word. "It's your choice: wear the helmet, or forget the ride."

Roxanne left the cowboy hat inside and took the helmet—reluctantly.

A gray quarter horse fifteen hands high paced toward Roxanne when she stopped by the corral gate, halter in hand. He stooped to touch noses with Gus, then shook his gray head and blew. The dog sniffed the horse's legs, then ambled toward the barn.

Watching Roxanne stroke Duke's nose, Jonathan felt the texture of the stiff bale under him and asked, "Have you worked with him much?"

Roxanne beamed. "Before you were injured, your mom gave me lessons almost every afternoon. She hasn't had time lately, but I still come out every day to talk to him, feed him, and muck out his stall." She lay her head against the horse. "We're best friends, aren't we, Duke?"

The horse blew and put his head down so she could slip the halter on. She led him to a hitching post near Jonathan and tied Duke with a slipknot. While she was cleaning Duke's feet, he hobbled sideways toward Jonathan and turned his head, snuffling Jonathan's shirt, his hand, his head.

"Do you think he remembers you?" Roxanne asked, prying out a rock with a hoof pick.

Jonathan laughed when Duke nibbled at his pocket. "Maybe. It's been a lot of years."

Duke put his head down, and Jonathan rubbed his face. The horse snorted then nickered. "Hmm, maybe he does," Jonathan said.

"You had him a long time." Roxanne tugged at the back of Duke's right rear leg, and he raised it for her to hold over her knee.

"My. . .dad got him for me when I was ten. He was just a two year old then. But what a fast learner! When he was a five year old, we won the regional junior calf-roping championship."

He rubbed the underside of Duke's jaw, speaking more to the horse than to Roxanne. "Duke is the best horse I've ever known. He never tried to throw me. When I fell off due to my own stupidity, he'd stop and come back." He swallowed hard. "I forgot how much I miss this guy." He hugged the gelding's head, smelling that distinctive odor that said "horse." "Sure been a long time, Fella." Duke nickered again.

"I've sure enjoyed him," Roxanne said. "He's so easy to ride."

"He's twenty-seven years old. There isn't too much he hasn't seen or done."

Roxanne's blue eyes locked with Jonathan's. "That's pretty old for a horse, isn't it?"

Jonathan nodded. "He's getting up there, all right. But he's always been sound. He's had the best of care and feed. That helps. Unfortunately, he's had no one to work him for a long time."

BETRAYED

Roxanne beamed. She looked cute, even in a black helmet. "If you don't mind too much, I'd like to take that job."

Jonathan tapped his left leg with the cane. "I may not be able to ride for a long time."

Moving like a pro, Roxanne saddled and bridled the horse. Grabbing the reins, she led him through the corral gate and closed it behind them. Jonathan was just about to open his mouth, when Roxanne checked the cinch strap and tightened it some more. He smiled and relaxed. His mother had taught her right. He should have known.

Roxanne had Duke walk around the arena. She was taking it easy with him, warming him up. Gus watched for awhile from the fence, yawned, and lay down. After an hour, she brought Duke back to the hitching rail.

"You did good," Jonathan said, his eyes approving.

"Thank you." Her face had a healthy flush.

Maybe Danny was right. Maybe she was a good kid in a bad situation.

In twenty minutes, she unsaddled Duke, groomed him, fed him, and released him into the corral. Enjoying the warm sun, the smell of the stable, the clear air, Jonathan stayed put as she strode toward him, Gus at her heels.

Roxanne dropped her slender frame onto a bale nearby, her hand absently scratching the dog's ruff. "Mr. Corrigan," she said, a little breathless, "do you mind if I ask you something?" She pulled off her helmet and smoothed her wispy hair.

"Call me Jon. Sure, what do you want to know?"

"This is the nicest place in the whole world. Why didn't you want to come here?"

He tensed. "Who said that?"

"When you were still in L.A., I used to hear your mother pray that God would soften your heart and bring you home." She looked into his face. "Your mother is a living angel, but you're tearing her heart out. She says you're angry at God."

Jonathan was getting irritated. Roxanne was treading in an area marked, NO TRESPASSING. "Not angry," he said shortly, "just not on speaking terms."

"I never even knew who God was before I met your mom," she said softly. "He's changed my life so much I can't even explain it all."

"How? By giving you a nice place to live, a horse to ride, a better school?"

She plucked at straw from the bale and studied it. "Those things are good, but the biggest thing was when He helped me forgive my parents."

Jonathan softened his tone. Here was a chance to get to the heart of something that had been troubling him. "Want to tell me about it?" he asked.

"When the application to terminate my parents' rights came to court, they didn't attend the hearing." She stared at Duke munching grass. "I hated them for it. I wished they were dead." She glanced at Jonathan. "You have a mother who cries over you and prays for you, and you don't appreciate her."

Jonathan ignored the part about his mother. "Terminate parental rights? Who filed the application?"

Roxanne looked up, surprised. "Didn't anyone tell you? Your mother is adopting me."

Jonathan stared at her innocent face. So that was her game. He considered the situation a full minute then said, "Boy, Roxanne, you are good."

"What do you mean?" She looked scared.

"My mom is a trusting sort. My brother, too. But I'm with the CIA, and we're not that easily fooled."

Roxanne's little-girl look vanished. Her cobalt eyes had shutters behind them.

Sensing a change in her, Jonathan pushed ahead. "I know what happened. You found a lonely old lady and wheedled your way into her heart." His voice grew louder. "Now you've convinced her to adopt you, so you can inherit a chunk of this farm."

Roxanne stared at him, tears slowly forming in the corners of her eyes. Ears pulled forward, Gus tilted his head, watching her. In a moment he whined and pushed his nose into her face. Sniffing, she jerked back and pushed him away. "Not now, Gus." The dog lay his head on her knee.

Fueled by his own anger, he said, "Tears work on most people, but not me. Here's a news flash, Roxanne. My mom doesn't own this farm. I do. The farm has been passed down to the eldest son in the Corrigan family for four generations. All my mother has is the right to live here until she dies. Ownership of the property remains with me or my heirs. Sorry, Kiddo, the pot at the end of the rainbow won't go to you."

Roxanne stood, shaking, tears streaming. She spoke in gasps. "When I first came here, I was terrible to your mom. I swore at her; I disobeyed her; I destroyed things. Finally, I ran away. She always brought me back

BETRAYED

and loved me." A sob slipped out. "You don't know it, but your mother is the most wonderful person in the world. I want her to love me, that's all." She glared at him. "It's too bad you're so stupid you can't see what you've got." Roxanne's hands flew to her face, and she ran toward the house. Gus bounded after her, his tail down.

Jonathan stared at the hay-strewn ground by his feet. What an actress. She was almost believable.

The smell of the barn, the hay, the pine-scented breeze brought back a flood of memories. Watching the horses, he became so absorbed that he didn't hear footsteps behind him. Suddenly, his ear exploded in pain. He spun around. . .and cowered.

Moving fast for a stout man, Laura's kidnapper jumped out of the Cougar and came for her from the left. Her only way of escape was to the right, across heavy traffic. Still half blinded by the glaring sunlight after being in the trunk, she darted into the street. A horn blared and air whooshed as a bus slammed on its brakes. It bumped her. She stumbled, but kept on running.

Another horn and Laura stopped short as a car brushed past her. Behind her, angry voices yelled, but she kept on going.

Laura made it to the sidewalk and looked around. Spotting a uniform, she raced toward a policeman talking to half a dozen teenagers. Laura ran to the man in blue and grabbed his arm.

The officer looked down at her, annoyed. He was writing on a clipboard. "What's the trouble?"

"I'm. . .I'm being chased." Laura bent over, gasping for air.

The policeman scanned the area. "By who?"

She spun around, pointing. Both cars were gone. She gulped. "They're not there anymore." She brushed stiff fingers through her tangled hair, staring at the place they used to be.

"Look, Lady, seems you're safe for the moment. Let me finish what I'm doing here, then we'll talk about your problem."

Laura stepped back a few feet, watching for the dark car, not daring to leave the officer's shadow. Glancing around, she recognized the courtyard of Westlake Center. She'd come here several times to shop.

About ten minutes later, the police officer's radio crackled. "All units in the vicinity of Turgeon-Raine Jewelers—robbery in progress—please respond."

The policeman ran toward Union Street, leaving Laura on the sidewalk feeling very small and very alone. She hurried toward the entrance of the shopping center. The more people, the better she'd feel.

When she entered the mall, hunger suddenly hit her, and she rode the escalator to the top-floor Food Court. Fortunately, she had a couple of fives in the pocket of her jeans. The Food Court offered a variety of options, everything from McDonald's to Vietnamese fare. She bought a cheeseburger, fries, and a Coke, and found a table near a window.

A rumble told her the monorail that ran from Seattle Center to Westlake Center had entered the station. As she popped the last bite of cheeseburger into her mouth, the stout man with a guttural accent slipped into the seat across from her.

"Miss McIvor," he muttered, "you are becoming much nuisance." He leaned closer, looking into her eyes. "We have men at every exit. You cannot get away. Be cooperative, and we not hurt you."

Stalling, searching for a way to escape, Laura picked up her Coke. "You'll have to excuse me if I'm a little skeptical. After all, you did just drag me to Seattle in the trunk of your car." She sipped from the straw.

"An unfortunate occurrence. The man in your apartment made it necessary. I could not let him hurt you."

Over the loudspeaker came, "All aboard for Seattle Center." Throwing her Coke at her tormentor, Laura sprinted toward the monorail, jumped the turnstile, and squeezed through sliding doors as they closed.

Her heart thumping like it would burst from her chest, she sank into a seat and tried to breathe. For a few minutes she was safe. No one could reach the Seattle Center before the monorail.

At the Seattle Center, Laura fast-walked out of the monorail station, then stopped. What an idiot she was. They knew where she was going. Laura spun around, this time paying the one-dollar fare, and rode the monorail back to the Westlake Center. Why go to where they expected? She'd be much safer at the last place they'd look. Where she'd come from.

Laura wandered around the Westlake mall. She was in big trouble—no doubt. These guys were serious and possibly deadly. She needed help—but from whom?

The answer came to her mind immediately. Wesley.

For an instant, she hesitated. The man who nabbed her had a foreign accent. He spoke about her father. Maybe this was something for the CIA to handle. Weren't foreign spies their thing? Years ago, Jonathan had given her a number to call if she needed him. He'd made her memorize it, and she still remembered it.

Laura found a pay phone and lifted the receiver. She dropped a coin in, then noticed a newspaper vending machine nearby. On the front of today's paper was a huge picture of a man in a wheelchair. Holding the phone near her ear, she glanced at it, then stared. That was Jonathan. A gorgeous blond in a negligée leaned toward him with a teasing, intimate smile. Bold and red, the headline shouted, HERO IN LOVE?

Turning away, Laura called the only man she could trust. Wesley.

CHAPTER FIFTEEN

Sandra Corrigan's eyes burned into her son. "What did you do to poor Roxanne?"

Jonathan held his hands up, ready to ward off another blow. Danny Corrigan wasn't the only one in the family with a wicked right.

Leaning away from her, Jonathan winced. "I just set her straight, that's all."

His mother backed off and came around to sit on the hay bale beside him. She looked like a hillbilly avenger in a jean skirt and a faded flannel coat of red plaid, her gray hair pulled into a loose ponytail.

He rubbed his sore ear where she'd boxed him. "That hurt."

Sandra's blue eyes still blazed. "No kidding. If you were younger, it would have been your rear." She shifted farther toward him. "Just how did you set her straight?"

He cleared his throat and tried to drag up some dignity. "I made sure she understood how things worked around here."

She raised her eyebrows, feigning surprise. "Really? And just how do things work around here? It must be something awful. She ran into the house crying, then she started packing."

He got his second wind, and his chin jutted forward. "Hey, Mom, ease off a bit. This is really your fault, you know."

"My fault?" Her mouth formed an O.

"You should have told me you're adopting her."

Some of the fight went out of her. "You've only been home two days, Jonathan. With you sick, I didn't want to hit you with too much at once."

She bore in on him. "But you need to keep in mind that you've been away for years. My plans for Roxanne started long before you came back into our lives."

He grunted and tore at the bit of straw in his hand. "Well, it's a stupid plan. Can't you see what she's after?"

Sandra Corrigan cocked her head. "Why don't you tell me?"

"It's the farm. You know, she worms her way into your heart, gets you to adopt her, then when you push off, she gets a chunk of the place."

"For someone so smart, you can be such an idiot, Jonathan."

His temper flared. "You're the one who's not so swift. That girl played you for a sucker."

Sandra drew up, her round face tight with indignation, her words thick. "For the record, Sherlock, I decided to adopt Roxanne the day I first saw her. . .in the courthouse. The Lord said to me, 'Make her as if she were your own.' "

He raised a hand, palm up. "You didn't know anything about her." He shook his head, disgusted. "Now that she knows she won't get any part of the place, she's sure booking out fast enough."

Sandra's voice grew louder. "Will you listen for a change? When I first talked to Roxanne about adopting her, I told her the farm belonged to you, and the only thing I could promise her was my love. An inheritance has never been an issue with her!"

Roxanne's stricken face and teary eyes waved through his consciousness. Jonathan gulped. He had a sinking feeling in the pit of his stomach. Why did he get himself into these situations?

He gazed at the hitching post and wondered if he should bang his head against it now, or wait for his mother to go to the house.

He darted a sheepish glance at her. "Is she really leaving?"

Sandra shook her head. "No, I calmed her down."

Letting out a relieved breath, he said, "I'll apologize to her later."

"You'll apologize to her now." When his mother motioned, Roxanne poked her head out the front door. "Come on out!" Sandra yelled toward the house. "He's tame now."

Shoulders bent, scuffing the grass, Roxanne shambled to them. Jonathan looked into her tear-streaked face and wanted to kick himself. How could he have missed it? She was a little girl hiding inside a woman's body.

He coughed, stalling to think of the right words. Looking into the girl's bleary eyes, he gently said, "I'm really sorry for what I said, Roxanne.

I'm a shortsighted idiot. Please, don't ever think about leaving here. This is your home."

Fresh tears slid down her cheeks. She threw her arms around him, knocking him back so that he almost lost his balance. She jostled his sore leg and planted a firm kiss on his cheek. "Thank you," she said, her face glowing as she stepped back.

Grinning, he rubbed his left leg. "I take it I'm forgiven."

"Oh, yes," she cried and attacked Sandra with a hug, too.

"Back to the house with you now," Sandra said, patting the girl's back. "I'll be along in a second, and we'll start on those pies."

"Yes, Ma'am." Arms wide, Roxanne flew back to the house, a jump and a skip in her step.

"How do they go from the depths of despair to the heights of joy in a split second?" Jonathan asked, his hand still on his wound.

Light came into Sandra's eyes. "I don't know. I raised two boys, remember?" She chuckled, a girlish look peeking out from her lined face. "I think it's a female thing."

"At least she doesn't hold a grudge. In my experience, women usually hold on to their hurts for awhile." A long while.

"Since Jesus came into her heart, Roxanne has learned the art of forgiving. Something we all need lessons in." She stood and brushed off the back of her skirt. "You'd better get yourself to the house. It's still winter, you know."

He gazed into the distance. "I'll be there in awhile. I need some time to think."

Her wide boots leaving a trail on the straw-covered ground, Sandra headed toward the house without a backward glance.

Jonathan sat like a stone. Mighty Corrigan turned into a bumbler every time he turned around. What was wrong with him? Even a girl like Roxanne was more on the ball than he.

He heard his mother's words again, "Since Jesus came into her heart." Swallowing back a lump pressing against his Adam's apple, he remembered when Jesus used to be in his heart. Life had been so much simpler back then—the farm, school, his friends at youth group. . .church. When Dad died, all that died, too.

Or did it? Did Jesus really leave him, or was it his own bitterness which blocked out that sweet voice? Using his cane and the fence for support, he paced into the barn. He had to get alone where anxious eyes at a window couldn't see him.

Inside, holding onto the door of Duke's empty stall, he rested his forehead on the top rail. *God, forgive me.* Tears melted away the anger that had haunted him for more than fifteen years. Sobbing out his grief for his father, he saw that dear, weathered face, heard his rough-yet-tender voice, and felt that calloused hand rumple his hair once more.

"Dad, I miss you so much," he murmured half aloud.

Rubbing away his tears, he raised his head and looked around. At the silo door, his mind's eye saw his father shoveling grain into a wheelbarrow, laughing, and calling Jonathan "Yogi" because he loved the cartoon so much. At the tack room Dad was there, fixing a lead halter for their new horse named Duke. As he worked, he gave Jonathan gentle instruction on caring for the horse. He was in the hayloft, the feed room, in the saw marks on the board under Jonathan's hand.

Looking up into the eaves of the horse barn, tears flowing freely again, Jonathan said, "You've been here all the time, haven't you, Dad?" He drew in a shaky breath and squeezed his eyes tight. *Thank You, God, for letting me remember.*

Sweet warmth filled his soul as he bowed again, lost in the goodness and all-encompassing love of his Savior. At long last, Jonathan had come home.

Minutes passed unheeded. Finally, his leg began to ache.

Someone behind him cleared his throat. Reaching for a handkerchief in his back pocket, Jonathan glanced around, wiping his eyes. "Perkins."

The big man's granite face had a red tinge. "Sorry, Sir. I didn't realize you were. . ."

"Praying?" Jonathan smiled, unashamed.

"Uh, yeah." Perkins turned away. "I'll come back later."

Jonathan cleared his throat and put away his handkerchief. "Now's fine. What have you got?"

Perkins moved closer. "I did some checking—like you asked—into Laura McIvor, aka Shannon Masterson. In the last three days, her apartment was robbed and her car stolen."

Jonathan said, "From the way she stormed in here, she must think we're involved."

Perkins nodded. "Your people could be doing something. They wouldn't tell you now that you're retired."

Corrigan thought about it. "I used my own resources to hide her. If the agency needed to find her, they'd have to ask me where to start looking."

"Maybe she slipped up somewhere and gave out her real name."

As scared as Laura was when he left her in Phoenix, Corrigan doubted that. "Even so," he said, "she was never involved in her father's treachery. That's why I got to her so easy when I was undercover. She had no reason to be suspicious."

"What's your take on it?" Perkins asked.

"I don't know. I'll have to think about it."

Perkins started to move away, then stopped. "About this morning, I'm sorry I got so rough with the McIvor girl."

Corrigan suddenly saw Perkins in a new light. "I haven't been very easy on you, have I, Sam?" he asked softly. "Don't sweat it. You were just doing your job, and a pretty good job at that."

Perkins's head came around "You okay?"

"I am now." Leaning heavily on the cane, he stepped forward. "Look, let's stop questioning everyone who comes down the driveway. No one's going to kill me, and if the odd photographer gets a picture, big deal."

Perkins looked doubtful.

Jonathan went on. "Let's cut down the troops to two guards who stick close by the house. That'll be plenty."

"The director won't like it."

"He'll get over it." Jonathan reached the other man and stood so they were face-to-face. "And Perkins—what happened in L.A.—that's water under the bridge, all right?"

The big man looked at him, wondering, and nodded. "Yeah, thanks."

Laura wrapped her coat tighter as she walked across the courtyard. The afternoon air was cooling fast. Meeting at Westlake Center was the safest move.

After fifteen minutes, she saw Wesley's head bobbing toward her. His face was grim, concerned, and to Laura the most beautiful sight in the world. As soon as he reached her, she threw her arms around him and held on tight, feeling safe as his powerful arms pulled her close. With her face against his chest, she let tears come. "I'm so scared," she said in a moment.

He pushed her back a bit and wiped away tears with his fingers. "Hey, it's okay now. I'm here." He looked at her light coat. "You must be freezing. Let's go inside and find a cup of coffee."

"That'd be great," Laura said, sniffing and fighting for control.

BETRAYED

Arm in arm, they headed for the Food Court. Inside the building, the warm air felt so good, and she snuggled closer to Wesley, as though he were a safe haven. He found a table near the back and pulled out a chair for her. "Wait here. I'll get some coffee."

Laura watched him make his way to the coffee bar. How much should she tell him? She already knew the answer. Wesley had shown her nothing but kindness since they first met. He would understand.

When he returned, he handed her a foam cup of steaming black brew. "Thank you," Laura said, her hands soaking in the warmth from the cup.

He sat across from her and sipped his coffee, his eyes searching hers. "What kind of trouble are you in?"

Laura held the cup near her face, enjoying the smell and the steam. Setting it down, she said, "Today a man attacked me in my apartment."

Wesley's voice was loud and harsh. "What?"

Glancing around to see who may be listening, she leaned forward, keeping her voice low, encouraging him to do the same. "He tried to snatch my purse this morning, and when he failed, he tracked me down to my apartment."

He whispered, "Why didn't you call me?"

"I thought I knew who was responsible."

Wesley scratched his red head. "This isn't making sense, Shannon."

"It won't until I give you the whole story."

Wesley set down his cup. "I'm all ears."

She hesitated. "Are you angry with me?"

His eyes softened. "I'm a little hurt that you didn't come to me first, that's all."

Laura drew in a breath and plunged in. "Do you remember that big trial a couple of years back for Harrison McIvor?"

"Sure, the guy that was selling secrets to the Russians and Chinese."

She paused for effect. "I'm his daughter."

His eyes widened. "You're Harrison McIvor's daughter?"

"My real name is Laura McIvor."

"Wow! No wonder you kept it a secret."

She ran a finger around the rim of her cup. "When that guy attacked me in the apartment, I whacked him with a baseball bat and knocked him unconscious."

"Good for you," Wesley said, impressed.

BETRAYED

"That's when another man showed up with a gun. He forced me into the trunk of his car and drove me here."

Wesley rubbed his head. "I can't believe all that happened to you." He watched her as though seeing her for the first time. "How did you get away?"

"I pried open the trunk with a car jack and ran toward a cop." She told him about the kidnapper reappearing and her dash for the monorail. Shivering, she glanced around. "They're still looking for me. I can feel it."

She leaned forward, her voice intense. "Wesley, the guy with the gun had an accent. It sounded Russian to me."

"Whoa!" A scared look came over his boyish face. He held up both hands as though he were surrendering. "This is more than a Bellingham cop can handle. We need big-time help here, but from who?"

"That's what I've been wondering. I mean, how do we know for sure that he's Russian? Maybe he's an FBI agent undercover still looking for something my father had." Desperation creased her soft features. "That's why I called you, Wesley. I don't know who else to trust."

He covered her hands with his. "I'm not sure how, but I'll get you out of this mess. I've got a few friends in the FBI. Maybe they can do some discreet digging and find out who's responsible. In the meantime, you have to hide."

"Where?"

His brows drew together as he considered. "I'd like to say my place, but if these guys are any good at all, they'll make a connection between us in no time. You'll have to go to a motel." He smiled. "I know just the one."

They finished their coffee and left the mall. In the parking lot, Wesley held open the door of his Camry, and she slid inside. When he got in beside her, he glanced into the rearview mirror. "In case we're being followed, I'll give you a tour of Seattle."

For the next half hour, Wesley drove all over town, turning suddenly, parking without warning, ducking down alleys. Finally satisfied, he headed north on Interstate 5. They traveled past Everett, turned at Arlington, and drove east for ten minutes. Pulling into the gravel parking lot of the Snowcap Motel, he parked and shut off the engine.

The single-level building had a pink exterior with a flat tar-and-gravel roof. A couple of cars sat in front of it. Laura gasped when she read the motel's faded sign. "Wesley, they have hourly rates. This place is a place where. . .you know."

Wesley nodded ruefully. "Last year I worked on a drug case, and we hid a witness here. The owner asks no questions, and he keeps his mouth shut." He touched her hand. "Wait here while I register."

Huddled in the car, afraid someone—anyone—would see her, Laura stared at the crumbling sidewalk and the broken-and-taped window in front of her. She'd gone from a villa in California, to a bachelor apartment in Bellingham, to a seedy motel. She forced back a wave of despair. Something had to change soon.

In short order Wesley returned, key in hand. Laura got out of the car and joined him at the door to Room 106. The musty atmosphere inside didn't surprise her. The carpets had bare spots, the bedspread had holes, and the white ceiling was browned from years of cigarette smoke.

Laura poked her head into the tiny bathroom. The toilet seat was split, and there was no bath, just a rusty shower stall. The small kitchenette was probably the room's best feature, but then it probably didn't get used much.

"I know, it's pretty grim," Wesley said, watching her disgusted expression, "but at least it's safe."

Laura sat on the edge of the bed. Creaky springs sank under her weight. "It'll have to do," she murmured.

"I've given the guy a week's rent in cash, so he won't bother you. Make me a list, and I'll bring you whatever you'll need."

Laura shuddered. "At the top of the list you can put a sleeping bag. I couldn't force myself to crawl into those sheets."

"Not a problem," Wesley answered, grinning. "Anything else?"

Laura found a notepad in the room's small desk and started writing.

Sitting on the edge of a leather desk chair in a plush, private office at the Russian Federation Consulate in Seattle, Alex Popov trembled as he picked up the ringing phone attached to a secured line. "Popov here," he said in Russian. He glanced around. The expansive room was empty, but he still felt as though someone watched him.

"Please hold for General Yuri Prokofiev," a woman's clipped voice answered in the same language.

"Popov!" A throaty male voice came on the line. "Do you have her?"

Swallowing and shaking, Popov forced himself to answer. "She escaped."

The other end of the line remained quiet for ten seconds. Dragging a nervous hand over a brass bear on the desk, Popov resisted the urge to say something just to fill dead-air space. The less he said, the less trouble he'd have.

The next words hit him like bullets. "You let her escape?"

Popov jumped as though he'd been struck. "Yes, my general. She ran toward a policeman." He hesitated. "I can't afford trouble with American authorities. So I just kept an eye on her."

"Where is she?"

Popov gulped. "I don't know."

Prokofiev exploded. "Why didn't you shoot the American policeman and take her?"

Sweat formed on Popov's face. "No one authorized such extreme measures, General. My mission was to bring her in unharmed."

The general bellowed, "She must be captured. Whatever it takes, whatever it costs, she must be found immediately!"

"General," Popov said, panting, "why is she so important?"

A pause. Prokofiev spoke carefully. "If you repeat what you are about to hear, you will die. Is that understood?"

"Yes, my general."

Popov's breath left him as he listened. A few minutes later, perspiring freely, he set down the phone. The next time he found her, there would be no escape and no mercy for anyone who helped her.

CHAPTER SIXTEEN

Hanging up the phone, Jonathan wore a worried frown. Over the past three days, he'd left more than a dozen messages on Laura's answering machine, and she'd never returned his calls. Today, a computerized voice told him the tape was full.

His renewed fellowship with the Lord had caused him to think about many things—especially Laura. He wanted desperately to ask her forgiveness. He stared at green intertwining vines on the den's wallpaper. Where could she be?

Still using a cane, but with hardly a trace of his limp showing, he left the den, passed a suitcase in the hall, and found Andrea at the kitchen table. She stopped sipping Coke from a can long enough to smile when he strode in. "You're sure looking good," she said with a teasing smile.

"Thanks to you. Those exercises worked miracles."

Andrea nodded to the wheelchair folded up in the corner. "Not much use for that anymore."

"Nope." He held up his cane. "Another week, and this becomes an ornament for sympathy purposes only."

She watched him, a slant to her eyes. "Do you still have any use for me?"

Jonathan studied her face—the high cheekbones, the slim nose, the full, curved lips. Andrea was a candidate for a glamor magazine. But she had no spark, at least not to him. "You'll always be a good friend," he said.

"Hmm." Her head tilted to a provocative pose. "For some reason, that statement brings back memories from Bellingham High, two days before the prom." She stood and made a show of straightening her narrow skirt. "It's that woman that came here Monday morning, isn't it?"

When he didn't answer, she pulled out her most seductive smile. "Boy, she must really be under your skin."

"Deeper than that, Andrea," he said softly, his face serious.

She set down her soda can and moved toward him, Charlie perfume wafting with her. Her lips gently brushed his cheek, and he felt her breath when she said, "I hope she blows it big-time. If she does, you know where I am."

He started to speak, but she held up her hand. "Don't say anything. I hate these kinds of good-byes."

Jonathan let his lips curve upward a little and stepped aside for her to pass. The front door opened, then closed. Waiting for the sound of her car crunching gravel in the driveway, he paced to the front door where he pulled on his cowboy boots and slipped into a sheepskin-lined jean jacket.

He found Perkins in the front yard watching Andrea's cherry-colored Camero disappear into the trees.

"Sam," Corrigan called.

Perkins turned toward him, a pleasant expression on his craggy face. "Yeah, Jon?"

Holding the rail, Jonathan stepped down the ramp. "I've been trying to reach Laura McIvor since Monday. When I phoned this morning, her answering machine was full. She's not picking up her messages."

Perkins's wide shoulders moved. "Maybe she went on vacation."

"She didn't seem in a holiday mood when she was here," Corrigan said, running a hand through his dark hair. "In any case, I'm concerned. I want you to come with me to her apartment."

Striding fifty feet down the driveway, Perkins got into the navy Caprice the FBI had assigned to him and backed the car closer to Jonathan.

Twenty minutes later, they parked in front of Laura's apartment building and got out. Jonathan looked over the parking lot. "What kind of car did the report say she drives?"

"A red Ford Tempo."

Corrigan nodded toward the battered Ford Tempo in the parking lot and walked toward it, Perkins following him. They leaned over to peer at the slashed interior. "What a mess," Corrigan said. His internal trouble alarm was screeching like a wounded cat.

BETRAYED

"Someone was searching for something," Perkins commented.

"Go to the head of the class," Corrigan said, straightening. He gazed at the brick apartment building.

Perkins said, "I know you're gone on that girl, but with her background, there's no telling what she might be involved in."

Corrigan's frown deepened. "If she was up to something, why'd she barge in on me? That would only attract attention."

Perkins chuckled. "She got your attention, all right."

Corrigan sent him a wry smile and tapped the dented fender. "The car's here, so she should be at home. Let's check out her apartment."

Crossing the lot, Perkins tried the doorknob, but it wouldn't give. "Locked," he muttered.

"What kind of apartment building is this?" Corrigan asked, looking around. "There's no panel to buzz in a visitor."

Perkins pounded on the door. When no one came, he pounded again, the window rattling.

"Hey, careful; you're going to break it."

Perkins leaned out to look up and down the street, ending with a hard stare at Corrigan. "You really want to get in there, don't you?"

"C'mon, Perkins, ask me something you don't already know."

The big man reached for Corrigan's cane. "Glass can't cost that much." He jabbed the handle of the cane at the window, and the glass shattered.

Corrigan looked up at the sky. "I can't believe you just did that."

Perkins grinned. "Service is our guarantee." He started to slip his hand through the opening to unlock the door, when the apartment closest to them flew open.

"Just great," Corrigan said in a stage whisper. "Now you've done it."

A grizzled old man staggered into the hallway. He glared at them. "What's going on here?" he rasped.

Perkins pointed down the street. "Some kids just threw a rock at us, and it hit the door. What kind of neighborhood is this?"

"A tough one. What do you want?"

Holding up his badge, Perkins asked, "Who are you?"

The old fellow glanced at the ID. "My name's Iverson. I'm the landlord. What are you guys after?"

"We're here to see. . ." Perkins looked over at Corrigan.

"Shannon Masterson," Corrigan finished. "Would you mind letting us in?"

Iverson opened the door. "It's about time you guys showed up," he said.

Perkins glanced at Corrigan, then said, "Why do you say that?"

"I phoned the Bellingham police when she left with that Russkie. They forgot to send anyone over." He rubbed a hand over his month-old T-shirt. "I'm glad the Bureau's on it."

Corrigan moved into the lobby and sat on the steps. He'd learned to conserve his energy as much as possible. "You're talking about Miss Masterson leaving with a stranger?"

"Who else?" Iverson asked, stepping toward Jonathan. The old man's breath was ninety proof. "Last Monday afternoon, I heard someone coming downstairs. I'd just changed the lock, so I came to the door to give her the new key, but she didn't want it.

"She had this guy with her. He was shorter than you," he nodded at Perkins, "and older. I didn't like the looks of him, I tell you. I asked if everything was all right, and she said, 'Yes,' but she didn't sound like herself. When I asked who the guy was, he said he was an old family friend."

His face crinkled into a wise expression. "He didn't fool me none. He called her Laura, not Shannon." The old man grinned at Perkins. "I just look stupid. I see a lot more than people give me credit for."

"I don't doubt it," said Perkins.

"Sure, you do." Iverson pointed to the glass on the floor. "If some kids threw a rock, where's the rock?"

Perkins shifted his feet. "I guess I owe you for a window."

Iverson waved a hand, dismissing the idea. "Not if you find Shannon, you don't. She's a great kid. If anything's happened to her, I'll be mighty tore up."

"Can we see her apartment?" Corrigan asked.

"Sure thing." He reached for the fist-size bundle of rattling keys hanging from his belt. "It's on the second floor."

Standing aside so Iverson could pass him on the narrow stairs, Jonathan followed him with Perkins at the rear. Steadying himself with the banister, Jonathan kept up with the old man. His leg took the punishment fairly well.

The upstairs hall was dim even on a bright afternoon. Iverson led them to number 212 and unlocked the door. Stepping inside, Jonathan drew up short, a dull ache coming up on the left side of his chest. What Laura must have endured all these months, living in a place like this when she was used to luxury.

Across the room, the mattress on the bed was a shredded lump. The sagging green sofa had its cushions sliced and gutted. A makeshift mattress lay in the center of the room on a matted brown carpet.

"I've been meaning to take that mattress away for her," Iverson said, rubbing what was left of his thinning white hair. "I'll have to get a truck to come and get it."

"When did that happen?" Corrigan asked as he moved into the room.

"Sunday afternoon around two she came down and got me because someone broke her lock. I came up with her and found this." He shook his head, his whiskery jowls quivering. "She didn't deserve it, Mister. That Miss Masterson is a first-rate lady."

"Jon, look at this," Perkins said from a doorway to the right.

Iverson followed Corrigan into the kitchenette where Perkins stood over a spot of dried blood on the floor and a baseball bat with a stain to match.

"Any ideas about this?" Corrigan asked Iverson.

"That bat's mine. I lent it to her for protection. I don't know about the blood. Neither of them looked hurt when they left here."

"You said you heard banging around up here?"

"Yeah."

Perkins pulled the tiny fridge away from the wall. A sharp squeal made him jump back as a large rat shot across the floor. He jerked, stifling a scream.

Corrigan chuckled. "She probably nailed a rat and made that spot."

"I hate those things," Perkins muttered, wiping his hands against each other.

Corrigan prowled around the apartment. The place was rough, but he could feel Laura's presence here. He opened the closet door and smelled Elige perfume on the hanging clothes. Some things never changed.

He picked up the stuffed bear from the small dresser and stared at the taped repair on its abdomen. "Whoever trashed the place did a thorough job." He set the bear down. "I hope to meet them someday." His voice was low, threatening.

The two men poked around for half an hour. "Not much to go on," Perkins said, kneeling to peer under the ruined sofa. He reached under it, then jerked his hand back and cursed as a rat raced out.

"You got something?" Corrigan asked.

"Nah," Perkins said, getting to his feet. "All that's under there is a dusty rat's nest." He sent Corrigan a meaningful look. "If you want to sift through it, go right ahead. I'm not sticking my hand under there again."

Corrigan turned to Iverson. "You wouldn't happen to know where she works, would you?"

"PTL Computers by Meridian and Monroe."

"Want to go there next?" Perkins asked, getting to his feet.

Corrigan considered. "Let's stop by the police station first. I'd like to know why they never came."

As they left the apartment, Corrigan had an uneasy feeling in his stomach. *Laura, where are you?*

Ten minutes later, Perkins wheeled the Caprice into one of the visitors' slots at the Bellingham Police Station.

When they reached the front desk, a uniformed officer with a gray flattop haircut yawned and looked up. "Can I help you gentle. . .Mr. Corrigan, what a surprise!" He turned and yelled into the back of the building. "Hey guys, Corrigan's here!"

Jonathan rubbed the back of his neck, partially hiding his face as half a dozen uniformed and plainclothes officers came out, some smiling, some simply curious.

"Good job on those Iraqis," the desk sergeant said, beaming. "You made us proud."

"Thanks, guys," Corrigan said, trying to squelch the flush he felt rising over his face. "Actually, I'm here on business."

A tall man with thick eyebrows and coal-gray eyes stepped forward, extending his hand. "I'm Detective Carswell. Why don't we go into my office?"

The detective led them down a hallway to a room the size of a walk-in closet without a single window. He motioned for each of them to take a seat in a metal folding chair in front of a metal desk strewn with papers.

"Who's your friend?" Carswell asked Jonathan.

Perkins dropped his badge on the desk. Carswell held it up. "FBI, huh?" He closed the blue case and handed it back. "What can I do for you?"

Corrigan said, "We're here to talk about Shannon Masterson. You got a missing persons report on her a few days ago."

Sitting behind the desk, the detective rubbed his face. "The name doesn't ring a bell." He picked up his phone. "Hang on a second."

Pressing a couple of buttons, he said, "Kowalski, come in here for a minute, will you?"

Less than a minute later, the desk sergeant appeared at the door.

Carswell asked him, "Does the name Shannon Masterson mean anything to you?"

Kowalski nodded, showing a thin spot on top of his head. "That's the girl Anderson's been dating."

Carswell's face lightened. "Oh, yeah, Wesley's girl."

"Does Officer Anderson know that Miss Masterson is missing?" Perkins asked.

"She's not missing," Kowalski said, stepping into the room.

"We just talked to her landlord, a Mr. Iverson," Corrigan said. "He reported her missing, and your department took no action."

Both Bellingham officers laughed. "Iverson?" Carswell said, leaning back in his creaky chair. "That guy sees a crook under every pinecone. We've got a whole file dedicated to him. I wouldn't take him too seriously, Corrigan."

"No one even bothered to talk to the guy?" Perkins asked.

Kowalski nodded. "Wesley did. He phoned Iverson and told him that Shannon was with him."

"Can we speak to Officer Anderson?" Corrigan asked.

Carswell said, "He's taken a week's vacation."

"Personally, I think he and the girl went to Vancouver or something," Kowalski offered.

Corrigan bristled. "That doesn't sound like Miss Masterson."

The slant to Carswell's smile made him look sly. "You don't know Wesley. He can really charm them."

Kowalski added, "He's got that innocent-puppy look that girls go for. A real heartbreaker."

"Listen," Carswell said, "she's dating Wesley, so you don't have to worry about her. If she were missing, we'd all be pounding the pavement right now."

Corrigan stood and picked up his cane. "When Officer Anderson comes in, would you have him call me?" he asked, stepping away from the chair.

"No problem," Carswell said, standing to shake hands. "It's great to have you home, Jonathan."

Corrigan shook a few more hands as he and Perkins left the building.

When they got into the car, Corrigan sat staring at the latch on the glove box.

"I guess you don't know her as well as you thought," Perkins said, fitting his key into the ignition.

Hearing him as from a distance, Corrigan didn't answer.

Putting the car into reverse, Perkins hesitated. "You want to go home now?"

Corrigan came out of his stupor. "Let's go to PTL Computers first."

Easing out of the parking lot, Perkins glanced at the glum man beside him. "I take it you're not satisfied."

"Just drive, will you?" Corrigan growled.

Perkins drove.

When Perkins and Corrigan entered the well-lighted display room of PTL Computers, a wide woman with a wide smile came from behind the counter and held out her hand. "Jonathan Corrigan, you're looking so well. Praise God."

Corrigan peered at her. "You know me?" he asked.

"Don't you remember me? Olivia Donner. I taught your sixth-grade Sunday school class."

Jonathan took another look. Miss Donner. He remembered now. She was fifty pounds lighter back then, but that big smile was the same. She used the power of home-baked chocolate chip cookies to keep the boys in line.

"I remember you now," he said, grinning. "Keep in mind I was only twelve then." Suddenly, he gasped, engulfed in a big hug with no advance warning.

"It's so good to see you walking," she gushed when she let him go. She turned toward Perkins. "Are you with him?"

The tall man held out his badge. "Special Agent Perkins, FBI."

Olivia looked shocked. She turned to Corrigan. "Have I done something?"

Jonathan said, "We're here about Shannon Masterson. I understand she works for you."

"That's right." Olivia stumped to a chair beside the register. "Shannon's a jewel."

"Has she been to work recently?" Perkins asked.

"Not since Monday."

"Has she called?" Corrigan asked, stepping closer to her.

"No, but Wesley did." She glanced from one man to the other, a frown creasing her brow. "He said Shannon needed some time off. I wasn't surprised. She was a real mess Monday morning, even came in late. She and Wesley must have had a huge fight."

"What makes you say that?" Corrigan asked.

"They were man-trouble tears, Jonathan." She cocked an eyebrow, coquettish in spite of her size and said, "A woman knows, Dear."

Corrigan felt a jolt in his middle but tried to hide it. Laura's tears were from Jonathan trouble at the farm. Noticing how closely Olivia watched him, he moved on to another question. "How well does she know Wesley?"

Olivia glanced at a wall calendar beside her, moving a red fingernail along the large numbers, remembering. "The first time she mentioned him was Monday morning." She tapped the paper, then dropped her hand. "She had a kind of dreamy expression when she spoke his name."

Jonathan didn't want to know more, but he had to. What if she was in trouble? "Do you think she knew him well enough to go away with him for a whole week?"

Olivia looked doubtful. "Jonathan, I don't think Shannon's that kind of a girl. She's been coming to my church and seems interested in the Lord. Of course, I can't say for sure what she would do."

"Is she a Christian?" He asked the question a little too quickly and a little too loud.

Olivia shook her curly head. "We talked about it, but she backed away." She looked from him to Perkins. "Why are you interested? Aren't you with the CIA?"

Jonathan backed away from the counter, smiling to soften his answer. "I'm sorry, Miss Donner, but I can't tell you. Thanks for your help." He glanced at Perkins.

The agent had picked up a computer game box from a nearby rack and was reading a back cover smeared with purple, laser-wielding aliens.

"You ready, Champ?" Corrigan asked, sarcastic.

Perkins dropped the box like it had scalded him and bustled out the door. Leaning on his cane, Jonathan followed with more dignity. He paused, touching the collapsible steel grate outside the doors, to wave good-bye as Olivia called after them, "Thanks for coming in!"

He caught up with Perkins on the sidewalk. "What now?" the agent asked, unlocking Jonathan's door for him.

"I guess we go home," Corrigan said with a deep sigh. "It looks like Laura did exactly what I told her to do. She's made a new life for herself."

Perkins put a hand on his shoulder. "Tough break."

As they headed home, Jonathan replayed the comments of all the parties they'd spoken to. The case seemed airtight. Laura had a boyfriend and went off for a vacation with him. He tried to dismiss it, but he couldn't. Something was wrong.

As the Caprice turned into his lane, Jonathan's shoulders sagged. *You haven't learned much in all your years with the agency,* he scolded himself. *The only thing wrong is that you don't like to think of Laura with another man. Face it, Chump, you blew it. You and Laura are history.*

Sprawled on top of her sleeping bag with a romance novel in her hands, Laura fought off discouraged tears. She'd been cooped up in this place for four days without a single breath of fresh air. The walls were closing in fast despite the shopping bag full of secondhand books Wesley had brought her. Even his evening visits were becoming a strain. Last night before he left, he'd grabbed her shoulders and tried to kiss her.

When she pulled away, he let her go, but anger sparked in his eyes. "What's the matter?" he demanded. "I thought we had something going."

Uncomfortable, she turned away. "I don't mean it that way, Wesley." She paused, then faltered, "It's just that. . ." How do you tell someone about a ghost from your past that refuses to stay buried?

When she didn't go on, Wesley slammed out without saying goodbye. Would he come back tonight or let her stew in this pot alone? Honestly, she didn't know which she preferred.

Her hand moved across the sleeping bag and a ragged nail caught on the fabric. In a sudden flash of temper, she muttered a word that would have shocked her mother and threw the romance novel at the towering stack on her bedside stand. They crashed into a heap on the rag that passed for a rug.

Using her teeth, she tried to correct the nail. If only she'd thought to pick up her purse, at least she'd have her nail file. Oh, how did she get into this predicament?

Lying back, staring at a crablike stain on the ceiling, she remembered the verse she'd asked Olivia about. She heard the young pastor quote it again, "Come unto Me all who are heavy laden, and I will give you rest."

BETRAYED

Or something like that.

Covering her eyes with her hand, she let out a deep sob. *God, are You there? I'm so scared, and I don't have anyplace left to turn. Every single person in my entire life has let me down. All I have left is You. If You're real, please give me a new life. I can't stand the old one anymore. Whatever You want for me, that's what I'll do. Just show me. Please!*

She rolled onto her stomach and buried her wet face in the stale pillowcase. Were there some special words she was supposed to say? *God, if I messed up that prayer, please let me know. I want what Olivia has. I want to belong to You.*

After awhile, her emotions exhausted, she slept deep and sound for the first time in days.

Headlights shone through the orange curtains and woke her. Blinking, Laura sat up and touched her tousled hair. That must be Wesley. A moment later, three knocks sounded on the door, two loud and one soft. Turning on the lamp, she fumbled with the lock, and the door swung in.

"Good news," he said, setting a fast-food bag beside the broken television. The smell of burgers and fries made Laura cringe. Not again.

She raked fingers through her bangs, sweeping them back. She must look a sight.

Wesley grinned down at her. "My FBI friends found the source of your trouble." He plopped into the only chair in the room. "It's some deep government operation."

Laura sat on the edge of the bed. "I was afraid of that."

He leaned his elbows on his knees. "The Feds want to talk to you."

She wasn't surprised. "When?"

"Tomorrow. They're setting up a safe house for you." He reached for her hand. "Best of all, you'll be under their protection. No one will be able to hurt you."

She wanted to cry from sheer relief, but she felt numb. "How will I get there. . .to the safe house?"

"I'll take you to meet the agents at ten in the morning."

She put a shaking hand to her forehead. "I can't believe it's over."

He moved next to her, their sides touching. "This will be your last night here." He touched her cheek. "It's also the last time we'll see each other for awhile. They told me I'll have to stay away for your safety."

He cradled her chin. "I care for you, Laura, like I've never cared for a woman before."

Mesmerized, Laura looked into his warm green eyes. She wanted to feel protected more than anything in the world. She ached for it.

Leaning down, tenderly pulling her chin, he aimed for her lips.

At the last second, Laura turned her face, and he kissed her cheek. Once, twice. Speaking against her skin, he murmured, "Laura."

Pulling away, she got to her feet, hugging her middle. "I'm sorry, Wesley, but I think you'd better go." Reaching for the doorknob, she pulled it open.

"Laura!" he said, exasperated. "Why?"

Between the door and the wall, she waited. "I'm just not that kind of girl. I'll be ready when you get here in the morning."

Muttering, he paused beside her as though deciding his next action. He raised the back of his hand to her cheek.

"Please!" she whispered, intense.

Closing the door after him, she slid the chain into the lock and leaned her head against the door. She felt awful for hurting Wesley. She should have explained her feelings instead of just throwing him out. He would have understood. Jonathan had.

Sitting on the bed, she rubbed her forehead with both hands, those dark chiseled features tormenting her again. With a deep moan, she threw herself onto her pillow. Why couldn't she erase Jonathan Corrigan from her mind and get on with her life?

BETRAYED

CHAPTER SEVENTEEN

After holding cupped hands over his white beard to blow on them, Harrison McIvor wrapped his prison-issue overcoat tightly around his thin chest. Wherever this was, the evenings were much cooler than they were in California.

The powers that be had moved him four times since his conviction two years ago—each time to a solitary jail block, each time with strict orders that he know nothing of his location. For that reason, they wouldn't let him into the exercise yard with the other inmates during the day. Instead, he got one hour at night. Shivering, he looked upward. He couldn't see the stars.

When the military had discovered that he'd tinkered with their computer systems, Federal marshals showed up at his cell and whisked him onto a Lear jet with the windows covered. Off they flew to. . .somewhere.

At first, he was terrified that his broad-shouldered marine-type escorts were really from the CIA or some foreign power. He wondered if he'd end up tortured or worse. But, they were legitimate. His strategy was working. In federal custody no one could touch him.

Cool air and high humidity told him the ocean wasn't far away. He guessed that he was somewhere on the Eastern Seaboard. Maybe the Feds wanted him near Washington. Still, he couldn't figure out why his location had to be such a grand mystery. It wasn't as if he could tell anyone even if he wanted to.

An orange dot glowed by the door to the segregated custody area, his entrance. Standing near it, Marv, his guard, called, "Time's up, McIvor." He had a voice like an iron griddle, flat and hard.

Harrison glanced at the sky, hoping for just one twinkling light, but only darkness showed overhead. He trudged across the yard, dampening his shoes in the dewy grass. Marv pulled open the door, and Harrison plodded down the concrete hallway that led to his home.

With Marv following five feet behind him, they made a right into a block of ten cells, five on each side of a narrow aisle. Each cell's front wall consisted of steel bars painted a muddy yellow. The stench of an unwashed toilet made it difficult to breathe. McIvor had almost forgotten the meaning of privacy.

He paced to the middle cell on the left, the sole occupant on the block except for Marv, who would spend the evening sitting in a chair on the other side of the bars. No television, no books, no radio. Just Marv.

"Open cell five," Marv called to the two guards at the outer door.

A deep, grating buzz, and the door slid back. Harrison McIvor plodded inside, hands in his coat pockets. The door slid shut with a thump. On a small stand in front of him sat a tin plate filled with cold meat loaf, mashed potatoes coated with congealed gravy, and a limp salad—his supper. Pulling off his coat, he sat on the cot and picked up his fork.

A wide man with a paunch, Marv sank into his metal folding chair, his eyes on the prisoner.

"Do you think the Phillies will do much this year?" Harrison asked him, lifting a cube of potatoes. His voice was husky with a cultured undertone.

Marv's pudgy cheeks swelled as he chuckled. "Nice try, McIvor. You find out my favorite sports team, and you'll know where you are." He leaned back and crossed his arms across his belly. "No soap."

McIvor pressed the side of his fork into a slab of meat loaf. "If we can't talk about sports, what can we talk about?"

Marv leaned forward in his chair, resting one elbow on his knee. "If you really wanna talk, you could tell me what all this fuss is about. Why are you on ice?"

Harrison shook his head. "I'm sorry, my friend. That is top secret. In fact, I believe you were ordered not to ask me about it."

Marv smiled. "Yeah, but a guy can always try. Listen, there is one thing that has always bugged me."

McIvor shoved away his plate. Two bites of that stuff was more than enough. "What is it?" he asked Marv.

"Is it true what they said in the papers? That you betrayed your country for nothing but money?"

Harrison looked up at the yellow bulb set into the ceiling and protected by a steel web. He turned to Marv, his voice stiff and emotionless. "Yes," he said, "it is true."

"I thought you computer guys made tons of money. How much does one man need?"

Harrison ran slim fingers over his beard, feeling it carefully. It needed a trim. "I earned two hundred thousand dollars a year for restoring integrity to our high-tech defense systems while children barely out of their teens were bringing in millions from websites and computer games." He smiled, a sad expression. "I'm afraid I wanted to even the score."

Marv peered at him as though trying to figure him out. "What about your family? Weren't you worried about what would happen to them if you were caught?"

"No one plans to get caught." Harrison clenched his teeth, highly insulted at Marv's question, and all the while knowing that he was lying. He'd always known he'd be caught. The espionage money was supposed to hide his wife and daughter until he got out of prison. He'd planned his release, too. That still lay ahead.

"But you did get caught," Marv said. "What happened to your daughter? Where is she now? I saw her picture once. She's gorgeous."

McIvor picked up his plate and flung it at the bars. Gravy and potato flecked Marv's brown khaki uniform. He jumped out of his chair, turning it over. "Hey! Watch it!" He swelled up like he wanted to fight. Then slowly a wary, knowing expression came across his face. He righted his chair to sit down again. Leaning back, he brought an ankle up to lay across his wide knee.

Ignoring him, Harrison pulled off his shoes and damp socks. He stretched out on the cot with his back to the bars. He wasn't worried about a reprimand for his outburst. What more could they do to him, put him in a black hole?

He slept lightly and awoke to the tramp of heavy footsteps coming down the hall. Turning over, he shielded his eyes from sudden brilliant light. Marv and Ellard—one of the other guards—stood beside his cell with a short, heavy man dressed in an expensive suit and a black overcoat.

Marv said, "Your lawyer showed up at the gate with a court order allowing him to visit you."

McIvor studied the man's face. He had a broad forehead, thick lips, and black coals for eyes. "He isn't my lawyer," the old gentleman said, sitting up. "I've never seen him before."

Marv and Ellard stared at him, their faces blank. "Open cell five," Marvin loudly called.

At the buzz, the door opened. The three men rushed in and tackled the scientist. He lashed out and caught Ellard on the jaw. The guard's head snapped back, and he went down. Marv took over and landed his bulk on the older man, knocking the breath from his chest.

McIvor's fist crashed into the face of the fake lawyer who, unfazed, fastened a handcuff around his wrist, then clipped the cuff to the bed rail above his head. He grabbed McIvor's other arm and pinned it to the bed as well.

"What are you doing?" McIvor demanded, frothing at the mouth as he continued to flail his legs, trying to clobber one of them with a number ten shoe.

Back on his feet, Ellard helped Marv grab McIvor's ankles and shackle them to the bed.

The prisoner shouted, "If anything happens to me, there'll be so much heat you'll never live to spend the money you're getting for this!"

Marv leaned over him, his face contorted. "We know exactly how important you are. But by the time you're discovered, we'll be out of reach." He yanked open the button on McIvor's sleeve cuff and pulled the cloth upward about six inches. Turning to the newcomer, he said, "Mr. Chekov, he's all yours."

As Marv and Ellard stepped back, Chekov sat on the edge of the bed. It squealed under the combined weight of both men. McIvor could smell his own fear.

"You may wait down the hall," Chekov called over his shoulder to the guards. He had a slow Midwestern drawl of practiced precision. With the air of a man who has the situation under control, he turned his attention to the prisoner.

"Dr. McIvor, I'm here to learn the encryption code."

Harrison spat out, "The price is ten billion dollars."

Chekov shook his head sadly. "You don't understand. I came to get the key, and I won't leave without it." He slipped a slim, black case from his overcoat pocket and unzipped it. Light glinted off two hypodermic needles nestled in velveteen. "Perhaps this will help you remember." He pulled one of the needles from its loop, squirted a stream of clear liquid

BETRAYED

into the air, and lowered it to the inside of McIvor's bare forearm.

Jonathan limped down a California beach, his game leg moving heavily across the sand. His surroundings were familiar yet strange—dark waves lashing at the sand, the sky rolling with heavy clouds, a foggy mist swirling about his knees. A wicked wind ruffled his dark hair and pierced his flesh with chilly fingers. He was alone and terribly lonely.

From behind him came laughter, two voices mingling into one. Jonathan whirled around, his body twisting awkwardly to swing his left leg forward. It was Laura, her copper hair glinting though there was no sun, her emerald eyes flashing, her smile dazzling. . .but not for him.

A tall, dark man without a face walked beside her. Arm in arm, they ambled toward Jonathan, so lost in each other they didn't notice him. Shoulders back, head erect, Jonathan stared, a loud roaring in his ears that didn't come from the raging surf.

Finally, Laura looked up and her expression changed. "Jonathan, what are you doing here?"

"Walking," he said, his heart hammering.

She looked at his leg and laughed. "Walking? With that dead stump?"

Jonathan turned to go.

"Wait!" Her voice sounded breathy and unreal. "You have to meet Wesley," she said.

Faceless Wesley held out his hand. Jonathan's fingers formed a fist. He drew it back, but before he could land a punch, Laura and Wesley faded into the silver mist; their shrill, mocking laughter clawing at his vitals.

Thunder pounded the house as Jonathan pulled himself from the nightmare. The second loud bang jolted him awake—a slamming door, not a storm. Roxanne's loud, angry voice followed with his mother's as loud and firm, then feet thumping and more slamming.

Jonathan slid out of bed. His left leg wasn't the dead stump in his dream. It was a tingly nuisance. He couldn't do the long jump anymore, but who wanted to anyway?

Slipping on his bathrobe, he left his room to see what had destroyed peace in the valley on a bright Saturday morning. As he opened the bedroom door, the dream still weighed him down. He'd found Laura only to lose her again. Maybe Perkins was right. Maybe she'd changed. He let out a heavy sigh. Somehow he couldn't accept it.

He met his mother at the bottom of the stairs. "What's up, Mom?"

he asked her.

She frowned. "Roxanne and I had a difference of opinion."

"A difference! The whole house rattled."

She sent him a calculating look. "Why don't you ask her about it?"

Catching her signal, Jonathan took the cue and, mahogany cane in hand, made his way up the straight staircase to the next floor. He knocked on the first door to the right and opened it at a muffled, "Come in!"

Roxanne looked up at him from her seat on the edge of her single bed, tears smudging her face. Jonathan stepped into a world of stuffed animals, horse pictures, and frilly girl stuff, another reminder of Laura. Gus came over to meet him.

"Hey, Kid, what's up?" he asked, bending to touch the dog's head.

"She says I can't ride Duke today." Roxanne sniffled into a tissue.

"That's odd. Why not?"

Her words came in a rush. "Because I got up an hour late and didn't go out and feed him right away." She sniffed. "She wanted me to go to youth group last night. Is it my fault we were bowling until two in the morning? Give me a break! I only had four hours of sleep.

"One hour wouldn't matter," she went on. "I was going to feed him as soon as I could." She flung her tissue into the trash can. "I don't understand."

Jonathan held up his hand. "Okay, Roxanne, I get it." He sat in the white wicker chair beside the bed. Gus lay down on the rug at the end of the bed. "I hate to tell you this, but I agree with her."

"But. . ."

"Let me finish. Duke is an old horse. I admit that missing his hay and grain by an hour or so every now and then won't hurt him, but that's not the point." He softened his tone. "He's locked in his stall, Roxanne. He depends on you to feed him. For that hour while you're sleeping, he's anxious, wondering when you'll come. It's not fair to him."

Roxanne huffed. "I said I was sorry. It's a beautiful Saturday." She gestured toward brilliant sunlight streaming through her gauzy curtains. "What else can I do with my day?"

He leaned back, the wooden cane resting against his thigh. "You can forget about riding. Mom won't give in on that one even if I demand it. However, you can still do things with Duke that aren't technically riding."

She brightened. "What?"

"You had breakfast yet?"

"A piece of toast. I'm not really that hungry."

"Go out and get him saddled, but don't put on his bridle. I'll meet you out there in a few minutes."

"Okay!" She reached for her dirt-stained sneakers on the rug beside the bed.

Jonathan returned to his room to dress, then he hit the kitchen. Since his mobility had improved, the kitchen had become self-service. Grabbing a bowl from an oak cabinet, he poured himself some dry cereal, added milk, and sat down at the table. He caught a glimpse of his mother hurrying down the hall wearing green overalls with a red bandanna over her hair.

"Not talking?" he called out.

She came back to the doorway. "Sorry, Son. It's Billy and Ida's day off, and I've got to do the milking."

"Hey, want some help?"

She shook her head. "Bending under cows to hook up milking machines wouldn't be good for your stomach. I've been doing it alone for plenty of years now. Besides, Danny said he'll be over later; he can help with the evening milking."

"Why don't you get Roxanne to help?"

Sandra Corrigan stepped into the kitchen. "No. I won't ask her to do that."

"I bet she'd be thrilled to do it."

Her mouth formed a firm line. "When I first brought Roxanne home, you know what people said?"

Jonathan didn't answer. What people said never bothered him.

"They said, 'Good idea, Sandra. You need help around the farm.'"

"So?"

"I took her in because the Lord said to. She's not a servant." She adjusted the bandanna over her right ear. "And just so you know, the state pays me a fixed allowance to meet her needs. Every penny of it is sitting in a separate bank account for her college. I don't want anyone to ever say I took advantage of Roxanne."

Cradling his red cereal bowl in both hands, Jonathan grinned at her. "You bucking for sainthood or something?"

She smiled and sent a playful swat to his cheek. "I'm already a saint, Son. I'm just trying to follow the Lord as best I can." She turned toward the door. "See you at lunch."

By the time he finished his breakfast, fought with his cowboy boots, and got out to the barn, Roxanne had Duke saddled and waiting. He grabbed a coiled-up line and a whip from the tack room. The smell of leather took him back to his teenage days and made him want to ride.

When he reached the corral, Roxanne looked at his hand and asked, "What's that for?"

He held them up. "This is a lunge line and whip to put Duke through his paces without getting on his back."

Leading Duke to the edge of the corral, Jonathan attached the line to his halter and led him to the center. He flicked the whip behind Duke, and the horse began to move at an easy walk. As he worked, Jonathan gave Roxanne instructions. Ten minutes later, in a sweat, he called, "Whoa!" to Duke, then summoned Roxanne into the corral, saying, "Here, you take over. I'm beat."

Retreating to a cedar lawn chair with Gus at his side, Jonathan watched Roxanne put into practice what he'd taught her. The girl had a natural gift. After about fifteen minutes, she stopped Duke and turned to him. "Why did you want me to saddle him?"

He grinned like a kid. "Unhook the lunge line and get the bridle."

When Roxanne returned, he said, "Put it on him."

Her face questioning, she slipped the bridle over Duke's head. She glanced at Jonathan. "You're going to let me ride, aren't you?"

He got to his feet, smiling. "Not a chance. If I crossed Mom, she'd have me in the woodshed." He moved toward her. "That's for me."

She glanced at his cane. "You sure you can?"

"Nope, but I'm sick and tired of watching you have all the fun."

Approaching the animal from the right side, he said, "Most people mount from the left, but I don't have a choice." He handed her his cane. "When I get up, I may need you to push my left leg over." Sticking the toe of his cowboy boot into the right stirrup, Jonathan pushed himself up. As he feared, he couldn't quite bend his left knee enough to clear Duke's rump. Roxanne reached from the left side to pull his bad leg over the rest of the way and stuck his boot into the other stirrup.

"Thanks," he said. "Now hand me my cane. I may need it if I fall off."

Roxanne passed it up to him. "You look good up there," she said grudgingly.

He felt good, too. It had been years since he sat astride Duke. Clucking his tongue, Jonathan set the horse into an easy walk. He knew that being in the saddle at all was pushing the limit, so he kept the pace slow. Boyhood memories rushed back—rodeo ribbons, long trail rides with his father. He waited for his chest to tighten, for the old pain to wash over him. Instead, he felt soft warmth and gentle joy.

With Gus trailing them, he headed Duke out of the corral and onto bush trails that had doubled as much-used dirt-bike tracks in his younger days. Out of sight of the house, he felt great. In the past week, he'd healed much faster than anyone had expected. Yesterday, Dr. Parker had told Jonathan he was a couple of weeks ahead of schedule. Maybe all that praying was doing some good, after all.

On his way back to the stable, the sound of a loud muffler reached him through the woods. The hair on his back standing up, Gus growled deep in his throat, then barked. Jonathan urged the horse to a faster pace.

Emerging from the trees, he saw an orange Mustang parked by the front ramp. Three teenage toughs stood in a half circle around Roxanne. The one in the center wore baggy corduroy pants and an oversized combat jacket. As big as Jonathan, he had his shoulders far back, chest out, chin up. Roxanne had the same stance.

Setting off at a full run, Gus barked his way toward the intruders. Setting Duke up to a trot, Jonathan reached them as Roxanne grabbed Gus's collar and held him back.

"What's up, Roxanne?" Jonathan asked.

Eyes on the ground, she didn't answer. Gus was doing all the talking for her.

Calling the dog down, Corrigan turned his attention to the teenagers wearing leather jackets and gold earrings. They looked like reform-school rejects. "I'm Jonathan Corrigan," he said. "Who are you?"

"I used to hang around with them," Roxanne answered, keeping a tight hold on Gus's collar. "This is Kurt, my old boyfriend." She nodded toward the eyebrow-pierced soldier wannabe whose black hair looked like a thorny bush.

Jonathan held out his hand. "Hi, Kurt." The teenager ignored him and spoke to Roxanne. "I'm not her old boyfriend. I'm still your boyfriend, Roxanne."

Jonathan slipped his left foot out of the stirrup. "Roxanne, give me a hand here, will you?"

Darting quick glances at her friends, Roxanne helped him get off Duke, and he reached up for his cane.

"You a gimp or something?" Kurt asked, eyeing the stick.

"Yeah," Corrigan answered. "I've got a bum leg." He stepped closer to Roxanne and asked, "How do you all know each other?"

"These are the guys I almost went to detention with," she murmured, shying back. Gus let out a single menacing bark.

"Did you just get out?" Jonathan asked them, letting his eyes pause on each of them. The one on the right had his head shaved on the sides with a thick hank of hair on top. The other had a greasy, slicked-back look from the fifties. They reeked of body odor and cheap cologne.

Jonathan spoke to Roxanne. "Are they still your friends?"

She squinted at Kurt, her eyes burning. "No!"

Kurt puffed up his shoulders a few millimeters more. "It ain't that simple, Roxy. You just don't unjoin the gang." He tried to reason with her. "Besides, we were good together. You know that."

Corrigan took a step toward Kurt, only three feet separating them. "You'd best go."

Kurt swore and shuffled his army boots on the grass. "Why are you butting in? She ain't nothing to you but a street punk you took in like a stray dog."

"Wrong, Pal." Jonathan stared into the boy's dark eyes. "She's my sister."

Kurt looked at Roxanne. "Roxy ain't got no brother."

Jonathan glanced over at the girl beside him. "Is that right, Roxanne?"

She looked smug. "He's my brother, Kurt."

"See, Punk." Jonathan bore down. "Playtime's over. You guys get out of here and leave my sister alone."

Kurt raised his fists. "Who's going to make me, Gimp? You?"

Jonathan's eyes narrowed. He stepped back. "Take your best shot, Kid."

Kurt faked with a left, then sent his right fist flying at Jonathan's face. Corrigan caught it with his right hand as if the punch had just been a throw to first base. Jonathan squeezed his steel-like fingers between Kurt's knuckles until sweat broke out on the boy's forehead.

Jonathan bent Kurt's hand back, driving him to his knees as a blue Windstar pulled up to the house. No one noticed but Jonathan. All were too mesmerized by the battle of wills.

Finally, Kurt let out a grunt, fell to his knees, and pulled his fist away. Springing to his feet, he assumed a boxing stance, pumping his fists before his chin. "Okay, big man, let's see if you can take all three of us."

Jonathan held up his hand. "No, please. I don't think I can do that."

Kurt laughed. "Then back off."

Jonathan scratched the side of his face. "Be reasonable, fellas, and you'll

BETRAYED

save yourself some trouble. Don't you ever watch the news or read a paper?"

Covering her mouth, Roxanne stifled a giggle.

The boys crowded closer to Corrigan. "You getting out of the way, Gimp?" Kurt said. "Or are we moving you?"

Holding up both hands, palms out, Corrigan said, "Let's be clear about what you're getting into here before you jump me. My name is Jonathan Corrigan, and I work for the CIA. That bruiser standing behind you is Roxanne's other brother, Danny Corrigan, of the Seattle police."

All three of them looked back. . .then up. . .way up.

"Hi, guys," Danny said, beaming good humor. He looked at Jonathan. "We got a problem here, Bro?"

Kurt and company moved closer together. The one on the left touched the back of his hand to his mouth. "Is this for real?" Kurt asked.

Jonathan said, "Roxanne is our little sister. If you toughs so much as spit in her direction, we'll make you hurt in places you never even knew you had." He jabbed his cane toward Kurt's middle. "Got it?"

Kurt looked at Roxanne as though trying to think of a parting jab.

"Get out of here!" Corrigan said. "I'm giving you ten seconds."

They shuffled off, trying to act as if they weren't in a hurry, but moving fast anyway. Ducking into the Mustang, Kurt waited until the third guy slammed his door before he peeled out, showering stones into the lawn.

Roxanne turned to Jonathan. "Did you mean what you said?"

"Every word," he answered, smiling softly.

"Goes for me, too," Danny said, stepping near them. "You're part of the family, Roxanne. We want it that way."

"I'm so sorry for this," she said, tucking loose hair behind her ear. "I tried to get rid of them before you came back, but they wouldn't go. I kept telling them that I'm not that kind of girl anymore." She picked up Duke's lead. Dropping her grip on Gus, she led both horse and dog toward the barn.

Suddenly, Jonathan's head jerked, startled. Of course! Laura wasn't that kind of girl, either! How could he have been so blind?

"Danny," he said, excitedly, "I know you came to do the milking, but I need some help. It's Perkins's day off, and I've gotta do something that just can't wait."

"Sure, Bro," Danny said, pulling out his keys. "Where to?"

At that moment, Wesley turned his Toyota Camry down a gravel road.

BETRAYED

Sitting beside him, Laura said, "I'm surprised they're having the meeting anywhere near Bellingham." She chewed at a ragged thumbnail. "Aren't they afraid of being found?"

"Hey, we're talking about the FBI. If they're not worried, I'm not worried either. Besides, I think they plan to move you after I've gone. Last night was our last for awhile."

She put her hand on his arm. "I'm sorry, Wesley. I didn't mean to hurt you."

He covered her hand with his. "Don't worry about it. It's history."

They turned off the gravel road, then drove deep into a wooded area. When they pulled up to the safe house, Laura frowned at the mobile home. Its sheet-metal siding had pulled away in places. Rust stains streaked down the sides, and the front window was broken. The lawn was a patch of straggly weeds. "Is this the best they could do?" she asked.

"No one can see it," Wesley answered. "That's the whole point, isn't it?" He parked his car in the rutted driveway beside a dark limousine and a white Monte Carlo.

"A limousine?" Laura asked.

"You rate the top brass, my dear." He kissed her cheek. "Good-bye, Laura. I'll say it now before we have company."

She smiled into his eyes. "Thanks for your help, Wesley. I'll call you when this is over." Stepping out of the car, she drew in a deep breath of the pine-scented air. "I sure can't complain about the scenery."

Ten strides later, Wesley held open the mobile home door, and Laura walked in to face two men sitting in deep upholstered chairs, one bald and stocky, the other fine-featured, almost feminine.

"Come in, Miss McIvor," the thinner man said. "I've looked forward to meeting you." He held out his hand. "I'm Alistair Crane."

"Alistair Crane," Laura repeated, her senses on red alert. "You own Puget Information Systems."

"Precisely," he said. His thin lips curved into an icy smile.

She spun on her heels to go out, but Wesley stood against the door, powerful arms folded across his chest. "Wesley?" she squealed. "Where's the FBI?"

"Sorry, Laura," he said, avoiding her eyes. "I needed Uncle Alistair's help. In exchange, I had to solve a problem for him. You."

She went numb. This was impossible.

"Miss McIvor, you've gone white," Crane said. "Come, sit down." He

BETRAYED

189

waved a slender hand at the worn sofa. "We need to discuss your future."

As they drove to Laura's apartment, Jonathan told Danny about his relationship with Laura—all of it.

Danny scowled at a green light as they passed under it. "So, I take it you're suffering now," he said.

"That's a major understatement," Corrigan said.

"Serves you right." He turned the car into the parking lot. "If I'd done something like that to Rita, I wouldn't be able to sleep or eat—ever."

"I didn't know her at first," Corrigan said, defensive and angry. "After we got acquainted, I couldn't back out. I've been in a lose-lose situation since I first laid eyes on her." He jerked the door handle.

"Careful, Bro," Danny said. "You'll tear it off." He sized Jonathan up. "You've got it bad, don't you?" Opening his own door, he didn't wait for an answer.

They roused Iverson from a drunken stupor long enough to let them into Laura's apartment again. "Lock up when you're through," he said, then returned to his apartment to finish sleeping it off.

"You look under stuff," Jonathan said. "I can bend down with this leg, but I have a hard time getting back up."

They searched in silence for ten minutes. Jonathan looked in places he'd already seen five times. If only he knew what he was after.

"Say, what's that?" Danny said, peering under the couch. Standing, he walked around the sofa, its back facing the door. Bending down, he pulled out a black leather handbag, dusty, the handles broken.

"That looks like something the last tenant left," Jonathan said.

"Let's see what's inside," Danny said, unsnapping the clasp. Kneeling, he turned the purse upside down on the carpet. A wallet, a folded wad of bills, makeup, a key ring. He picked up the wallet and opened it. "Well, looky here," he drawled. He held it up to Jonathan.

"Laura's driver's license." Jonathan said, staring at the photograph. He flipped through the inner flaps. "Her credit cards, everything." He glanced at Danny. "She'd never leave this and go on vacation."

"I wonder how it got in such bad shape." Danny pulled at the loose straps.

"Or how it landed under the back of the couch."

"You know," Danny said, "it is possible that she and her boyfriend got so wrapped up in each other that they took off on the spur of the moment and she forgot her purse? Rita leaves hers everywhere."

"Not Laura." His statement had a definite ring.

"How can you be so sure?"

"When Roxanne said, 'I'm just not that kind of girl,' it hit me." He rubbed his hand across the black leather wallet. "Almost a year after I met Laura, I got a little too free and easy with her. She shut me right down. I can still hear her say, 'I'm just not that kind of girl.' "

He handed Danny the wallet. "If she turned me down after almost a year, she didn't say yes to someone after less than a week." He headed for the door. "Bring the purse along. We're going back to the police station and talk to that detective again. Someone is holding something back."

CHAPTER EIGHTEEN

Light-headed, Laura shambled to a matted couch which had two springs sticking through its brown upholstery. When one of the springs made contact with her tender flesh, her shock turned to anger. She turned on Crane. "Maybe we should talk about your future instead of mine. I know about the viruses you're installing into your customers' computers."

Crane steepled his fingers and tapped his mouth. Dropping his hands he smiled, well mannered and cold. "You are your father's equal, Miss McIvor. The way you repaired those systems—especially the one at Archon Energy—we knew you couldn't be a mere correspondence-school graduate.

"That's why we had to turn Wesley's irresistible charm loose on you." For an instant, he let his plastic smile move to Wesley at the door. "Thanks to his good work, we know who you are."

"So?" Laura demanded, chin high, ready to fight. She hadn't come this far to be hijacked by some two-bit crook.

Crane sobered. "How do you think the good people of Bellingham will react when they learn that Shannon Masterson is the daughter of world-famous traitors?"

Glancing from Crane to his fat, ugly friend, Laura said, "Is that what this is about? Blackmail?"

Still smiling, Crane nodded. "You are very astute."

Laura seemed to grow taller. "If I have to face up to my past, I'll do it. I have friends who care about me." Her stare focused on Crane. "At least what I am won't put me in jail. How about you?"

"I told you," the stocky man said to Crane.

Crane sighed. "You were correct, Mr. Dagg. She is pathetically honest."

Laura jumped to her feet. "I've had enough. I'm leaving." She marched to the door, but Wesley blocked her way. "Step aside, Wesley!"

"I can't, Laura," he muttered. Feet wide, his crossed arms warded her off.

"Yes, you can." She grabbed his wrists and pulled, but he stood like a marble statue.

Dagg spoke, his voice as rough as a bundle of tied weeds. "Miss McIvor, let me tell you the facts of life. Wesley likes to shoot dice. Last year he got into debt in Las Vegas. With the mob, no less. He'd be six feet under if Mr. Crane hadn't picked up his IOUs. Unfortunately, he's already run up a big tab in Seattle, and it's deja vu for poor Wesley."

Laura peered into the young policeman's red face. "Is that true?"

Turning his head away, he muttered, "Yeah."

Laura stepped to the center of the room and demanded, "Are you going to keep me a prisoner or what?" She curled up two fists. "If you hurt me, it'll be the biggest mistake you ever made. Someone else is looking for me, too. The CIA. They searched my apartment and my car." Her lips formed a straight line. "You're in over your head, Crane."

Both Crane and Dagg chuckled. Crane paused long enough to tell her, "We trashed your apartment and stole your car, so you'd run into Wesley's arms."

While they laughed, Laura wanted to wipe the smile off of Crane's face in the worst way, but she forced herself to think instead. There had to be some way out of this.

"Gentlemen," Dagg called down the hall, "please come in." A door opened, and the fight suddenly went out of Laura. Her knees buckled as her Russian kidnapper paced toward her, followed by two dark-haired bodybuilders.

Her stone-faced enemy clasped her arm. "Miss McIvor, you cause me much trouble," he said, his voice guttural.

"Meet Alex Popov, agent of the Russian Federation," Crane said. "When Wesley told us some Russians were after you, well, we just couldn't resist. We had to know exactly who. Fortunately, Mr. Dagg has some. . . useful contacts. It took a few days, but we learned who was looking for you, and—what a surprise—their problem solves ours."

She glanced from Popov to Crane. "What's going to happen to me?"

"We have Mr. Popov's word that within hours you will be on your way

BETRAYED

to Russia and out of our way. As a bonus, he's already put a million dollars into a numbered account." He tapped manicured fingers on his cashmere lapel. "You've been a very profitable venture. We do thank you."

Laura turned to Popov. "If you think I'm going to stay quiet while you haul me through the airport, you can forget it."

Popov shook his head. "We have a ship leaving Seattle tonight. You can help us with our problem while we sail."

"What problem?" Laura asked. What on earth could she do to help the Russians—even if she wanted to?

Popov didn't answer.

"That concludes our business," Crane said, standing. Ever the gentleman, he held out his hand to shake on the deal.

Popov said, "As agreed, we leave first, and you wait here five minutes. Yes?"

"Yes," said Crane, nodding.

Popov put a strong hand on Laura's shoulder. "We go now."

As she passed Wesley, Laura squinted up at him. "How could you?"

"If it. . .helps," he stammered, swallowing, "I really did. . ."

"Don't even say it," she ground out as she stepped into the afternoon sun.

Standing in the doorway, Wesley watched Laura duck into the back of the limo. In his life he'd used lots of women, but it had never hurt like this. If only he hadn't owed so much money. He could have really fallen for that girl.

The limo backed over the weed-infested lawn to get around Wesley's Camry. As it pulled onto the gravel road and sped off, Dagg said, "Something stinks."

A roaring blast rocketed Wesley through the air, his back searing in pain. He slammed onto the ground, air exploding from his lungs. At that instant everything went black.

Turning on the blue velour seat to look out the limousine's wide rear window, Popov grunted his approval as the fireball soared thirty feet into the air.

In the rear-facing seat, Laura watched, mesmerized. She felt an icy chill and began to tremble. "You killed them," she gasped.

Popov shook his closely cropped head. "Not us. Propane explosion. People need to check their gas lines more often." He chuckled at his own twisted attempt at humor.

Suddenly, he sobered and gestured to the tinted glass and thickly carpeted floor. "No trunk for you this time. You can ride in style."

Laura bit her fist as it knocked against her lips.

"Ivan," Popov called to the driver, "turn up the heat. Miss McIvor is cold."

No amount of warm air could stop Laura's shivering. She had no idea what these insane people wanted from her. What would they do to her if she couldn't give them what they asked?

For fifteen minutes, Jonathan and Danny cooled their heels in the dingy rear waiting room of the Bellingham police station before Detective Carswell could see them.

Finally, Carswell strode into the room with the attitude of a man in a hurry. "Sorry to keep you, Corrigan. I've been on the radio. We've got a possible arson outside of town with a couple of burn victims. I've got to get out there." His eyebrows lifted slightly. "What can I do for you?"

Jonathan said, "I just learned that Shannon Masterson couldn't have gone away with Wesley for a week."

"How do you know that?" Carswell asked.

"We found her purse in her apartment. No woman leaves for a week without her purse."

Carswell lifted a pen from between two stacks on his desk. "That doesn't change the fact that Wesley said she was with him. Wesley wouldn't lie about something like that. Why should he?"

Jonathan wasn't buying it. "Anyone could have called Iverson and claimed to be Wesley."

"You may have something there," Carswell said, nodding. "Wesley Anderson was found at the fire scene I just told you about. He's burned over 80 percent of his body."

"Only Anderson was found?" Corrigan asked.

"There are two other bodies, burned beyond immediate recognition."

Jonathan's breath left him. His mind instantly rejected the first thought that sprang up.

Carswell continued, "The other bodies are male, but we'll have to get dental records to ID them."

Corrigan glanced at his brother. "Let's get to the hospital." He nodded to the detective. "Thanks, Carswell."

BETRAYED

Pushing his leg to the max, Jonathan rushed out of the police station. When Danny reached the driver's side of the Windstar and slid into the seat, Corrigan barked at him, "Do some of your cop stuff and get me to the hospital pronto. I've got to talk to that guy before they put him out."

Without a word, Danny shoved the shift lever into drive and piloted his automobile to St. Joseph Hospital.

Facedown on the gurney, Wesley heard the wailing ambulance siren as though from far away. A rubber mask poured cool oxygen into his nostrils. An IV dripped the maximum dosage of morphine into his veins, but he couldn't tell it. Pain ebbed and flowed from excruciating to unbearable. He no longer feared that he'd die. Now he hungered for it.

But not yet. He had only one chance to make things right. He must live long enough to tell Corrigan about Laura.

The ambulance swayed, then stopped. The siren faded, and the back doors popped open. As the gurney slid into the emergency room, a gray-haired doctor shone a light into Wesley's eyes and the paramedics recited his statistics.

"Corrigan," he whispered through the mask.

"That's right, Son," the doctor said. "We'll look after you."

Wesley shook his head, but the doctor wasn't paying attention. The gurney rattled down an endless white hall. Automatic doors *whooshed* open, then closed. He felt himself lifted, then set down again. A nurse wearing green touched his face, smiled. "You're going to be fine," she said.

No. He was going to die. First, he had to tell Corrigan. Bellingham's hero would know what to do. Grinding his teeth, he groaned as he moved his burned arm up to pull the mask from his face. "Corrigan! I have to see Jonathan Corrigan!" he rasped.

"Later," the doctor said from behind him.

"Now!" he called out, pleading with all his being.

"Andrea," the doctor said, "ask someone at the station to call the farm, will you?"

"Yes, Dr. Henley," she said and padded away as Wesley drifted into an agonized fog. Sometime later, he woke up to see a man's haggard face peering at him. "Wesley? I'm Jonathan Corrigan," he said. "Where is Laura?"

The injured man tried to talk, then groaned under a massive spasm of pain.

Corrigan waited a moment, then said, "Please, try to tell me where Laura is."

"The Russians," Wesley gasped. "The Russians have her."

Corrigan moved closer, his face inches from Wesley. "Where?"

"Boat. . .taking her to Russia."

Corrigan stepped back.

"Wait!" Wesley cried with his last strength. "Tell her. . .sorry."

Corrigan's face softened. "I'll tell her."

Another spasm, and Wesley's world went dark.

Outside the examining room, Corrigan bumped into Andrea and asked her, "How's it look for him?"

She shook her head. "Not good. As soon as he's stable, we're airlifting him to Seattle. He needs a miracle." She hurried back to her patient, and Jonathan headed toward the exit.

Danny met him in the hospital lobby. "Did he say anything important?" he asked.

"I'll tell you in a second," Corrigan said, stopping at a pay phone. He dropped in some coins. "Mom? Hi. . .sorry, we didn't have time to explain. Still don't. . . Who called me? . . . I'll call him later; it's probably just something about my pension."

He shifted the phone to his other ear. "Now listen, Mom, Danny and I are going to Seattle. Can you do me a favor and come to the hospital? There's a guy here named Wesley Anderson. He really needs your prayers. Andrea will show you who he is. . . Thanks, Mom. I can't talk anymore. I really have to get going."

Hanging up the phone, Jonathan turned to his brother. "We've got to get to Seattle ASAP."

"Why?" Danny asked, reaching for his keys.

Jonathan headed for the double-glass doors. Speaking over his shoulder he said, "I'll explain on the way."

Elijah Stone stood when bulldog Feretti and tall, lean Jefferson entered the spacious office at CIA headquarters in Langley, Virginia. He motioned for them to sit on the west end of the room in burgundy leather chairs surrounding a small conference table containing a phone and some folders.

"Thanks for coming so quickly," the CIA director said after they were seated.

"What happened to the need for secrecy?" Major-General Feretti asked, his fleshy face anxious. "I thought you didn't want us to be seen together."

"We're left with few options, gentlemen," Stone said. "Secrecy has fallen from the list. National security has been jeopardized like never before in our history."

"What's up?" Jefferson asked. As usual he remained cool and in control. His head resembled a brown bowling ball with a face carved on the front of it.

"The morning prison guards found Harrison McIvor's body in his cell. Three of the night shift guards are missing as well as the security videotape for his cell." He lifted a folder from the table. "Our pathology people sent me this an hour ago. McIvor's blood was loaded with truth serum." Stone leaned forward, a strange gleam in his dark eyes. "Some foreign power infiltrated the prison and interrogated McIvor."

"How?" Jefferson asked.

"A man posing as McIvor's lawyer showed up at the prison with a forged federal court order allowing him to visit his client."

"And those idiots let him in?" Jefferson demanded, his black eyes flashing.

"The papers were in order. No one questioned them until McIvor's body was found this morning. The judge's name and signature were bogus. So was the attorney."

"Who did it?" Feretti asked. "The Israelis?"

"Our best guess is the Russians," Stone said. "A background check showed that one of the guards has a brother-in-law who works for a Russian shipping company."

Jefferson spoke. "What did they milk from him? They killed him, didn't they? They wouldn't have done that if he'd held out."

Stone relaxed enough to tap an index finger on polished mahogany. "When Mrs. McIvor found out about her husband's death, she started talking." Excitement made his voice waver. "She said that Laura McIvor is the encryption key."

"I thought she was clean," Jefferson said.

Stone ran fingertips along the edge of the blue file folder lying on the table. "According to Mrs. McIvor, her husband left instructions that if anything happened to him she was to say, 'Laura is the key.' That's all."

Feretti ran stiff fingers through the black brush on top of his head. "Where's the girl?"

"Jonathan Corrigan used his own resources to hide her. He left no records. She could be anywhere in the world."

Jowls quivering, Feretti glared at the director. "This is incredible."

Jefferson asked, "Where's Corrigan?"

"We're trying to locate him," Stone said. "We phoned his home. His mother says he's out, and she's not sure where he is." He adjusted the gold band on his watch. "Give us ninety minutes, and we'll have him. I'm sure he'll cooperate."

Stone's cell phone beeped. He snatched it up. "Stone here. . . Put him on." He cupped his hand over the receiver. "It's Corrigan. He's calling from Seattle."

CHAPTER NINETEEN

The sleek limousine streaked south on a country road to Highway 9, then onto Highway 542 and Interstate 5. From there, they glided across ninety miles to Seattle. Too shocked even for tears, Laura stared glassy-eyed out tinted windows and ran an index finger around and around a blue upholstery button beside her thigh.

How could God let this happen to her? Hadn't she just given everything to Him? She drew in a shaky breath and sent up a silent prayer. *You're the only One who can help me now.*

They traveled along country roads, mostly through dense forests with few houses along the way. When the car paused for its final turn, Laura shifted on the seat to look forward. The car parked beside a wide, grassy meadow with an old airplane hangar on one end, one corner of its roof sagging almost to the ground.

"This is where your freighter is?" Laura asked Popov.

He ignored her.

The limousine bumped over a rutted road with grass growing across most of it and parked near the hangar. Three minutes later, a gleaming black helicopter hovered for a moment, then gently sat down, blasting the tall grass flat in a wide circle around it.

Popov grabbed Laura's left hand and slapped on a handcuff. He did the same to the right one. Once again, pain brought her to full alertness. She let him lead her out of the car and, ducking low, toward the roaring cyclone caused by the helicopter.

Her senses crying for action, Laura waited for the moment when

Popov's massive hand relaxed to shift its position. Timing it to the second, she jerked back and pounded her heel into the back of his knee. Spinning left, she raced toward the nearest grove of pines like a wide receiver sprinting down the sideline.

Her head filled with a rushing sound that didn't come from the helicopter. She wanted to scream, to beg someone to help her, but she hadn't breath for screaming. Every ounce of oxygen must power her pumping legs. Always a strong runner, this mad dash was a personal record for her.

Thirty feet from the end zone, one of Popov's friends came around for a shoestring tackle.

She felt clawing hands on a back loop of her jeans, felt a tug, then sailed forward. She hit the grass with an "oof" that knocked the wind from her aching lungs and tore flesh from her cheek. Rolling over, she tried to scratch him, to kick her way to freedom, but other arms grabbed her handcuffs by the center link and jerked her upward.

Mouth wide to suck in air, sobbing and shrieking by turns, she writhed and flailed as the burly Russians dragged her toward the whipping black beast that waited to swallow her up.

Seconds later, she landed on a hard flight chair, and they strapped her in. Popov and his men sat one on each side of her and one behind her. The whir of the chopper blades grew still louder as the ancient landing field grew small below them.

Head rolled back, moaning from pain and raw fear, Laura knew she'd never see the United States again. Her last hope had just been ground into the dirt.

"Corrigan," Stone said into the phone, "please call me back on my secure line." He waited about a minute for the table phone to ring. This time he hit the button for the speakerphone. "Go ahead, Jonathan."

Deep and strong, Corrigan's voice came into the room. "This morning a Bellingham police officer who's been seeing Laura McIvor was badly burned from an explosion that smells like arson. He told me that the Russians have Laura. They're taking her to a freighter that's headed for the motherland."

Stone's face became mottled red and white. His fist thumped the table, and he swore.

"What gives, Director?" Corrigan asked. "Is her father up to something again?"

Ignoring Feretti's disapproving expression, Stone told Corrigan of malfunctioning missiles and Harrison McIvor's death. "Mrs. McIvor now says that Laura is the key."

"That's impossible," Corrigan declared.

"How can you be so sure?" Jefferson asked suddenly.

"Who's that?" Corrigan asked.

"Gary Jefferson, NSA," Jefferson said. "How do you know the girl's clean?"

"She trusted me. She told me everything."

Stone grunted. "C'mon, Corrigan. Do you honestly believe that Harrison McIvor would put his daughter in danger for no reason?"

After a pause, Corrigan said, "It looks like she made a fool of me."

Stone leaned toward the phone. "I'm counting on you, Corrigan. You pull off one last assignment for me, and I'll triple your pension."

"Just name it, Director," Corrigan said without hesitating.

"Go to TSCOMM Whidbey Island. I'll meet you there and brief you."

"Yes, Sir," Corrigan said.

Scowling, the CIA director hung up the phone.

"Did you have to spill your guts to him?" Feretti demanded. He had his head pulled down between his shoulders. "What are you doing, Elijah?"

Stone glared at him. "Extreme circumstances call for extreme action. Before his injury, Corrigan headed up a special unit that answered only to me. He's familiar with the McIvor case, and I want him in this."

His tone became more congenial. "I'll need your help, Tony. Dispatch a couple of SEAL teams to Whidbey. Once we figure out where the ship is, we've got to move. That girl must be secured at all costs."

Feretti nodded. "You've got it."

Stone stood and reached for his briefcase. "Thank you for coming, gentlemen. If you'll excuse me, I've got to find a plane."

At the Blaine crossing of the Canadian border, Ruben Abrams drummed on the steering wheel of his Grand Marquis. He looked at his fine fingers. They could make a violin sing. His parents had swelled with pride when he told them he wanted to be a concert violinist. He'd never told them that he made that decision because such an occupation allowed him to travel freely and without question.

They wouldn't be so proud if they knew how many times his index finger had pulled a trigger and silenced a life. Who would suspect that a man of the fine arts was also an assassin?

"Citizenship?" the gray-haired Customs officer asked.

Ruben said, "American."

"Do you have anything to declare?"

"No."

"Please drive through."

He pressed on the accelerator and merged onto Interstate 5 toward Bellingham. His mission was simple. Find the girl and get her out of the country. The car already had a false bottom in the trunk for that purpose.

However, the closer he got to the Bellingham turnoff, the more those nagging doubts surfaced. Capturing Laura McIvor may mean killing Jonathan Corrigan, the man who had saved his life in Lebanon last year. Could he do it? When he had received this assignment, he told himself there was no problem. Now that he was here, he wasn't so sure.

Five hours after talking to Stone, Corrigan sat on a hard sofa in a gray military-style office at the Tactical Support Center Communications located on Whidbey Island, Washington State. He'd been waiting an hour and wanted to pace in the worst way, but he had to be content with bouncing his right knee twice a second. Stone's plane should be landing any minute now.

When Stone had told him that Laura was the key, he felt like he'd been trampled by a bull. Now that he'd had time to think it over, Harrison McIvor's plan made perfect sense. The scientist had wanted to be caught. All he had to do was wait in the safety of a prison lockup until his program brought the U.S. to its knees. A jail was the safest place in the world for him. At least, he'd thought so.

Laura is the key. Had she played Corrigan for a fool? Maybe she was waiting for her father to rise from the ashes and restore what they'd lost. As reasonable as that sounded, he just couldn't accept it.

The office door opened. Corrigan came to his feet as Director Elijah Stone entered. The older man scarcely glanced at his top agent as he strode to the metal desk by the only window in the room.

Dropping his briefcase to the desktop, he turned to Corrigan and said, "Radar logs show a helicopter leaving the roof of the Russian Consulate and landing at an old airstrip north of Seattle. It was tracked from there to a freighter that's now in the Georgia Strait. Canadian waters."

Moving behind the desk as he unbuttoned his rumpled trench coat,

BETRAYED

he dropped into the straight-backed chair. "We've obtained permission from Canada to go after it. SEALs will attack tonight, coming in at the boat at low altitude from behind."

"Why do you need me?" Corrigan asked. "I can't swim or run."

"I need your knowledge of the girl. We've got to decide whether to bring her back alive or just kill her there." He dug inside his coat for a cigar. "The latter would be more practical," he added.

Jonathan steeled himself. He must not show any emotional reaction when he asked, "What about the code? We can't get it if she's taken out."

"Neither could anyone else," Stone said. He unwrapped the cigar and reached into another pocket for his cutter.

"The Russkies have had her for six hours," Corrigan continued. "Who's to say they haven't drugged her and already gotten the answer?"

"In that case, she's already dead." Stone's voice was flat. He flicked open a brass-plated lighter and held a flame to his cigar.

Corrigan's stomach did somersaults. How could he think when his emotions were on the rampage? Drawing in a slow, quiet breath, he let it out and drew on his intensive training for stress management. Finally, he said, "I doubt they'd kill her. They'd want to make absolutely sure that her answer actually works. If she's given them the code, we need her alive so we can get it, too. If they've been unsuccessful, then we need her alive to get it for ourselves."

He paused as a thought occurred to him. "You know, there's another possibility."

"What's that?"

"There might be something rattling around in her head that only she and her father knew. She may not know that she has the answer."

Leaning forward, smoke billowing above him, Stone grunted. "That doesn't sound likely to me."

"What are your plans for her once she's ours?" Corrigan asked carefully.

"That's where you come in. You gained her confidence once; you can do it again. Get her to tell you what she knows."

"She's still got me on her list of world-class liars and villains. I don't think I've much chance of snowing her again." He shifted in his chair.

Stone's flinty eyes narrowed. "What do you suggest as an alternative?"

Corrigan grinned. "I know this may sound far-fetched at first, but hear me out before you make a decision. It may just work." He relayed a harebrained scheme with the exacting finesse of a politician speaking at a ten-thousand-dollar-a-plate dinner.

When he finished, Stone allowed himself a small smile. He said, "I knew you were the man for this operation."

Corrigan added, "Once we get the encryption problem solved, it would be best if Miss McIvor went six feet under for good this time. We can't have anyone else getting to her, can we?"

"Take care of the details, Corrigan. I've got to brief the SEAL commander." He scraped back his chair and trudged out, still puffing away.

Corrigan waited until Stone closed the door, then whipped out his cell phone. He listened a moment, then said, "Danny? I need a big favor."

Ruben Abrams of the Mossad stayed four cars back from the navy Caprice he was tailing. Last night, Israeli intelligence had heard from a wiretap that Corrigan wanted his brother to bring him a vehicle. Immediately, Ruben had staked out Danny Corrigan's home.

It had paid off this morning when Special Agent Perkins had showed up at Danny Corrigan's home, and the two men left together. Abrams followed them. Danny had promised he'd get a car to his brother. Eventually, he'd come through.

The men left Seattle and headed straight to Bellingham. They traveled north on Guide Meridian Road. When they turned left on Axton, Abrams realized that they were going to Corrigan's farmhouse and drove on by. In ten minutes, he'd double back and pick up their trail when they came out.

Abrams crossed the Nooksack River, then turned around and parked his Marquis half a mile from Corrigan's driveway. He slouched down in the seat and opened the glove compartment. Reaching inside, he flipped open a false bottom and pulled out his Glock. His former weapon of choice had been a Walther P88. Jonathan Corrigan had introduced him to the Glock 17, and he liked it much better.

He caressed the weapon and bit down on his lower lip. Why had the Mossad given him this mission? They knew about him and Corrigan. Could he really aim this Glock at the man who'd saved his life?

He leaned his head back against the seat and closed his eyes for an instant. Blast Corrigan. Blast the Mossad. Why did they have to put him in this position?

Crunching wheels on the gravel driveway brought Abrams up. A Ford Bronco pulled out followed by the navy Caprice. They turned toward him.

BETRAYED

Ducking below the dash, he waited for them to pass.

Two minutes later, Ruben did a U-turn and followed. When they worked their way into the Wenatchee National Forest, Ruben had to stay closer than he liked so he wouldn't get lost.

He smirked. These men must not be too sharp. A good agent would have detected him long ago.

The two lead vehicles turned onto a dirt road, but Abrams didn't follow. He knew this area from a previous mission. Wherever they were going, they'd have to come out the same way. He'd wait for them to leave, then check out the woods for himself.

He pulled off the road behind a wide stand of brush and relaxed. His eyes had sharp needles behind them. He wanted to sleep in the worst way, but sheer force of will kept him awake.

Forty minutes later, Abrams sat up at the sound of a car's engine. The navy Caprice cruised past with both men in it. What had happened to the Bronco?

Abrams hit the ignition and headed down the dirt road, his body jarring with each pothole. Piles of brush littered the grassy clearings on both sides of the road. This area had been logged years ago, and now was only a forgotten maze of dead-end roads. He'd been here before to meet a contact and had almost lost his way. Watching carefully ahead, he hoped they hadn't left the vehicle too far inside. If he couldn't find it easily, he'd wait out at the main highway. There was only one way out of this place, and Corrigan would have to use it.

There it was—the Bronco parked at the side of the road. Ruben did a three-point turn and headed back toward the main road. This was the break he'd been waiting for.

Seated in the back of a Seahawk helicopter skimming the chilly Pacific waters northwest of Seattle, Commander Percy Schell took stock of eight men in black fatigues seated in front of him. This team—Group A—and Group B in the Seahawk behind them were the best the navy had to offer—combat-seasoned men who knew their business.

Their mission was simple. Get aboard the ship and recover the woman alive.

When he'd learned that a CIA agent had final command of this operation, Schell had bristled until he learned that the man was Jonathan Corrigan, a former colleague and a friend. Corrigan was top drawer, a man

Schell respected, a man now seated behind the copilot of this helicopter.

Once his men landed on the ship, Schell was in charge. Corrigan would stay in the chopper and transport the woman out the moment they had her.

The helicopter sharply dropped altitude, causing Schell's stomach to turn a flip. The men ahead of him must have felt it, too, but not one of them flinched or even shifted in his seat.

In total darkness, Schell couldn't see the ocean, but he knew they were almost touching the waves to approach the ship below deck level. At the last moment, they'd rise over the stern and drop the men to the deck.

These pilots could fly through a mountain range in a blizzard while blindfolded, or so it seemed to Schell.

His earpiece crackled. "Five minutes," the pilot said. In one movement, his men looked back at him. He nodded. Eight weapons were drawn, checked, and replaced.

A dozen sparkling white lights outlined a ship dead ahead. The helicopter slowed, then rose over the rear deck and hovered. Schell slid open the door, and his men lowered themselves by rope into the darkness below.

When Schell dropped to the steel deck, he yanked the rope, signaling the chopper to back off. On the other rear corner, the second Seahawk dropped its load. The entire sequence took less than two minutes before the helicopters vanished into a starry night of salty winds and pervasive dampness.

Group B led by Commander Ray Wilson moved along the port side of the ship through a wide aisle between metal freight containers the size of railroad cars while Group A moved along the starboard side. Crouched behind a vent, Schell listened to deep silence. Fifty more containers blocked the bridge from view.

Except for loading and unloading, the crew had little to do on deck. This time of night they were probably below playing cards or snoozing. He hoped they'd all tied one on and were sleeping it off.

Keeping low, Schell quickstepped toward the nearest door. Flattening himself against the steel bulkhead, he waited for his men to line up beside him.

On the other side of the ship, Wilson and his men made their way toward the bridge.

Five minutes passed. A small eternity. Finally, his earpiece came to life. "She's on the second floor," Wilson said abruptly. "At the top of the stairs, make a right, third door down on the left."

Schell held up his hand, palm left. He unlatched the steel door beside him and slipped into the heart of the ship.

The interior felt warm and smelled dank. The dull green galley way had bare twenty-five-watt bulbs at long intervals ahead of them. Surprisingly quiet for men their size, Group A moved along the corridor to stairs which resembled a steel ladder with handles on each side.

Beretta upright at ear level, Schell eased his head around the corner then jerked back. After a second look, he motioned for his men to follow.

At the top of the stairs, Schell almost bumped noses with a sailor dressed in a bathrobe. Moving instinctively, he slammed the man's jaw with an iron fist, knocking him unconscious. The last man in line would apply duct tape to the sailor's mouth, wrists, and ankles.

Two men peeled out of line to guard the stairway, two more to guard the entrance door. Heading down the next galley way, Schell hoped no one else was wandering around. He'd have to kill anyone who tried to sound an alarm.

Huddled on a creaking metal cot with a thin piece of bare foam for a mattress, Laura stared at her guard, a blunt-featured giant wearing jeans and a black fisherman-knit sweater. She was desperate for sleep, but she couldn't relax with a thug in her room staring at her.

Sometime between midnight and dawn, a key rattled in the metal lock. The guard jumped to his feet as Popov strode in.

Laura's grim-faced captor didn't waste words. "Moscow sent a message," he said. "You must tell us what the key is now."

Laura shrank back, her heart skipping in her throat. "A key to what? I don't have a key. I never had a key."

Popov's thunderous expression relaxed a fraction. He sat beside her and spoke softer. "Miss McIvor, I don't want to hurt you, but Moscow must be obeyed. If you refuse to tell me, I must force you. Please, make it easy on yourself."

"What are you going to do. . .torture me?"

He shook his big square head. "Torture takes too long." He slipped a filled hypodermic syringe from his coat pocket and repeated, "What is the key?"

"You mean *where* is the key, don't you?" she gasped.

"Don't play games," he said. Sharp, slim, gleaming metal came toward her. "What is the key to your father's missile encryption?"

"I don't know!" she cried, pressing her back harder against the metal wall. "He never told me."

His mouth hardened. "You leave me no choice." He glanced at the guard. "Danov, assist me."

Working with practiced skill, the guard shoved her backward on the groaning cot, held down her legs with one massive knee, and gripped her elbows. In less than three seconds, she lay helpless.

Screaming, she threw her head from side to side. Popov slapped her hard, back and forth, until she had no strength left to fight. A primal moan came from deep in her throat. Tears coursed toward her ears. *God, where are You?*

Pulling up the bottom of her sleeve a few inches, Popov squirted a bit of liquid into the air.

The door banged open, followed by spitting noises and an acrid smell. The guard collapsed across Laura's knees. Popov fell on her chest. She felt faint. Maybe she was hallucinating.

Weight crushed the breath from her. Suddenly, it vanished, and she looked up into a blackened face with a black knit cap on top.

"Commander Schell, U.S. Navy SEALs, Ma'am," he said. "We've come to take you home."

Laura couldn't speak. She moaned and trembled, her mouth hanging loose and open.

"We've got control of the ship," Schell said, kneeling beside her. "You're safe now."

He put a solid arm around her shoulders and helped her to stand. Moving his forearm under her armpit, he called for another SEAL to support her on the other side. Sixty seconds after they'd entered the room, the men half carried her through the ship, her feet stumbling along. She scarcely knew what was happening. She felt sick to her stomach and wondered if she'd vomit.

Cold ocean air blasted her face and chased the shocked numbness from her brain. When her legs began to function again, one of her escorts turned toward the other side of the ship. Commander Schell led her through a maze of containers with a massive crane in the center.

When they reached the aft of the ship, a helicopter hovered over the deck. A cable with a chair attached to it tumbled down. Schell snagged it and held it steady. "Get in, please," he said, pushing her into the seat.

The moment he'd belted her in, the helicopter lifted up and away while a winch hoisted her closer to the aircraft. Swirling through the darkness, Laura knew she must be dreaming. Any moment she'd wake up in the freighter with a Russian goon staring at her.

Hands pulled the chair into the chopper. The door slid closed, and a flashlight clicked on. Jonathan Corrigan grinned at her as though she were a long-lost friend.

Numb, she stared at him while he unsnapped her safety harness. The next thing she knew she was in his arms, held tight to his chest. "You're okay now, Laura," he told her. "Safe."

Heavy sobs caught her breath. Clinging to him with all her remaining strength, she soaked his black pullover with hot tears.

After a long while, he loosened his hold on her and wiped her cheeks with his fingers. "How are you feeling?" he whispered.

She tried twice before she could gasp out, "They came just in time."

He helped her to a seat and buckled her in. "You're safe now, Laura. Sit here a few minutes and catch your breath. I've got something to do."

With burning eyes, she watched Jonathan make his way up the aisle to the front of the copter. In one lithe motion, he pulled a handgun and pointed it at the pilot's head.

CHAPTER TWENTY

At Whidbey Headquarters in the bustling communications center, Stone sat at a long table and sipped coffee from a Styrofoam cup while he listened to a radio report from Commander Schell. The commander's voice blocked out the beeps and clicks of a dozen machines jammed together in a line with four men monitoring every blip and squeak.

The commander's message was succinct: Laura McIvor was in the chopper with Corrigan.

Suddenly exhausted, Elijah Stone heaved a deep sigh. The fight was only half over. They still had to secure the code. Leaning back in his metal folding chair, Stone rubbed his neck at the hairline.

To confide in someone would be such a relief. But he couldn't. He had an objective. Sticky points of law and high-sounding talk about ethics couldn't interfere with it. Even Feretti and Jefferson couldn't know what he had in mind. This was a solo flight—winner take all.

His gaze settled on the green tactical screen as he noted the various positions of the key players. One helicopter was near the ship retrieving SEAL operatives. The other moved toward the States. Unwilling to admit what they had done, the Russian freighter would continue on course as though nothing had happened.

Two hours before dawn, Stone left the communications room and returned to the office where he'd spoken with Corrigan. It had a comfortable couch, and he was tired. Someone would wake him when the chopper touched down. Pulling off his shoes, he stretched out and closed his eyes.

It seemed like seconds later when a loud knock roused him. "What?" he called out, irritated.

The door opened, and the light glared down at him. Stone blinked as a lieutenant poked his head in the door. "Sir, we've got a missing chopper."

Stone came upright in one motion and felt a wave of dizziness. He groped for his shoes and jammed his feet into them.

When he reached the communications center, the captain in charge— a slight man with a face like a frog—pointed to the glowing green screen. "It dropped from radar coverage over Puget Sound, and the transponder shut off."

"Is that all?" Stone asked, disgusted.

"Sir?" The captain's beady eyes narrowed.

"You woke me for this?" Stone demanded.

The small man stiffened. "Sir, it may have crashed. All attempts to contact the pilots have failed."

Stone yawned. "Everything is under control, Captain." He yawned again and turned away. "I'm going to catch some sleep. Don't wake me again unless something drastic happens."

At the door, Stone turned back. "Just to be clear. What you people saw today is classified. If it ever comes out in the media, all of you—no matter who is responsible—will get a posting north. Way north."

Jonathan held his Glock steady, ignoring the shocked fear on Ken Judson's face. He and Jonathan were friends years ago, before Corrigan joined the CIA. "Relax, guys," Jonathan said. "I'm not going to shoot you unless I have to. Do me a favor and don't be a hero, okay?"

"You can't shoot us," Judson said, his dark moustache twitching. "Who'd fly the chopper?"

"It's been about eight years since I sat at the controls," Corrigan said, "but I think I could manage. Do as I say, and no one gets hurt." He handed the pilot a paper. "These are the coordinates of our destination. Get down low, shut off the transponder, and take us there."

The helicopter dropped to twenty feet above the ocean and skimmed toward the shoreline. An hour later, they increased height to clear some trees and set down in an old logging area.

Keeping one eye on the pilots, Corrigan motioned for Laura to come forward. She unbuckled and was beside him in five seconds. He pulled a small flashlight from his pocket and handed it to her. "A short way from here—straight ahead—you'll come across a road. There'll be a Bronco parked on it. Wait for me there."

"What about bears and wolves?" Laura asked, her eyes round.

"You'll be fine," he told her, squeezing her lower arm. "The chopper's landing scared pretty much everything away." He smiled encouragingly. "Hurry. I'll be with you as soon as I can."

Wearing a doubtful expression, Laura jumped from the chopper and headed into the darkness, her light bouncing along the ground as she moved.

The moment she got out of hearing range, Corrigan ordered the pilots out of the helicopter. Hands clasped behind their heads, each husky man stepped clear of the chopper. The wind had a biting chill that reached the bone.

Corrigan barked, "Facedown on the ground." He searched them and removed their weapons. "Stay down," he said, "or you won't be eating cake on your next birthday."

Returning to the chopper, he fired two rounds into the radio and another two into the controls.

Before he left the area, he paused for one more word with the prone men shivering on the ground. "We're about ten miles from civilization. There are bears in this country, so I'll leave your weapons near the road. When you walk out, stay on the road and head east. West of here the country is a maze of dead-end trails."

Limping across the rutted field, he used his aluminum cane for balance. Laura was waiting for him inside the Bronco. The moment she saw him she got out, a stubborn tilt to her chin.

"Let's go," he said, catching his breath. "We don't have much time."

"What if I say no?" Laura asked. She sounded like she wanted a fight.

He let out a frustrated gasp and spoke loudly. "I'm trying to help you, Laura!"

Her words flew at him. "Since I woke up this morning, a 'friend' of mine handed me over to some Russians who almost shot me full of drugs. Then the U.S. Navy came in at the last minute and rescued me. Now someone who betrayed me pulls a gun on my rescuers and says he wants to help me." Her eyes stretched wide. "Do you see where I'm having a problem with this?"

He considered picking her up and throwing her into the Bronco, like it or not. Even as he thought it, he knew he couldn't do it. Instead, he

BETRAYED

said, "I'm telling you, we don't have much time." He stretched out his hand. "Look, if it'll make you feel better, keep the gun. On top of that, you can drive." He held the keys toward her. "What more can I do?" His tone softened. "Please, Laura. A lot is at stake for both of us."

She shied away from the gun. "The way I see it, if I stick with the helicopter, the navy will come, and I'll be safe for sure. If I go with you, who knows what could happen."

Jonathan shook his head. "As soon as they picked you up, the nightmare would start all over again. The Russians still want you, and they're not the only ones—so do the CIA, the Mossad, and the Chinese. I have a plan that gives you a chance." He sucked in a breath. "I'm trying to save your life, for crying out loud!" He pushed the Glock toward her. "Here, take the gun."

Laura bit her lower lip. "Keep the gun. I'll drive."

Taking the keys, she then handed him the flashlight, darted around the Bronco, and jerked open the door. Corrigan tossed the pilots' weapons to the ground, then limped to the passenger side. As he touched the handle, the Bronco spun gravel and peeled out.

Yelling after her, he threw his cane to the ground. What a stubborn woman!

Finally, he picked up the cane. He searched the ground with the flashlight until he found a grassy patch by the road and hobbled toward it. He may as well sit down while he waited.

A few minutes later, when he'd had a chance to cool off, he almost laughed. For once, Perkins had done something right. He'd left the Bronco facing west.

Fifteen minutes later, headlights appeared. Getting to his feet, he stood in the center of the road and held up his hands. She pulled up beside him, opening the window just a crack. "How do I get out of here?" she demanded.

Corrigan formed his words carefully, each with its own force. "Why don't you let me show you?"

"No! You tell me."

What did he have to lose? She wouldn't let him inside the Bronco either way. All she had to do was drive straight ahead, and she'd find the highway.

He pointed east. "Drive for about ten miles. When you get to a paved road, left takes you toward Interstate 5; right takes you nowhere." He reached for the door handle. "Will you let me in? My leg's killing me."

The next moment, Laura showered him with gravel. Corrigan said a few choice words about women in general and Laura in particular, then sat down again.

Twenty minutes later, he was getting worried. If she kept driving she'd be captured within an hour or two. No matter who got to her, she'd die. He thumped a fist into his palm. Why hadn't he shot out the tires?

"Hey, Corrigan," Pilot Judson yelled, "we're freezing. Can we at least wait in the chopper until you get your mess straightened out?"

Jonathan shot a sour look in that direction, still shrouded in darkness. A moment later, he second-guessed himself. Why shouldn't those guys wait in the helicopter? There was no point in making them suffer unnecessarily. "Yeah, go ahead," he called.

"Lord," he whispered, "talk to Laura and bring her back."

Thirty seconds later, headlights shone through the forest ahead of him. A few seconds later, the Bronco stopped beside him. She rolled down the window. "Get in, Corrigan."

He hobbled to the passenger side and pulled open the door. He was circling the door to climb in when glass exploded beside him.

He threw himself inside, yelling, "Get down!"

Laura lay across his lap. He grabbed the steering wheel, yanking it hard so that the wheels were fully turned. A couple of dull thuds told him the door was taking punishment.

"Hit the gas!" he told Laura.

The Bronco spun in a semicircle, and Jonathan straightened the wheel, keeping his head barely above the dash. The rear window exploded. A bullet whistled past his ear.

"Why are they shooting at us?" Laura cried, hands over her ears.

"I don't know," Jonathan said. "Let's not hang around to find out." The Bronco bumped and swayed down the forest road. Once they were out of range, Jonathan returned control of the Bronco to Laura.

"I thought you took their guns," Laura said, her breathing deep and long.

"When you took off, I let them go back into the chopper."

"Why'd you do that?"

"It's cold out there." His mouth twisted. "There must've been more weapons hidden in the helicopter."

She glanced at him. "And you're supposed to be a top agent?"

"I'm a little rusty, so shoot me." His joke fell flat. They rode in silence to the highway. Finally, he asked, "Why did you come back?"

Eyes still on the road, Laura said, "You told me the truth about how to get out of there. I figured that I'd better trust you just a little bit." She shot him an arch look. "But just a little."

The road ahead suddenly went blurry. Jonathan squeezed his eyes shut and opened them again.

Laura said, "I want to know why I'm not safe with the U.S. Navy."

The Bronco was spinning. Jonathan's eyes drifted closed.

Laura said, "You're pale to the lips." Her voice was a distant echo.

"Go to Seattle," he mumbled, and all went comfortably dark.

After spending hours cramped on the front seat of the Grand Marquis with nothing for company but some chirping crickets and an occasional hooting owl, Ruben saw the Bronco sail out of the forest and turn left with only the McIvor woman inside. He hit his ignition. Maybe he could take the woman without having to shoot Corrigan. Things were looking up.

He followed her down Highway 20, but before he reached a straight stretch where he could force her off the road, she pulled into a farmhouse driveway.

He thought maybe she'd detected him, but after he drove past, he saw her turn around and head back down the forest road again. About twenty minutes later, she reappeared with Corrigan, smashing Ruben's hope for an incident-free capture.

Not wanting a shootout with Corrigan on a dark country road, Abrams settled down to bide his time. Somewhere ahead lay the opportunity he needed.

Hunkered down on the Bronco's seat with his head level with the back, Corrigan felt the Bronco lurch to a stop and pried his eyes open. "Where are we?" he asked.

Laura said, "We're going through a fast-food drive-thru. I'm feeling faint, I'm so hungry. My last meal was breakfast yesterday. It's time for breakfast again."

She spoke into the microphone beside a wide, lighted sign, "Two orders of pancakes with eggs and sausage, a bagel with cream cheese, two blueberry muffins and two milks." She glanced at him. "Do you want anything?"

"Why would I want anything?" he asked, staring at her. "You're set to feed a Boy Scout troop."

She stared back. "I'm not going to eat all that now, Doofus. I want to have some reserves in case we can't stop to eat for awhile."

"Get me a jelly biscuit and some milk," he said, rubbing his stomach. "I need sleep more than food at the moment."

While they waited for their order, she said, "My last meal was a Danish and coffee on the way to the trailer yesterday when I thought I was meeting the FBI. Last night, the Russians sent me some kind of greasy cabbage soup, but I couldn't force myself to taste it." She shivered. "As hungry as I am now, I still don't think I could have put down a spoonful of that stuff." She reached out the window for the large bag held by a smiling Asian-American girl with a long, black braid.

With the bag between them sending up a tempting aroma, she turned right on Aurora, heading north into Seattle. "Get me something, will you?" she asked. "I can't wait until we stop."

He dug around and pulled out the bagel. She grabbed it and took a huge bite.

Looking ahead, Jonathan caught sight of a large orange sign. "There's a Howard Johnson's up ahead. Pull in there."

She swallowed and glanced at him. "You're awfully pale," she said. "Maybe we should go to the hospital."

"Can't. It's not safe."

"For who? Me or you?"

He turned his head toward her, his eyes seeking hers. "For you." For an instant, he had a glimpse of the scared girl inside the willful woman. She turned back to driving and eating.

"Don't worry about me," he went on. "I'm still not 100 percent recovered, but I'll be okay. It's the stomach wound more than anything. If I get too tired, I pay. As long as I can rest, I'll be fine."

Laura turned into the covered front entrance of the hotel and put the Bronco in park. Corrigan started to get out, then stopped. "Will you be here when I get back?"

She paused to clear her mouth, then said, "If I wouldn't leave a wounded dog to suffer, I guess I'll stick around for you."

"Right. Thanks." She sure knew how to lay it on.

While she turned her full attention to the food, Corrigan pushed open the glass door and entered a dimly lit lobby decorated in deep greens and gold. The smell of old coffee lingered in the air.

Behind the high counter to the left, the wall held a rack full of pamphlets describing points of interest in Seattle. Corrigan limped to the desk and rested his elbows on it.

A sleepy-eyed clerk of Middle-Eastern descent looked up. "Yes, Sir?" He had a slight accent.

"One room, one night. Two beds."

The clerk stood. "I'm sorry. I've only one room left, but the bed is a king size."

Jonathan looked out the glass door at Laura sitting in the Bronco drinking milk from a carton. What would she think of this arrangement? He was tempted to look for another place. The burning in his gut ruled out that idea. He must rest.

"I'll take it," he said, reaching for his wallet.

The clerk passed him a registration card. Jonathan wrote Mr. and Mrs. Tom Henna in the top blank.

"Cash or credit?" the clerk asked.

"I'm paying cash," Jonathan said, peeling out four twenties.

"That's fine, Sir." He picked up the money. "Here's your key card. Checkout time is eleven. Enjoy your stay."

Jonathan's limp was more pronounced as he returned to the Bronco. He got in and gently shut the door to keep the ragged glass in place.

Because the motel was full, Laura had to park behind the main building, a good eighty feet from their room. As Jonathan limped toward the unit, he looked the place over in the light of a new dawn. The hotel was oddly laid out in three buildings. The single-story front structure contained the lobby and office with two condo-style towers behind it.

Fortunately, the elevator was close to the entrance. Down a short hallway—past a soda and snack machine where Laura paused to buy two candy bars—they came to room 308. Jonathan inserted the key card, and a green light flashed.

He pushed open the heavy door to meet the pine scent of industrial cleaner and the sound of a humming heater. Dominating the room was a king-sized bed covered with a rust-and-green comforter exactly the shade of the rust carpet. On the far end of the room, double sliding glass doors showed a tiny balcony.

Jonathan headed straight for those doors to pull the drapes closed.

"There's only one bed," Laura said behind him.

"It's all they had," he answered over his shoulder, his hand on the drapery cord. "Believe me, the way I feel right now, I'm no threat."

Cradling the food bag in her arms, she looked him over. "Just the same, I'll sleep on the chair."

"Suit yourself. I'm too sick to argue." He sat on the edge of the bed, then gave a quick gasp as he tried to reach down and untie his hiking boots. Laura dropped the sack on the bed and bent down to unlace them and pull them off.

"Need help with anything else?" she asked.

"No. I think I'll sleep in my clothes." He put his feet up and got comfortable. "Hand me that carton of milk, will you? That may ease my stomach a little."

She gave him the white-and-red container, then pulled an ottoman toward a soft corner chair with a high back. Lifting a Styrofoam carton from the bag, she tore open a silverware packet with her teeth. "You said something back there about having a plan. What is it?" she asked. She forked up some eggs and leaned down for a big bite.

"Later." He yawned and closed his eyes.

Abrams cursed when she pulled into Howard Johnson's without a blinker light, and he couldn't follow. He missed the turnaround and had to cross the bridge. By the time he found a way to get back on North Aurora, he'd wasted fifteen minutes. This was the most confusing and frustrating street he'd ever been on. When he reached the motel, he spotted the Bronco. But which room were they in? He decided the best thing to do was to park down the alley and settle in for a long, cold wait. Maybe an opportunity would present itself tomorrow.

Light peeked through the crack in the long drapes when Laura stretched her cramped legs. Now she wished she'd taken half of that massive bed. She felt like a limp pretzel. With her head against the chair's back, she watched Jonathan's sleeping face and felt a familiar twinge.

Was he telling the truth this time? She hoped so.

Unable to stay still any longer, she stood and reached for the ceiling, urging her muscles to loosen up. She peeked out the side of the drapes, then pulled the curtain back farther.

The hotel sat on a hill overlooking a glistening blue harbor dotted with small boats. Suddenly, overwhelmed by an urge to breathe in some salty air, she unlocked the sliding glass door and stepped outside. A cool breeze caressed her face. Laura pulled in a full breath and felt cleansed. Looking across the green hillsides, she understood why they called Seattle the Emerald City.

Below her, traffic was light. This morning she should be meeting Olivia at Starbucks for coffee and a muffin, then go with her to a warm service for worship. When would she be able to go to church again? Did she need a building to find God? Standing on the balcony admiring creation, Laura closed her eyes and worshipped the Creator.

In the silence of her heart, she spilled out her problems, her fears, her hopes. She knew He was there.

A deep voice behind her held a gentle tone. "Is this a private party?"

Still lost in God's presence, she turned.

He peered at her. "Is that a smile?"

Inwardly, she took a step backward. "Don't take it personally," she said. "Someone else put me in a good mood."

He looked around. "Who?"

"You don't know Him."

"Maybe I do," he said quietly. He stood away from the door. "How about coming inside? We need to talk."

Laura followed him and sat in her chair, not sure what was coming next. He sat on the ottoman facing her. Watching him, she said, "The last time you sat across from me like that, I slapped you."

He nodded. "I deserved it."

She couldn't believe he said that. "At least you admit it," she said.

Jonathan shifted on the ottoman. "Getting back to this person you were talking about. . . I've met Wesley."

Laura wondered if he'd lost his mind. "You think Wesley put me in a good mood?"

Corrigan stayed serious. "I know how much you mean to him, Laura. Didn't he get burned trying to save you?" He spread his hands. "He called me to the hospital and asked me to tell you he was sorry."

Laura made a choking noise and sat bolt upright. "Wesley's alive?"

"He's badly burned, Laura. The doctors didn't hold much hope for him. I've gotta give the guy credit, though. He made sure he told me where you were. That's all he cared about. He's really in love with you."

Laura shook her head. "Not by a country mile."

"What?"

"When the Russian's first grabbed me, I escaped and called Wesley for help. He hid me in a motel until his uncle could find out who was after me." She paused. "That's where I was last week." She started to shake. Her next words wavered. "Wesley and his uncle sold me to the Russians for a million dollars. That's how I got on that ship."

Corrigan's forehead tensed. So did his fists. "Wesley sold you to the Russians?"

She sent him an icy look. "Don't get too self-righteous. Your hands aren't clean either."

Jonathan looked down and consciously relaxed his fingers. "I want to make it up to you. I want to help you."

She relaxed against the chair's soft back. "What's your plan?"

Jonathan reached for her hands. She started to pull away, but something in his eyes made her stop. "For starters, Laura, I have some bad news. Your father died two days ago."

At first, she thought she'd heard him wrong. Her dad dead? It couldn't be. She gasped and started to shiver, suddenly feeling bitterly cold. She hated her father. She should be glad. Why were tears flooding her eyes?

CHAPTER TWENTY-ONE

Suddenly, Laura stiffened and rubbed the tears from her cheeks. Her stare grew so intense that Jonathan forgot to breathe. When she spoke, he felt like she'd delivered a roundhouse punch to his midsection.

"How do I know you're telling the truth?"

He gulped. "Laura, I wouldn't lie about something like that."

An edge came into her voice. "You could think that Dad's death would scare me into obeying you." She shook her head. "You've got to prove it."

Jonathan stood up and rubbed the back of his neck. There weren't any instructions in the CIA manual for this one. What if the agency had killed the story of McIvor's murder? She'd never believe him.

Crossing the rust carpet, he grabbed the TV's remote control, pressed a couple of buttons, and found CNN. He tossed the black bit of plastic to Laura. "Here. Sooner or later it'll show up on CNN. I'm going to the Bronco for our luggage."

"Luggage?" she cried. "You brought luggage, and I slept in my jeans last night?"

He felt more like a heel every minute. "I was hurting so bad when we arrived," he told her, "that I forgot about the suitcase. I was pretty woozy, remember?" He headed for the door, speaking over his shoulder. "I got some stuff from your apartment."

Jonathan crossed the parking lot at a good clip. The day was sunny and crisp, the way he liked it. His leg was cooperating nicely. He hardly limped.

He stopped short. What an idiot. He'd forgotten his cane. Another mistake like that, and they could be dead meat.

He shook his head at the sorry state of the Bronco. Windows shot out, bullet holes in the side. He'd have to replace it right away. Driving this thing around Seattle would be like wearing a placard saying, "Look at us. We're up to no good." If he hadn't been so out of it last night, he would have ditched it then.

He unlocked the rear door to haul out a single suitcase and Laura's handbag. Back at the room, he dropped the bag on the table near the balcony windows and tossed the mangled purse to Laura. She perched on the end of the bed, her attention on the TV screen. She hadn't looked up when he came in.

"Anything yet?" he asked.

"Just sports," she mumbled. Rubbing her fingers over the handbag, she looked up at him, grudging gratitude in her eyes. "Thank you for this."

He gave her an ironic smile. "I'm glad I have one redeeming quality." He tucked his key card back into his pocket. "I'm going down to the breakfast bar and get some coffee. You want anything?"

"Two of each," she said. "Whatever they have."

He returned fifteen minutes later with four plastic-wrapped Danish pastries stacked on top of two large coffees. Pausing long enough to swallow his share of the food, he unzipped the suitcase and said, "I'll take a shower while you finish watching the news."

Absently nibbling her second pastry, she didn't answer him. She hadn't spoken to him since he told her about Harrison McIvor's death. At first, he thought she was grief-stricken. Now he wasn't sure.

He hung his fresh clothes on the bathroom hook when a light rap sounded on the door. He froze. Another knock, louder.

Rushing into the room, he saw Laura staring at the door like it had a grizzly behind it.

"Lie down on the floor beside the bed!" he stage-whispered.

When he removed the Glock from his jacket hanging over the back of a chair, she dropped the Danish to the bed and threw herself to the carpet, hands covering her head.

Jonathan tiptoed to the door and peeped out the hole. A woman on the other side put knuckles to wood again. He couldn't see to the left or right of her. It could be a trap.

Unlatching the safety, he put tension on the trigger. Opening the

BETRAYED

door with his right hand, he hid the weapon behind his left leg.

A haggard blond, the woman spoke with a European accent. "Mr. Henna?"

Corrigan's eyes darted left and right. She was alone. "Yes?" he asked.

She held out a ten-dollar bill. "I am the manager. Our night clerk overcharged you. Please, take this refund with my apologies."

"Uh, thanks."

She smiled. "I hope you enjoy the rest of your stay."

Jonathan shut the door, uncocked the weapon, and put the safety back on. He leaned against the door and let out a long, slow breath.

Laura appeared beside him. "Who was it?" He could see gold flecks in her green eyes.

"It was the manager. She gave me a ten-dollar refund on the room."

"Wow. Such honesty is refreshing," she said, a bite to her words. "You should take lessons."

He turned to the door on the right. "I'm hitting the shower," he said.

Bored, Laura stretched out on the bed to watch CNN. Tears sprang up again. What if Jonathan had told her the truth? Bitterness against her father had consumed her for so long, she was surprised at the pain-filled emptiness his death would cause her. If he really was gone, he'd never have another chance to ask her forgiveness or tell her that, yes, he really had loved her after all.

She lurched upright as her father's face filled the TV screen. The announcer confirmed Jonathan's words. Harrison McIvor had died in prison after a short illness.

The next moment, Laura cried out in blind panic. She jumped from the bed and ran to the bathroom door. Banging hard, she yelled, "Come quick! Now!"

She sprinted back to the TV. Seconds later, Jonathan dashed out of the bathroom dripping water, a white towel draped around his midsection. His eyes darted about the room, shoulders tense, hands up.

"What's wrong?" he demanded.

"I'm on the news!"

His expression grew intense when he focused on her picture. Laura turned up the sound.

"Further into our story on the death of Harrison McIvor. . . Bellingham police are asking for help in locating this woman. She's using the name Shannon Masterson, but CNN archive photos identify her as Laura McIvor, daughter of Harrison McIvor. Bellingham police say that she is wanted for questioning in regard to the critical wounding of a police officer and the deaths of two unidentified men."

Jonathan groaned when his picture appeared next. "Bellingham police also advise that Miss McIvor may be in the company of Jonathan Corrigan, the local hero who broke a terrorist plot in L.A. last month. Mr. Corrigan is not a suspect in any way. He is only wanted for questioning."

Jonathan's shoulders slumped. He tilted his face toward the tiled ceiling. "This is a disaster!"

"Should I turn myself in?" Laura asked.

"Don't even think it!"

"Why not? They only want to ask us some questions."

"That's what they say, but it's not true. Your life is in danger, Laura. You can't trust the police or the CIA or anyone else but me."

A firm knock at the door made them jump.

Jonathan ducked into the bathroom.

Another knock followed, more insistent.

Thirty seconds later, Jonathan came out wearing jeans and a black pullover, the back of the shirt still halfway up his back. "Lie down beside the bed again," he said.

Laura rolled to the carpet and heard his gun click again. Squeezing herself against the wooden base on the bed, she was tempted to look out and see what was happening.

"Danny!" Jonathan exclaimed.

"Hi. Can I come in?"

"No."

"What?"

"I'm busy," Corrigan said.

Danny's voice hardened. "Can the cute answers, Jonathan. I know Laura McIvor is in there. We have orders to take her into custody."

"Show me a warrant."

"Probable cause. Get out of the way!"

After a pause, Jonathan said, "Okay, you can come in, Danny, but not him."

The door closed and footsteps drew closer. Laura held her breath as though that could make her invisible.

"Go ahead and get up, Laura," Jonathan said.

BETRAYED

What was Jonathan up to now? She slowly got to her feet. Danny's blue uniform made him look massive. She noticed some similarities between the Corrigan men but a lot of differences as well.

Danny stepped forward, "Miss McIvor, I need to take you in for questioning regarding the explosion near Bellingham yesterday."

"You can't take her, Danny," Jonathan insisted, reaching for his brother's arm. "She won't be safe."

Danny turned back, eyebrows slanted. "Not safe in police custody?"

"She was in police custody with Wesley, remember? Just before that explosion. She barely escaped." He couldn't tell him the whole story. There wasn't time.

"I have orders to take her in," Danny said. He sounded as stubborn as Jonathan. "You're lucky it's me who got the call, or you'd both be on the floor with your hands cuffed."

Jonathan pursed his lips. "Any other cop would be on the floor wounded." He spoke quickly. "This is a national security issue, Bro. I can't let her out of my care."

Danny shifted his weight and cocked his head. "Okay, make a call and get this straightened out. I know you CIA guys have someone to call for times like this. Do it."

Jonathan shook his head. "I can't."

"Then I have to take her in."

Jonathan dropped his hands loosely to his side. "I'm sorry, Laura. He's my brother, and I can't hurt him. You'll have to go. I'll do the best I can to look out for you."

Laura stared at Jonathan. After what he'd just told her about not trusting anyone, he was letting someone have her.

Danny reached forward to grip her arm.

Jonathan's right fist drove into Danny's kidneys, causing him to drop to the right. A solid uppercut and the big man's head snapped back. From behind, Jonathan wrapped his arm around Danny's neck and squeezed firmly.

The big man clawed at his sleeve, trying to breathe. His face turned from red to purple. Finally, he collapsed to the floor.

Jonathan leaned down next to him, checked his pulse, and put his cheek near his brother's mouth. The older Corrigan sighed, relieved. "He's breathing. I hated doing that, but I couldn't let him do this." He dragged his brother behind the bed.

Stepping toward her, he told Laura, "It's time for Act Two. Keep your hands behind your back as if you're handcuffed."

When she did, he opened the door and nodded to the other police officer—a small, stout man with a baby face.

"Okay, you can take her now," Corrigan said.

The policeman got two feet past Jonathan before the Glock pressed the back of his head. "Keep going, Pal," Corrigan said.

"You wouldn't shoot an officer," he stammered.

"I wouldn't shoot my brother, but I'll shoot you. You guys are in way over your heads. Cooperate, and you'll go home to your family tonight."

Jonathan knocked the man to his knees and cuffed him to the leg of a large built-in dresser. He drove a right fist into the man's jaw, and the policeman laid out, unconscious.

Reaching behind the dresser, Jonathan ripped the phone out of the wall. Then he cuffed his brother's arm to his partner's leg. "They can keep each other company," he said wryly.

He turned to Laura huddled by the wall. "We've got to hit the road. I'm sorry you didn't get a chance to change."

She stared at him as though he were a scary stranger. "Is this what you do for a living?"

Jonathan's eyes softened. He touched her hand. "After you're out of danger, I'm retiring—for good."

Elijah Stone enjoyed morning coffee in the offices of the Cascade International Shipping Company—a CIA controlled corporation—when the CNN special edition came across the tiny TV bolted to the ceiling.

The china cup smashed to the floor when the photographs of Laura McIvor and Jonathan Corrigan appeared side by side.

He swore. If Corrigan had let him know about the Bellingham police action, a call from Stone to the U.S. attorney would have calmed the situation down. Instead, Maverick Corrigan had mauled two of Seattle's finest. Warrants had been issued for assault.

Now the Russians, Chinese, and even some of their NATO allies would be looking for the fugitives. Corrigan was burnt. Stone would have to bring them in. Whether the woman talked or not, she must eventually be terminated.

He pressed an intercom button. "Brown, get in here."

A tall man with thin, sandy hair and a potato nose entered the office.

"Yes, Director?"

"The mission is blown. Where is Corrigan?"

"He's traveling east from the downtown core."

"Have them brought in."

"Sir, Mr. Corrigan can be a problem. If he should resist?"

"Take him out. Bring in the woman alive."

Jonathan threw the luggage into the back of the Bronco while Laura hopped in the passenger side. He threw his cane in the back with everything else.

When he got in beside her, Laura was shivering. With the broken windows, the heater was useless. "Where are we going?" she asked.

"I have no idea," he said. He paused to wait for a red Ferrari to pass before turning right on Aurora. "We need to go somewhere private where we can talk."

"I know a place." She sounded a little smug.

"You do?" He smiled at the confidence in her freckled face. He really loved this girl.

"Head north on I-5, and I'll tell you which exit."

"First we have to find new wheels. This thing is worse than a beacon."

Five minutes later, he saw a gaudy sign: Pioneer Used Cars. "I've got some cash. We can buy a clunker up there." He nodded toward the car dealership and turned down the next alley.

"Is it safe to go there?" Laura asked. "Everyone in Seattle knows our faces by now."

Corrigan took two pairs of black plastic sunglasses from the glove box. He handed one pair to Laura. "Put these on. You'd be surprised how much they'll change your appearance."

Laura looked in the mirror and made a face. "They aren't my style." She giggled with a hint of hysteria. "Just kidding."

As they paced down the alley, she asked, "Should I hold your hand? You know, to make us look like a couple?"

Jonathan looked her over. For all she'd been through, she was holding up remarkably well. "Good idea," he said.

Her hand slipped into his. It fit just right.

"You don't need your cane anymore?" she asked.

"Just sometimes. Right now I feel pretty good."

Suddenly, Jonathan stopped in his tracks.

"What's wrong?" Laura asked, looking around for hidden gunmen.

"It's Sunday. They're closed."

She groaned. "So what do we do, drive the Bronco?"

"We switch plans, that's all." He continued down the sidewalk. "The good news is we won't have to worry about being recognized."

The car lot contained older vehicles of every make. "Pick one," Jonathan said.

Laura walked around the lot and stopped beside a blue Ford Tempo.

"That's what you want? A Tempo?" he asked, his voice unbelieving.

"Yes. My other car is a Ford Tempo, and it's never let me down."

"You got it." He read the sign on the car's window. "The price tag says $2,199.00. You know as well as I that they'll sell it cheaper. So, here's what I'm going to do."

He sauntered to the little trailer that served as the sales office, slammed the weathered door with his shoulder until it popped open. A minute later, he returned holding car keys and a license plate that fastened with magnets.

"I left two thousand dollars in cash on the guy's desk. His alarm just went off. We've got to hurry."

He unlocked the door, started to get in, then his expression changed. "I don't believe this!" he said, getting out.

"What's wrong with it?" Laura asked.

"It's a standard. I can't shift a standard with my bum leg. You'll have to drive."

"But I can't drive a standard," Laura said. "My Ford Tempo was automatic." She looked scared again.

"The cops will be here in about three minutes. You'll have to learn fast."

They slid into blue bucket seats, and she took the keys from him. On the passenger side, Jonathan barked instructions. "Push the clutch in and turn the key."

The motor sputtered to life. She revved the engine.

"Now, give it a little gas and slowly release the clutch." The car shot back and crunched the vehicle behind them.

"What are you doing?" he shouted.

"What you told me," she shot back. Her freckles had disappeared beneath a red glow.

"I said to let it out slowly."

"I thought I did."

He lowered his chin and tried to stay calm. "Push in the clutch and start the motor again. This time put it in first."

"Where's that?" She touched the shift stick with tentative fingers.

"Never mind," Corrigan said, trying to keep his voice low. How many minutes had passed? "Just start the car. I'll shift."

Jerking to the edge of the parking lot, the blue Tempo made a right on Aurora. "What about our stuff?" Laura asked a moment later.

"We'll go back for it."

Lurching and swaying, Laura took the first right, went down the side street, and made another right at the next street.

"Stop here," Jonathan said when they reached an alley. "I don't want to be any closer to the dealership than I have to with this car. We can walk to get our stuff."

Hustling and puffing out white clouds as they walked, they covered the short distance to the Bronco in less than five minutes. Jonathan had just grabbed the suitcase when a navy Caprice squealed to a stop in front of them. Two men in dark suits got out. Each held a handgun with a silencer.

CHAPTER TWENTY-TWO

The small hairs on the back of Jonathan's neck stood up when he saw two goons with guns bearing down on Laura and him, but he forced his face to stay calm. Idiots! What were they doing?

"Don't move, Corrigan," said the taller agent, a man whose face was all nose and chin. He stood near the open passenger door of the Caprice and gripped his Beretta like he knew how to use it.

Corrigan's shock turned to anger. "Brown! What are you doing here?"

The big man wasn't smiling. "We're taking you both in. Stone's orders."

Laura grasped Corrigan's arm. "Jon, what's going on?"

"I'm not sure," he told her, then moved his body between her and the CIA agents.

"Well, Corrigan, are you coming peacefully or the hard way?" Brown asked.

To give himself some time to think, Jonathan decided to stall.

"Get Stone on the radio," he told Brown. "If he gives me a direct order, we'll come along."

Hesitating, the nose of his weapon rising, Brown glanced at his partner, then plopped onto the car's seat with one leg hanging out the door. A second later, he held a cell phone to his mouth.

Recognition flitted behind Jonathan's eyes as he glimpsed the lithe form of a dark-haired man moving quietly toward the back of the Caprice, using parked cars for cover.

Keeping an eye on the scene before him, Corrigan whispered to Laura, "These guys are from the CIA. They plan to kill you after they get the code. I want to get you out of this alive. Will you do as I say?"

He saw something in her eyes that he hadn't seen for a long time: trust. "All right," she whispered.

He squeezed the hand gripping his arm and murmured, "Go to the back of the Bronco and stay low."

A minute later, Brown stepped out of the car holding the mike. "Okay, I've got the director on the phone."

Corrigan paced toward the navy Caprice, hands wide, his Glock tucked into the back of his pants, hidden by his coat. Laura moved behind the Bronco.

"Where's she going?" Brown demanded, his eyes flicking from Corrigan to the girl.

"Just getting some of her stuff," Corrigan said, still moving.

Brown lifted his weapon. "Stop right there, Corrigan. Miss McIvor," he yelled, "come out in the open!"

"Or you'll do what?" a throaty voice asked from behind him.

Against their training, both agents whirled to see the source of the voice. Jonathan pulled his weapon and aimed it at Brown's slim belly.

"Nice to see you again, Ruben," Corrigan told the wiry Israeli holding twin Glock 17s on the CIA agents.

Ruben's narrow face held an ironic expression. "You are having a problem, I see." His voice had a definite Middle-Eastern flavor.

"Are you willing to help me out?" Corrigan asked. He still held his gun level.

"I think so."

Still holding the phone, Brown's hands wavered around his ears as he asked Corrigan, "Who's this?"

Jonathan smiled. "That's Ruben Abrams of the Mossad. You know, the Israeli secret service."

"Don't get smart," Brown shot back. His pale cheeks turned red to match his nose.

"He looks like he has plans to shoot you if you shoot me," Corrigan said. "Is that right, Ruben?"

"Exactly." The Israeli's eyebrows lifted, a silent question.

Corrigan nodded, then said, "So, Brown, what's it to be? Abrams is an excellent shot; he'll nail you, and I'll get your partner."

"But I'll get you," Brown said, his Beretta rock steady on Corrigan's head.

Jonathan's chin raised a fraction. He said, "I only care about Miss McIvor's safety, not my own." He put tension on his trigger. "What's it going to be? Will your wives be shopping for black tonight?"

"Put your weapon down, Conroy," Brown said, disgusted. A Beretta and a Glock clattered to the asphalt.

Shoving his left gun into a shoulder holster, Abrams came behind Conroy and frisked him for more weapons. He pulled a knife from behind the agent's neck and pitched it down the alley. Digging a thumb into the man's skinny neck, Abrams stepped back as the agent collapsed. Three seconds later, a karate chop put Brown out.

Stepping around the unconscious lumps sprawled in the alley, Corrigan picked up the black cell phone on the asphalt near Brown's hand. He spoke into it. "Listen, Stone, you fouled up your end of the deal, but I'm going to keep mine. If you send any more men after us, they'll pay the piper."

He tossed the phone to the car seat and slammed the door. The receiver squawked, but he ignored it.

"How long have you been following me?" Jonathan asked Abrams.

"Since you came out of that logging area." Abrams looked at the scarred Bronco and grinned, his teeth long and white. "Looks like you've had your share of trouble, my friend."

Corrigan wasn't in the mood for small talk. He held his Glock steady at waist height. "Why are you here, Ruben?" he asked. "The truth."

The Israeli scratched his dark head. "Intelligence says that Miss McIvor knows the missile code. I have come for her."

"You can't have her," Jonathan said firmly. The Glock tilted slightly.

Abrams let his level eyes rest on Corrigan. "This is a great dilemma. You are my very good friend, Jon. You saved my life, and yet I love my country, too." He raised his shoulders. "What am I to do?" he asked sadly.

"If we find the solution, I guarantee that your people will get it."

Abrams shook his head regretfully. "I want to believe you, Jon, but sometimes you'll promise the moon when you don't even have a rocket ship."

"I'm talking straight, Ruben," Jonathan said, an edge to his words. "If Miss McIvor finds the answer, I will make sure you get it. You have my word."

Suddenly, the second Glock lay in the Israeli's left hand. One gun aimed at Corrigan's middle, the other at the Bronco. "Put your gun down,

Jonathan," Abrams said carefully. "I don't want to kill you, my friend."

Corrigan's chest puffed out. The ball was in his court, but he wasn't sure how to make the play. Finally, he bent at the knees and lay his Glock on the ground.

Abrams nodded and stepped forward. "A wise. . ."

His sentence died as a hiking boot crunched his chin upward, knocking him off balance. Both guns flew up and out, still clenched in iron fingers. A second kick pulled his feet out, and he landed hard on his back, gasping for air.

Corrigan stepped from one of the Israeli's hands to the other, giant steps with his heels grinding down.

Abrams screamed.

Jonathan bent over to pull the weapons from the Israeli's mangled fingers and tuck them into his own waistband. "I'm sorry, Ruben. You left me no choice." A hard right to the jaw put him out of his pain, at least temporarily.

Jonathan dashed to Laura, who was still bent down behind the Bronco. Her face was wet and shiny. She jerked when he came around the vehicle then cowered against the back door. "I can't go on." Her voice was shrill. "We'll never be safe."

He cupped her cheek in his hand. "I'm going to get you out of this, Laura." Pulling her up and holding her shoulders with his left arm, he jerked open the Bronco's back door—ignoring the shower of glass chips from the shattered window—and grabbed the suitcase.

"What about your cane?" Laura asked.

Hustling her toward the Ford Tempo, he said, "I don't need it anymore."

Elijah Stone sputtered into the cell phone for two full minutes before he realized that Corrigan wasn't answering. Finally, he stabbed the off button and sent for his assistant. "Get a new team and find out what happened in that alley!" he barked.

Two hours later, Brown and Conroy stood before him with hangdog expressions.

"What happened?" Stone demanded.

"Ruben Abrams of the Mossad came at us from behind," Brown said, rubbing his bruised neck. "He must have taken off with Corrigan and the girl. He wasn't there when we came around."

Stone leaned back in his stiff chair and massaged his weary face. "Take a couple weeks of vacation, both of you. And don't bother to come for your checks on Friday. Get out of my office."

When he was alone, Stone stared at the gray plastered wall in front of him. Corrigan had about an hour's head start on the new team. As soon as the police reported which car was missing from Pioneer Used Cars, he'd put every asset he had in the air for a massive search.

As an ace in the hole, his agents had located a cousin to Wesley Anderson and paid him ten thousand dollars to put up a fifty-thousand-dollar reward for information leading to the fugitives. The CIA would pick up the tab for the reward, of course.

A soft knock brought Stone out of his daydream. He straightened and called, "Come in."

Brown peeked his head in the door. "I forgot to tell you one thing."

"Yes?"

"Corrigan said that even though you weren't willing to keep your part of the deal, he would keep his."

"Yes. He told me the same thing on the phone."

Brown closed the door, and Stone's brow came down. Corrigan's mind games didn't matter. Laura McIvor must be brought in. . .regardless of the cost.

With Laura at the wheel of the Tempo, the fleeing couple drove along a secondary road, passing farm after farm. "Isn't there a restaurant or even a grocery store around here?" Laura wailed.

"I know what you mean," Jonathan said. "My belly button is almost touching my backbone."

She laughed. "That's gross."

He smiled and said, "Sorry." But he wasn't.

Rounding a curve, Laura cried, "Aha!" Ahead on the left sat a low, flat building with a weathered sign hanging from an iron pole—ROSE'S CAFE. She pulled into the lot and turned the key. "If someone comes along to shoot us, let him bang away. I've got to have something hot to eat or I'll die anyway. Do you realize it's been over a week since I've had a decent meal?"

He reached for the door handle. "Let's go. We'll wolf down a dinner and get moving." He grinned at her. "Just don't order half a cow; we don't have time to wait for the butcher to bring one."

Instead of half a cow, they settled for steaks that covered their plates, fat baked potatoes smothered with sour cream, and garlic bread on the side. Laura couldn't finish her potato, so she brought it along in a small box for a bedtime snack.

Ten minutes later, they reached Laura's hideaway. Jonathan raised an eyebrow at the Snowcap Inn, a blight on the rolling landscape.

"This is where Wesley hid me," she told him when the Tempo pulled into the ragged parking lot.

"What makes you think this is safe?" Jonathan asked, taking in the broken and taped windows, the missing shingles. "All kinds of shady characters come here."

She said, "We'll fit in, won't we?"

"Beggars have to take what they can get, I guess." He reached for the door handle. "Wait here. I'll go in and pay for a room."

Striding down a cracked sidewalk, he pushed open the weathered wooden door and entered the office.

A cloud of smoke hung around a scraggly, thin man wearing a yellowed undershirt and gray sweatpants. "Yeah?" the attendant asked through tobacco-stained teeth.

"I need a room."

"How long?"

"Two days at the most."

"A hundred bucks, cash."

Jonathan tossed a hundred-dollar bill on the counter. "Where do I sign?"

The man's grin looked like a rotting picket fence. "No one ever signs. Here's your key, room 125. It's the one farthest at the end. There's parking behind the building."

"Thanks." Jonathan grabbed the key, turned, and opened the door, almost bumping into a well-dressed businessman coming in. Their eyes made brief contact. The man mumbled an apology, and a shot of electricity jolted through Jonathan as he hurried back the way he'd come. Would that man turn them in?

When he hopped into the Tempo, Laura asked, "What room?"

"One-twenty-five. It's at the end."

"Hmm, last time he gave me 106. I hope this one is better."

Laura entered the room ahead of Jonathan while he lugged the suitcase. While he locked the door and set the suitcase on the leaning dresser, she stood hand on hip, looking the place over.

"Any better?" he asked, taking off his jacket. As shoddy as the place was, at least it was warm.

Getting out of her wool coat, Laura shook her head. "This time the bed isn't even a queen size." She lay her coat beside Jonathan's across the table by the window.

"We can sleep in shifts. I'd prefer that anyway," Jonathan said. "We need to keep watch. With our faces on TV, we can't be too careful."

She looked him straight in the eye. "Before we sleep, eat, or do anything, I want a complete and honest explanation of what is going on."

Jonathan set the suitcase down and motioned to the bed. "Have a seat."

Laura sat on the brown spread, crossing her legs and resting her hands on her lap, face upright, waiting.

Jonathan stood before her and said, "Recently your father's missile guidance system crashed and produced a worldwide crisis. His system contains an encrypted program that no one can crack. The Russians infiltrated the prison and overdosed your father on truth drugs trying to learn the code. When your father died, your mother said that you were the key. So, the Russians grabbed you.

"While they were planning to snatch you from the Russians," he continued, "the CIA considered killing you on the ship so no one would have the answer. I talked them out of it."

Tears filled her eyes.

Jonathan sat beside her, speaking steadily. "The CIA plans to drug you so you'll tell them the answer. Then, they'll dispose of you."

"Why?" She sounded broken. "I haven't done a single thing."

"So no other country can get the solution. Director Stone is out of control. He wants total nuclear supremacy for the U.S."

She plucked at her collar. "He told you this?"

"Not in so many words, but I know how his mind works. He's gone over the edge, Laura, and there's no one to stop him. . .but us."

She wiped her eyes on the sleeve of her shirt. "I'm going to spend the rest of my life on the run, aren't I?"

Jonathan shook his head. "Not if my plan works." He reached for her hand. "Do you know what the key is?"

Laura shook her head until her short hair swayed. "I never worked on that project. You know that."

"Did your father say anything to you that would help us figure out the code?"

BETRAYED

Laura's voice quavered. "My father and I did a lot of encryption together, but nothing the government's computers couldn't crack in a couple of weeks."

Jonathan slowly exhaled. "Then we're sunk."

"Can't you make me disappear again?" she asked.

"No. I mean. . .I could, but they'd eventually find you. We're going to have to go to the press with the story. It's the only way."

Laura peered at him. "You'd do that?"

"Why not?"

"You're still a CIA agent. Wouldn't you get into trouble?"

His lips formed an ironic smile. "We're talking jail time for breaching national security."

"Then let me go alone."

Jonathan's smile softened. "It's nice of you to offer, but it wouldn't help. I'd still go to jail for purposely sabotaging my own mission."

He went on, "The CIA told me to make you think you were being chased, so I could be a hero. When you trusted me, you'd tell me the code. Afterward, I'd hand the code and you over to them."

Life came into her expression. The old Laura stared at him. "That episode in the alley was staged?"

"No, that was real. When the Bellingham police put our faces on TV, the CIA considered us burnt. That's why they sent those goons to bring you in."

He went on, "If you knew the key to the encryption, you could put it on the Internet so everyone would have access to it at once. Once the world has it, you're no longer a threat." He raised his hands, palms up. "At least, that was my plan."

"And it failed."

"Yeah. You don't know the key."

Laura stood and peeked out the window through the crack between the mossy green drapes. A moment later, she turned to him. "How do I know you aren't lying to me again, making this all up?"

"You have no reason to believe me, Laura. I know that."

The room stayed silent for a full five minutes. Laura wandered about the room, then returned to the window and stared out the crack in the drapes.

Was he lying? There was only one way to know for sure. She turned to Corrigan who was still sitting on the sagging bed. "All right, I have the key."

His face had a strange expression. "You were holding out on me?"

"I think you can understand why."

He hesitated, then asked, "What is it?"

"My father's grandmother was a Navajo. She lived with his parents when he was child and taught him the language. Sometimes for fun, he would base encryption programs on it."

"It's that simple?"

Laura nodded. She clenched her hands together. "Where do we go from here?"

"We find a computer, and you post it on the Internet."

She watched his eyes. Did he mean it? Maybe he'd get her to a computer, watch what she wrote, then stop her at the last second. Maybe he was just stringing her along. She ran a hand through her hair. "Any idea where we can find one?"

Jonathan rubbed his bristly chin. "I'll bet the motel manager has one. He grabbed his leather jacket and tossed Laura her wool one. "Let's go!"

A late afternoon rain had just started. "Run ahead," he told Laura. "There's no sense in both of us getting soaked."

Staying mostly on her toes, Laura ran to the office, and Jonathan speed-walked behind her. His leg felt like a stick of week-old bologna.

When they burst inside the door, the scraggly attendant strolled out of a back room, a beer in one hand, a cigarette in the other. "Yeah?" he asked.

Pulling out a friendly smile, Jonathan said, "We were wondering if the manager had a computer."

He lowered his cigarette to get a better look at them. "I'm the manager, Matt Hardy. Why do you need a computer?"

"We need to send some E-mail," Laura answered. "Do you have Internet access?"

Hardy bristled. "Who says I have a computer?"

"Do you?" asked Jonathan.

The manager looked them over. "Your pictures don't do you justice." He focused on Jonathan. "Do you know there's a fifty-thousand dollar reward for you two?"

Corrigan's smile faded. "Are you going to turn us in?"

Hardy drew on his cigarette and let out a cloud of smoke. "The last thing I need is to have the heat crawling over my place. Fifty thousand isn't half enough to cover the investments I'd lose in the process." He

BETRAYED

stepped away from the door. "The computer's back here."

He led them into a living room the size of a postage stamp. The couch's rust-colored upholstery was shiny on the arms. Full ashtrays and empty beer bottles littered the landscape. On a cluttered corner desk, its blue eye gleaming, was the computer.

Laura sat in front of the screen, her fingers on the keyboard.

"What's the first step?" Jonathan asked, peering over her shoulder.

"I have to search out the government E-mail addresses of all the countries involved. Russia, China, and Israel. . . ."

Corrigan added, "Britain, France, Italy, Canada, and Spain."

"That's it?" Under her hands the keys sang a metallic tune.

"That's enough to accomplish our purposes."

Half an hour later, she had everything she needed. She said, "I'm going to set his computer so the message will come from my E-mail address instead of his. Then they'll be able to verify the return address as mine."

She paused. "Oh, no!"

Jonathan stared at the blinking screen. "What happened?"

"It's downloading my new mail onto his computer. The powers that be will be able to trace my location within a couple of hours." She looked up at Jonathan. "We'll have to find a new hideout."

Corrigan kept watching the screen. "Don't worry, Laura. We'll be okay. This is what I'm trained for, remember?" He glanced at his watch. It's fifteen past four. We should have at least an hour, maybe more. If you post the solution on the Internet, we're home free."

When the messages finally finished downloading, Laura typed in the solution. She had spasms in her stomach, and her fingers kept fumbling at the keyboard. How long would it take for those hated black sedans to reach the broken-up parking lot and take them away? Was this little ploy worth the time?

But she couldn't stop now. She had to know where Jonathan's loyalties lay once and for all. She plowed ahead as quickly as she could. When she finished, she paused and looked at the tall man behind her shoulder.

"Once I click send, there's no bringing it back," she told him, watching his face. "The world will know the key."

"By all means click it," he said.

Instead, Laura moved the bear pointer to the x in the upper right corner of the screen and closed the E-mail program.

Gazing up at his puzzled face, she loved him. He hadn't tried to stop her from posting the solution. He'd gone through all that danger to protect her.

"What's wrong?" he asked, his face alert.

"Let's go back to the room," she said quietly. "We don't have much time."

They thanked Matt Hardy for the use of his computer and stepped into the rain. Keeping close to the partial shelter of the roof's overhang, Laura glanced at Jonathan's wondering expression and smiled—fully, radiantly.

Despite their imminent danger, for the first time in months she felt free. She wanted to dash out into the falling droplets, arms wide, face heavenward, and twirl until she felt too dizzy to stand.

Instead, she laughed up at him, a girlish sound.

Suddenly, he grinned, a wide disarming smile that used to take her breath away. It still did. "This is our door," he said, holding up a metal key.

"Know what I wish?" she asked.

"What?" His eyes lingered on her face.

"I wish we were at the beach getting ready to take a walk on the sand."

He leaned toward her, his hair dark with rain. "I second the motion." He touched her chin. "How about a rain check?" Still smiling, he turned the knob, and they entered the room.

Laura tried to fluff up her wet hair with her fingers.

Helping her get out of her coat, Jonathan said, "You'd best put on something warmer. We're going to be out in the weather most of the night, probably." He reached into the suitcase and pulled out a thick pullover sweater. "I'll wait in the bathroom."

He disappeared into the cubicle at the back left, and Laura pulled blue jeans, a pink sweater, and a warm sweatshirt from the suitcase.

"Okay," she called out a few minutes later.

Jonathan's damp hair had a combed, slicked-down look when he emerged. "What happened in there?" he asked her. "Why didn't you send the code?"

"I don't know the encryption key," she said. "I was just pretending."

He stood still for a moment, his eyes searching hers. "You were testing me?"

"Yes."

"Did I pass?"

BETRAYED

"Yes." Her smile started deep inside and worked its way out to her face.

Jonathan's slow, warm grin came out again. Laura felt giddy and shy, and she had a strange desire to burst into tears.

He stepped closer. "This year has been a living agony for me, Laura. I've ripped myself apart every single day because of what happened to you. That day at the villa . . ." He looked deep into her eyes. "I never wanted that. I tried to stop it."

She opened her mouth to speak, but he lay his fingers across her lips.

"The worst thing," he went on, moving closer to her, "was not knowing where you were and if you had everything you needed. And wondering," his eyes lingered on her lips, "if you missed me half as much as I missed you."

He touched her cheek with the back of his hand. "I love you, Laura." Tears swam in his eyes. "I always will."

She put her hands on his cheeks and gently brought his face down for a gentle, affirming kiss. He drew her into a warm hug, her cheek on his shoulder, and Laura felt completely safe. She wanted to stay there forever.

"I love you, Jonathan," she whispered after awhile. "But there's something I have to tell you right away."

CHAPTER TWENTY-THREE

The Cascade International Shipping Company had doubled its size in twenty-four hours. Electronic equipment filled its dozen offices where grim-faced men and women worked feverishly. Stone had called in all the troops.

On the ground, agents scoured Seattle. In the air, a dozen military helicopters scoured the countryside.

A gray-haired woman in a navy suit stepped into Stone's makeshift office. "Director?" she said in a well-modulated voice.

He looked up from the papers on his desk. "Yes, Ida?"

"We've got a lead. Almost an hour ago, Miss McIvor used her E-mail account. We've just located the source—a motel outside of Arlington."

Stone jumped from his seat and went to a wall map, his index finger locating Arlington. "That's not too far from here. Get on the radio and direct the nearest units to that motel!"

When Jonathan heard Laura say she had something to tell him, a dozen thoughts flashed through his brain—she still had feelings for Wesley. . . she'd secretly married Wesley. . .and the list got worse.

"I'm not the woman you knew in California," she went on, pulling away so she could look at his face. She had a glow that he'd never seen before when she said, "I belong to God now. Is that a problem for you?"

A problem? Was she kidding? He looked into her green eyes, "Laura, I came back to God myself at the farm while I was recovering. It's a long story, and I don't have time to go into it now." He cupped his hand around her cheek. "But you've made me the happiest man alive today. Even Stone can't take this away."

He forced himself to look at his watch. "It's been an hour since you downloaded that mail," he said. "We've got to go. Now."

He tossed her coat to her. "We won't be able to take any luggage this time."

Laura wrapped her black coat around her. "Where are we going?"

"We'll have to run across the back field and trust God for the rest."

They turned out the lights, and Jonathan cracked the door open. Dusk had fallen, and two security lights shone down on the parking lot. He opened the door, and the crisp evening air rushed in, the cold after a hard rain. Laura shivered.

They rounded the corner of the building to the back. The Tempo sat there, waiting for them.

"Should we take the car?" Laura asked.

"I'll take the car and lead them away from you. You take off across the field."

She stared into the black expanse of pasture. "No way. I'm not going out there alone. We go together."

He tried to sound stern, but his heart wasn't in it. "Laura, it's best if we split. They'll chase me."

She turned to him, her face inches from his. "Without you, I am not safe."

Three black sedans roared down the road to their right. They churned gravel and squealing brakes into the motel's parking lot.

Jonathan grabbed Laura's hand. "Let's go!"

They dashed across the back lot to a barbed-wire fence. Jonathan pushed down the second from the bottom strand with his foot, lifted the third strand with his hand, and Laura slipped through.

She then did the same for him. Jonathan found it awkward; his leg still a problem. The back of his coat snagged on a barb.

"I'm stuck," he said, trying to reach around to loosen the barb. "I'll have to leave the coat."

"It's too cold," she said. Gasping with frustration, Laura jerked the coat. It seemed like hours later when he broke free, and they stumbled onto the wet grass.

Hand in hand, they hurried through the damp-scented darkness. Light flickered in the distance. They automatically aimed toward it.

The uneven ground made walking a chore for Jonathan. His leg throbbed after only five minutes. Could he make that tingly limb carry him far enough to find safety?

Behind them a spotlight swept the parking lot and edged toward the field. Jonathan glanced back every few steps, gauging its progress.

"Get down!" He pulled Laura's hand as he flung himself flat on the ground. She landed beside him with an "oomph" sound.

"Sorry," he said. "The light's almost on us."

When she caught her breath she asked, "What are we going to do after we cross the field?"

"I'll steal a car. With wheels we can get to Seattle."

"Will they have the roads blocked?"

"That depends on whether they call in the police and the FBI."

"Why wouldn't they?"

Puffs of vapor coming from his mouth, Jonathan said, "Stone plans to kill us. The FBI wouldn't go for that."

A wave of brilliant yellow passed a yard from their feet. When it moved down the pasture, they scrambled up.

"Oh!" Laura gasped. "There's something wet on my knee."

"Don't touch it!" Jonathan told her, pulling her along with him. "This is grazing land for cows. You don't want to know what it is."

The light across the meadow had come from the security light in a farmyard. When they drew near, a dog started barking. "Stay down," Jonathan whispered to the girl beside him.

Side by side they lay in the damp grass. It had a pleasant earthy smell. On one side of the yard stood a two-story farmhouse with shingled siding. A weathered barn stood a hundred and fifty feet from the house with two vintage oaks in the yard between.

The back door of the house opened, and a plump woman in a tent dress stepped out on the porch. She shouted, her voice nasal and harsh, "Whatcha barking at, Brutus?"

A howl sounded in the distance. "It's just coyotes, ya stupid mutt," she said. The door closed.

Jonathan pressed Laura's arm. "Wait here. I'm going in for a closer look."

He crept closer to the house and stood in the shadow of a wide oak trunk, its bare branches wide over his head. Both vehicles parked in the driveway—a red pickup truck and a dented Buick—were within reach of the chained dog.

Jonathan's leg pounded. His stomach felt like it had been stepped on. He couldn't travel on foot much farther. Then a welcome sound came from the barn—the snort of a horse.

Jonathan returned to Laura, but before he could speak the *whump-whump* of helicopter blades came from overhead. Once more, they flattened themselves into the earth, hiding their faces, as the chopper passed over them. When it reached the motel, it lit up its spotlight and hovered a few minutes, then shot down the road, the beam still searching.

"God is definitely on our side tonight," Jonathan told Laura as he sat up. "If we'd left in the Tempo, they'd have us by now." He leaned toward her until he could see her glistening eyes. "We have a better way to get across country than a car."

"What's that? A tractor?" she asked, peering at the barn.

"No. A horse."

"I can't ride a horse," she said.

"Don't worry. I can. You can sit behind me."

Laura sounded doubtful. "I don't know."

"Come on. It'll be fun."

"Fun? We're being chased by the CIA, and it'll be fun?"

Jonathan grabbed her hand and helped her up. They trekked to the barn and entered through a side door. That distinctive horse odor and the stamping of hooves met them inside.

The yard light shone through cracks in the barn walls. Laura could see Jonathan move between the half-dozen horse stalls. He'd walk up to a horse, stroke its nose, then lunge forward. The animal would snort and shy away.

"What are you doing?" she whispered.

"No time to explain," he said, his face striped with light.

At the fourth horse—a large black—when Jonathan jumped, the horse looked at him and practically yawned. Jonathan grinned at Laura. "This is the one. He's not skittish. He'll be safer to ride."

"Safer? Not safe?"

Jonathan came over and took her hand. "He's safer than a car chased by a helicopter." He put his arm around her. "Laura, it'll be all right. I've owned horses all my life."

"If you say so." She didn't sound convinced.

"There's a door at the back. It's probably the tack room. I'll get a saddle and bridle."

He went to the back of the barn and came out carrying a saddle with a bridle hanging over the horn and a blanket resting on top. In about ten minutes, he had the horse saddled.

"Now comes the hard part," he whispered.

"What?"

"Getting the horse out of here without being noticed. That dog is going to start yapping as soon as he hears us. Hopefully, the lady will think he's barking at coyotes again."

Laura followed a good ten paces behind as Jonathan led the black horse out of the barn. Sure enough, the instant the horse stepped outside, the dog barked. Moving quickly, Jonathan led the docile animal to the dark side of the barn, and Laura skedaddled after them.

They froze when the woman bellowed, "Brutus! Shut up!"

The dog barked louder, insisting that its owner pay attention.

"You trying to tell me something, Brutus?"

"Yeah, he's telling you it's a nice night and to go back inside," Jonathan murmured near Laura's ear. She shivered.

The dog kept yapping.

"Okay. You get your way, dog. Come on inside."

Laura let out a sigh when the door banged shut.

They moved through the darkness to a barbed-wire fence and walked along it until they found a gate. Laura opened it, and Jonathan led the horse through.

"Come here," Jonathan said, motioning her closer.

Laura moved to the front of the horse.

"Hold the reins here near the bit." He touched the place. "Some horses like to step away when the rider mounts up. He'll stand in place if you're holding him."

The horse looked friendly enough, but the closest Laura had ever been to a horse before this was at a petting zoo. Gingerly, she wrapped her hand around the leather reins, her fingers resting against the horse's mouth. It felt warm and fuzzy.

"If he should start to run," Jonathan said, "let go immediately."

"Don't worry," Laura replied, keeping her arm stretched out and stiff.

Jonathan swung himself up. "Laura?" he said in the darkness.

"What?"

"Let the horse go. Come over here and shove my bad leg the rest of

BETRAYED

the way up. I can't get it over."

Laura did as asked, and soon Jonathan sat astride the saddle. He took his foot out of the stirrup. "Put your foot in there, then grab onto my right arm. I'll pull you up."

Laura stretched to put her foot into the stirrup. It seemed so high off the ground. Jonathan's powerful hand grabbed her forearm. He swung her up, and she landed behind him, none too graceful, but she stayed put.

He said, "Grab around my middle and hold on. Not too tight, though. Remember my stomach wound. We won't go fast. Just a nice, easy walk."

From the cool night air and the dampness of lying on the ground, Laura was chilled clear through. The heat from the horse's back and heat from Jonathan next to her warmed her up.

She felt good, her arms around his waist, her cheek against his jacket. Her eyes drifted closed. After awhile, the jogging motion stopped, and Jonathan said, "You need to get down and open a gate."

She climbed off the horse, opened the steel gate, and Jonathan rode through. Laura closed it, then climbed to her perch.

They continued for an hour, heading west. In the distance, they saw a building with a neon light flashing the word *Tavern*. Jonathan headed the horse toward the building and drew up within three hundred feet of it at another barbed-wire fence.

They dismounted. Jonathan unbridled the horse, then released it. Crossing the fence, they came on the building from behind. A frame structure, it had cedar siding. Kitchen garbage and empty beer cases littered the back.

Stepping carefully, they reached the corner of the building and moved along the side. Laura kept close to Jonathan.

When he poked his head around the corner to the parking lot, he drew back, disgusted. "Take a look," he said.

In a row, like soldiers prepared to do battle, stood eight motorcycles. They glittered with chrome, long forks, and banana seats.

"It's a biker bar," he told her. "You know, long greasy hair, black leather jackets. Guys who beat up people like me for fun."

"Do you know how to steal a motorcycle?"

"I think so, but do I want to? If those guys catch us, it won't be pretty."

"Do we have another option?"

Jonathan shook his head. "We're fresh out of options, I'm afraid." He limped around the corner and approached the chopper nearest them.

He'd never stolen a motorcycle before, but it couldn't be too much different than a car.

He had unfastened two wires when he heard a muffled scream behind him.

He spun around to see a big, bald man dressed in leather. He had his hand clamped over Laura's mouth, a sawed-off shotgun to her head.

"What are you doing near that bike?" the man yelled. His voice could saw lumber.

Jonathan held up his hands. "Hey. . .careful with that gun. Don't hurt her."

The man shoved Laura aside. She stumbled and fell on the gravel. He turned the weapon on Corrigan. Gritting his teeth, Jonathan forced himself to stay still, his stance harmless.

"What are you doing sneaking around the back of my place in the dark?" The gun pressed against Jonathan's chest.

"I was just admiring the bikes."

"Yeah, right." The man's bushy, black eyebrows drew together. "Hey, I know you," he said. He looked down at Laura. "You're on TV. There's fifty thousand bucks out for you two. I could sure use fifty thousand bucks." The man stepped back, and the weapon lowered a bit.

Jonathan had to keep him talking. "I don't suppose you'd consider letting us go if we promise to give you sixty thousand in cash later?"

The biker shook his head. "I don't think so."

Laura picked herself up off the gravel and stood behind Jonathan. "Laura, get out of the way," he whispered.

"No, I'm standing right here with you," she said loudly. He felt her hand on his lower back. How he loved this woman.

"Do you mind if I put my hands down?"

The biker laughed. "What, you think I'm some kind of a nut? I know what you do for a living, Mr. CIA Agent. In fact, get up against that wall. I'm going to search you."

Jonathan did as commanded, placing his hands against the rough cedar. The bar owner's hand ran along his sides and pants legs.

"See, I told you I wasn't armed," Jonathan said.

"Turn around," the big man said.

There was a definite click. "You turn around," said Laura.

She had Jonathan's Glock aimed at the biker's chest, cocked and ready to fire. Jonathan grabbed the sawed-off shotgun and kicked the man's legs out so he fell.

Pressing the gun against his head, Jonathan said, "I should kill you for threatening her. Now which bike is yours? And give me the keys."

"Fourth one over," the man mumbled as he dug keys out of his pocket.

"You lie here until we're gone. Then, if you want, you can run inside and get all your biker buddies to chase us. But keep this in mind. My Glock holds nineteen rounds plus whatever's in this shotgun. Is your bike worth it? I'll kill you and as many of your buddies as I can."

Keeping the shotgun on the biker, Jonathan took the keys and moved to the Harley Davidson chopper. He threw his good leg over the seat and found the electric starter. Inserting the key, he revved the motor. "Get on," he called to Laura over the engine's blast.

Laura jumped on the backseat, the Glock still in her hand. Jonathan handed her the shotgun, and they roared into the darkness, anxious to put distance between them and the tavern, in case the bikers decided it was a good day to die.

When they'd traveled five miles with no signs of pursuit, Jonathan pulled the motorbike off the road beside a field. "Give me the shotgun," he said.

Laura handed it to him. He cocked it half a dozen times and shells fell onto the ground. He flung the weapon into a field.

"The Glock."

Laura gave him the handgun, and he tucked it under his back waistband again. Only stars lit the sky, but he could see the shadowy form of Laura's face. She had saved their hides with her fast thinking.

"You are one fantastic woman," he said and pulled her into a hug. His lips found hers for a tender moment.

Turning her loose, he fired up the Harley, and they roared toward Seattle.

CHAPTER TWENTY-FOUR

Whizzing down the dark country road, her hair flapping in her face, Laura felt that she was watching herself from somewhere high above. So many sensations had hit her in the past twenty-four hours that she thought she was past feeling anything anymore. All she could do was hold on and whisper a constant, silent prayer for help.

As farm after farm blew past, the Harley's single headlight lit up several entrance signs: Double P Ranch, Crazy Eight Cattle, Marsden Dairy, Julie's Piano Lessons.

Piano lessons? Someone must be running a music studio out of her home.

Laura had spent ten years studying piano. It had been a passion with her. Her father had taken great delight in finding difficult pieces of music and watching her master them.

"Stop the bike!" Laura yelled above the rushing wind.

Jonathan brought the bike to a halt beside the road.

"I know what the key is," she cried, so excited she bounced on the seat behind him. She rushed on, "About a year into the missile project, my dad brought me this obscure piece of music to learn. I was surprised at the time because it had been years since he'd done that. He was very adamant that I learn it and not forget it.

"When I asked him why it was so important, he said it might make me rich someday." She grabbed his jacket by the side seams and shook. "That has to be the key!"

Throwing her arms around him, she squeezed his middle until he gasped. "Sorry," she said, calming a little. "I forgot your wound."

He half turned on the seat. "You mean that we can get on the Internet and tell everyone the name of the music piece?"

Laura shook her head. "It's not that easy. My dad changed ordinary things—such as a book or music—into an encryption key by converting it to letters and numbers. For example, if the note is a C quarter note, but is in the lowest octave, then you multiply. . ."

"Never mind," he said. "I get the idea."

Laura's enthusiasm faded. "I need my laptop. It's at PTL Computers in Bellingham."

"No other computer will do?"

"Who else would have the right software?"

Jonathan sounded doubtful. "Stone will have your normal haunts staked out. It'll take a miracle to get you in there."

Suddenly, red and blue lights strobed toward them from the front. "Hold on tight!" he cried.

He opened the throttle, and the bike shot down the road, passing the oncoming police car. Jonathan glanced in the mirror and saw the cruiser making a U-turn.

"Can you outrun them?" Laura shouted in his ear.

He yelled back. "Not likely. I'm going to have to outsmart them."

As fields whipped past, Jonathan watched for something he knew every rural area had. Behind him, the police car gained ground, its siren growing louder by the second.

Then Jonathan squeezed the brake and edged off the road. He bounced across a ditch and onto a narrow path. Every kid in the country had a track for his dirt bike.

The motorcycle tore down the rutted path and disappeared into some trees. He could hear the siren die out as the police car gave up the chase. They'd radio to headquarters, and all the units on patrol would keep an eye out for the stolen Harley. If the CIA found out about the stolen-chopper chase, a helicopter would show up shortly.

The path wound through the trees. An occasional bump gave Laura and Jonathan a thrill as the bike sailed and settled back down. He'd never been so thankful for having grown up on a farm.

At the edge of the trees, Jonathan stopped the bike and turned it off. They got to the ground, and he pushed down the kickstand with his boot.

"What's the matter?" Laura asked, fear in her voice.

"Shh." He touched her arm. "I want to listen." In the distance, a helicopter buzzed across the dark sky. Soon, a bright light would be on them.

"I wish their bulb would burn out," Laura burst out.

Jonathan touched her shoulder. "You are so smart!"

"What did I say?"

"Wait here!" He walked into the field a hundred paces and lay on his back. Laura stayed in the trees beside the motorcycle. Zigzagging through the sky, the helicopter worked its way toward them, the spotlight a blinding shaft that skimmed the ground.

Taking careful aim, Jonathan fired one shot, and the light vanished in sparks. Jogging as best he could, he returned to Laura. "We've gotta go. They're going to land that baby and come in here looking for us."

The Harley roared to life once more. Jonathan and Laura took off across the field. When they reached a paved road, they shot ahead until they came to an all-night convenience store, a Mom-and-Pop affair with a gas pump.

Coasting the bike to just outside the scope of the parking lot's lights, he brought the machine to a stop.

"We've got to make some phone calls," Jonathan said.

"You never did tell me how you'll get me into PTL Computers," Laura said, hopping off the bike. Her legs felt like soggy spaghetti.

"I'm going to bluff our way in." He took her hand. "Come along and listen."

At Cascade Shipping, Stone's staff tried to stay clear of their chief—and for good reason. The director of the CIA was in the mood to find a scapegoat, and no one wanted the position.

After fouling up the motel sting, the agency's best helicopter had its searchlight blown out, and Corrigan managed to slip away again. What was the man? A ghost?

Stone's office phone rang, and he grabbed it, anxious to vent his frustration.

"Director?" a familiar voice asked.

"Corrigan!" Stone's face turned the color of a ripe plum. "Where are you?"

Ignoring the question, Corrigan said, "I have to be quick. She's just gone to the bathroom." His words were clipped. "Director, Miss McIvor knows the code."

Stone's left hand scrabbled on his cluttered desk for a notepad. "What is it?" he demanded, picking up his pen.

"It's some piece of obscure music."

"Did she give you the name?"

"No. But it wouldn't matter. She says her father had some kind of method for changing music to code. Even if you knew the music, you'd never know what to do with it."

Corrigan grew adamant. "I still want to do my job, Director Stone. Call off the troops and let me play this to the end. She needs to get to her computer where she can convert the music into the encryption key, and I intend to see that she does."

Stone let his pen fall to the desk. He leaned back in his soft leather chair, his expression tight. "I don't think I can trust you."

"Why not?" Corrigan sounded properly offended.

"You knocked out two of my agents."

"You sent them after me contrary to our agreement," Corrigan countered.

"You ditched your cane with the homing device."

"Is that a surprise? I had no idea what your guys would do next."

"I'm sorry, Corrigan," Stone said, authority in his words. "You'll have to bring her in. We'll give her a computer here."

"She won't tell you the code willingly," Corrigan said.

"Then we'll drug her."

Corrigan kept his tone reasonable. "She tried to explain the transfer code to me and lost me after the first sentence. If you drug her, she won't be able to unravel it. Check with your own people. See if someone can explain detailed encryption technology while flying high on truth drugs." He drew in a short breath. "Sir, she's willing to do it without being forced as long as she stays with me."

Stone's words rang with suspicion. "What did you promise her?"

"I told her we'd broadcast the solution over the Internet. Once the world knows, she'll be safe." Corrigan chuckled ironically. "One good thing about all this chasing, she's convinced that I'm on her side."

Stone listened carefully. Corrigan had his full attention. "What do you propose, Jonathan?"

"I want to take her to PTL Computers in Bellingham where her software is and let her figure out the answer. As soon as she's got it, I'll shut her down, and we can take her into custody."

Stone's fingers showed white on the phone receiver. "How do I know you're not working an angle, Corrigan?"

"Sir, is there anything in my record that would make you doubt me? As we speak, the Chinese or the Russians could figure out the code and overrun our country. We're on the same side, Director."

Corrigan paused to draw a breath, then said, "You can monitor PTL's phone lines. If a modem tries to dial out, cut the wire."

Stone tilted his head back against the chair's upholstery, thinking it over. "Go to PTL," he said, finally. "I'll check with our people about the effects of the truth drug on a person's reasoning ability. If your story washes, you'll have no troubles. If it doesn't, it's over. Deal?"

"Deal," Jonathan said.

Stone hung up the phone.

"Ida!" he called.

A worried look on her seamed face, his secretary appeared at his door.

Stone said, "I want three units to join the men watching PTL Computers. Tell them all to stay hidden until I get there." He stood up and reached for his coat. "Get me a chopper. I have to go to Bellingham."

Sam Perkins sat at the wheel of his navy Crown Victoria on the Canadian side of the border when his cell phone rang. "Perkins," he said, bored.

"It's me," a deep voice said.

"Well, hello. Everyone is searching for you, including your mom. She's upset because you punched out your brother. Where are you?"

The caller ignored the question and said, "Is that big favor you owe me still on the table?"

"Sure."

"I need to call it in. I can't tell you much, but I need you at PTL Computers in about an hour and a half." He paused, then asked, "Where are you anyway?"

"I'm in a mile-and-a-half lineup at the Canadian border at Blaine. Someone phoned in a terrorist threat, and they're searching every car."

"You've got to be kidding. What are you doing in Canada?"

"Someone said Vancouver was a pretty city, so I went to see for myself."

"Get to Bellingham as fast as you can. It's life or death, Sam. I wouldn't kid you on that."

Perkins heard desperation in Corrigan's voice. He knew that Corrigan was on the run. That was one of the reasons he'd pulled vacation time and left the country. He didn't want to be on a search team if the Seattle police asked for FBI assistance.

"I'll get there somehow," Perkins promised. He closed the phone and lay it on the seat beside him. Leave it to Corrigan to ask him for the impossible when he couldn't bow out.

Olivia Donner usually went to sleep by ten o'clock, but tonight she stared into the darkness, Laura's tear-filled eyes hovering in her mind. In the short time she'd known her, Laura had become like a daughter. Olivia had been shocked when CNN announced that Shannon Masterson was really Laura McIvor, but that fact hadn't changed Olivia's feelings for the girl. After what the poor girl had been through, she couldn't blame her for changing her name.

Dropping to her knees on the Oriental runner beside her king-sized bed, Olivia prayed that God would protect Laura and make everything right. Then she prayed that if she could help Laura herself, He'd show her how.

Jonathan hung up the phone and looked down at Laura close beside him. "I hope it worked," he said.

Laura gave him a nervous smile. "You were so convincing I started to wonder if you were telling him the truth and lying to me."

Brushing hair from her cheek, Jonathan gazed into her emerald eyes. He leaned forward to kiss her forehead. "Do you want to hold the gun again?" he asked, grinning. "If I'm lying, you can shoot me."

She smiled, eyebrows lifted. "If you're lying, I'll find a more painful way to kill you." She glanced around the empty parking lot. "How do we get to Bellingham? Steal a car or a motorcycle? How about another horse? Or should we look for a canoe?"

Jonathan looked over her head. "How about a cab?"

Laura turned to see a yellow taxi at the gas pump. "That's the best idea I've heard all day," she said. "But first let me pick up a couple of honey buns and a bottle of water." She stepped toward the door and turned back. "Hey, they have a cappuccino machine!"

They rode to Bellingham sipping hot hazelnut coffee and enjoying each other's company. Watching Jonathan's face, Laura saw a confident exterior, but she knew he had the same doubts as she. Everything could go terribly wrong.

Halfway to Bellingham, Laura drained her cup and suddenly felt a panic attack coming on. What if Director Stone went back on his word again? What if she couldn't solve the encryption?

She forced herself to breathe slowly. Jonathan looked at her, squeezed her hand, and smiled, his eyes full of love. She leaned her forehead against his cheek and closed her eyes. If everything fell apart, at least she had learned that this man truly loved her.

Meridian Street was deserted when the taxi pulled up in front of PTL Computers. Jonathan tossed the driver several bills and helped Laura out of the car.

He looked up and down the dark street. Laura started to talk, but a flicker of his eyes stopped her.

Punching a code into the security keypad, Laura unlocked the steel security mesh, then the glass front doors to the computer store. Inside, she locked the door behind them and turned on the main lights. Jonathan put his finger to his lips, then made a spider motion with his hand.

"Bugs?" Laura mouthed.

Jonathan glanced across the showroom. "Maybe," he mouthed back.

Beside the register he found a piece of paper and wrote, *They may have bugged the place. Be sure to talk like you have no idea I called Stone.*

Laura nodded.

"So, Laura," he said aloud, "what do you need to break this encryption code?"

Putting his Crown Victoria in park, Perkins got out and stretched. Even the preauthorized lane was jammed. Traffic spread out ahead as far as he could see. Nothing was moving.

Thankful that he was dressed in loose khaki pants and running shoes, he jogged along the shoulder of the road. Whew, was he glad he'd shed those twenty pounds.

Alternating running and walking, fifteen minutes later he reached the U.S. Customs checkpoint, breathing heavily. Without slowing much, he kept moving past the booth.

A Border Patrol officer burst out of the building, aimed for Perkins. "Hold it right there," he yelled.

Puffing, Perkins turned and reached inside his coat.

"Don't move!" The officer drew his weapon. "Down on the ground. Now!"

Perkins read the man's name badge. "Hi, Mark, look, I'm. . ."

Mark clicked back the hammer of his gun. "Down! I won't say it again."

Perkins dropped to the cold macadam. Two more officers ran out of their headquarters, weapons ready.

"I'm FBI," Perkins shouted from the ground.

"What's going on, Mark?" the taller of the two officers asked when he reached them.

"This guy tried to walk through without checking in, Phil. He went for something inside his coat, so I ordered him down. Now he says he's FBI."

"Yeah, and I'm Elliot Ness," Phil said. He had the voice of a twelve year old.

"Cuff him, Brett," Phil told the third man. Built like a prizefighter, Brett was none too gentle. Once their prisoner was cuffed, Phil and Brett grabbed under his armpits and hoisted him to his feet.

"Where's your ID?" Phil asked Perkins, watching him warily.

Perkins glared at them. "In my coat pocket." His expression sagged when Phil's hand reached into his windbreaker pocket and drew out a "Things To Do in Vancouver" brochure. He waved it for the other officers to see.

Patting him down, Phil pulled a Beretta out of his shoulder holster.

Mark said, "You realize this doesn't look good."

Perkins started to sweat in earnest. "I left my badge in my car. I am FBI."

"Uh-huh," Phil said. "Why were you trying to cross the border on foot?"

"With you guys checking every car, it'll take at least two hours for me to clear. I can't wait. There's an emergency call I have to make."

"You know," Mark said, "he does look like FBI."

Phil shot Mark a hard look and said, "Terrorists don't usually come with a T stamped on their forehead."

"Tell you what," Perkins said. "One of you guys come back with me to my car."

Phil scratched behind his left ear. He turned to Mark. "He's your catch. Go with him to his car."

Perkins turned halfway, wiggling his hands. "What about these?"

"They stay on until we check out your story," Phil said.

Thoroughly disgusted, Perkins set out at a half trot.

"Hey, slow down," Mark called after him.

Perkins stopped to glare at him. "Didn't you hear? I'm in a hurry."

"Hey," Mark said. "I'm in charge here."

Perkins stepped close to the officer. "If I'm really an FBI agent—which I am—and you keep me from my duty by making me late, I'll make sure you spend the rest of your life in New Mexico pulling northbound swimmers out of the Rio Grande."

Mark got in gear. At the Crown Victoria, he dug Perkins's keys out of his jacket pocket, opened the door, and pulled out the green plaid blazer. Reaching for the inside pocket, he found the ID folder, and his face turned red. "Well. . .what do you know."

"Just uncuff me!"

Mark fumbled with the key and unlocked the cuffs. Without another word, Perkins grabbed his ID folder and aimed toward the checkpoint.

Reaching down for energy he never knew he had, the big man managed to keep his legs pumping. The image of Corrigan falling, wounded by bullets from Perkins's gun flashed through his mind like an old rerun. He couldn't let Corrigan down again.

His badge high, he ran to the waiting Phil. "Satisfied?" Perkins panted.

"Yes, Sir. I'm sorry, but we had to be sure."

"I understand," Perkins said. He looked at four squad cars parked fifty feet away. "I need one of your cars."

"No can do," Phil said. "We're on full alert for terrorist activity."

CHAPTER TWENTY-FIVE

In a frustrated fury, Perkins left the border checkpoint and continued a stumbling run along the highway toward Blaine. Five minutes later, his legs were rubber. He had a sharp pain in his chest. When a blue-and-white cab passed him, he used the last of his wind to shout, "Wait!" Frantic, he waved at the back of the taxi. Its brake lights lit up.

Sweat pouring from his face, Perkins jumped into the taxi's front seat. He gasped five times before he could choke out, "Bellingham. . . hurry!"

The cab driver had a small head that was all nose with three chins hanging down to his chest. "No problem," he said, his voice shrill. "But first I gotta. . ."

Perkins flipped open his badge. "No stops, Bud!" he growled, still fighting to breathe. "It's an emergency. Step on it."

The cabby glanced at the dash panel. "You're the boss. I guess we'll make it okay."

"You got a cell phone?" Perkins asked.

"Nah, just that." He pointed at a scuffed citizen band radio below the dash.

Not wanting to take time to stop and look for a pay phone, Perkins clamped his jaw, hunched forward in his seat, and sweated away the miles.

Zipping through Blaine, they entered Interstate 5. With Perkins goading the driver every three minutes, they traveled over eighty miles an hour. Just before the Ferndale exchange, the car chug-chugged, and the driver pulled onto the shoulder.

"What's wrong?" Perkins demanded. His blood pressure would have broken the gauge.

"Out of gas. I waited so long in that border lineup I was low on fuel."

"Why didn't you tell me?" Perkins had an urge to belt the guy. Instead, he gestured toward the CB and said, "Radio for another cab."

The driver lifted the mike with a slim hand that could have been a woman's. "Whatever you say, but this is a Seattle company. It'll have to come from there."

Throwing a bill at him, Perkins cursed and got out of the cab. Drenched and wheezing, he pounded up the exit ramp and did a fumbling jog to a phone booth outside of a gas station. His hands shaking so bad he could hardly hit the correct buttons, he punched in a number from memory and babbled into the receiver. Since it was the weekend, Bellingham's FBI resident agency was closed. That put the nearest FBI post an hour and a half away in Seattle. Any agents they sent over would probably miss all the action. Still, he had to try.

Plopping the receiver to its hook, he turned to see a kid with a Mohawk haircut hurrying out of the station, slipping his wallet into the back pocket of his ragged jeans as he walked. Perkins met the boy at a yellow Volkswagen Beetle with a lighted sign for JimBo's Pizza on top.

The delivery boy hopped in and set the engine whirring. At that moment, Perkins shoved his Beretta against the guy's cheek and ground out, "Get out. I need your car."

The kid wasn't impressed. "You can't do that. I'm late already." He flung a hand over the seat toward a leaning tower of pizza boxes, a dozen at least. "I'm delivering to the mayor's house. His daughter's birthday party."

Perkins had heard enough. He pulled open the door and grabbed the boy's jean jacket. "I said, 'I need your car!'" He jerked. The kid fell out and scrambled up. He grabbed the back door handle and started to open it, but Perkins knocked him down.

He folded his big frame around the tiny seat and reached for the shift lever. Sounding like a chain saw on overdrive, he roared onto the highway. The back door rattled. Its latch had loosened when the boy grabbed it. Perkins ignored the irritating noise and kept the pedal to the floor. If the police stopped him, he'd use his badge. He only hoped he wasn't too late already.

Jonathan watched anxiously as Laura tapped away at her laptop.

BETRAYED

Meaningless letters and numbers filled the screen. He bent down next to her ear and whispered. "How much longer?"

In answer, she typed on the screen, "I'm going as fast as I can. Another fifteen minutes for sure."

Jonathan straightened and gave her some space, pacing and praying that she'd finish sooner than she expected.

The front door rattled. In one motion, Jonathan pulled Laura away from the desk and pushed her behind it. He whipped out his Glock and trained it at the door. The handle turned, and Olivia Donner walked in, leaving the steel security mesh pushed back.

"Oh, no," Jonathan groaned. He uncocked his weapon and ran a hand through his short hair.

"What now?" Laura asked, her face white and scared.

"They're going to bust through the door any second." He looked around, his mind racing.

Her keys dangling from her hand, Olivia stepped closer. "Jonathan, what are you doing with that gun?"

Jonathan gestured, palm up. "Laura's father did something to put her in danger. Another fifteen minutes and we'd be home free." He turned around, scanning the barred windows and the steel doors. "They'll be on us any second. We've got to find a place to hide."

Olivia's chin came up. She moved into his personal space. "There is a place."

"Keep your voice down," Jonathan whispered. "The place is bugged."

She wheezed, "I've never told Laura about it. I'm embarrassed to tell you now. . . But it may be what you need."

When the big woman entered PTL Computers, Stone didn't like it, but he decided to wait in his Buick LaSabre and listen to the conversation inside. Three minutes later, he gave an order and agents descended upon PTL Computers from all sides. They blew open the steel back door and battered in the front door's glass. At the same time, they cut the power and phone lines.

In his car, listening to radio traffic, Stone tapped his knee with square-cut fingernails, waiting to hear that his men had the McIvor woman in custody. Finally, he barked into his wrist mike. "What's going on?"

"No one's here," Brown answered.

"What!" Stone jumped out of his car and ran down Meridian Street.

He lunged into PTL Computers—glass crunching under his feet—and turned full circle. No one was there. "What about in back?" he shouted.

"We've been all through it," Brown said. "It's empty."

Stone clenched his fists. "They're hiding. Tear the place apart."

He paced back and forth in front of the mangled glass doors. He had violated federal law. Bellingham cops would be here any second asking questions.

Brown and two others turned over tables, smashed computers, and ripped open walls. At Stone's order, agents entered the two adjacent businesses just in case there was a common door they hadn't found. Corrigan and McIvor hadn't gone out through the roof—agents had been there from the beginning.

Screaming sirens split the air. Two Bellingham patrol cars pulled up on the sidewalk, and four officers jumped out. Stone rushed toward them, an FBI badge in his hand.

"Special Agent Carter, FBI," he called to the approaching officers.

"Sergeant Bill Dade," the leader said, hands on hips. He was two inches shorter than Stone. "What's going on here?"

"We've got terrorists holed up inside there," Stone said, jerking his head toward the back room. "It's a national security issue. We hoped they'd come out quietly, but they're making it tough. Now, if you gentlemen would just stay back a bit, we'll finish up here."

The four officers looked at each other. "Come on, guys," Dade said, sending Stone a measuring glance. "The Feds don't need us local yokels butting in."

The policemen retreated down the road a block. Frowning, Stone watched them a moment, then returned inside.

Brown emerged from the back room. "We found something."

Stepping over broken monitors, dented computer towers, and chunks of wallboard, the CIA director walked into the back room to find two agents staring at a steel plate on the floor. He knelt and grabbed the steel ring attached to it.

"We tried it, Sir," Brown said. "It must be locked from the other side."

Stone stamped on the plate. "Corrigan! I know you're in there. Open up!"

Silence.

Stone told Brown, "Blast it open."

"With what? We only had enough explosives for the back door. This place is like Fort Knox."

Stone burst out with a string of profanity. "That's it. I've had enough." He waved a hand. "Torch the place."

"Sir," Brown said, staring at his superior, "we're breaking a new law every two minutes. You may not mind a few years in prison, but I've got a family."

Stone's glare skewered him. "Either you obey my orders, or I'll lock you in here and have Neilson do it."

Backing down, Brown hurried out the rear door and called outside, "Neilson, there's a gas station at the end of this street. Buy some cans and get us some gas."

Stone banged his heel on the plate. "Hear that, Corrigan! We're going to torch this place. You're going to fry alive!"

Ten feet below Stone, Laura looked up from her desk chair when he screamed those words. She raised trembling hands to cover her ears. "I can't think, Jonathan. I can't!" Her voice raised a full octave and cracked.

Jonathan knelt beside her, peering at her through the yellow glow of a candle flame. "You're almost done, aren't you, Honey?" He pulled her head onto his shoulder and held her close. She even smelled good in a musty place like this.

"Whether we get out of this or not, we'll still be together," he whispered and blinked away his own wrought-up emotion.

He kissed her damp cheek. "What's left? Is there something I can help you with?"

Rubbing her cheeks and sniffing, she gestured to her laptop's blue screen. "I have to send the file attachment to the government addresses I printed from the motel's computer." She pulled a folded page from her jeans pocket.

Standing beside a shelf filled with canned goods and camping gear, Olivia spoke. "Let me do it, Laura. I can type a hundred words a minute. My nerves haven't been torn up by a midnight chase." She stepped to the cardboard folding table where Laura worked. "God is on our side, you know. If you didn't have a cellular modem, we'd be sunk."

Corrigan sent her a grateful glance. He wondered if Olivia's nerves ever got torn up. This would be a prime opportunity if they did.

Laura stood and Olivia draped herself over the metal folding chair. She opened the paper saying, "When Jim from the hardware next door convinced me to convert our joint basement into a Y2K shelter, I never dreamed I'd use it to survive a CIA attack." She set the list on the desk. "Take a breather, children. I'll have this sent out in no time."

Huddled in Jonathan's arms, Laura said, "Even if we get the message sent out, how will we get out of here? They've got the place surrounded."

He kissed her temple. "Relax. I've already got that covered."

Hands deep in the pockets of his tan trench coat, Stone trudged out the front door of PTL Computers five minutes later. Three agents scrambled out of the building behind him, giving Stone a guarded look as they passed him.

Ten minutes after that, a wisp of smoke curled out the front door as Brown raced outside. Within seconds, flames engulfed the store—black, yellow, and dark red, reaching far above the roof. It roared and cackled like a laughing demon.

Stone crossed the street to watch at a safer distance. A crowd had gathered, and sirens wailed somewhere to the east.

Brown said, "That'll be the fire department."

"Don't worry, by the time they get in place, those traitors will be fried," Stone said and glanced at the patrol cars down the street. "I think it's time for us to go."

A deep voice, mildly ironic, sounded from the shadow of the building behind him. "Nice fire, Director."

Stone spun, mouth gaping. Jonathan Corrigan stepped out holding Laura McIvor's hand, Olivia Donner following them. Stone's face contorted, he let out an insane war cry and lunged for Corrigan shouting, "How did you get out?"

Pulling his Glock, Jonathan brought the director up short. "As soon as your men cleared out for the bonfire, we left through the basement door of the hardware store."

"Brown," Stone said, "shoot this man and take Miss McIvor."

"Go ahead and shoot, Brown. You'll go to jail for nothing. The key to the encryption is already on the World Wide Web. You can read it there along with the Russians, the Israelis, and half a dozen other countries."

"You're bluffing, Corrigan. We cut the lines. You didn't get the message out."

Laura spoke for the first time. "Ever hear of a cellular modem, Director?"

BETRAYED

Stone glared at her. "You're both going to jail for treason."

"For what?" Corrigan asked. "For restoring everything to the way it was before Dr. McIvor fouled up the works? C'mon, Stone. I don't think the courts will see it your way." Corrigan smirked. "You're just a sore loser."

Stone nodded to four agents standing in a huddle on the sidewalk. "Take them into custody." To Corrigan, he said, "You people are going to have an unfortunate accident."

Holding weapons, Stone's men slowly spread out, watching Corrigan's gun hand, edging around him and Laura.

Suddenly, a yellow Volkswagen Beetle with a lighted sign flashing JimBo's Pizza zoomed in, followed by four Bellingham police cars. The Beetle skidded to a stop, two wheels scraping the curb for ten feet, leaving a long black streak and jolting the back door open. A dozen pizza boxes torpedoed across the ground, tripping up one of the CIA agents so that he fell on his face.

A large man burst out of the VW's front door. Eight police officers jumped from their cars, guns held out before them with both hands.

"Sam Perkins, FBI," the big man roared at them. "Back off! All of you!"

Jonathan took a firmer grip on Laura's hand and said, "You know, Mr. Stone, somehow I get the idea that you're the one who's going to prison."

Three red fire trucks screamed onto the scene, filling the remaining spaces in the street. They draped black hoses over police car hoods and around bumpers to reach the fire hydrants. Soon, a wide white spray arched up and into the building, a hopeless gesture. PTL Computers had already become a skeleton with empty, glowing eye sockets.

After telling local officers the whole story, Perkins held a gun on Stone while they cuffed him and his men. The CIA renegade stood with his chin resting midway down his chest while his men huddled a short distance away, constantly glancing around but avoiding eye contact with any individual.

While everyone else was occupied, Jonathan pulled Laura into the doorway of a closed hairdresser's shop. He wrapped his arms around her and cradled her near his heart, swaying with her from side to side.

"I've got you now, Laura McIvor," he murmured into her hair. "You're not getting away from me again. This time I'm going to marry you." He bent to kiss her, but she turned her head away.

"I can't marry anyone with the CIA," she whispered, her voice hoarse. "Knowing you're in danger all the time would send me over the edge.

I couldn't handle it." Tears filled her eyes. She tried to pull away.

"Oh, no, you don't." He held on tighter. "For your information, Miss McIvor, I'm not CIA any more. From now on, I'm FBIL."

She tilted her head. "FBI. . .L?"

"Yeah." He grinned and leaned down so their noses almost touched. "Farming, Babies, and In Love. . .with you." He kissed her eyelids. "I've been so miserable without you, Laura. Please, say you'll marry me."

She melted against him, her forehead resting against his temple. With a deep sigh, she murmured, "Yes, yes, yes, yes, yes. . ."

Bending, he silenced her lips for a long, warm moment, staking claim to his own private niche of heaven, soft as the breath of an angel, sweet as. . .

"Uh-humph!"

Startled, they looked up to see Perkins beside them holding a flat box in each hand. His chin had a tomato-sauce smudge. Shoving a box toward them, he asked, "You guys want pepperoni or triple cheese?"

ABOUT THE AUTHORS

ROSEY DOW is a popular speaker, best-selling author, and homeschooling mother of seven. A missionary to the tiny Caribbean island of Grenada for fourteen years, she is now a pastor's wife in Mississippi. Rosey has written four historical mysteries, including *Reaping the Whirlwind*, the true account of the Scopes "Monkey" trial wrapped inside a compelling whodunit. Check out her web site at www.roseydow.com.

ANDREW SNADEN is a Certified General Accountant who lives on an eighty-acre farm in Prince George, B.C., Canada. Andrew has written articles for Christian magazines such as *On Mission, The Evangelical Beacon,* and *Live. Betrayed* is his first published novel. Andrew and his wife have one daughter. Check out his web site at www.andrewsnaden.com.

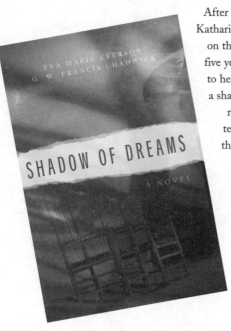